To: Shel[illegible]

Worde[illegible]ng

you [illegible]

Hope this challenges

& entertains you

[illegible]

A CONVENIENT RUSE

SUZEN FROMSTEIN
AND
TJ STOATE

A CONVENIENT RUSE

Suzen Fromstein &TJ Stoate

Print ISBN: 978-1-77242-137-8

Carrick Publishing

Cover Art, Sara Carrick

For information address:
415 St. Clair Avenue East
Toronto, ON M4T 1P6, Canada

Dedications

To Mikel, Carley, Dustin, Irina, Benjy, Abby & Gabby—thank you for adding depth, texture, fun & laughter to my life. ~ *Suzen*

To my family and closest friends. All of you have had a major impact on my life and especially to my granddaughter Mathilda, who always makes me want to be a better person and has brought more joy into our lives than one could imagine. ~ *Tim*

Character Legend

Ada Adelmann: student at INSEAD, member of the Sustainable Investing Club, one of the "Leave Only Shadows" co-authors

Alyosha Foundation for Financial Literacy and Education: not for profit educational institute and Misha Mikhalov's passion project headquartered in Russia, OhMy EAU!! shareholder

Bob Merilees: President of St. Clair Associates LLC, a private security/cyber security firm

Butch Badger: Junior Democratic Senator, chair of the Senate Subcommittee on Communications, Technology and the Internet, married to Financial Analyst, Edie Li, One of Christina Sinclair-Sanchez language clients

Camp Orlyonyk: month-long computer camp for mis adventured youth held at the Mikhalov's Corsica estate

Christina Sinclair-Sanchez: former Bears Stand Associate Vice President Private Equity and Alternative Investments, freelance language coach and yogi, ESURE/ESHURE co-creator, Melodie Beaudoin's best friend, ESHURE trader and Jacques Beaudoin's girlfriend

Constantine "Onassis" Smith: Republican Senator, vice-chair of The United States Senate Committee on Armed Services, one of Melodie Beaudoin's language clients

Cosimo Calderella: student at INSEAD, member of the Sustainable Investing Club, one of the "Leave Only Shadows" co-authors, sworn enemy of Melodie Beaudoin and Misha Mikhalov

Denzel Sun Mah/Ted Chen Williams: Temp Reynolds' best friend, former CIA, computer whiz, brother of harpist Jade Chen-Williams, student at INSEAD, member of the Sustainable Investing Club, one of the "Leave Only Shadows" co-authors, ESHURE software developer, webmaster and trader, acting director of The Alyosha Foundation for Financial Literacy and Education

Dmitri Mikhalov: one of Sergei/Elena's twin sons and spy

Edie Teresa Li: George and Edith Li's daughter, computer expert, Junior Analyst on Temp Reynold's team, sabotaged Temp/Treasury, married to Butch Badger

Elena Popov/Mikhalov: Model, married to Sergei Mikhalov, mother of twins Misha and Dmitri, owner and principal shareholder of OhMy EAU!!, sole beneficiary of the Otto Lacuna estate

ESURE/ESHURE: Melodie Beaudoin/Christina Sinclair-Sanchez insider trading scheme

George and Edith Li: George was an expert in the use, misuse and development of drone technology for military and commercial purposes. Edith was a world-renowned virologist and bio weapons specialist. They, along with their daughter, Edie Theresa Li, were all spying on behalf of Russian mob boss, Sergei Mikhalov

Guy St. Cloud: Computer hacker and Owen Talbot-Mercer's best friend

Ivan/Okie: Russian butcher and Sergei Mikhalov's freelance muscle/hitman. The Iceman's mentor and partner

Jack Edelstein: the onsite custodian at Melodie Beaudoin's townhouse development

Jackson Temple (Temp) Reynolds III/Jackson Tiggs/Hercule: retired soldier, former head of the Financial Crimes and Enforcement Network, an agency within the US Department of the Treasury, best friend of Ted Chen Williams, Gold USB winner, former employee of St. Clair, Melodie Beaudoin's boyfriend, Owen Talbot-Mercer's biological father

Jade Chen-Williams: Ted Chen-Williams' biological sister, world renowned harpist, Misha Mikhalov's fiancée

James Brown (JB) Washington: student at the INSEAD, member of the Sustainable Investing Club, Melodie's co-author and ESHURE trader, brought the Camp Orlyonyk concept to the US

John Berlin: Office Manager at St. Clair Associates LLC

Leave Only Shadows: the definitive co-authored guide for measuring economic return on eco-investments co-authored by members of the Sustainable Investing Club and their professor

Leonardo Capilano: INSEAD professor/Melodie's mentor, founder of the Sustainable Investing and the Ethical Investing clubs, ESG advocate, Paula Da Silva's lover

Melodie Marie Beaudoin/Watson: former Assistant Analyst at Investment Brothers, student at the INSEAD, Leave Only Shadows co-author, language and physiotherapy coach, ESURE/ESHURE co-creator, Temp Reynold's girlfriend, detective Jacques Beaudoin's sister

Miles Worthington: retired three star General, Republican Senator, chair of the United States Committee on Armed Services, insider trader/serial philanderer, one of Melodie Beaudoin's language clients

Misha Mikhalov: one of Sergei/Elena Mikhalov's twin sons, harpist Jade Chen-Williams' fiancé, computer expert, founder of The Alyosha Financial Literacy and Educational Foundation, student at the INSEAD, member of. The Sustainable Investing Club, Leave Only Shadows co-author, ESHURE trader

Mr. Ogiyevich: The Li's handler and Sergei Mikhalov go-between

OhMy EAU!!: Elena Mikhalov's international bathing suit and lingerie business

Otto Lacuna: Elena Mikhalov's guardian/mentor and successful swimsuit retailer

Owen Talbot-Mercer: Temp Reynolds biological, teenaged son, computer hacker and gamer

Paula Da Silva: INSEAD student, Melodie's roommate, member of the Sustainable Investing Club, Professor Capilano's lover, Leave Only Shadows co-author and ESHURE trader

Philadelphia Romualdez: Pulitzer Prize-Winning Reporter with *30 Minutes*

Prince Sayid al Farah: 14th Saudi prince, student at INSEAD, member of the Sustainable Investing Club, Leave Only Shadows co-author

ReID: Misha Mikhalov's customized software that scrambled the features of OhMy EAU!! customers

Roberta Fromme: US Senator, Chair of the Senate Foreign Relations Subcommittee on International Development, one of Melodie Beaudoin's language clients

Sandra Makalowsky, US Senator, chair of the Senate Appropriations Committee, one of Christina Sinclair-Sanchez language clients

Sergei Mikhalov: vicious Russian gangster, married to Elena, father of twins Misha and Dmitri

Stanislav Kuzentsova/The Iceman: Ivan's partner/Sergei's exclusive hit man and master of disguises

Svetlana Tretiak: INSEAD student, member of the Sustainable Investing Club, Leave Only Shadows co-author and ESHURE trader

ubdqt.com: Sergei Mikhalov's Peeping Tom subscriber website that-live streams OhMy EAU!! customers

Viktor Vasilevich: Russian policeman and informant

Vladimir Alexandroff: Sergei Mikhalov's friend, President of Russia and honorary patron of the Alyosha Financial Literacy and Educational Foundation

Vladimir Naumovski, went to university and hunted boar with Sergei Mikhalov, US Senator, chair of the Senate Sub-Committee on Security and International Trade and Finance, one of Christina Sinclair-Sanchez language clients

Wayne Lee: INSEAD student and member of the Sustainable Investing Club, Melodie's co-author and ESHURE trader

Prologue

Washington DC 2012

Temp was running late. He had stopped at the office to collect the engagement ring which now rested comfortably in the inside right pocket of his navy-blue sports jacket. Parking was even more of a nightmare than usual and the first vacant spot he found was four blocks away.

It was hard to wipe the happy smile from his face. It was well past time to set things right. As he rounded the corner to Melodie's townhouse complex, he glanced down at the new Patek Phillippe Nautilus Chronograph watch he had purchased yesterday at the Paris airport duty free. The matching women's watch was in his briefcase at the office. He didn't want something as insignificant as a watch to distract his sexy fiancée from the special moment he had planned.

As he rounded the corner he stopped in his tracks. The end unit, the townhouse Melodie rented, was engulfed in flames.

The media, medics and police were already there. Sergeant Walter Wilkes, badge 73973, was in charge of the scene. Earlier, the officer had used his cell phone to shoot a video of the bystanders, the street, and the front and back of the high-end townhouse complex.

The Sergeant walked towards a slightly paunchy middle-aged man who was clutching the leash of a golden retriever puppy, who was dancing excitedly between his master's legs.

Notebook in hand, the Sergeant approached the man who introduced himself as Jack Edelstein, the onsite custodian. The officer asked for and received his contact information, his Neighborhood Watch affiliation, and reviewed his conceal carry permit and passport. He then asked Edelstein to describe exactly what had happened and when.

Edelstein was nervous. He had never been part of a police investigation before. He cleared his throat, took a deep breath to steady himself, and said, "At 11:00 p.m., as Sunny and I were returning from our last walk of the evening, we saw a middle-aged man, in a grey uniform, on the sidewalk in front of Melodie's townhouse. He was wearing a Washington Nationals baseball cap. He had a bushy mustache and a bit of a beer belly."

Edelstein took another deep breath and continued. "The man carried a portable black tool chest in one hand and a clipboard in the other. A tool belt was hanging off of his waist. Because Melodie had mentioned she was having trouble with her stove earlier in the week, Sunny and I just assumed the man was from one of the big box stores making a late house call." Unfortunately, in his excitement of being part of a real investigation, the custodian neglected to mention the unexplained bang he heard around 11:25 p.m.

Sergeant Wilkes then asked Edelstein if he knew who lived in the burning townhouse. "Of course," Edelstein continued conversationally. I know everyone that lives here. Mademoiselle Melodie Marie Beaudoin rents the end unit. Lovely French-Canadian woman. She moved here a couple of years ago. She teaches languages, Mandarin, French and Spanish for politicians and does some physiotherapy for professional athletes, mostly hockey players, I think. She also wrote a best-selling book on some financial thing. I can't recall the title. I'm sure you can Google it. Is Melodie OK? Sunny and I are really worried about her."

"When I can share any information, I will do so," Sergeant Wilkes replied. He then asked Edelstein if there was any particular reason he was worried about Ms. Beaudoin. A bit taken aback at the question, Edelstein replied, "Her townhouse is burning. Isn't it reasonable to worry about our neighbor's safety?"

Sergeant Wilkes replied. "Of course, besides the fire I mean." "No there isn't," Edelstein emphatically said.

Sergeant Wilkes then asked Edelstein if Melodie lived alone. "Yes, although her boyfriend often slept over."

The policeman then asked Edelstein if he had observed any problems between Ms. Beaudoin and her boyfriend. "No, the only thing Sunny and I ever saw them do was hold hands and hug, and the only thing we ever heard them do was laugh. Melodie Beaudoin has a very distinctive, musical laugh. Her parents must have named her for that laugh. It was obvious to anyone with eyes in their head that they were very much in love. One afternoon not that long ago, while we were sharing recipes, we often did that, Melodie mentioned that her boyfriend was trying to talk her into marrying him, and that she was seriously considering his proposal. Since she was a cancer survivor, she was unwilling to say 'Yes' until she was reasonably certain about her health prospects. But based on their loving behavior, Sunny and I believe it was only a matter of time before she agreed. We sure hope she's ok."

Temp found it difficult to move and his feet seemed cemented to the ground. It would be hours before the police and other emergency responders completed their on-site investigations. Since he had no official role he saw no reason to stay.

Even with all of his native intelligence, cunning and investigative experience, Temp had not foreseen this unexpected turn of events. He thought things were bad when his best friend, Ted, died and then, when one of his work colleagues, Edie, had betrayed him. As bad as those things were, the thought that something had happened to Melodie was even worse.

He allowed himself one minute of self-indulgent emotionalism before his training kicked in. Earlier that same week Melodie had mentioned that she felt like she was being watched. He had dismissed her concerns to being overtired because she had taken on several new language clients and had been working extra-long hours.

Usually, he had excellent instincts. Had he missed something? Even if it was the last thing he did, he swore he would not rest until he figured it out. He used his St. Clair work phone to call Melodie's eldest brother, Jacques. The two men didn't speak or meet in person until Melodie's memorial service thirty days after the fire.

Chapter 1

The Russian

Just by looking at him you would never suspect that Sergei Mikhalov was a cold-blooded killer and the head of Russia's largest and most successful crime family. Not only did the mob boss have excellent leadership skills, he also had a PhD. in Economics from The London School of Economics.

His attire was sophisticated and understated. His manners were impeccable. His voice was measured and reassuring. On meeting him casually you would have placed him as a successful CEO. Sergei was also one of the rare individuals that could perform well on four hours of sleep.

The mob boss was also positively obsessive about his health. He only smoked the odd cigar and, unlike many of his countrymen, drank nominally. Everything he did was calculated to be top drawer. His lieutenants joked that he only blinked when he decided that it was necessary to do so. Self-discipline was in his DNA. He wanted to control every situation, which some found intimidating. That was exactly why he acted that way.

But appearances can be deceiving. Although Sergei Mikhalov was a sophisticated CEO, he was also a premier member of the underworld. His education taught him how to hide his mountains of illegal cash. In many cases, his legitimate businesses (which included nightclubs, hotels and casinos in major offshore centers with favorable secrecy laws) reported higher revenues than the businesses themselves actually earned.

Sergei laundered money by taking over failing businesses. He revived them with new infusions of cash. Eventually, he controlled one hundred companies that took in dirty money as "payment" for goods and services that were provided at inflated prices. These companies traded with the public and with each other.

Although inflated, the bills of sale created the appearance of legitimate transactions. Sergei augmented this significant legitimate cash flow with drugs, prostitution, blackmail, identity theft and clandestine corporate espionage which included selling information to the highest bidder.

His hands were never close to any of the sources of the funds which were capably managed by well-paid and loyal surrogates. With constantly changing runners, burner phones, and random email addresses, his lieutenants maintained a low community profile, and had minimal direct contact with each other or with the public. The encryption codes used by his team were as sophisticated as those used by professional intelligence agencies which is why his clandestine activities were never discovered.

Chapter 2

Brass Balls

None of his well-educated business colleagues suspected that Sergei was responsible for the deaths of both his father, Nikolay, and his mother, Svetlana. He choked the life out of his father in the family's Olympic-sized swimming pool—his father had made the unforgivable mistake of naming his head capo, Antonio Tesdeco, rather than his only son, Sergei, as his successor. His father's betrayal was made worse when his weak mother told her son that, although she understood his disappointment, for the sake of his father's legacy, she supported his decision. Their son should know by now that the health of the business always came first.

Sergei's father, Nikolay, made his choice of successor for what he thought were practical reasons—he was not sure his only son had the brass balls needed to make the tough business decisions that came with being a mob boss. He came to this conclusion reluctantly, and only after he found out that Sergei, who was responsible for "collections," failed to follow a direct order to execute Sergei's lover, Dominika, the beautiful daughter of a client refusing to pay protection money.

Sergei didn't have the heart to kill his lover just to "send a message" to her parents. Instead, he hid her in one of their family properties and visited whenever he could. When Nikolay learned of his son's insubordination, he decided to teach Sergei a lesson. At gunpoint, he forced Dominika to call Sergei. She asked her lover to visit her on an urgent basis. When he asked why, she hung up.

When Sergei arrived, he didn't find a distraught Dominika in the living room. That's strange, he thought. Maybe she's taking a shower. But Dominika was not in the shower either—she was in bed—with his father—who was obviously enjoying himself as her head bobbed up and down on the old man's rock hard erection.

When Nikolay finished, he patted Dominika on the head. Then, his left hand moved to caress her neck. His right hand joined the left. Without warning his two hands tightened around her larynx in a stranglehold.

As the girl slowly died, his father turned to Sergei and calmly said, "You don't have the balls needed to run the family business. You'll receive a generous allowance. But I'm choosing a different successor who won't squander what I've worked so hard to build." Sergei was shocked and angry at his father's words. He resolved to show his mob boss father that he was more vicious than Nikolay gave him credit for.

Sergei bribed the coroner to declare that his father had a heart attack and drowned in the family pool. A grateful associate, masquerading as a guide, took care of his mother while she was skiing off-piste. He used the cash from his parents $12.5 million life insurance policies to purchase a twenty-bedroom estate in Corsica where he wined and dined his capos, and members of the political, business, and media elite. One month each summer, he turned the Corsica estate into a computer camp for underprivileged teens.

After his parents' funerals, Sergei invited his father's twelve lieutenants to a will reading at the Corsica estate. All twelve capos were in the boardroom, including Antonio, Nikolay's preferred successor. "I'm here to tell you that regardless of what the will says, what my father promised or even how many of you think you should lead this organization. I am the rightful successor and fully intend to take my father's place. You can either pledge loyalty to me or advance your own claim," Sergei calmly said.

Seven of the twelve lieutenants pledged loyalty to Sergei on the spot. Sergei thanked them and invited them to the library where his household staff had laid out a beautiful spread. "Looks like I have more work to do to convince your colleagues of my rightful claim," Sergei said with a brief, evil smile. He stood up and said, "Excuse me for a moment, gentlemen. I'm just going to show your colleagues how to get to the library. I'll be back shortly."

Two minutes later Sergei returned to the boardroom. He walked to the head of the table, smiled briefly at his five remaining colleagues, and raised a glass of water to his lips. That was the signal for the oil paintings on the boardroom wall to flip up. The hidden machine guns took care of business. Sergei was grateful for the earplugs he had inserted when he walked the seven loyalists out of the room. His household staff, who had already proven their loyalty, knew where to take out the trash.

Chapter 3

A New Friend

Sergei met police officer, Viktor Vasilyevich by accident one fall evening. He had just stepped into the shadows of the unoccupied patio located at the rear of the Myaso Dichi restaurant on Gogolevsky Blvd. He had just finished another delicious, late dinner of Siberian game meat, wild fruits, berries, and pinecones.

He was on the back patio because he didn't want to stink up his new car with a rare after-dinner cigar. Because of the late hour, Sergei hadn't expected anyone else to be on the patio. He was in the shadows, just about to light up, when he observed an overweight cop threaten Fredrik, the restaurant owner, with bodily harm, should he fail to pay protection money.

Since he had not yet lit his cigar, neither Viktor nor Fredrik, knew Sergei was there. Fredrik, who was 130-pounds soaking wet, was doing his best to reason with Viktor who outweighed him by close to one hundred pounds. When Sergei watched Viktor slowly remove a pair of well-used brass knuckles from the breast pocket of his uniform, he realized that if he ever wanted to eat Frederik's delicious food again, he would have to do something.

Although he didn't know Viktor personally, he could tell by his uniform that the man shaking down Viktor was a member of the Russian politsiya. Sergei dropped his unlit cigar onto the flagstones by his feet. Quick as a cat, the mob boss crossed the patio and delivered a round house kick to Viktor's solar plexus that would have made his 8th degree black belt Taekwondo Grand Master proud.

As the air left his lungs with a whoosh, Viktor collapsed onto the patio stones. When his head hit the cobble stones with a resounding thud, Fredrik started to cry. "Is he dead?"

Sergei turned to Fredrik and said, "Lock up, go home and leave the big bad policeman to me. I'll make sure he doesn't bother you again. And Fredrik, reserve my usual table for 9:00 p.m., next Friday." Fredrik stuttered his thanks and scurried back into the restaurant. Within a minute, Myaso Dichi was plunged into darkness.

Two minutes later, the policeman regained consciousness. The first thing he smelled was carbon and some kind of a spice. As his eyes focused, he saw the sole of a custom-tailored leather shoe, hovering two inches above his face. As his vision cleared, Viktor observed that the well-dressed, good-looking man at the end of the expensive shoe, had expertly placed the same brass knuckles Viktor had threatened Fredrik with, onto his own, well-manicured left hand.

"Do you know who I am?" Sergei said. Everyone in Moscow knew Sergei Mikhalov. Viktor, who seemed to have lost his voice, nodded yes.

"Being a policeman is hard work and probably doesn't pay very well. I admire your efforts to supplement your income. But it is far too labor intensive to shake down people like Fredrik, who have so little, and who struggle to just to make ends meet. I have a proposition for you. Interested?" Viktor again nodded yes.

"I have need of someone with your talents. I'm expanding my operation and want to grow my team. I am prepared to pay you $25,000 USD cash a year, for as long as you continue to prove your value and loyalty. In exchange, I require advance knowledge of any police activities that might affect me or mine. If things work out, our arrangement will automatically renew every year. And Viktor, the $25,000 is just the base salary; there will be cash bonuses for any 'special' information, if you know what I mean."

"Just to be clear, this is a one-time offer. But before you give me your answer, I want you to know that I sit on a number of non-profit boards with Police Commissioner, Georges Malkin. I'm sure my good friend, Georges, would like to know that one of his officers was seen shaking down a law-abiding citizen. So, what do you say? Will you accept my very generous offer, or do I call Georges?"

As Viktor once again nodded Yes, Sergei put his foot back on the ground, held out his right hand, and helped Viktor to his feet. He slipped Viktor's brass knuckles off of his left hand and returned them to the cop. Then, he reached into his impeccably tailored suit jacket and pulled out a soft, kid leather wallet. He removed ten crisp, one hundred USD bills and extended them to his new employee.

"This is a good faith down payment. One of my colleagues will deliver the other $24,000 to you this Sunday, during afternoon mass at The Cathedral of Christ the Saviour on the northern bank of the Moskva River, a few hundred metres southwest of the Kremlin. Do you know it?" Viktor nodded yes, placed the brass knuckles in his left-hand pants pocket, and slowly walked away.

Sergei finished his cigar and congratulated himself on turning another good crisis to his advantage. This chance meeting turned into a 25-year, mutually beneficial "relationship."

Chapter 4

A Born Killer

Some people are born killers. In Stanislav Kuznetsova's case, it would have been a miracle had he not become one.

His mother, Katia Kuznetsova, was a fourteen-year-old runaway with a serious drug problem. She lived in Chertanovo, one of Moscow's most criminally active districts. She survived by selling the only thing that she had to trade—her body. She never knew which one of her so-called clients fathered her son.

Stanislav Kuznetsova was born after a five-hour labor on April 6, 1970. Katia registered his birth at the civil registry office, the Zapis Aktov Grazhdanskogo Sostoyaniy or ZAGS.

Because Katia was stoned most of the time, she often forgot to feed baby Stanislav or to change his diapers. Were it not for an occasional customer, and Ivan, the local butcher who lived in the same housing block, it was likely the Kuzentsova's would have starved.

Ivan was a mean drunk with a wicked temper. When he had been drinking, which was a daily occurrence, Ivan beat Stanislav, Katia, or both of them. When he sobered up, he recognized that he had brutalized the only two people in the world that smiled at him when he entered a room. On the odd occasion when these regretful emotions crept in, he beat mother and child even harder. Didn't they know that he drank to excess so as to not feel anything, especially guilt?

Chapter 5

A Dark Apprenticeship

As the local butcher, Ivan was very strong and focused. His attention to detail ensured he made the cleanest and best cuts of meat. His signature brown leather apron, decorated rusty red by the blood of a variety of animals, was a grim reminder of his skill. He operated his butcher shop from a nondescript shop on Gidrostroevskaya Street in the city of Tolyatti. But being the neighborhood butcher was not the only place he worked. Ivan supplemented his modest butcher's income as a freelance enforcer and hitman, the job that he enjoyed the best.

One of the reasons Ivan was so successful in both of his chosen careers was his incredible observation skills. He knew all of his regular meat customers. He not only greeted each by name he remembered each of their favorite cuts. His off-the-charts observation skills meant that he could walk into any room and within minutes tell you everything about what was in it including what people were wearing, to an exact level of detail. When he was on a freelance assignment, Ivan worked in disguise. To ensure his two careers did not intersect, he only operated his secondary business outside the City of Tolyatti. Anyone that lived long enough to file a police report described a wide range of male and female perpetrators. With such different body signatures, none of his victims ever made the connection between the local butcher and the string of robberies, beatings, and murders that plagued Moscow.

Stanislav broke Ivan's nose when he fought back after a particularly vicious beating Ivan administered after his young ward was expelled from The Red Square Public School. That was the last time Ivan beat him. It was also the first day the teenager became Ivan's apprentice and partner.

Ivan taught Stanislav everything he knew about creating a disguise including the effective use of clothing, hats, wigs, makeup, and lifts. As his young protégé gained prowess Ivan rewarded him with extra food. Ivan also taught Stanislav that, especially when he was on assignment, he needed to keep a low profile. Poor manners and loud obnoxious behavior brought too much attention from curious neighbors and witnesses.

Over time, Stanislav's powers of recall and subterfuge surpassed Ivan's. Just like a professional golfer who could recall every detail of every shot, the teenager could go back a year and describe everything he had seen. It almost seemed as if he photographed everything he saw and then digitized it.

Unlike Ivan who barely spoke passable Russian, Stanislav excelled at languages. Besides Russian, Latin and French, the only other classes he attended regularly were history and drama. When they bothered with him at all, his classmates at The Red Square Public School described Stanislav as an unwashed, boorish bully.

When he was fifteen years of age, Stanislav was expelled for beating and raping Galina, another student because she had dared to make fun of his mother. Galina became pregnant and because of her strict, religious upbringing, did not terminate the pregnancy. Stanislav quit school and he and his mother moved in with Ivan to avoid answering questions from the local constabulary. Seven months later, Galina gave birth to a 5 lb. 4 oz. boy she called Andrei.

Despite his formal education being cut short, there was nothing wrong with the teen's mind. He was a voracious reader and a devout fan of Zuo Zongtang (General Tso) one of China's greatest military leaders, of the late Qing dynasty. He knew every weapon the General used, every military tactic he employed, and every battle he fought. He was also a big fan of the sleight of hand employed by Russian magicians, Igor and Alexei Kovax, and was even a passable magician himself.

By the time he was fifteen, Stanislav spoke passable English, Latin, Russian, French, Italian, Spanish and German.

He would continue to refine his language skills by listening to foreign films at the local library. More importantly, he would use all of these language skills in his future career as Sergei Mikhalov's assassin and enforcer.

Chapter 6

Full Partners

In the beginning, Ivan only used his young apprentice as a lookout. Things changed when the teen saved his mentor's life. Early in their new partnership, Ivan and Stanislav were paid to steal some records from a warehouse, and then to torch the place. The men collected the gear they needed, put on their disguises, stole a car, and headed to the warehouse.

Ivan was the first person to climb through the window Stanislav broke with his elbow. He had been told the landlord owned a nasty pit bull and that, before the duo arrived, his client would take care of drugging the animal. But Ivan, who was essentially illiterate, had misread his own poorly scribbled notes—and thought the job was scheduled for the evening of Sunday July 11th rather than the evening of Saturday July 10th.

As he landed on his feet, Ivan was surprised by a snarling pit bull, inappropriately named "Princess," who was awake and on the job. Ivan was slow to react to the dog's charge. Princess knocked Ivan to the ground and clamped her lock-jaws onto the intruder's right femur. The leg bone snapped under the pressure. Because of the pain, Ivan couldn't land a decent punch or dislodge the beast.

When Stanislav heard Ivan's screams, he crawled through the broken window to help him. The teenager was so focused on getting to Ivan, he didn't notice that he sliced the underside of his forearm on the broken glass.

Stanislav did not wait for Princess to react to his presence. Five long strides took him from the window to where Ivan was writhing in pain on the warehouse floor.

The teen punched Princess in the head and simultaneously plunged the double-edged Akela knife he always carried in his right boot, into the Pit's spine. The dog died instantly.

"You are shrewd, strong, and street smart. You know what our assignment is. Get the records. Set the fire and come back and get me the hell out of here," Ivan whispered painfully. Stanislav didn't need to be told twice.

The records were surprisingly easy to locate. Stanislav poured gasoline onto all the office surfaces on the second floor from a canister he retrieved from the car, and then lit a wooden match which he threw onto the soaked surfaces. He didn't return to Ivan until he saw the fire had taken hold.

The teen made his way to the first floor of the warehouse, put Ivan in a fireman's hold, and carried his friend and mentor out the front door, which he didn't bother to close. He knew fire needed oxygen to spread and was confident the open front door would ensure the warehouse would shortly be nothing more than smoking rubble.

He loved the adrenalin rush and didn't feel guilty about the property damage. "That's what you get from putting your faith in a dumb dog. The owner should have invested in sprinklers, not that sprinklers would have stopped us for long," Stanislav said with a wicked grin.

The local abortionist had enough medical skills to set Ivan's leg and stitch Stanislav's arm. Although the teen would be required to do most of the heavy lifting from that point forward, and Ivan's leg always ached, especially when it rained or snowed, which was often the case in Russia, the team was functioning again within six weeks.

After the incident, Stanislav gave Ivan, the hated nickname, "Otklyuchen," (Russian for disabled), "Okie" for short. Stanislav loved the nickname Ivan gave him. He believed "The Iceman" suited him perfectly—not only was it accurate it was aspirational and perfectly reflected all that he was and all that he aspired to be.

Business was brisk. Local gangs and shady businessmen, including mob boss, Sergei Mikhalov, retained Okie and The Iceman to intimidate witnesses and to collect debts. The two men received a premium if broken bones were involved. There was a further bonus if wet work was required.

When their services were required, Sergei placed an ad for a handyman with magical hands in The Moscow Times. When Okie called for the mob boss' instructions he said, "I'm replying to your ad for a handyman." To ensure he was talking to the right handyman, Sergei would ask, "Do you have written references?" Okie would reply, "I've done a lot of work for The Kovax Brothers. I'm sure they would be happy to provide a reference." The system worked perfectly.

One summer's day, it occurred to The Iceman that he was more than satisfied with the life that he and Okie had carved out for themselves. Although they shared many of the same traits, and Stanislav greatly admired Ivan's strength and courage, he was determined to surpass his mentor's skill level.

Several months after the warehouse fire, Stanislav's mother Katia died of a drug overdose. Her death didn't bother him much. A couple of weeks after that, Okie was killed in a knife fight at his favorite watering hole, the Hammer and Sickle Bar on Bolshawya Nikitskaya Street. That death bothered him much more.

Chapter 7

Payback

The Hammer and Sickle bartender was an informant for the local Militsiya. His information often helped them solve crimes, except the one that was dearest to his own heart. Several years earlier, the bartender, and his wife, Karine, had been in The Moscow Bank, when it was robbed at gunpoint. Karine was so frightened, she had a fatal heart attack. She was dead before she hit the floor. Everything happened so quickly, that he and their two children, never had a chance to say goodbye. The incompetent police never caught the perpetrators nor did any of the locals take him up on his $5,000 ruble reward for any information that led to a successful arrest. Sadly, it appeared that his wife's accidental death and the bank robbery case were colder than his dead love.

Because it was his mother-in-law's birthday and he wanted to treat her to some juicy steaks, the bartender was happy to see the butcher, who also happened to be a regular customer, enter the bar. He placed a couple of free shots of vodka in front of Okie to butter him up. The butcher was already drunk and didn't seem to notice that several of the regular customers were offended by the blood-stained work apron he had neglected to remove. When added to the shots the butcher had already consumed at the tavern down the street, Okie didn't have any of his usual filters and started to mumble about a civilian's death during a bank robbery and something about mothers crying and babies dying.

Okie's drunken reminiscences got the bartender's attention. Although inebriated, and spouting silliness, the butcher seemed to have too many details of the event not to have been involved. Could the butcher be one of the two men who were responsible for Karine's heart attack death?

Although it had been a couple of years since Karine had passed, his young daughters still cried for their mother. Blinded by mounting rage and frustrated by the lack of interest by the authorities, the bartender decided to take matters into his own hands.

He crushed several valium in the mortar and pestle he kept under the bar and usually only used for crushing something as innocuous as mint and laced the vodka shot with the valium powder. He placed the drink in front of the butcher and excused himself. He called the leader of a local gang, who owed him a favor, from the payphone located in the dingy hallway. It seemed that the only tasty steak he was likely to get was the one he would ask the local gang to stab into the butcher's heart. That would be the most delicious steak by far.

A half an hour later, Okie decided he had enough to drink. He intended to splash some water on his face and to "see a man about a horse" before he tackled the ten-minute walk home. He never made it. He was jumped by two masked men just as he exited the men's room. A third masked man stood guard in the dirty hallway.

The first attacker threw a wild punch with his left hand. Okie deflected the blow with his right elbow. Then, the butcher grabbed the first attacker in one beefy hand, and the second attacker in the other, and smashed their two heads together. Stunned, the two attackers crashed to the floor.

When he saw what was going on, the third hood, who was acting as lookout, grabbed the fire axe from the wall. He swung the axe at Okie's head, missed, and almost lost his balance from the momentum. The butcher easily ducked the swing and then delivered a roundhouse kick to the lookout-turned-attacker's balls. The lookout writhed in pain on the scarred wooden floor.

While he was busy fighting off the lookout, Okie hadn't noticed that the first attacker had recovered enough to sneak up behind him. He successfully jammed a knife into the back of the butcher's left shoulder. The knife was in so deep it was impossible for Ivan to reach or dislodge it. He tried his best to ignore it.

Despite the drugs in his system, the alcohol dulling his reflexes, and the knife sticking out of his shoulder, Okie still managed to pivot and grab the first attacker. But by then, the second attacker had recovered enough to take out a set of well-used brass knuckles from his jeans. He slipped them on and delivered a powerful Haymaker to the back of the butcher's head.

Although his knees started to buckle, Okie still managed to hook his left leg behind the second attacker's right knee. The butcher and the second attacker crashed to the floor. Just as Okie was starting to get up, the lookout regained his hold on the axe and swung it at the right knee on the same leg that had never completely recovered from the dog bite.

The pain was excruciating which made it difficult to focus. The tranquilizers in his system, further dulled the butcher's normally lightning quick reflexes. Which was why Okie never realized that the second attacker had regained his feet and was advancing towards him with the knife that had dislodged from his shoulder while he fought with the lookout.

The second attacker plunged the knife into the butcher's carotid artery. As Okie painted the scarred hallway floor the same color of rusty red as his leather apron, the second attacker delivered the kill shot to the butcher's head. He then collected his two dazed comrades, and went out the back door. Okie's last conscious thought was, "I'm done. It's up to The Iceman now."

There were no witnesses willing to come forward, and the tranquilizers in Okie's system could have been self-administered. Although the Militsiya went through the motions they were unsuccessful in locating the butcher's three attackers. It didn't matter. The Iceman was on the job.

Two weeks later, Stanislav put on a new disguise, and entered the bar from the alley entrance. He was dressed as a pretty blonde woman. He was determined to find out what really had happened to his partner and to get the names of all of Okie's attackers. At first, the bartender told the Iceman to take a hike.

When the Iceman held the bartender's throat in one gloved hand, he asked for the names of the hoods that attacked the butcher. As the Iceman started to squeeze, he began to describe in gory detail what he would do to the bartender's mother, mother-in-law and two young daughters, should the bartender fail to give him the names of Okie's attackers. The bartender squealed like a stuck pig.

Once he had the information he needed, The Iceman started to walk away. He was not surprised when he sensed the bartender reach under the bar for a shotgun. He reached into the left pocket of his custom-made trench coat and removed a hammer, which he had secreted in one of the deep pockets. In one fluid motion, he threw the hammer at the bartender's head. It connected. The bartender went down and didn't get up. The pretty blonde nonchalantly slipped out the back door. He had what he needed. Time to get the revenge party started.

A month later the Iceman put on another disguise and caught up with assassin #1. He drowned him in his own toilet, while his children and wife looked on. A week later, the Iceman donned another disguise. He beat the second attacker to death with a tire iron he stole from the trunk of the second assassin's wife's car. Just as the third attacker was starting to relax, The Iceman surprised him. Because he wanted the torture to last, he took his time loosening and tightening the garotte around the third assassin's throat. It took three hours before the man finally died.

Although he missed his friend and mentor, The Iceman knew all of Okie's clients and communications protocols. He was confident that he had even better technical skills and could run the business effectively on his own. He liked the idea of being an entrepreneur and looked forward to what he was sure to be many future opportunities to test his own clandestine mettle.

Chapter 8

The Iceman

Local mob boss Sergei Mikhalov made it his business to keep his finger on the pulse of his territory. Over the years, he had occasionally used the butcher as freelance talent. One of his twin sons, Dmitri, had mentioned that the Butcher had a young, crackerjack assistant and that this person had picked up much of the slack since his partner was injured.

When Dmitri told Sergei about the butcher's grisly death, he wondered if Okie had briefed his young protégé about their communications protocol. To ensure he was talking to the correct handyman, Sergei always asked for written references. When Ivan answered that he did a lot of work for the Kovax Brothers Sergei would know he was talking to the correct handyman.

On a "what the heck" basis the mob boss placed an ad for a handyman with magical hands in the Help Wanted section of the Moscow Times. He was always interested in growing his stable of talent and hoped that the butcher's young assistant would be interested in continuing their mutually beneficial relationship.

The Iceman spent part of each day honing his language skills by reading books and watching foreign films at the library. He smiled to himself when he read Sergei's ad. He called the mob boss from the public pay phone conveniently located in the library rotunda. The two men agreed to meet at the Hammer and Sickle bar. Because it had failed without the owner, Sergei had purchased it from the family and was now using it to launder money. Win/Win. Before what was supposed to be his one and only personal meeting with the mob boss, The Iceman transformed himself into a beefy construction worker.

The meeting itself was anti-climactic. Sergei confirmed he wanted The Iceman to be permanently on call and that he was prepared to pay a premium for an exclusive arrangement. He would continue to use the communications protocols the mob boss and Okie had set up and would be in touch when there was an assignment that required The Iceman's specialized skills. He encouraged The Iceman to keep training.

The Iceman gave Sergei new banking information and asked the mob boss to alternate payment between ten accounts. What a beautiful way to celebrate his 19th birthday!

The Iceman enjoyed wet work and his expertise was as broad as it was deep. He had perfected a wide variety of killing methods, including strangulation, suffocation, garrotting, fire, explosives, dismembering a live victim with a chainsaw or a knife, or shooting them in the head with a crossbow. He was also a crack shot and an expert in Russian fist fighting. In addition, he knew how to use potassium and cyanide because both of these substances could be put in drinks, brushed on skin, injected or breathed in, and the symptoms would mimic a heart attack.

Every time he undertook a job for Sergei, he created a new name and identity for that specific assignment. Because of this his work became more and more invisible and off the grid. His network of forgers and counterfeiters were located outside of Russia which was why he wasn't really worried about betrayal. The Iceman knew where they all lived and had so much information on their families that even witness protection wouldn't save them if they were stupid enough to double-cross him.

He always introduced himself with the words, "The Iceman sent me." None of the forgers knew what The Iceman actually looked like, because he was always in disguise. He made it a point to purchase a minimum of four identities at the same time. He needed multiples and used identities from different forgers to avoid detection. This system worked so well, he never had to improvise on the fly which had been how others had been caught.

After he received the documentation for a new identity, The Iceman changed into a slightly altered disguise, completed the assignment, and then changed again before he left the area. Although more time consuming, his system of multiple identity changes worked perfectly.

Although several of these identities were on Interpol's Most Wanted List, The Iceman was never captured. Like his mentors General Tso and the Kovax brothers, he was a master of the art of the ruse. He knew how to move seamlessly between looking like an executive one minute and a bum the next. He could quickly modify his eye color and hair length, alter his height by as much as six inches, and change his sex and weight by as much as one hundred pounds.

After the assignment was complete and the target was eliminated, The Iceman retired any identities used for the job. If Sergei was ever compromised, or if he was ever tempted to ice him, his employer would not know what name he was using and would be unable to give an accurate description to the police.

Sergei told The Iceman, that he had very well-connected police insiders including Viktor the police insider and who was available to help if needed. Between The Iceman and Viktor, Sergei was confident that he had all of his bases covered.

Chapter 9

A Hitman's Strategy

Sergei respected and trusted The Iceman's judgment and believed his skills were as good if not better than his own. He was most impressed with the assassin's combination of physical and mental capacities as well as his creativity.

He told his sons, Misha and Dmitri, that he thought his Iceman was the most accomplished hit man in the world. Throughout their association nothing his loyal retainer had done had splattered back on the family in any way.

While the assassin was probably the most expensive, his meticulous planning and 100% success rate without detection, was priceless. He believed the Iceman was successful because he never deviated from four rules:

1) If there was no time to plan the job, The Iceman refused the assignment. If Sergei wanted it done yesterday, he was encouraged to find someone else.

2) If the moment on the job that he had planned for went away for any reason—that was meant to be—there would always be another moment—the cost of failure was just too high. After all, his patron's and his own life was on the line.

3) The Iceman never asked any questions about why Sergei wanted him to do the job. Knowing this information was irrelevant to a successful outcome.

He never explained his tactics—not knowing preserved his secrets.

When the internet came to Russia, Sergei would post the ad on the website InterNationals.com. The Iceman monitored the website from a library computer. Although the two men would work together for more than two decades, they only met in person twice—the initial meet and greet and when Sergei issued his final instructions.

The mob boss was The Iceman's only client and he was paid handsomely for his exclusive services. In fact, he had more than $40 million reasons to be grateful for Sergei's patronage. The Iceman placed the funds in a number of offshore bank accounts, opened under various identities, none of which were ever used for any of his paid assignments.

Although he had enough money to enjoy any lifestyle he desired, The Iceman kept a low profile. He lived modestly, in a low-cost, concrete paneled, five-story Khrushchyovka apartment building on Nikita Perculok. His neighbors believed he was a travelling shoe salesman.

He rebuffed all of their well-meaning efforts to set him up on dates with their single relatives or to join them for dinner or a friendly glass of vodka. He did not want to have any distractions or human entanglements while he was working with Sergei.

His wealth allowed him to pay for several apartments, homes and storage units that were located in strategic locations around the world. He used these locations to store his huge inventory of stage makeup, wigs, clothing, lifts, and other disguises. He also kept several changes of clothes and clown wigs in his vehicle. If he was ever pulled over, he would tell the police that he was a magician on his way to perform at a kid's birthday party.

The Iceman occasionally thought about Galina and his son, Andrei. Despite his career, he didn't consider himself a complete monster. Because he could afford to do so, he set up an anonymous education fund for his son. He also purchased Galina a modest, two-storey, brick house in the Moscow suburb of Novye Cheryomushi.

He instructed the lawyer that handled the real estate transaction to tell Galina that a distant relative had left her the house and established the education fund. Galina who worked as a char woman, was so grateful for the help that she didn't inquire further.

After the transaction was completed, the lawyer, who was cycling home after a busy day at the office, fell off his bike and hit his head on the sidewalk. He was dead before he hit the ground. The autopsy indicated he had died instantly from a massive heart attack. Nothing personal—his business required a "no-loose-ends" policy.

Chapter 10

Lust

When Sergei first laid eyes on Elena Popov, the breathtakingly beautiful blonde Lacuna lingerie model at the 1975 Waterways show, his cock almost burned through the zipper of his custom Josef Knize suit pants. When he imagined the hot sex he was sure they would enjoy, he resolved to do whatever it took to get the green-eyed witch into his bed.

It was one of the few moments in his life that he couldn't control himself. He was so overcome by the pheromones that he was just lost to the beautiful model. Had he had bothered to learn anything about Elena's background, he would also have been impressed by her pedigree.

Elena Popov's grandfather, Alexei, was a member of the Polish underground, and had provided useful intelligence to the Allies during World War I. Her grandmother, Veronika, was a Russian spy. Her parents, Peter and Alexandra Popov, had been upwardly mobile executives in the Communist Party before they were poisoned. Elena was just twelve years old when her parents were assassinated. Otto Lacuna, a family friend, took her under his wing, mentored her, and when she was 16, gave her a job as one of his swimsuit models.

Although he had two biological nephews, Otto, who did not have any children of his own, treated Elena like a daughter. Because she showed a keen interest in his business, he taught her everything he knew about building a successful brand and retail empire. Otto never told her that she was the sole beneficiary of his considerable estate

Sergei wasn't interested in Elena's pedigree or her net worth. He needed an heir, and was sure Elena Popov would give him many strapping sons. He planned on unleashing his considerable powers of persuasion to induce the gorgeous 5' 8" Lacuna model to marry him.

He pursued the leggy blonde for three months. Elena was more than a little intimidated by Sergei's intensity and was tired of saying No! to his daily gifts and marriage proposals. She finally agreed to marry him when the powerful businessman promised to bankroll her own retail business. Little did she know the extent of the betrayal and future heartbreak that would come from that one decision.

Uncle Otto made some perfunctory inquiries about Elena's suiter. Although he was a bit overbearing, everyone he asked, spoke highly of Sergei's personal style, wealth, and education. Since there didn't appear to be anything to worry about, he gave his blessing to the union and the couple was married that same month. Otto proudly walked his de facto daughter down the aisle of The Cathedral of Christ the Saviour.

Chapter 11

Another Funeral

Soon after they were married Elena realized that Sergei was extremely possessive and jealous of her close relationship with Uncle Otto.

One night over dinner, she asked "Why do we have all these bodyguards? I've never noticed so many people in our home before."

"They are here to deal with anyone who wants to kidnap me. As my wife, you are also a kidnap target. I may have enemies I don't even know about that would do just about anything to see me fail and that want to hurt my family," Sergei said.

"Some people even suspect that I am a mob boss," he added.

"Are you?" Elena asked.

"Every businessman has enemies. Because I go for the jugular, I have more enemies than most."

"Is there anything illegal about your work?"

"I sometimes color outside of the lines."

"And my darling girl, I hope you understand that if you ever betray me the consequences will be much more serious than a divorce," Sergei said.

"Are you threatening me?" Elena asked.

"No, I'm just suggesting there are many benefits of being married to me, like starting your own retail swimsuit and lingerie line," he reminded her.

Elena was shocked. Although she suspected that Sergei was not a white knight, she had no idea that he was a mob boss. So much for Uncle Otto's due diligence. She decided the only way to survive the marriage was to spend as little time as possible with her new husband and to concentrate on building her retail empire.

Sergei's controlling nature was one of the reasons that he was so successful in business. He believed that the sooner his new wife got pregnant the better. But that happy event took several years longer than originally anticipated. And he knew it wasn't because he was sterile, as he already had two, DNA-confirmed bastard sons that he secretly supported. Their mothers had either lied to him about using birth control or the condoms he used had been faulty. No matter. He always did his duty inside and outside of the bedroom. And his generous child support payments combined with his promise to unleash The Iceman guaranteed loyalty and the appropriate level of gratitude.

Six months after that conversation, Uncle Otto died unexpectedly, of complications from a stroke. His estate, worth some $100 million dollars, included a $5 million-dollar life insurance policy, several properties, stocks and bonds, three original Rembrandts, $10 million in cash, and ownership of his Lacuna retail business. Elena was the sole beneficiary.

Otto's sister, Liliya, and his nephews, Konstantin and Leonid, disputed the will. Sergei didn't want any complications and reached out to the Iceman in the usual way. Two months later, Liliya, and her two sons, drowned when their fishing boat capsized after it was swamped by another boat. They weren't wearing life jackets. Elena would have been horrified to learn that Sergei's Iceman was responsible for the deaths. But she never learned the truth and believed their deaths were nothing more than a tragic accident.

The mob boss originally assumed that someone as beautiful as Elena, was also stupid. He was wrong. Besides being gorgeous, Elena possessed a laser sharp mind. Thanks to Uncle Otto, she had no need of Sergei's cash. But a promise was a promise, and she would never have accepted his marriage proposal had Sergei not agreed to bankroll her own lingerie and swimsuit company.

Elena knew Sergei wanted to start a family. But that was his priority, not hers. She wanted to create a successful business before she would consider having children. Despite his network of informants and spies, Sergei never learned about the secret stash of birth control pills Elena kept in her locker at the gym.

A year after they were married, the couple were at their Corsica estate for a "spontaneous" dirty weekend. Elena's birth control pills were back in the city. When they returned to Moscow, she visited her doctor who prescribed the morning after pill. Her husband may have had plans but so did she. And being barefoot and pregnant before her business was established was not one of them.

Chapter 12

OhMy EAU!!

Elena had been designing her own clothes since she was twelve years of age. She knew all of the super models, fashion media, and the manufacturers from her Lacuna modeling days. Uncle Leo's Lacuna business was well established and basically ran itself. But it was his baby, not hers. She wanted her own brand and one that was not geared to the mass market. When she publicly announced her intention to open her first store, everyone that knew the beautiful, even-tempered model, was happy to lend their support.

She called her brand *OhMy EAU!!*, a word play on Maillot, the French word for swim suit. Elena opened her flagship store in her hometown, Moscow, in a 3,500 sq. ft. facility on Tversjata Street 3, close to the Glitz Carlsberg Hotel.

Because Elena understood fashion, glamor and style, she knew what to do to keep the business fresh. The ability to move product between stores, lent itself to expanding the business to other countries. A chain of stores meant very little overstock. And because they knew, liked and trusted Elena, the manufacturers were happy to provide huge volume discounts which allowed her to offer competitive pricing. Her aggressive business plan called for opening ten different stores in various tourist hot spots around the globe each and every year.

OhMy EAU!! was brilliant at promoting itself and Elena's marketing team worked hard at ensuring "Fashion Club Members" were engaged and loyal. The company's tag line, "We're All in For Under Things," played really well, especially in Vegas!

One of the ways *OhMy EAU!!* lived its tagline, "We're All in For Under Things," was to provide rewards for purchasing intimates for someone else.

The words, "What better way to go under cover!" appeared in bold embossed ink on all marketing materials including customer membership cards and the company website.

Chapter 13

Membership Perks

Clients had to be eighteen years of age to be a Fashion Club member. *OhMy EAU!!* worked hard to connect its customers to a unique "sensory" experience aroused by the items of clothing they intended to try on. Customers could enhance their customer experience by donning a virtual reality headset which generated realistic images, sounds and other sensations that were either romantic and sexy to match the beautiful lingerie or beach-oriented, consistent with a potential swim wear purchase.

The *OhMy EAU!!* ambassador, who was conveniently stationed outside the change rooms, offered the head set and instructed the customer to put it on as soon as they were in the privacy of the dressing room. If the customer didn't want to have a virtual reality experience, the clerk would manually select the lighting and the sounds that most closely reflected their potential purchase.

As part of its member engagement strategy, all *OhMy EAU!!* stores hosted bi-monthly fashion events with local designers and in January and October of each year, the different stores sponsored an "*OhMy EAU!!* Fashion Week." Members and the media loved Fashion Week because beautiful local models were always on "display" in the store windows during business hours.

Besides Fashion Week, fashion icons hosted fashion trends seminars at select stores. All content and special promotions were included in the monthly member newsletter Elena's administration staff blasted out to members.

Every Valentine's Day (Otto Lacuna's birthday and the day Elena opened her first store, *OhMy EAU!!* Moscow), there was a draw for three, USD $1,000 *OhMy EAU!!* gift cards.

Only Fashion Club Members were eligible to enter the Valentine's draw.

Elena's customers loved the pricing, appreciated the educational glamor of the bi-monthly events and Fashion Week, and enjoyed the discounts, the newsletter and the draw. The business was so successful that after accepting initial start-up funds for her first store, *OhMy EAU!!* Russia, Elena never needed to take another dollar from her husband.

But there was trouble in paradise. Although she ran a successful business and had everything money could buy, Elena felt like a prisoner. She missed the easy relationship she had with Uncle Otto. She was only able to cope with Sergei's controlling ways because she knew she could get away on her own when she was on her quarterly buying trips. It was only when *OhMy EAU!!* Moscow had been operating for two years, and she had successfully opened 25 additional stores that Elena stopped taking her birth control pills. In 1981, she gave birth to twin sons, Misha and Dmitri. Sergei was ecstatic.

Chapter 14

The Twins

From the time they were three years of age (that was when Sergei decided that Misha rather than Dmitri would be his public successor), the twins had been on different life paths. Sergei spent hours teaching Misha mathematics and geometry and hired a tutor to teach him coding. To the world, it appeared as if he left the more adventurous, artistic, and outspoken Dmitri to the gentle ministrations of his mother.

As a result, the brothers never developed the deep bond that usually exists between twins. They were not best friends, nor did they appear to understand or even to like each other. And unlike most twins, neither brother automatically knew what the other brother was thinking.

To the world at large, it appeared as if Sergei favoured his dark-haired business minded son, Misha. But appearances can be deceiving. Sergei's apparent disdain for his dreamy, blue-eyed, golden-haired, son Dmitri, was just a ruse. The truth was, Sergei depended upon Dmitri for the market intelligence he needed to keep growing the ever-expanding tentacles of his legal and illegal business empire.

Unlike his more introverted, technologically minded, business-oriented twin, Dmitri was charming, witty, and outgoing. He was welcomed in boardrooms and bedrooms around the world and was comfortable with everyone—from politicians to heads of the world's largest corporations, to musicians, actors and even media types. He also had sex with most of them.

Sergei relied on Dmitri for market intelligence on potential mergers, acquisitions and takeovers, wars, power plays, and gun and drug running opportunities. He needed this information to stay ahead of all of his legal and illegal enemies and competitors. Because Dmitri was very good at his job,

Sergei made millions of dollars, buying and selling stocks, shorting the market, blackmail, and identity theft.

Unlike Misha, Dmitri was not a good student and barely made it through the Hanzel University of Applied Arts and Sciences. Truth be told, he would rather take photos of street signs than to pick up a book. The only person Dmitri appeared to love was himself and he often joked that if the silver spoon stayed firmly in his mouth, he couldn't care less how it got there. But the pretty package/empty box persona was just a ruse as Dmitri possessed the razor sharp mind and cunningness of his mob boss father.

When he wasn't playing polo, raising polo ponies, or attending a black-tie event, Dmitri could be found painting or developing film in his art studio. His photos and paintings hung on the walls of The Mikhalov Center for Photography and Contemporary Art on Syromyatnicheskly Perculok, the art gallery his father custom-built for him.

Unlike his more artistic twin, Misha earned a Computer Science Degree from Novosibirsk State Technical University. Sergei and Misha could often be found with their heads together, discussing business into the early morning hours. Elena often joked that she thought that her husband and Misha, rather than her two sons, were the fraternal twins.

Chapter 15

A Welcome Reprieve

Elena relished the freedom of her *OhMy EAU!!* buying trips. As much as she loved her sons, it was always a relief to get away from her dominating husband, and the demands of running her two businesses. She never knew The Iceman always stood guard when she was on one of her solo trips. Sergei would not tolerate disloyalty—if she was foolish enough to bed another man, The Iceman would ensure she wouldn't have a chance to do it a second time.

But having an affair was the furthest thing from her mind. After Elena visited three factories in Milan on January 13, 1998, she checked into a five-star hotel near the Basilica di Santa Maria Delle Grazie's refectory. She was looking forward to again seeing da Vinci's famous mural, The Last Supper, the next day. Elena ordered her favorite liver offal dish, a salad and several brandies from the hotel's room service menu.

Dmitri was more than a son. He was also her best friend and confidante as well as her pusher. When she was finished with her dinner, Elena opened her purse and took out the small package Dmitri had carefully gift wrapped in star-studded birthday wrap for an evening of solo partying. "That boy has such a great sense of humor," she said out loud.

She changed into a pair of *OhMy EAU!!* muted puce, silk sleepwear, turned on the television, and swallowed two tablets. She washed everything down with the one remaining shot of brandy and looked forward to a blissful evening alone. As Elena turned down the bed, she welcomed the first waves of pleasure.

An hour later, her blood pressure had risen to 232/180 and her heart was clattering like a runaway train. She started to sweat and barely made it to the bathroom to throw up. Her severe jaw pain ensured she stayed conscious long enough to call Dmitri, who knew both her location and her schedule. Dmitri called the concierge who entered his mother's room with the hotel doctor.

When she awoke five hours later, Dmitri and the hotel doctor were both standing by her bedside. There was an IV in her right arm. Although his mother looked very frail, Dmitri was not really worried. This had happened before. Once the drugs were out of her system, his mother would be as good as new.

As the doctor took her pulse, he informed Elena that the Ecstasy overdose had caused a miscarriage. Elena hadn't even realized she was two months' pregnant! She was expanding the business, and just assumed that stress, not a pregnancy, was responsible for her missed periods. It looked like she dodged a bullet. As far as she was concerned, Misha and Dmitri were more than enough and the baby factory was closed!

Chapter 16

Heir Apparent

By the time he was thirty-two years of age, Misha was as important to the Mikhalov family business as was his father. Sergei told him he was grooming him to take over the whole network of legal and illegal drug, oil, diamond and blackmail businesses within the next ten years.

As the future CEO, Misha knew everything about all of his father's legal and illegal business activities including the fact that his father often employed violence and intimidation to achieve his business goals. When Sergei offered Misha The Iceman's coordinates and their communications protocol, Misha laughed and said, "I can't imagine ever needing the services of a hired gun However, for added peace of mind, I will take the information." He didn't know that everything his father told him was also shared with his twin.

Misha naively believed that if his father did not provide these customer-driven, illegal services, someone else would do so. He rationalized his involvement because their legitimate businesses paid taxes and created hundreds of well-paying jobs throughout the world. In his mind at least, the good that Sergei did, more than balanced out the bad.

He rationalized that the illegal activities funded Sergei's numerous not-for-profit and charitable projects, including Alyosha, his own educational foundation. His father's most recent philanthropic enterprise involved paying all expenses (including transportation, lodging, equipment, food, entertainment and the best teachers that money could buy) for fifteen underprivileged, technologically minded, 13-15-year-old "misadventured" youth, at Camp Orlyonyk, a month-long computer camp held at the family's Corsica estate in July of each year.

Chapter 17

Camp Orlyonyk

Camp Orlyonyk recruits were referred to Misha through Dmitri's police contacts. Like a modern-day Fagan, Misha met with each camper candidate personally. The purpose of the meeting was to assess the camper's attitude, technological aptitude, and most importantly, moral compass.

Despite what was printed in the promotional brochure, Misha only enrolled youth whose past activities demonstrated they would do just about anything for a price. The more desperate the candidate, the better. As their marketing material said, the Mikhalov's only focused on the saddest cases because they were committed to, "Helping the un-helpable help themselves."

Every July 1-31, Sergei turned his twenty-bedroom Corsica estate into Camp Orlyonyk where fifteen lucky recruits were taught advanced computer programming, gaming, and social media skills. When they weren't in class or working on homework assignments, the campers were welcome to swim, play tennis, or to go horseback riding on the beautiful estate grounds. An award-winning cordon bleu chef prepared and served all of the campers' meals.

Computer monitors in the private rooms played a "reveille-type" alarm at 6:00 a.m. Campers were expected to be showered (each private bedroom contained a private bathroom), changed, and seated in the main dining room by 6:30 a.m. when casually dressed wait staff served a healthy, hot breakfast.

Classes started promptly at 7:30 a.m. Lunch was served in the dining room at noon. Campers were welcome to help themselves to any of the hot and cold buffet style items that were laid out in the main dining room. Milk, water, fruit, along with healthy homemade cookies could be found in the main dining room from 10:00 a.m. to 11:00 a.m. and again from 2:00 p.m. to 4:00 p.m. every day.

Campers were served a healthy dinner at 6:00 p.m. and were expected to be in their private suites by 10:30 p.m. Another one of Misha's customized computer programs turned the overhead lights off at 11:00 p.m. Attendance was taken before all meals and at 11:00 p.m. Security cameras in the halls confirmed that the campers stayed put until the following morning. At the end of the month, regardless of aptitude, every camper received a graduation certificate, a mobile telephone, and an Apple Mac book computer.

The world at large praised Sergei for his corporate sponsorship of such a worthy cause. Sergei's philanthropic efforts were acknowledged in a personal letter from Russia's Human Rights Ombudsman. The camp also received the Order of the Badge of Honor from the Communist Union of Youth (Komsomol) organization, which was awarded for extraordinary social and civil accomplishments. All of these framed letters (along with several others) were prominently displayed on Sergei's office wall.

As a result of his work with at-risk youth, Sergei was invited to join a number of not-for-profit boards. He also donated significant sums of money to both of Moscow's children's mental health charities, three hospitals (one in Saint Petersburg, one in Moscow, and the other in Novosibirsk), breast cancer, Alzheimer's research, Right to Play, and Doctors Without Borders. In addition to his own charitable projects, Sergei was also the chief ambassador and fundraiser for Misha's Alyosha Foundation.

But like everything else the Mikhalov's did, most of their philanthropic activities were nothing more than a smokescreen for something more sinister. For example, Camp Orlyonyk was a recruitment tool for future employees that could demonstrate they had the right "mindset."

Each year, up to five campers were selected to be mentored by Misha who taught them how to hack, to create false identities, to steal corporate secrets and personal identities, and to access the dark web. Then, each of the five campers were employed in one of the family's illegal businesses or on their server farm. Generous salaries, perks, and The Iceman ensured the campers stayed loyal and engaged. The program was very popular and all of the camper candidates competed for the honor of being chosen for Misha's follow-on "employment" program.

Chapter 18

Memorial Service

Melodie Marie Beaudoin's memorial service was held at 11:00 a.m. on Friday September 17, 2012, at the Mother of Mercy Roman Catholic Church on Rene Levesque Street in downtown Trois-Rivières, Quebec. The service was well attended and took place exactly one month to the day that Melodie died in a fire at her rented D.C. townhouse.

In addition to Chief Denis Fornier, and thirty cops from The Service de police de la Ville de Montréal, there was an equal number of firefighters from his brothers' stations, the mayor, a regional executive from Tim Horton's, the goalie from the Washington Capitals Hockey team, fifteen Loups Du Bois (Timber Wolves) hockey alumni, and at least one hundred and fifty friends, neighbors and former classmates from Cornell and INSEAD. By the time Father Durand was ready to begin the service, there was standing room only at the back of the picturesque church.

Father Durand had known the family for over fifty years and had baptized and officiated at the communions for every one of the nine Beaudoin children. After a cycle of prayers, the funeral Mass, and the absolution, Father Durand invited Melodie's eldest brother, Jacques, to the podium to say a few words.

"Thank you all for coming, especially my fellow police officers from The Service de police de la Ville de Montréal and the firefighters from Stations 6 and 10 here in Trois-Rivières. My family and I appreciate your friendship and support during this very difficult time.

My sister, Melodie, was just thirty-two years old when she died in a fire in her D.C. home, one short month ago. It's still so hard to believe that she's actually gone, and not just out at another hot yoga class or at brunch with friends and colleagues at her favorite restaurant, the Vegan Delight in Washington D.C. The reason I'm assuming it must have been her favorite restaurant is because my health-conscious sister insisted we dine there every time I visited her in D.C.!

Because of my career, for those of you that don't know me, I am a police detective, I have seen more than my fair share of death. Even with all my experience, I was not prepared to lose my vivacious, intelligent, and funny younger sister. I'm half expecting her to bound up the aisle and tell us all that it was all just a sick joke. Melodie, I'm a cop. I always thought that that I would go before you. I never expected to be delivering the eulogy at YOUR funeral.

I still find it so hard to believe that I will never hear you laugh again. Wouldn't you all agree that my baby sister had the best laugh in the whole world? It was so contagious that everyone that heard it started laughing too, even if they didn't know what was so funny.

Melodie was the kind of kid who was interested in everything and because of this, she asked millions of questions. So much so that, that in order to maintain their sanity, from the time she was five years old, my parents limited their precocious daughter to just ten questions per day. That's why she carried a notebook and a pen with her everywhere she went, a habit she maintained until the day she died.

Her personality entered the room before she did. Young or old, white, black or brown, from Canada or abroad, English speakers, French speakers, Spanish speakers, or Mandarin speakers—everyone, including animals, loved her. Between the squirrels, raccoons, ferrets, birds, turtles, and snakes Melodie nursed back to health, our house often looked like an infirmary for injured creatures. Our mother, Dee, finally said "suffisamment," when Melodie wanted to bring an injured skunk into our home.

For those that don't know us well, we Baudouin's are an ambitious, loving and competitive family. Melodie had eight older brothers—Raphael, Luc, Alexandre, Louis, Jean,

Georges, Olivier, and of course, the eldest, and her all-time favorite brother, me!

As the only girl, and the youngest child, our parents, Dee and Pierre, and all of her brothers, spoiled her. But it never went to her head. Melodie wasn't a delicate flower or the kind of girl who just sat on a pillow and looked pretty. She had to be tough with the eight of us, and in a fight, she knew how to give as good as she got.

When she was a teenager, Melodie was the town's best hockey player. Our father, Pierre, managed the ice hockey rink here in Trois-Rivières, and later coached the Timber Wolves hockey team, where Melodie was MVP for all three of the years that she played with the team.

She was fiercely loyal to her friends and would never back down if she thought she was right. From a very early age, mon petite soeur demonstrated she had backbone, courage, and principles. I never saw her walk away from an injustice.

Here's an example. When she was just fifteen years old, Melodie exposed a former Timber Wolves hockey coach who was seducing the players. Because she had grown up with a cop as a brother, she knew that she needed proof of inappropriate behavior before the police would get involved. So, she recorded a sexually explicit conversation between Coach Lasalle and Suzanne St. Pierre, the team captain. She held onto the tape until she saw me a week later, when I was in Trois-Rivières for a family visit.

When I heard Melodie's recording, I went directly to Coach Lasalle's office and played him the tape. He admitted he had crossed the line, resigned his position as coach of the Timber Wolves, and left Trois-Rivières for good. Now you know why my private nickname for her was "Watson." When Coach Lasalle left, our dad, Pierre, stepped in to coach the Timber Wolves Girls' Hockey Team. In the ten years you coached the team, Dad, you have done a solid and inspiring job! Go Timber Wolves!

Melodie attended Cornell University on a full hockey scholarship. When I pointed out there are many other wonderful universities to choose from, she told me that if Cornell was good enough for her beloved brother, and for Ken Dryden, who was a hockey player, a lawyer, and a politician, it was good enough for her too!

Maybe you didn't know this, but while she was at Cornell, Melodie seriously considered a hockey career and was almost guaranteed a spot on the Canadian Women's Olympic Hockey Team which is why she stayed away from the slopes and her second love, skiing.

But for anyone that loves to ski, four years without enjoying the slopes, was just too long. Because summer training camp for the Olympic hockey team was three months away, Melodie agreed to join the rest of the family for a Mt. Tremblant ski weekend.

On the first day, she was content to find her feet. Because she wanted to get over boot shock, Melodie stuck strictly to the blue slopes, and avoided crowds and moguls. By day two however, she had found the center of her ski and was back to the same level of skill she had prior to her four-year timeout.

After warming up and then running some mid-level mogul runs, we found ourselves on Dynamite, the most challenging run at Tremblant. On the third run, Melodie's binding hit an ice boulder and released just as she was changing uphill skis. Down she went.

I could tell my sweet sister was seriously injured when she couldn't stand. I called the ski patrol on my cell phone. Thank goodness they arrived quickly. Melodie was ignominiously sledded down the slope and immediately put in an ambulance. And that was how an ACL tear sidelined her and her Olympic hockey dreams forever.

But did her accident keep her down? Not our Melodie Marie. That autumn my sister completed her physiotherapy studies at Georgetown University. It turned out she was also a talented physio therapist. After she moved to Washington, D.C., she provided part-time physiotherapy services to the Washington Capitals hockey players.

Melodie was smart and loved learning. She had a B.A.—she majored in finance and business—from Cornell University in New York and a Kinesiology & Sport Science degree from Georgetown. She augmented her studies with an M.B.A. in International Business Finance from INSEAD.

I know it wasn't a New York Times Best-Seller, but Melodie and her colleagues from the Sustainable Investing Club at INSEAD, many of whom have travelled from afar to be with us today, wrote a book on how to calculate R.O.I. on sustainable and eco-investments and to measure non-monetary returns from positive social change. Even after graduation, all of the Sustainable Investing Club members remained close friends. I'm sure that was largely because of Melodie, who collected people like some people collect stamps.

After she graduated from Cornell and Georgetown, Melodie had a great job with Investment Brothers before it collapsed in the financial crisis of 2008.

My little sister was also an avid boxer and yogi. Most recently, she and her best friend, Christina, were enjoying life as freelance Spanish, French, and Mandarin language coaches in Washington D.C. My sister worked with some very important and powerful people in the United States government as well as with many sports professionals.

Before she died so tragically, my sister had also found love.

Melodie, I miss you already. I can't believe you're gone. Rest easy baby sister. I love you. Always have. And always will.

And now for some announcements. Melodie will be interred in Section D of the Roman Catholic Cemetery on Boulevard de la Montagne Street. If you plan on being part of the funeral procession, please keep your lights on and drive slowly. Thanks to my colleagues from the Service de sécurité publique de Trois-Rivières, we have a police escort.

After the internment, please join my parents, brothers and I for some light refreshments at my parents' home at 454 Boulevard Oeust. In lieu of flowers the family would appreciate it if you made a donation in Melodie's memory to either The Canadian Breast Cancer Society or The Amateur Hockey Association of Canada."

Many people, including her boyfriend, her best friend, Christina, and her INSEAD colleagues, Denzel, Misha, JB, Wayne, Svetlana, and Paula, came back to the house where Jacques informed them about the coroner's ruling of accidental death. All of his sister's friends and colleagues were certain the coroner had made a mistake. Anyone that knew Melodie also knew that after her cancer diagnosis, she was obsessively committed to living a healthy life style.

She didn't smoke and only drank wine moderately and was always very responsible with her medications. They didn't believe Melodie would just pop a sleeping pill, light a candle, and indulge in alcohol. Despite the coroner's ruling, they believed their friend was a victim of foul play and encouraged Jacques to launch his own investigation.

Chapter 19

Shared Grief

The next morning, Jacques invited Melodie's boyfriend, her best friend, Christina, her INSEAD roommate, Paula Da Silva, and her other INSEAD friends, Denzel Sun Mah, Misha Mikhalov, Svetlana Tretiak, and Wayne Lee, to join him for a private celebration of life at one of Melodie's favorite local restaurants. They congregated at Café Gateux on rue des Forges at 11 a.m., before each of them left for their respective homes.

It was the first time Christina had an opportunity to meet Melodie's boyfriend, (Melodie had kept her updated on their evolving romance through their joint UPS mailbox) and her INSEAD friends, Denzel, Misha, Paula and Svetlana. Jacques already knew Christina from their 2008 Burning Man experience. Jacques also knew Misha from a cyber security seminar they both attended when Misha worked at the Caisse. Denzel was also at the same seminar, but didn't want to call attention to his previous persona, and didn't say anything.

The seven mourners laughed and cried together over chocolate croissants and dirty (double-shot) cappuccinos. Everyone agreed that Melodie was not only an exceptional human being, she was the bravest and most responsible person any of them had ever known. Everyone believed there was no way that she would have been so careless to have caused her own death.

"She was my hero," Christina said in a shaky voice. "One day I'll tell you, but not today, as I'm barely holding it together." As the brunch was winding down, everyone offered to help in any way that they could.

Svetlana was spending the rest of the weekend with Melodie's brother, Luc. Christina and her boyfriend were taking a late afternoon flight back to Washington. Wayne was returning to Japan and Paula to Spain on separate red eye flights. Denzel was returning to Mexico, and Misha to Russia the next day. Jacques, "Hercule," a real-life private detective, hugged Christina, and Wayne and Paula goodbye. "

Jacques then invited Misha and Denzel to join him for dinner at Steak Frit St. Georges on rue St. Georges at 7:00 p.m. Jacques, Misha and Denzel bonded over scotch on the rocks, a lively discussion of hockey, and their shared grief.

Before the mouth-watering medium rare steaks were served, Jacques said, "I don't know if you know this, but I gave Melodie her first pair of hockey skates and I seriously considered having a professional hockey career before I joined the police force."

"So, that explains Melodie's lopsided loyalty to the Montreal Canadiens hockey team, especially because the Washington Capitals, the team that she occasionally worked for, are a much better team," Denzel said with a sad smile. His eyes teared up as he added, "I'll never be able to watch another Montreal Canadiens hockey game without thinking about her."

"Your sister held all of us "Leave Only Shadows" co-authors' feet to the fire and made sure that we did what we said we were going to do, when we said we were going to do it. She was a fair and inspirational leader. I still haven't been able to figure out what she said or did to keep all of us focused on meeting her ridiculously tight deadlines," Misha added.

When he got back home, the first thing he did was complete a police search on Melodie's boyfriend, Misha, and Denzel. He had completed a cursory search on Christina before he, Melodie and Christina went to Burning Man together. Although he liked the three men, he always hoped for the best, and planned for the worst. Jacques needed to complete his personal research before he made a further emotional investment into these relationships.

Chapter 20

Professor Leonardo Capilano

It was September 2004, a couple of years before former U.S. Vice President Al Gore released his documentary film, "An Inconvenient Truth" (Gore would later receive a Nobel Peace Prize for his work). The world had just begun to think of climate change as the "most pressing issue faced by 21st century humanity."

Even before Gore's movie, Environmental, Social, Governance (ESG) or socially responsible, focused investing, was becoming more mainstream. His own fund, "Generation Investment Management," proved that it was possible to be environmentally responsible AND to make a lot of money.

As a leader in the area of socially responsible investing, INSEAD had a number of student-run clubs, including the Sustainable Investing and the Ethical Investing Clubs. These two clubs were founded by Professor Leonardo Capilano, who was consistently ranked as the most animated and entertaining professor in student polls. The Club provided additional opportunities for Professor Capilano (Professor C) to mentor and coach his students and also allowed him to fulfill the terms of his plea agreement.

Professor C believed it was possible to make money while doing good and often talked about the merits of "triple bottom line investing." He believed that every corporation should be working towards a social return, an environmental return, and a financial return.

At first, the students were skeptical and believed Professor C lived in an academic bubble. As far as they could tell shareholders only seemed to care about making money. They uniformly believed Professor C's approach would cause the public markets to react negatively which would reduce quarterly profits and imperil the market price for its shares.

In one lecture, Professor C said, "Making money is important of course. But there is more to it than that. Let me ask you a couple of questions. Do you believe you can do well financially by doing good? And if so, do you believe it is good for a business to build in attributes their clients and customers deem to be desirable? Two organizations, Panneaux Solaires, a solar company headquartered in France, and Starbucks, a coffee company, headquartered in the United States, prove the viability of a triple bottom line approach.

"Both businesses are very profitable. Last year, Panneaux Solaires, a relatively small company reported $3 Million in profits. That is the doing well part. Would you also agree that using solar power means you use less non-renewable fossil fuels? That's the doing good part! Now let's look at Starbucks. One of the things Starbucks does is to use fair trade coffee beans. Purchasing a more expensive fair trade product means that Starbucks has proven its commitment to not take advantage of people. Does Starbucks do well financially? You bet they do! You have to apply to buy the license to operate a Starbucks store and in 2001 the corporation had a little over two billion in net income. Yes, you heard me correctly. That's Billion with a B."

Professor C continued. "Do you think that not taking advantage of others extends to respect for employees in things like education, sick leave allowances, health benefits, and share ownership? Starbucks is a leader in all of these areas. So, what kind of company do you want to work for and hopefully lead in the future? I propose that you only want to work for a company that can demonstrate that doing good and making money are compatible, that takes a long-term view, that pulls together the many components that are necessary to achieve that objective, and that invests to drive profits?"

Here's your class assignment. Like the triple bottom line, it has three parts. Find the industry that has the worst track record and describe the harm that it has done to the environment. Ask yourself 1) is that harm being paid for in lost profits or is it being paid by the citizens through their taxes? 2) describe all the benefits that the industry provides the human race. I'm thinking of jobs, and taxes paid to the government and then money spent for the public good. 3) assume that the Board of one industry player has given you, the CEO, the mandate to transform the organization into doing the kind of "good" we have talked about without compromising the profitability and share price. How would you go about doing this?"

"I'm looking for a maximum of five single-spaced pages—due next class. I will pull one submission at random out of the pile and have that student present and defend his or her paper. I know this is a bit overwhelming for your first assignment, so I've decided that it is only worth ten percent of your overall grade. Please include all of your research sources in a separate appendix at the end."

At coffee after the class the students gossiped about the professor who had spent some time in the Big House for insider trading, had a lifetime trading ban, and had paid the highest fine ever levied by the courts on a Wall Street trader. Once he had paid his debt to society, Professor C entered Harvard's Business school. His innate business sense and sheer will meant he graduated top of his class.

Since the Professor was unable to trade on his own account he invested through others in a completely arm's length way—rumor had it that he had re-amassed the fortune he paid in fines. He only invested in companies that were ESG-focused and rooted out/outed the "Green washers" very publicly in his newsletter and blogs. His research—aided by students looking for extra credit, was rigorous and entirely accurate. He had been given a second chance and one of the students said what everyone else was thinking—we can learn a lot from people like Professor C.

Professor C founded the Sustainable Investing and the Ethical Investing Clubs. The student-run clubs provided the reformed stock trader with a golden opportunity to influence the next generation of CEO's. In fact, his plea agreement required that he use his own scam, as a case study and a warning about what not to do. His students were impressed by his integrity. Under his tutelage, most Club Members became enthusiastic ambassadors for financial literacy, and became responsible stewards of the environment and the triple bottom line.

In September 2004, there were ten members of the Sustainable Investing Club, including Melodie Beaudoin, Misha Mikhalov, Wayne Lee, Cosimo Calderella, Paula Da Silva, Svetlana Tretiak, Ada Adelmann, and Prince Sayid al Farah.

Chapter 21

Melodie Marie Beaudoin

Before she completed her M.B.A. at the INSEAD, Melodie Beaudoin was on a full hockey scholarship at Cornell University in New York. After she graduated, Melodie was hired by Investment Brothers as an Assistant Analyst reporting to the Director of Strategic Investments. She was hired almost one year to the day that she shattered her knee and her dream of representing Canada at the Olympics, on a double black diamond run in the Mount Tremblant Quebec mountains.

Her common sense and quick mind made her a natural investment banker. When Investment Brothers offered to pay her full salary and all tuition expenses to upgrade her skills at the INSEAD, she jumped at the opportunity. She joined, and then chaired, The Sustainability Investing Club. She wanted this role because she was in a position to influence capital investment in sustainable projects at Investment Brothers. Even after she graduated, Melodie remained very close to Professor C.

Melodie was also close to her mother Dee, and her father, Pierre, who owned and operated three Tim Horton's franchises in the province of Quebec, Canada and one franchise in the province of Ontario. She considered her eldest brother, Jacques, a police detective with The Service de police de la Ville de Montréal (SPVM), her best male friend.

Chapter 22

Misha Mikhalov

Misha had a Computer Science Degree from Novosibirsk State Technical University. When he was a student there, Misha developed the notion that financial literacy and economic independence were linked. He created a Foundation to support the advancement of financial literacy and capability programs in low and middle-income countries and to alleviate the guilt he had because of his association with his mob boss father.

He called his Foundation "Alyosha" Russian for, "One who helps people." Misha was so committed to Alyosha's mission that, each year since its inception in 2000, he donated one-half of the $500,000 allowance he received from the various family businesses to his foundation.

Sergei was a significant shareholder of Caissse Financiere, a major player in the life and health insurance and financial services industries, in Canada and knew the chairman, Roman Golovaka. The two men owned adjoining estates on Corsica and socialized regularly. Sergei had multiple business reasons for getting Misha a job, as assistant director of technology at the Caisse. Sergei wanted Misha to learn about all of the back doorways into financial institution servers in Canada.

While he was working at the Caisse, Misha developed proprietary software that identified and tracked suspicious trading activity. His grateful employer awarded him a bonus of $50,000 and 1,000 shares in the publicly traded company. Misha deeded the cash and the shares to his educational Foundation.

Misha met Melodie's brother, detective Jacques Beaudoin, and CIA computer whiz, Ted Chen-Williams, at an identity theft task force meeting in Quebec City, Canada.

Misha knew that Sergei was grooming him to take over the Mikhalov family businesses. His father directed Misha to continue his education with an MBA. After he left the Caisse, the always dutiful son enrolled at the INSEAD.

Misha was an extreme introvert. Unlike many of his fellow students who were far more sociable, he joined The Sustainable Investing Club and The Emerging Markets Club to push himself to socialize and to have an opportunity to talk to other humans rather than just stare at a computer screen all day.

Chapter 23

Wayne Lee

As far back as he could remember, Wayne loved numbers. His father, Aatami, was a senior bank executive with The Chinese Petroleum and Chemical Company. His mother, Minako, was the CEO at the company, one of the "top five" Chinese producers of crude oil.

Wayne completed his B.A. at the University of Hong Kong and was studying international business at the INSEAD. He planned on helping his mother develop the recycling side of the crude oil business. He possessed an undated offer of employment from Mitsubishi that would take effect the day after he graduated.

He joined the Sustainable Investing Club because he thought the committee chair, Melodie Beaudoin, was cute. Because he was painfully shy, he believed the club provided air cover and an opportunity to get to know the vivacious French Canadian, without the pressure, or the cost, of an actual date.

Wayne was an older and conscientious student. His favorite professor was the club sponsor, Professor Capilano. For Professor C's assignment, Wayne decided to focus on Canada's oil industry that consisted of three regions in the provinces of Alberta and Saskatchewan. From his research, he learned that Canada's "oil patch" covered more than 142,000 square km's and contributed about 10% of the country's GDP. The industry directly employed about 169,000 people; there were thousands more ancillary jobs. His preliminary research revealed that the company had been battling the federal government's oil policies for more than fifty years.

Wayne first analyzed the annual reports of every oil company that did any drilling in Canada. He was looking for any contingent liability associated with the responsibility to clean up any environmental damage. He was surprised to learn there didn't appear to be a line item that assessed this. This bore out Professor C's contention that the true cost of the extraction was not borne by the shareholder. Although the country benefited from the tax revenue, in the end, it was the taxpayer that bore the cost of any environmental clean-up. Not too many Canadian taxpayers had any idea they were subsidizing for-profit shareholders.

Wayne also observed that the province seemed to be overly dependent on the oil industry and the power and culture was so tied to the oil riches that politicians didn't seem to be willing to consider changing or diversifying. He concluded that it would be difficult if not impossible to maintain the status quo over the long term. Professor C's assignment forced him to revise his thinking about the industry and his future role in it. For that he was grateful. He was going to work in his mother's oil company which would give him an opportunity to put theory into practice and like the wise words of Mahatma Ghandi, to be the change he wanted to see in the world. Wayne concluded that any industry that did not recognize the full cost of the impact of all of their endeavors on their books was being dishonest.

Chapter 24

Cosimo Calderella

Cosimo had a B.A. from the University of Bologna. The Calderella family owned and operated a chain of sweatshops in Turkey, Indonesia, Cambodia, and China. Every year, hundreds of their workers died because of the poor and unsanitary working conditions in their properties. Cosimo believed the family business could be profitable as well as safe and was at the INSEAD to find out how to make that happen.

Cosimo met Misha Mikhalov at The Sustainable Investing Club. Because Cosimo didn't have many friends he enjoyed his time at the Club. He wanted to impress Misha, and disclosed more about his family's illegal business activities than he probably should have.

Misha, who was always on the lookout for investment opportunities to pass onto his father and brother, asked a lot of detailed questions. Assuming that Misha cared about what he was trying to accomplish, Cosimo offered Misha a senior job in the Calderella family business after graduation. Misha asked Cosimo for some time to consider his offer.

Since he already had the information about the Calderella family's business interests his father needed to devise a takeover strategy, Misha had no further need of his "friendship" with Cosimo. He also didn't want to have a daily reminder of his own treachery.

Misha, who had to work hard to be as devious as his father, told Melodie, a straight shooter and the glue that held The Sustainable Investing Club together, that he suspected Cosimo's family was mobbed up.

Although she wished Misha would have told her about this before they published their co-authored book, the idealistic, principled Melodie, felt that any hint of scandal would taint the credibility of the club's good work. Before their book was published, she asked for, and received, Cosimo's resignation.

Chapter 25

Paula Da Silva

Paula's great grandfather, Alejandro, was an executive with the Western Pacifica Railway Company, which was owned by Erroyo Alcoyo Gandío, one of the three companies that built the Transcontinental Railroad, the 1900-mile contiguous railroad line constructed in the United States between 1865 and 1868. Because he was astute enough to purchase stock in the enterprise, by 1900, Alejandro was a millionaire.

Paula had inherited her grandfather's love of rail travel. She liked big machinery almost as much as she liked to dress in fine clothing—her parents often joked that they didn't know if she was going to be an engineer or a fashion designer. After graduating with a B.A. from the Universitat de Barcelona, Paula asked for a train trip across Canada with her cousin, Maria, a self-employed wellness consultant, as a graduation present. The cousins had fallen in love with Algonquin Park and Canada when they attended Camp Tamakoon when they were teenagers.

Her parents and aunt and uncle were happy to oblige—both young women had demonstrated a commitment to their studies and a mature attitude. Paula was older than her first cousin by two months and two days. Although they studied at different universities, the young women remained very close, treasured their friendship and often confided in one another. Paula's parents joked the biggest potential issue would be if Maria, a minimalist, was going to give up space in her suitcase to make room for her cousin's extensive wardrobe!

Although she enjoyed the food and the service on the train, Paula was shocked that there didn't appear to be any high-speed rail links in Canada—even between populous cities like Toronto and Vancouver. She wondered if she had the knowledge and experience to bring Canadian railway travel into the 21st century. But that would have to wait.

Her current priority was to settle into her new job as Operations Manager at Riasayo High-Speed Rail Company (RHS). Her first operational challenge would be to make the railway more fuel efficient. Her new colleagues assumed that anyone who looked like Penelope Cruz wouldn't have a brain. They couldn't have been more wrong.

After four years at RHS, on the advice of her immediate superior, Paula decided to obtain an MBA. Her boss told her that she needed an MBA if she wanted to move into the C-suite. "Your background, work ethic, and leadership skills make you perfect for a top executive position here. You can apply for a leave and an interest-free loan that will be deducted from your salary, in equal payments, amortized over three years. Payments would start when you return. If you don't come back—and I recognize that's a possibility—the loan becomes due immediately. I went to the INSEAD for my second degree and highly recommend you consider going there. Take some time to think about it. If you need a reference, I am happy to provide one."

That night Paula called Maria to talk through her superior's recommendations. Maria said, "Look, it sounds like he's basically telling you that if you get your MBA, you will be on the executive track by the age of thirty. And access to an interest free loan is amazing. No one offered me an interest free loan. Besides, I seem to recall that a senior role at RHS was your dream job. What can I do to help you make a decision?" Maria said.

"The biggest thing I can think of right now is to help me talk through the pros and cons. I had thought about taking an MBA but I'm still not confident that it is the right strategic move, at this stage of my career. I'm also a bit concerned about the costs. Going to INSEAD in France isn't cheap. What if I don't return? How am I or my parents going to find the money to repay the loan?"

The next morning Paula called her father and mother and talked to them about her interest in pursuing an MBA at the INSEAD. The discussion was similar to the one she had with Maria. Her parents had the same reaction as her cousin. Her father said, "It sounds like your boss is advising you to do it now, which probably means he has great things in mind for you." Before Paula could raise the money issue, her mother said "Don't worry, we'll look after all of your living and tuition costs. After all, you are our only child and it is our pleasure to invest in your future." Since finances were no longer an impediment, Paula identified three schools that offered the curriculum she was interested in.

Paula met Melodie Beaudoin at a yoga class while she was on vacation in New York City. Melodie encouraged Paula to learn Mandarin and to join her at the INSEAD, the next stop on her own skills enhancement journey. Paula acted on Melodie's suggestion and was thrilled when INSEAD accepted her application. While at the INSEAD, the two friends roomed together, studied together, and joined The Sustainable Investing Club together, initially to meet smart guys.

Like Melodie, Paula loved Professor C's classes, and found his assignments thought-provoking and even sexy. Paula was a brilliant student and had no need for the Professor with whom she was having a passionate affair, to juice her grades. She would have happily screwed his brain if she had been able. Luckily, his body was a worthy substitute.

Professor C's latest assignment provided a great opportunity to look at transportation companies around the world. She was especially interested in those that had divested themselves from fossil fuels and was particularly impressed by the Sydney public transportation system.

During her research she also discovered an organization in Canada called Metrolinx. "I wonder if a job with a Canadian company would be fun?" Melodie is also from Canada and I would have an opportunity to see her more often. Bonus. I would even be willing to relocate for the right opportunity," Paula said to herself.

Three months before graduation from INSEAD Paula noticed that Metrolinx was expanding its team and had an opening for a Director of Sustainability. Without hesitation, she applied for the job. The recruiters were so impressed with her resume they flew her over for two days of interviews. Her signed offer letter was in her inbox before she returned to France.

Chapter 26

Metrolinx

With Maria along for a two-week Canadian holiday before she started her new job at Metrolinx, Paula found a perfect one-year executive condominium rental in Toronto, overlooking Lake Ontario. The owner had moved to Costa Rica for a year, to run a tourist property there. She gave first and last month's rent, signed the lease, and booked an Algonquin lodge for five nights and several remote camping sites for another five, and rented all the camping gear. The cousins looked forward to resting, relaxing and reconnecting.

During this pre-work trip, Maria fell hard for Pablo, a guide from Mexico she met while the cousins were picking up their gear from the tuck shop located in the in-park store at Lake Opeongo (access point #11). Pablo also loved the Park and had spent every summer there from the time he was a tween.

The attraction between Maria and Pablo was instantaneous. Both were minimalists and loved nature. Although Paula felt a little left out, she was happy for her cousin. After Paula returned to Toronto and her new job at Metrolinx. Maria extended her stay by four months so that she and Pablo could figure out if they had enough in common to make the four-month relationship trial, permanent.

Paula loved her new digs and new job. She knew her new role would be challenging and tough; linking the intercity trains and the commuter system within the cities and bringing it all together under a one-pay system was a big undertaking and would cross over two Ontario election cycles. She recognized that if she got it right her next move would be to COO.

As an added bonus, Melodie lived in New York, a quick Porter Flight or Amtrak away from Toronto. And if her cousin Maria was willing to extricate herself from Pablo's arms, she could meet her in the park in just under three hours.

Chapter 27

Svetlana Tretiak

Before enrolling at the INSEAD, Svetlana, Lana to her friends, studied the physiology of sports at the University of Moscow. Her mother, Anna, was one of Russia's leading autism doctors—her medical practice focused on autism because her youngest son, Konstantin, was autistic. Her dad, Ilya, was a cosmonaut. She had no idea that her father was leading a double life including a second wife, two additional kids, and a German Shepherd puppy named Graf.

Before being accepted at the INSEAD, Lana played centre on the Russian national women's hockey team. Ironically, thugs from the Calderella crime family had approached her to fix some games but she had refused. These same criminals had better luck with her teammate, goalie, Anastasia Sokolova, who managed to have a really bad night. Lana never made the connection between fellow club member, Cosimo Calderella, his family, or the thugs that tried to intimidate her several years earlier.

In Russia, Lana was the de facto face of The Russian Anti-Doping Agency. She believed steroid abuse had put her boyfriend and gold medalist, wrestler, Alexei Federova, into an early grave. Her anti-doping stance didn't seem to deter her Coach, Anton Kiselyov, who insisted that players in all of the top hockey teams, especially those that were on the American and the Canadian teams, all took performance-enhancing drugs and that there was nothing really wrong with taking a little extra to get an edge.

When she researched the veracity of the Coach's claims, Lana didn't find any evidence of anyone else doping to gain an advantage. When she mentioned this to Coach Kisliak he said, "Richard Frommer, the chief watch dog, is Canadian, and naturally, he is covering the doping up."

At the INSEAD, Lana, Melodie, and Paula, hit it off—they were all prepared to stand up for what they believed in, loved hockey, and spoke French—Lana had learned French as part of her bid to get into the INSEAD. Although Melodie and Lana often talked of past hockey glory most of their conversations at school revolved around their dreams of sustainability for the whole planet.

Lana's dream job was to work at/lead the IOC's environmental practice and she enrolled in the sustainability stream at the INSEAD. She wrote to Richard Frommer on a regular basis. One day he actually replied. "I have done my homework on you. I'm impressed. I'm interested in the anti-doping side of what you do—your country needs a face of respectability—so let's talk. If you can help me, I will help you with team green later on," he said.

A week later, Richard and Lana connected over the telephone. At the end of the call Lana asked for (and was offered) a job with the International Olympic Committee (IOC) in Montreal. A move to Canada would provide an opportunity to see, ski, and skate with her former classmates Melodie and Paula.

Melodie was happy to learn that Lana would be so close and believed that she would be a good romantic prospect for her brother, Luc. They had a lot in common—Luc had played forward on a Russian professional hockey team, spoke conversational Russian, and when he retired from playing, returned to Canada where he coached a junior hockey team in Montreal. She couldn't wait to introduce them.

Chapter 28

Ada Adelmann

Before she went to the INSEAD, Ada was a member of the Women's German Soccer Team where she gained a reputation for a hot left foot. While on the team she had the chance to travel to many countries. When they were on the road, the team often stayed at one of her mother's 26 hotels. In between practices and games, Ada and a couple of teammates, drank beer (clandestinely) and explored the different cities where they competed. When the occasion arrived, team members never missed an opportunity to watch Lionel Mesi or Ronaldo, arguably the world's best soccer players, burn up the pitch.

Ada's dad, José, was president of Extra-Terrestrial Global Networks, a multinational, public, electric company based in Barcelona, Spain. He not only spoke about solar power at conferences around the world, he published many peer-reviewed articles on the subject. Before she took a leave of absence to upgrade her skills at the INSEAD, Ada was employed by one of the biggest banks as a wind farm and renewable energy specialist. She joined the Sustainable Investing Club because she believed ESG would distinguish her mother's hotels from its competitors.

Ada spoke five languages, played the Cello, had a great singing voice and was on track to graduate in the top five percent of her class. She was also really approachable, down to earth and a natural leader. She was too busy acquiring great skills to have any serious romantic entanglements and had no intention of falling in love until she was well established in her career.

She was thinking seriously of leveraging her knowledge of finance and solar and teaming up with her father to help electrical utilities decarbonize their grids. She knew that solar and renewable energy needed storage—it was the glue that bound it all together. There was a lot of new interest in battery technologies—she couldn't wait to brainstorm some ideas with her dad.

She decided to look at how electricity was generated for Professor C's assignment and was not surprised to learn that over sixty percent of the world's electricity was generated by carbon. Not only was the industry "dirty," in many cases the world 's grid was antiquated which meant that a great deal of energy was lost across the lines.

Professor C really liked her research and thought process and gave her an A on the paper. He referred her to his colleague at a Korean company. The company made smart grid and storage solutions. Ada had an interview and received a great offer. As an added bonus, their plant was in Barcelona, close to her father's business. As she was worried her mother would be upset by the shift in career focus, Ada was excited to share a number of cost-effective ideas that would make her mother's hotel chain more energy efficient.

She ate in the Hotel Isabella on her first day in Barcelona and was surprised to be approached by a well-dressed businessman who introduced himself in perfect German as Mike Spencer from London, England.

"How did you know I spoke German?" Ada asked. "I've only spoken Spanish since I sat down and ordered."

"You are Ada Adelmann, aren't you—top point getter for the German women's team?"

Mike then told her that in his earlier career he had been a sports announcer and had seen her play several times. "I even interviewed you after the game in which you set a scoring record against a solid English team."

"It's nice to be recognized, she said with humility. What brings you to Barcelona?" Ada asked.

"I'm now a freelance environmental reporter. I am very interested in learning everything I can about the Spanish electrical grid. I understand that Spain has an enormous amount of solar energy and I've had a number of interviews to find out more, while I'm here. I'm hoping to interview José Adelmann, president of Extra-Terrestrial Global Networks. I just now realized you have the same last name. Is he a relative of yours?"

"A really close relative—he's my father!" Ada replied with a warm smile.

Ada then surprised herself and asked a question that she had not asked before, but all of a sudden seemed really important. "Is your wife or partner with you?"

Mike smiled and said "No, my long term relationship ended about two years ago, when my girlfriend passed away. Before I run off to an interview I was wondering if we could continue our conversation over dinner—I haven't even asked what you are up to—what kind of journalist am I, failing to ask the important questions?" he said with a shy smile.

Without hesitation Ada agreed and asked him to meet her in the lobby of her hotel at 7:30 p.m. When she arrived, her hair was down and she wore a simple blue dress with white buttons that gave her 34 C breasts just the right emphasis. A simple gold chain around her neck flirted with her cleavage. Mike also noticed that Ada wore the tiniest bit of makeup that accentuated her twinkling brown eyes. Lots of red toenail polish on those professionally buffed toes peaked out of white, open-toed, leather sandals. In a word, she was perfect.

Over dinner, Mike poured on the questions and as much charm as he could—what a great coincidence and Ada seemed genuinely interested in him as well. When he learned of the work she, her father and her mother were doing he was impressed—that night the conversation and the wine moved effortless between four languages and endless topics.

At the end of the evening Ada handed Mike her cell phone number and said, "There is a great run that follows the rambla. It's a very beautiful trail beside the waterfront. It's very nice at any time of the day but it's positively magical at 6:30 in the morning. Would you be interested in joining me?"

Without hesitation Mike agreed to join her the next morning and was even able to keep up with the pace she set.

After the run they grabbed some bixies and took a tour of the site of the 1992 Olympics. Ada couldn't help noticing that Mike was very fit, had a great sense of humor, and was an engaging conversationalist. He was also well travelled and an avid skier.

As morning turned into afternoon and afternoon turned into evening, Ada invited Mike to her room. She walked into the bathroom, peeled off her clothes, and asked him to join her there to see the new environmental plumbing. It didn't take Mike long to get the hint. He undressed quickly and followed her under the water.

Chapter 29

Prince Sayid al Farah

"Sy" was the 14th prince of Saudi Arabia. Unlike his playboy brother, D.J., Sy believed in meritocracy, not just birthright, and was prepared to earn his royal assignment. He graduated from both Eton and Cambridge cum laude and was on track to graduate in the top one percent of his class at the INSEAD. Thanks to his leadership, Saudi Arabia already had an impressive network of solar resources and cutting-edge green technologies including many geothermal resources related to the tectonic activity of the Red Sea, volcanic rocks and ridges.

The solar and geo potential was enormous. Fifty installations were planned in the first two years of the region's twenty-year plan. If the results were as expected the program would be expanded to 1500 installs. The project total was ambitious and included 200 GW of solar power by the year 2030. This compared to a global solar power installation forecast of 100 GW by 2017 with a total installed capacity of 77 GW target in Saudi Arabia by 2016.

The Prince was good friends with Ada Adelmann's father, José, and the two collaborated on many innovative solar projects together. He joined The Sustainable Investing Club because he took every opportunity to learn as much about sustainable investing and eco projects as humanly possible. He enthusiastically pursued every opportunity to turn his knowledge into projects that would bring power and prestige to his country. Being at the INSEAD had another important benefit—attendance would allow him to fulfill his commitment to keep a watchful eye on José's daughter, Ada, while they were both pursuing their studies.

Despite his energy and focus on alternative energies, the Prince was also human. Away from the confines of his country's rigid rules he indulged in drinking and orgies, especially with anonymous young, athletic, men. He especially enjoyed sexual intimacy with someone from the African colonies—just an extra layer of "je ne sais quoi" he said to himself. In addition to being extraordinarily fit and fabulous physical specimens, all of his male lovers had brains as well as balls.

One early morning, as he opened the driver's door to his Rolls Royce, he laughed out loud when he realized he had parked in a no-parking zone. He opened the glove compartment and took out the flask of brandy stashed there. As he put his key in the ignition, he took a few small sips. He didn't notice the gendarme approaching from the rear of the vehicle.

The gendarme said, "I saw you drinking something out of a flask. At that instant, the Prince realized he would need more than charm to talk himself out of the situation and that he had underestimated his need to use the restroom. "I need to go the toilette; we can talk when I return," the Prince said.

"Leave the flask," the gendarme replied. When he returned the gendarme was holding a portable breath machine and there was a ticket on the window of the Rolls.

"You need to blow in here. If you refuse—you will be arrested and your car will be impounded. If you blow over the limit—I will impound your vehicle. I will also issue a large fine and suspend your license for three months. If you blow under, I will cite you for drinking while driving, impound your vehicle, and suspend your license for a month. So, no matter which way you turn it, you lose and I win."

Even though he protested and the Rolls had diplomatic plates, a fact that he pointed out to the gendarme several times, the Prince was still charged with a DUI. Thankfully, the matter never made it to court. When his father learned of his wayward son's actions, he commanded him to return to Saudi Arabia.

Although he never completed the Professor's assignment, Sy's marks were high enough to pass the course. Eventually, he convinced his family to start an alternative investment fund that directed their oil profits into clean energy and tech. Two years later and with the help of his "suitable" wife, the crown prince started a program to allow women to drive.

Chapter 30

James Brown (JB) Washington

JB grew up in Louisiana and spoke French perfectly. From a genealogy site he learned he was a fifth generation American whose ancestors had been slaves. He also learned his great grandfather was a famous tribal king. His father was a Baptist Minister who tended to his flock with colorful word pictures of love and salvation; his mother was a freedom fighter who marched alongside Reverend Martin Luther King.

He graduated from Wiley College where he was the captain of their award-winning debating team. While he was in Texas for his studies, he'd learned about the Hispanic cultural influences as well as how to speak Spanish.

His language gifts and an undergraduate degree in economics landed him a "full ride" Master's degree in economics from the University of Chicago. Although he had originally envisioned a career as a university professor, he recognized that what really fascinated him was the stock market.

He augmented his skills with a Certified Financial Analyst designation earned while working at his first job at a local Chicago management consulting firm. He supplemented his income with some contract work advising a French firm looking to acquire a US brokerage firm.

The INSEAD, a leader in the field of sustainable investing, was a logical choice for his second MBA. He also believed a degree from INSEAD would give him the financial chops to credibly own his own boutique sustainable investing firm.

His persuasive nature and ability to debate Professor C made him a Sustainable Investing club member favorite. Fellow club member, Misha, often invited him to talk to the Camp Orlyonyk campers. Through these interactions, JB developed a passion for making a difference in young people's lives.

With Misha acting as interpreter, JB painted them a very detailed picture of his life in the US and what it meant growing up as a black person, in a middle-class household, with educated parents and a history of being successful in a world that was less kind.

The campers appreciated JB's honesty and philosophical balance—he was forthright but not bitter—and enjoyed his stories of all the racially enlightened people he had met over the years. He often talked about relationships, and how his life was better because he had learned how to trust.

JB asked the campers as many questions as they asked him. He wanted to know about their backgrounds, what inspired their interest in computers, and what they planned to do next. He was fascinated by their personal stories and loved the idea of how the Mikhalov's computer camp was changing lives at a local level. By taking misadventured teens with promise, giving them purpose and marketable skills, the campers had a chance to have a decent life. This improved their confidence and mental health and positioned them to become givers to society, rather than takers.

JB was so inspired by the Orlyonyk campers, he often thought about how he could replicate the Mikhalov's computer camp in the U.S. with a twist—his camp would cater to single parents and their "misachiever" offspring not as a reform school but as an upward-forming school. He believed that if he could grab the kids early, like those in the movie, Goodwill Hunting, he could change minds and hearts, and attract the interest and support of many foundations and corporate funders.

Two weeks after his last visit with Misha's campers, his credit card was compromised, and his bank account was defrauded. Because he was able to get everything back, he never suspected any of the campers.

By the time he returned to Louisiana, JB had a concrete plan for his single parents and kids camp, applied for a charitable number, and had checks in hand totalling $105,000 dollars from the Mikhalov Children's Foundation and his fellow Sustainable Investment Club members. He also found a location, completed his due diligence on six life skills and computer teachers and planned to beta test the program with six students for a camp he named, "A New Tomorrow."

Chapter 31

Denzel Sun Mah

Denzel was not using the name he was born with, which was Ted Chen-Williams. He got his new name, Denzel Sun Mah, courtesy of the CIA. Because he had always been interested in business and finance and had heard good things about the INSEAD, Denzel decided to pursue an MBA with a Finance specialty there. He excelled at his studies and didn't tell the faculty or his fellow students about his agency past or the extent of his computer knowledge and skills.

After he completed his first year, a visiting professor persuaded him to join France's Credit Agricole. This was the right career move and Denzel was given some very serious roles at the bank. He never finished his INSEAD degree. He never had to.

A couple of years later, Denzel left the French bank and joined an Asian bank, where he spoke passionately against, "Trash Mortgage Debt." But his employer had invested heavily in these instruments, and needed Denzel to stop his "trash" talk. To distract their new employee, the bank promoted him, changed his title and gave him a big raise in pay. The bank's strategy worked—Denzel was too busy meeting his objectives to think about Trash Mortgage Debt.

Although he liked everyone in the Club, Melodie Beaudoin was his favorite because she was as much of a hockey nut as was he. After they left the INSEAD, Melodie and Denzel continued to speak on the telephone and to meet for a beer or a quick bite whenever Denzel was in New York, or later, Washington, on business.

Chapter 32

Leave Only Shadows

Thanks to Professor C, all ten Club members had become convinced that a sustainable business model was a good business strategy and that it was only a matter of time before the world's investors would measure success by the sustainability of their investments. In fact, being good to the planet while making money was the impetus behind the club's critically acclaimed, co-authored book, "Leave Only Shadows."

Professor C wrote the foreword and Misha's father, Sergei, donated the printing and distribution costs. "Shadows" quickly became the definitive guide for measuring economic return on eco-investments. Although the Sustainable Investing Club members would never come close to duplicating Mr. Gore's financial success, their book, "Leave Only Shadows" made decent money.

Royalties were split equally between eleven people—the ten, outwardly idealistic, passionate, and committed co-authors, and their mentor, Professor C. The students were all green enough to believe that they could responsibly bring positive, sustainable, eco-friendly, business strategies to their respective employers.

After their studies, The Sustainable Investing Club Members continued to invest in stock in companies that could demonstrate that environmental and social stewardship practices were as good for the planet as they were for the bottom line. After Cosimo left the club, every two years after the initial print run, the nine remaining co-authors updated the content to reflect current ROI figures. Sergei continued to pay for printing and distribution and the Club members continued to direct their ongoing royalties to Misha's Alyosha Foundation.

Chapter 33

Alyosha

When he was a student at the INSEAD, Misha asked his father to chair Alyosha, his educational Foundation. Sergei agreed, and shortly thereafter, became the Foundation's principal fundraiser, marketer, and ambassador. Sergei didn't particularly care about Alyosha's good deeds. He only wanted to reward Misha for all his hard work and to keep him loyal. It also suited his purposes to have his competitors and colleagues think he was generous with both his time *and* his money.

In exchange for a tax receipt for in-kind services, Sergei purchased the computers and the cell phones for all of the Foundation's professional and administrative staff. He considered it a real coup when his riding buddy and President of Russia, Vladimir Alexandroff, agreed to be an honorary patron.

The Sustainable Investing Club members students engaged in many heated discussions about insider trading and manipulative sales practices and how these systems stacked the deck against the average investor. They were all frustrated with the existing system and often brainstormed ideas about what they could do to fix it.

Misha believed that a concrete step was to improve global financial literacy levels because financial education would both even the playing field and help prevent future system abuses. His long-term vision included making financial literacy an educational prerequisite for every degree everywhere in the world; setting academic standards, and establishing Alyosha as the global Financial Literacy Registrar.

To ensure that his vision had teeth, Misha believed that his Foundation needed both auditing and penalizing authority. Although he never articulated it as such, he considered his work on the Foundation as penance for his family's illicit business dealings and wealth that was built upon humanity's greed, perversions, and addictions.

Misha had a good relationship with the Dean of the INSEAD, and floated his idea of making financial literacy an educational prerequisite when they saw each other at a cocktail fundraising event at his parents' Corsica estate. The Dean was cautiously supportive and asked Misha to prepare a written business plan that he could present to the INSEAD board.

Sergei asked his friend and Alyosha's honorary patron, President Alexandroff, to help Misha get a speaking slot at the U.N. Economic and Finance Committee. Unfortunately, the earliest speaking opening was three years away. Misha was not discouraged. Regardless of how long it took, he was committed to presenting his views on the world stage. He wholeheartedly believed that every global citizen needed a basic understanding of the financial markets and that there was an urgent need to include financial literacy as a prerequisite for graduation from any post-secondary institution.

Misha also believed the Foundation staff was uniquely positioned to carry this important message out into the world—since inception, the organization had hosted financial literacy seminars in most major cities and could easily meet with the Deans of the local universities, whenever and wherever they traveled.

Chapter 34

Legacy Funding

The Sustainable Investing Club members supported the Foundation's good work by donating 75% of their "Leave Only Shadows" book royalties. To further consolidate the members' commitment to the Foundation, Misha suggested that Sergei invite the parents of several of the club's well-to-do students to join him on the Alyosha Board. Sergei thought this was excellent suggestion and reached out to Mohammed al Farah, Minako Lee, and José Adelmann. Vladimir Alexandroff, President of Russia, agreed to be an Honorary Board Member and Patron.

In the end, the Board of Directors of The Alyosha Foundation for Financial Literacy and Education consisted of five people.

1. Sergei Mikhalov, Chairman and CEO of The Mikhalov Family Trust

2. Misha Mikhalov, Chief Technology Officer and COO of The Mikhalov Family Trust

3. Mohammed al Farah, President and CEO of Saudi Basic Industries Corporation (agriculture, building and construction, electronics, healthcare and packaging)

4. Minako Lee, CEO of The China Petroleum and Chemical Company (oil and gas)

5. José Adelmann, 2nd Vice President and CEO of Extra-Terrestrial Networks (electric power company).

Because board members were leaders in a variety of unrelated industries and were also extremely wealthy in their own right, Sergei was confident he had secured the Foundation's ongoing cash flow.

During the monthly board meetings, using the most up-to-date, green, video conferencing technology, professional staff presented updates on all new donors, as well as budgets and work-back plans for current financial literacy and education projects. Each agenda devoted at least half an hour to a different client beneficiary. Every month, a representative of that organization, was invited to present how an Alyosha project had positively impacted his or her organization, community, or charity.

In addition to the monthly board meetings, once a year, in mid-May, board members were expected to attend a weekend retreat at Sergei's twenty-bedroom Corsica estate. The agenda was simple. Day 1 was devoted to identifying future financial literacy projects. Day 2 was spent on fundraising ideas and establishing financial targets. Spouses and significant others were also encouraged to participate in the May retreat.

The Spouses' Program was slightly different: Day 1 was devoted to generating ideas for new projects. Day 2 was devoted to designing a gala. On a rotating basis, the spouse of each Board Member was expected to host a gala on behalf of Alyosha. When they weren't working on these projects, the spouses were welcome to swim, play tennis, go horseback riding or indulge in the private spa on the property. Dress was casual. An award-winning cordon bleu chef prepared and served all of the Board members' meals.

Other than the monthly board meetings and the annual retreat, ongoing duties were minimal and primarily consisted of fundraising. All board members were expected to make a personal stretch donation, as well as to help identify and make introductions to other prospective donors.

Even with the addition of the three new Board members and one famous Patron, Misha continued to obsess about the consequences of running out of money before his Foundation could achieve its worldwide financial literacy mission. In January 2007, he asked his mother to transfer ownership of 200,000 preferred *OhMy EAU!!* shares to Alyosha. It was a good business move. Last year Elena, Misha and Dmitri, the three *OhMy EAU!!* preferred shareholders had received over ten million dollars in dividends.

Misha redirected his share to Alyosha. Dmitri purchased two new polo ponies and hosted a party at the Corsica estate for one hundred of his closest friends. He also paid for breast augmentation surgeries for a number of grateful female colleagues.

The share transfer would ensure a steady cash flow and meant the Foundation would never have to cut services. Elena thought Misha worked too hard and the gesture gave her a way to demonstrate her gratitude and love. She instructed her attorneys to prepare the necessary paperwork.

In exchange for its generosity, *OhMy EAU!!* received a tax receipt for a transfer value of four million USD, which effectively wiped out the company's tax liability for the previous three years. This benevolent act also consolidated The Mikhalov's standing as philanthropists. Elena received an award from the Russian Economic Think Tank for Corporate Social Responsibility.

She was also offered positions on several prestigious government boards, including Roswell, Russia's biggest oil company, and Alrossa, a Russian group of diamond mining companies. Citing business demands, she nominated Dmitri, to take her place. The various boards agreed to the substitution.

Chapter 35

Cosimo's Revenge

Cosimo Calderella had a secret crush on Melodie Beaudoin. It was just about the time that he was mustering the courage to ask her out that Misha Mikhalov betrayed his trust and disclosed his family's connection to sweat shops. When Melodie demanded that he leave The Sustainable Investing Group, Cosimo hid his hurt feelings and bruised ego, and immediately agreed to do so.

Truth be told, Cosimo was devastated. Although he knew his family was mobbed up, he hadn't yet been totally indoctrinated into the Cosa Nostra mindset. He had enrolled at the INSEAD to learn how to make life better for his family's employees. Because of his mob connections, no one had ever refused any of his requests before and he did not have the emotional fortitude to deal with what he saw as a betrayal by both Melodie and Misha. Cosimo never learned that Misha also came from the mob family that eventually took over his family's business interests and territories.

Every 'Leave Only Shadows' royalty check that he received rubbed salt in an already festering wound. Every night before he went to sleep, and the first thing every morning before he got up, Cosimo fantasized about how to get revenge on Melodie and Misha and their respective family members. When he couldn't stand the pity party for a minute longer, Cosimo reached out to local muscle, Enzo Mancini. He instructed him to cause Melodie and Misha extreme pain and suffering. He paid Enzo $100,000 USD for a total of six events, three in Melodie's life, and the same number in Misha's.

It was relatively easy for Enzo to think of three ways to disrupt Melodie's life.

Incident #1: One evening while she was out on a relaxing jog in the local park, a masked stranger snuck up on her from behind and knocked her to the ground. As she tried to fight back the stranger slashed her left forearm with a box cutter. The police never identified the perpetrator. The only long-term consequences to what police characterized as a "random attack" was that Melodie had a scar on her left forearm, no longer jogged on park paths, and carried a rape whistle and bear spray in her purse whenever she went out in public.

Incident #2: The next month, during reading week, Melodie and her roommate, Paula, decided to go on a shopping expedition to the Forum des Halles mall in the City Center. The dress store they were looking for was located on the second floor. Just in front of them, a clown wearing bicycle clothes, grasped the handlebars of his racing bike which he balanced precariously on the moving escalator steps. The girls were deep in conversation about their planned purchases and other than a quick glance at his firmly muscled behind, didn't pay attention to either the clown or his bike.

Side by side, the roommates stepped onto the lower escalator steps. Just as he was nearing the top, the clown stumbled and lost his grip on his bicycle. It came crashing down the escalator steps and plowed into the girls. The impact knocked Melodie and Paula onto the moving steps. The clown fled.

Because he was wearing clown makeup and a multicolored wig, it was impossible to visually identify him. The bicycle was a generic make and there was no DNA evidence because the clown wore white gloves. Although Melodie fractured her ankle and Paula her wrist, the girls considered themselves lucky. They abandoned their shopping expedition and hailed a taxi home. When they got there, they changed into comfortable clothes, opened a bottle of wine, and chalked the whole thing up to being in the wrong place, at the wrong time.

Chapter 36

Incident 3: Party Poopers

Melodie and Paula decided to co-host a spring break party. They posted notice of the happy BYOB affair on their university Facebook pages. Later that same night, when she was replaying the evening's events in her head, Melodie recognized that she had dismissed her instinctive reaction to the two muscular, Roma-looking men who knocked on their apartment door while Paula was out picking up beer.

Although she didn't recognize them, she assumed they were early party guests. Not wanting to appear to be racist, Melodie invited the two men in. As soon as they sat down, one of the men asked for a glass of water. Since the kitchen was in another room, Melodie had to leave the two men alone while she went to get the water. She thought of taking her purse with her but decided such an overt action would send the wrong message which would have horrified her family, especially her brother, Jacques.

When she returned, she glanced at her purse, was relieved to see that it was exactly where she had left it, and handed the glass of water to the man who asked for it. He drank it quickly and handed the empty glass to his friend who said that he too would like a glass of water.

On the way to get the second glass of water Melodie had a fleeting thought that something was amiss. Why didn't the second man ask for water at the same time as his friend? The rest of the party guests weren't expected to arrive for another hour or so and she didn't know when her roommate would return from the beer store. Maybe she should have asked the two strangers to come back when Paula was home. But it was too late for that now.

When Melodie returned with the second glass of water, the man that asked for the first glass of water, said that he had something he had to do and would return later that evening. After he left, Melodie was alone with the second man.

She sat down beside the stranger, who was slowly sipping his glass of water, and stuck out her hand and said, "I don't think we've been properly introduced. My name's Melodie, but I guess you knew that from the invitation. What's your name?"

"Bill, I'm a student at the INSEAD studying forensic accounting," he said. "What are you studying?" Melodie spent the next five minutes telling Bill about her studies, the Sustainable Investing Club and the club's Leave Only Shadows book. Talking to the stranger settled her nerves.

When "If I Ain't Got You," one of her favorite Alicia Keys songs, came on the radio, she smiled with contentment. She felt relaxed enough to close her eyes and began to sway with the music. Seconds later she felt both of Bill's muscular arms around her neck as he leaned in for a kiss. She almost gagged at the smell of pickled eggs. Why hadn't she noticed that obnoxious smell before?

Melodie wasn't really worried about her physical safety. Her brother, Jacques, a police detective, had taught her how to defend herself from both a sitting or standing position. Although she could hurt him, she only pushed Bill away and asked him to leave. But Bill had other things on his mind.

He reached into his boot and pulled out a blood red switchblade decorated with two silver bolsters. He pressed the silver-plated image of the Russian double headed eagle coat of arms located on the top of the exterior casing. A wicked blade fired free. His thumb caressed the shaft threateningly as he growled, "This time I'm asking. Next time I'll take."

Melodie couldn't believe she had invited this Neanderthal into her home. She was more angry than frightened when she yelled, "I can't believe you're doing this. Is this how you abuse my hospitality? Get out of here before I call the university police."

Bill smirked, pressed the image of the dragon slayer, St. George, the Patron Saint of Moscow, on the bottom bolster, and the blade slide back into its protective sheath. He then returned the knife into its hiding place in his right boot, blew Melodie a lecherous kiss, and walked nonchalantly out the front door.

Melodie poured herself a glass of red wine and sat down on the couch. Before she knew it, a half a bottle was gone. At least her hands weren't shaking anymore. By the time Paula returned with the beer, the party guests had started to trickle in and it seemed silly to let two strangers ruin what promised to be a wonderful evening. The house party was a lot of fun and ran very late. Since neither roommate knew all of each other's friends, they assumed any strangers had been invited by the other roommate.

When the girls were cleaning up the next day, Melodie laughingly mentioned the scene with Bill. Paula said, "Interesting. I don't know a Bill that is studying forensic accounting." Melodie was a bit taken aback by Paula's response, but there was nothing she could do about that now. She could just hear her brother Jacques' voice in her head, as he reminded her to stay vigilant and to always be aware of her immediate surroundings.

A couple of months later, Melodie received a disturbing collection call from the credit card division of The Central Bank of Switzerland, informing her that she had reached the $25,000 limit on her credit card and that her minimum monthly payment was two months in arrears. There was only one problem—she did not have a Central Bank of Switzerland credit card. Had she been a victim of identity theft?

After Melodie finished her call with the credit card collection company she nonchalantly asked, "Remember those two guys that crashed our spring break party? Is it possible that when you went out of the room to get them water, one or both of them went through your wallet?" "You're right! I can't recall any other time that my purse was out of my sight," Melodie replied.

She called her brother, Jacques, who promised to look into it. The police detective told the girls to install the best deadbolt locks that money could buy. Going forward, Melodie and Paula resolved not to let anyone they didn't know into their apartment. Eight months and $5,000 in legal fees later, the credit card matter was successfully resolved.

Melodie believed that her run of bad luck ended when she graduated, with high honors, from the INSEAD, and returned to her job at Investment Brothers in New York. The roommates never learned their run of "bad luck" had been financed by their former classmate and co-author, Cosimo Calderella.

Chapter 37

Cosimo's Revenge on Misha

It was more difficult for Enzo to harass Misha because he was working all the time and was rarely out of doors. It was, however, a lot easier to interfere with the lives of his twin brother, Dmitri, and his mother, Elena. He asked for and received permission from Cosimo to make the substitutions.

For his first act, Enzo broke into The Mikhalov Center for Photography and Contemporary Art on Syromyatnicheskly Perculok and slashed all the paintings and photographs hanging on the gallery walls. Enzo took special delight in the damage he inflicted on Dmitri's original work. He then threw a can of red paint onto the gallery walls and the floors. The insurance company assessed the damage at over one million USD.

The next month, he laced the feed of Dmitri's favorite polo pony, Nureyev, with poison. The animal suffered a horrible death.

Two months after that, a masked man pushed Elena into traffic, just as she got out of her limousine that had stopped in front of the Opera house. When she fell, she ripped her Versace gown, scraped both knees and twisted her right ankle.

Sergei wondered if his enemies were responsible for these three incidents and doubled the number of Elena and Dmitri's bodyguards. There were no further problems.

Cosimo congratulated Enzo on his innovative disruptions. He was especially pleased with the results and believed he had received a tremendous return on his $100,000 investment.

Chapter 38

Christina

Christina Sinclair-Sanchez's family had a long history of social activism. Her great grandfather, Señor Carlos Hermoso, was a sea captain. When he retired, he purchased and operated Dulce Nuevo Mundo (Spanish for Sweet New World), a sugarcane plantation near New Orleans.

In addition to sugar cane, Señor Hermoso's five hundred acre holding included the master's house, a separate residence for the overseer and his family, a separate residence for the teacher and her family, two segregated sleeping quarters for his fifty-five slaves, and a stable for his ten horses.

Señor Hermoso was light years ahead of his contemporaries in the way he treated his slaves. All of the adult males were employed as laborers in the sugarcane fields or as carpenters, grooms, or blacksmiths. The adult females worked as domestics or cooks. Señor Hermoso did not allow his overseer to beat, starve or rape his female slaves, nor did he indulge in any of these extracurricular activities himself.

The male fieldworkers were served a hearty breakfast at 5:00 a.m. The female slaves brought them lunch and a pail of water at noon. All Dulce Nuevo Mundo slaves ate dinner together at 6 p.m.

Weeknights, between 7:00 and 9:00 p.m., a credentialed teacher, hired and paid for by Señor Hermoso, taught the slaves how to read, write, and do basic arithmetic. Señor Hermoso expected all of his slaves to attend Sunday services and bible study classes on Sunday mornings. Everyone had the afternoon off to rest and to socialize with friends and family.

Señor Hermoso kept meticulous records of every birth and death on the plantation. Although few chose to do so, every adult slave (an adult slave was defined as a male or female over the age of fifteen) was entitled to petition for his or her freedom on their thirty-fifth birthday. No slave was required to work on either Christmas Day or Easter Sunday.

Every man, woman and child received twenty-five dollars in cash, a new pair of shoes, and a new set of clothes every 9th of May, which was Señor Hermoso's birthday. When the plantation owner sold Dulce Nuevo Mundo and moved to Napa Valley with his bride, Carmella, he freed all fifty-five slaves.

The Hermoso's established Casa Hermoso Jardin in Napa Valley in 1855. They cultivated Sauvignon Blanc grapes until they were killed in a flash flood in 1920. During their lifetime, their vineyard thrived because the Hermoso's operated Casa Hermoso Jardin in the same way that Señor Hermosa had operated his Dulce Nuevo Mundo plantation in New Orleans.

Their only daughter, Christina's grandmother, Adora, married a local vintner, Buddy Sinclair. Adora and Buddy continued the family tradition of innovation. Shortly after inheriting Casa Hermoso Jardin, the couple started cultivating olives. Because the same tractors and bins could be used for grapes and olives, there were no additional costs for machinery.

In addition to providing a steady cash flow for the Sinclair's, when they added the olive crop, the vineyard was able to stay open twelve months of the year which meant they did not have to lay off any of their hardworking staff. Five years later, the couple innovated again, and started raising sheep, goats and chickens and growing food for the local food bank and other needy people.

Adora and Buddy had one daughter, Christina's mother, Maria, who married Christina's father, Santiago Sanchez. In keeping with her parents and grandparent's legacy, Maria and Santiago looked for new ways to make a difference. They founded The Napa Valley Vintners Cooperative, a non-profit company, dedicated to inspiring vintners to produce wines in an environmentally responsible manner. Christina was their only child.

Chapter 39

Casa Hermoso Jardin

Casa Hermosa Jardin was not the typical migrant farm. The owners respected all races and cultures and employed a fully diverse workforce that included Whites, Hispanics, Native Americans, Asians and Blacks. Every year the Sanchez's contributed $50,000 to The Worker's Continuing Education Fund. Each worker family was entitled to access a $5,000 bursary to offset any continuing education costs. Any member of the worker's family, including the worker, was welcome to access the bursary. The only requirement was to achieve a passing grade.

In keeping with the Hermoso family tradition of honoring workers' rights and respecting everyone's contribution, the Sanchez's introduced a loyalty retention program in 1975. On their three-year employment anniversary, every full-time worker received one common share in the business.

In addition to higher-than-market wages, at the end of the year, 30% of Casa Hermoso Jardin's net profits were shared between all of the working shareholders. The money could be taken as a cash bonus, or the worker could purchase more shares. There was no pressure to select one option or the other. Most opted to grow their net worth by purchasing more shares.

Christina's parents were convinced that they owed their ongoing success to their cooperative business model—by a wide margin, yields at Casa Hermoso Jardin consistently outstripped those at the other farms. Because they were so much more successful than the other neighbors, vintners and ranchers, it was difficult to get people to join The Napa Valley Vintners Cooperative. But Maria and Santiago knew they were right. They continued to innovate and their vineyard continued to thrive.

Chapter 40

A Healthy, Happy Childhood

Until grade eight, blonde-haired, hazel-eyed Christina, and the workers' children, all studied together in an air-conditioned, school that her parents had built on site. There was also a state-of-the-art computer lab and sports facility attached to the school. Accredited teachers taught the full California school curriculum to the children.

Like the vineyard, the school was open seven days a week, 363 days a year to allow workers, as well as children, to take classes. In keeping with family tradition however, there were no classes on either Christmas Day or Easter Sunday.

A volunteer worker committee interviewed and hired the teachers and the early childhood educators for an on-site day care for the little ones. In each school year, Christina's parents paid the teachers and educators' salaries and benefits and sponsored two offsite, age appropriate, field trips (one fun and one educational) for each student.

After three years of steady, full-time employment, the teachers and early childhood educators were also welcomed to participate in the Sanchez's loyalty retention program.

By the time she was sixteen, the curvy, teenager was fluent in English, Spanish, and French. Christina credited the hours of being chased down by boys, especially her boyfriend, Alberto, for developing her field vision, and ability to dribble the soccer ball. As a result of these early experiences, Christina always knew where someone was and played two-touch as well as any of the boys.

Christina and Alberto used every opportunity to sneak away together, usually when everyone else was asleep. They kept the intensity of their growing relationship secret—her parents often told her that she would not reach her full potential by getting romantically involved with someone when she was so young. Although she loved her parents and didn't want to disappoint them, she didn't allow loyalty to them to get in the way of her growing affection for Alberto.

One especially hot summer's evening, Christina and Alberto decided to take their relationship to the next level. Alberto came prepared with a Mexi Cola, a picnic blanket, and several condoms. Afterwards, he looked lovingly at Christina, who was dozing in the crook of his right arm, with a contented half smile on her face. She was so sexy. He decided to wait until his pulse stopped racing before he kissed her again.

Since the cola had tipped over and the contents had dripped out onto the parched ground beneath the picnic blanket, he decided it would be very dashing to get up and fetch Christina a cold, refreshing drink of post coital water from the stream located about twenty yards east of their blanket. When he tried to stand up, he tripped on his shorts and crashed down on top of her. Christina couldn't stop laughing. She kissed him enthusiastically. Alberto warned her that if she kept that up, he would never be able to get her a drink. Christina wasn't particularly thirsty and didn't care.

Chapter 41

Sabotage

When he finally approached the stream with the empty cola bottle in hand, Alberto became aware of the sound of buzzing flies. He almost tripped again, this time over a coyote, several dead opossums, and a family of what looked like pygmy rabbits. That was odd—he always thought that wild animals slunk away somewhere private to die.

He knew Christina's parents were dealing with some push back from several of the other vintners, who were losing staff to the Sanchez's, likely because of their more employee-friendly policies. Could a jealous neighbor have done something to the vineyard's water?

Alberto called out to Christina who hadn't bothered to put her clothes back on and looked like a gorgeous wood nymph when she emerged from the shadows. She too was shocked by the number of dead animals. The two teenagers agreed to come back during the daylight to better assess the situation.

The young lovers dressed, kissed quickly, then hand in hand, raced back down the hill to the slumbering vineyard below. They kissed again at the edge of the property. Christina slipped quietly back into the main house where she lived with her parents. Alberto returned to his parents' more modest abode.

The following afternoon, the two teenagers returned to the stream. Christina, who had been blessed with excellent vision, noticed an empty brown bottle. It was easy to miss it because it was lying on its side and the glass bottle was camouflaged perfectly by the parched grass. As she went closer to read the label, she tripped over several more animal carcasses. As Alberto suspected, it looked like the stream had been poisoned with arsenic. Christina wondered if the vineyard well had also been affected.

She grabbed Alberto's hand, they kissed briefly, and the young lovers ran down the hill to tell her parents what they had discovered. Although they laughed and loved the rest of that summer, their budding relationship was cut short when Christina was accepted to UCLA on a soccer scholarship.

Chapter 42

Bears Stand

Scouted and recruited by UCLA, Christina played first string from the moment she arrived. But as good she was, Christina was still not good enough to secure a spot on the U.S. soccer team.

As part of managing her disappointment, Christina immersed herself in her studies. She also became interested in Jivanmukta Yoga. Their core philosophy—a path to enlightenment through compassion for all beings—resonated with her.

During her first year at UCLA, Christina started dating Sidney Chu, a second year MBA student enrolled in the Global CEO Program for China. Sidney encouraged Christina to study Mandarin because he believed China's rising economic power would create many business opportunities for anyone who knew how to speak the language.

She took his advice and was well on her way to also becoming proficient in Mandarin when Sidney accepted a junior executive role as C.E.O. at Wingsunlee Technologies Co. Ltd., the largest telecommunications equipment manufacturer in the world, which was run by his father. Chu's employment choice and return to China kyboshed their budding romance.

Christina graduated from UCLA with an honors degree in economics, and a minor in forensic accounting. During the summer when she wasn't training or playing soccer, she worked as a forensic accountant with a firm in Los Angeles that assisted the Government Accounting Office (GAO) with its toughest cases. The GAO's job was to confirm whether Government funds were being used for their intended purposes and to identify any individuals and/or businesses that broke the rules.

Christina was both appalled and incensed by the amount of fraud and seriously considered forensic accounting as a career. Her firm, Writer, Feldman and Ovitz (WFO), was impressed by her instincts and work ethic. When she quit WFO to obtain a master's degree at Harvard, her boss told her that she was welcome to return any time. That summer, Christina also graduated from a 300+ hour, month-long Jivanmukta Yoga teacher/training program.

Christina always thought that she would have a private sector career in forensic accounting. No one was more surprised than she was, when her final paper at Harvard, "The Economics of the Migrant Farm Worker—Virtual Slavery in the Modern Day—Reliving the Cotton Generation Through Grapes," captured the attention of the president of Bears Stand.

She was a bit taken aback when the company offered her a job as an Associate Vice President, Private Equity and Alternative Investments. Her mandate included identifying promising private companies in the wine and spirits industries. The year was January 2006.

That February, her boss introduced her to lobbyist, Sterling Smith, at The Art League's Patrons' Show. Because she found him easy on the ears as well as on the eyes, she was happy to continue their conversation over drinks in the lobby bar. Over the next few months, Christina and Sterling discovered that they had a great deal in common, including finance, soccer, and a love of all things Spanish. The couple planned to elope during a ten-day summer holiday to Don Quioxte Tapas & Spanish Wine Academy in the Andalusian village of Vejer de la Frontera.

Their relationship fell apart after Sterling lost 95% percent of his net worth in the 2008 global financial crisis. After several very worrying incidents, his family committed Sterling to the Western State Psychiatric Hospital.

While she was still recovering from what happened to Sterling, a few months later, on April 6, 2008, two days before Christina's 32nd birthday, Bears Stand, and the U.S. investment industry, failed.

Chapter 43

A Natural Friendship

Because they were unemployed, Melodie and Christina had lots of time for networking, self-reflection, and recreation. In March 2008, the two women met at a two-day Mindfulness and Jivanmukta Yoga retreat in Tucson, Arizona. At one of the scheduled breaks, the two fit and fabulous females found themselves standing next to each other. When they introduced themselves, Melodie remarked with a warm smile that Christina's first two names were almost identical to the first two names of Christine Sinclair, Canada's top soccer player.

Returning Melodie's smile, Christina replied. "I went to UCLA on a soccer scholarship and at one point I even wanted to play professionally. Unfortunately for me, but good for the Olympic team that went on to win Gold that year, they chose a much better player. I still play for fun whenever I get a chance, which isn't nearly as often as I would like."

Melodie was charmed by Christina's openness and honesty. She invited Christina to continue their conversation over lunch. It wasn't too long before they discovered they both lived in the "Big Apple," and were proficient in French, English, Spanish, and Mandarin. And the similarities didn't end there.

Until the global financial markets started their downward slide, Melodie and Christina had both enjoyed upwardly mobile, management roles with respected financial services companies. When the markets crashed, the two strong women, along with hundreds of other middle managers, lost their financial services jobs.

Christina and Melodie believed they had been betrayed by their bosses and were convinced the system was stacked against the average person. They wanted to do something about the "broken system" but didn't know what two, unemployed, private citizens could do that might make a measurable difference.

After the retreat, Christina and Melodie ate lunch together and spoke on the phone as often as possible. Their friendship deepened over these conversations. In addition to yoga, sports, entrepreneurial friends, family members, and dating, they spent a lot of time talking about life before the crash, when they were each a part of their respective "hot" investment banker teams. Notwithstanding the dog-eat-dog nature of the financial services industry, they both believed they had done good work.

After many such conversations they recognized that their philosophies about business and life were surprisingly similar. Both women believed that you earned respect by giving it and that you built trust by being trustworthy. They were not afraid to say what they meant and meant what they said. Their finely tuned people skills ensured they were well liked by colleagues and employers, who all said they would be happy to rehire them when the markets improved. Their professional references confirmed they played well with others, and would cope well in a quick moving, high stress environment.

Both women also had their own trading accounts. Although most of transactions were in the black, returns were not enough to survive on in the absence of a good base salary, especially in an expensive city like New York.

Chapter 44

2008 Burning Man

Several months after the yoga retreat, Melodie received an unexpected telephone call from Christina. Her new friend laughingly explained she was in a bit of a jam and hoped Melodie would be willing to help.

"The two people I was counting on joining me and sharing expenses for the 2008 Burning Man in the Black Rock Desert, unexpectedly cancelled. Given my current state of employment, I can't go unless I share expenses with at least two other people. When I reread the 2008 marketing material and saw that the theme—nationality, identity and the nature of patriotism—I thought of you immediately," Christina said with a smile in her voice.

As Christina read Melodie the rest of the marketing material, Melodie got goosebumps. "In 2008, leave narrow and exclusive ideologies at home; forget the blue states and the red; let parties, factions and divisive issues fall away, and carefully consider your immediate experience. What has America achieved that you admire? What has it done, or failed to do that fills you with dismay? What is laudable? What is ludicrous? Put blame aside, let humor thrive, and dare to contemplate a larger question: What can America, this stumbling, roused, half-conscious giant, still contribute to the world?"

Melodie was intrigued. Participating in the 2008 Burning Man with Christina, sounded perfect! But Christina said she was looking for two people, not just one. "Just thinking out loud here, but why don't I see if my brother, Jacques, would like to join us? I think he would love Burning Man. Although Jacques is a cop, please don't hold that against him, he is also a creative thinker. More importantly, he has cash flow and a secure job. So, can I invite him? And Christina, I'm so glad you called. I can't wait to experience Burning Man with you and Jacques," Melodie said.

"Me too. I think we'll all love it! When I went to last year's event, it was a life-changing experience. Given our current circumstances, I'm confident we'll both get even more out of this year's event!" Christina replied.

After she said goodbye to Christina, Melodie called her brother, Jacques. Because of his seniority, he was able to get ten day's holiday on short notice.

Chapter 45

The Beginning of an Idea

A week later, Christina and Melodie met for lunch at Just Greens, an upscale organic vegan restaurant on 9th Avenue. Over several green smoothies, and the best bowl of vegetarian chili either of them had ever tasted, they finalized their travel arrangements.

Reluctant to leave the restaurant or each other, their conversation turned to their lack of employment and future prospects. Both agreed that it was unlikely that, at least in the near term, either of them would be able to secure a comparable position in another financial services company.

As Melodie took a sip of her second green smoothie she said, "Even though it was really well hidden I suspected that our firm was profiting from insider trading information. I even made a written complaint to the Management Committee. I never got a response. Then, the world went tilt and I lost my job. After that, everything is a bit of a blur."

Christina answered, "Yes, something similar happened to me. It seems as if the average person is the only one playing by the rules."

Melodie responded, "Wall Street is so corrupt. Insider trading is an out and out violation, yet it seems that no one is held accountable. Unfortunately, there doesn't appear to be any equality in the marketplace. My brother, Jacques, told me he thought that there were more laws broken on Wall Street on any given day than in the rest of North America combined."

Both agreed that something had to be done. "Just think," said Christina, "Our parents, and the parents of most people we both know, work hard for their money. It's not fair that numerous executives get to profit from insider trading. That hurts everyday people."

"You're not kidding,' Melodie said. "The only people the corporate elite and their buddies, the politicians, seem to be serving, is themselves. And what about the very clever, top brass at the big trading firms who get to trade on that information too? The average person loses out because he or she doesn't have access to the same information."

"Or are bound by iron-clad confidentiality rules, and cannot act on anything that they learn. Firms, including the ones we worked for, collapsed under the weight of their own greed and nearly crippled the global financial system. The taxpayers, who never benefitted from any of these deals, bailed the disintegrating financial organizations out. Typical—taxpayers had all of the costs but none of the benefits. Of course, the greedy executives profited from their trades, and also kept their jobs, while hard-working underlings like you and me, were thrown out with the trash," Christina replied with a sad smile.

The more they talked, the angrier Melodie and Christina got. They railed at a system that rewarded this type of abusive behavior. From the time they were students, Melodie at the INSEAD, and Christina, at Harvard, they believed that it was possible to invest ethically and to realize a decent profit. Melodie had even co-authored a book on that same subject.

There must be something they could do to right this obvious wrong. They left their delicious lunch feeling frustrated and powerless. They hoped that the 2008 Burning Man, and perhaps some insight from Melodie's brother, Jacques, would provide some clarity and inspiration.

Chapter 46

The Three Amigos

Christina, Melodie, and Jacques met in the lobby of Christina's New York apartment. The three of them were splitting the driving and all of the costs associated with joining the 45,000+ like-minded people gathering at Black Rock City, Nevada. Like their fellow travelers Christina, Melodie and Jacques each had their own, highly personal reasons for going on the trip.

Jacques had just closed three extremely challenging, emotionally draining murder cases. He was worn out and needed some time to rest, relax and refocus. Although he had thought that looked more like a white sandy beach and unlimited cerveza's, one of his key strengths was his flexibility. When Melodie read him the marketing material he was immediately intrigued. Besides, spending time with two beautiful and intelligent women, one of whom was his best friend and only sister, sounded just about perfect.

More importantly, he was a little worried about his sister, who was sounding mildly depressed. The last time they talked, Melodie mentioned she was more tired than usual and was frustrated by the lack of progress in her job search. During their last conversation, Melodie casually mentioned that she was on the verge of giving up and heading home to Quebec. Jacques had always been able to talk his sister out of the very occasional dark mood. Maybe some time with her big brother was exactly what they both needed right now.

And maybe it was also time to have her meds rechecked. Melodie couldn't afford to get sick again and they both knew that too much stress might cause the cancer to return. She seemed more like her old self when she talked about participating in the 2008 Burning Man. Jacques being Jacques, didn't have the heart to turn her down.

Melodie didn't want to admit to anyone, especially herself, how emotionally devastated and frightened she was. These days, the only thing she looked forward to was spending time at the local boxing gym. Like Christina, she was quickly running through her savings and was concerned about how long she could last without a steady job in an expensive city like New York. She relied on her company medical benefits which thankfully, still had eight more months to run, to pay for the absurdly expensive cancer medications she was still taking.

It was not like her to be directionless and lethargic, and she was relieved Christina had suggested participating in the 2008 Burning Man. It sounded perfect. She was over the moon when Jacques agreed to join them and was looking forward to spending some quality time with her two favorite people.

Christina was also looking for inspiration and was finding it difficult to get any traction on her job search. She had never been unemployed before and was finding it challenging to fill so many empty days. And she was sick of drinking coffee and faking optimism about the future with strangers, who only agreed to meet her because they were returning the favor to someone in their network or who recalled how coffee and conversation got them through when they too were looking for employment.

Because she had always had a great paying job, Christina had never noticed that living in New York was ridiculously expensive. At the rate she was going, she would be dead broke in less than a year. Tapping into her 401K's, selling at a loss, or borrowing money from her parents wasn't her idea of long-term financial planning. "Even Wonder Woman would find it difficult to lose her job, and her boyfriend, within weeks of each other. I definitely need a new game plan," she thought to herself.

"I don't like how much I'm sounding like a victim. Wasn't it singer/songwriter Billy Ocean that said, when the going gets tough the tough get going? Time for an attitude adjustment. Burning Man, here I come," Christina said out loud.

Chapter 47

Life After Burning Man

Three months after the 2008 Burning Man, Melodie and Christina met for lunch at the Peach Bistro, which was quickly turning into their favorite New York restaurant. After enjoying two vegetarian lasagnas and two house salads, the young women relaxed over a couple of almond/date smoothies.

"Since our Burning Man experience, thank you so much again for inviting me by the way, I've been seriously thinking about the future. And here's what I've come up with. I think that the only sensible thing for both of us to do is to start our own consulting practices in an area of the country that will never melt down, regardless of what is going on in the financial markets. Of course, I'm talking about Washington D.C."

Christina said, "What a great idea! I've always wanted to live in D.C. I think every red-white and blue-blooded American girl should live in our Capital at least once. And I must admit that there is something about running my own business that I find really appealing."

Forty-five days later, Melodie and Christina shared the cost of a moving van, found places to live in D.C., and launched their respective consulting practices. Both women offered language coaching. In Melodie's case, she also offered physiotherapy services. In addition to language coaching, Christina was also a freelance yogi and consulted on acquisitions in the wine and spirits industries.

Chapter 48

A Soft Launch

Melodie's freelance career took off like a rocket when she was hired as an interim physiotherapist for two amateur hockey players—David had a frozen shoulder and Earl suffered from a severe rotator cuff injury. Chase Costanzia, the team captain of the Washington Capitals professional hockey team, was David's older brother.

One night during the off season, when the brothers were unwinding over a bucket of barbecued wings and mugs of frothy beer, Chase mentioned that the Capital's senior physiotherapist had quit unexpectedly to participate in a UN mission to the Congo.

David asked, "Would you like me to refer you to the most amazing physiotherapist in all of D.C.? Melodie Marie Beaudoin unfroze my shoulder and returned me to game play faster than I ever imagined possible. Why don't I send you her coordinates?"

Within a week of that conversation, Melodie signed a temporary consulting contract for physiotherapist services—she would fill in until the Capitals found a permanent employee. Her French accent, friendly personality, and XX chromosomes were a big hit in the testosterone-dominated locker room. Because her physiotherapy skills were also top notch, the team continued to hire her whenever permanent staff was ill, on vacation, or away for an extended period of time, which as it turned out, was surprisingly often.

The vivacious professional welcomed these part-time physiotherapy roles because they were lucrative and leveled out the cash flow peaks and valleys that were inevitable for someone who had just launched a freelance language business.

Chapter 49

Melodie's Clients

Luckily, after she had finished her first contract with the Capitals, her language coaching business began to gain traction. Melodie was hired to teach Mandarin to three Senators and was very excited about the possibilities of working with them as well as other government officials.

Virginia Senator Miles Worthington, a Republican, was a narcissistic, three-star General with an insatiable appetite for younger women. He entertained an endless stream of barely legal, curvy young females in a suite he rented at The Jefferson Hotel under the name of George Washington III.

The General was always upfront about his intentions and told his young conquests that he didn't want anything permanent and to not get any ideas because he had no intention of leaving his wife, Gladys, even for the, "Best screw north of the equator." When he got tired of the sex, or if it appeared that any young beauty wanted something more permanent, he decisively terminated their connection.

When it ended, and it always ended, none of his conquests left his bed, or his life, without several tokens of his appreciation. Each young beauty received $3,000 in mad money, a $2,000 credit at Quinn's Goldsmith, a world-renowned, high-end jewelry store, and a $1,000 credit at The Glitz Carlton spa. All of these tokens of the General's affection were tucked into the current season's must-have Coach purse. Everyone was satisfied with the arrangement.

In between seducing young women, the General chaired The United States Senate Committee on Armed Services. It oversaw defense policy, as well as military research and development and was considered to be one of the most powerful Senate Committees. Many of his Committee members, including Vice-Chair, Constantine Smith, the

Republican Senator from Alabama whose nickname was "Onassis" because he was the heir to a shipping fortune, had major ship building contracts in his home state.

As part of their civic duties, the Senators made sure the financial support of generous pre-qualified, constituents like CACE, All Season and Bluewater received lucrative government defense contracts. Before the contracts were announced, the Senators purchased stock in these companies because there was absolutely nothing in the existing rules that prevented them from doing so.

Melodie also provided language coaching services to Roberta Fromme, the Democratic Senator from Washington. Senator Fromme was an international financial executive before she married dotcom multi-millionaire, Tim Fromme. After their five brainy kids (two girls and three boys) left for college, Roberta had the time to devote herself to the public good. She ran for public office and won her seat in a landslide.

Unlike many of her colleagues, Roberta Fromme was not your typical career politician. She did not have the time, the energy, or the interest in indulging in any extra-curricular shenanigans. When, and if, she thought about sex, it was always with her husband, Tim. Nor was she in the role for the money or the power. She already had plenty of both. She only went into politics because she honestly believed she could make a difference.

Senator Fromme was the Chair of The Senate Foreign Relations Subcommittee on International Development. Her Subcommittee oversaw international development policy, and foreign assistance to international organizations including the U.N. It was responsible for foreign economic policy, international investment and U.S. participation in international financial institutions and trade organizations.

Although Senator Fromme was not religious per se, she tried to live according to the Ten Commandments. Unfortunately, she also had a human ego. When she learned that the China River Power Group was going to build a new hydroelectric dam, she bragged about it in Mandarin, to her language coach, Melodie Marie.

Melodie wondered if her Senator clients were just boasting or if they were actually trading upon what sounded like insider information. She also questioned if they even realized that by talking about it to her, they were disclosing information they had sworn to protect.

She decided to test her insider trading suspicions and set up a spread sheet that tracked the share prices of the companies her Senators discussed. Then, she shadow-traded the same stocks on the insider information she received from Senators Worthington, Onassis, and Fromme. After three months, the value of her imaginary portfolio had grown from an initial investment of $500,000 to $715,000—a 43% increase! If this could be repeated 4x a year, gains would be over 170%! It looked like her Senators' insider trading tips were legit.

"Is this my shot? Can I finally be the insider for a change? Would my parents and siblings approve? Can I live with breaking the law? What would Jacques say? Wouldn't it be ironic if something as illegal as insider trading was the thing I used to finally stick it to The Man?"

The increases in her imaginary portfolio inspired the creation of a payback scheme she playfully dubbed "ESUR," essentially RUSE in reverse. She couldn't wait to share the results of her investigation with Christina.

Chapter 50

Christina's Clients

Because of her vineyard experience, and her role as an Associate Vice President, Private Equity and Alternative Investment Funds at Bears Stand, Christina was the North American subject matter expert on the wine and spirits industry. After she lost her job, a number of mutual fund companies retained her to consult on potential investments in these sectors. She was grateful for the work as these lucrative contracts overshadowed the revenues from her start-up language business.

For the past six months Christina had worked with Senators Vladimir Naumovski, and Junior Senators Butch Badger, and Sandra Makalowsky on their Mandarin speaking skills.

Christina knew the executive assistant to Senator Vladimir Naumovski the Republican Senator from Rhode Island because they were both members of the same gym. She often talked about her boss, Senator Naumovski, one of Washington's most eligible bachelors. He was a vegan, a marathon runner, and the captain of the 47-person crew that won Gold at the 2006-2007 Sailing World Cup Series in Australia. An expert marksman, at least once a year, he hunted boar (his ancestral passion), with Sergei Mikhalov, an old friend from university days. He always looked forward to their annual get togethers especially because Sergei was a wonderful host, an accredited sommelier, an expert marksman, a financial genius, and most importantly, had close connections to the European elite.

Because the Senator was an early adopter of technology, he was also independently wealthy. He made his fortune because he had the foresight to purchase stock in Amazon, Apple, and eBay when he was a young MBA student at The London School of Economics.

The Senator enjoyed relations with both male and female partners. To date, no one from either sex had captured his heart or occupied his bed for longer than a month. And because he was serially monogamous with his partner du jour, and was painfully honest about his intentions, he avoided most of the drama when these amorous relationships inevitably ended.

The handsome Senator chaired the Senate Subcommittee on Security and International Trade and Finance. His Subcommittee oversaw international economic policy, including the development of international financial institutions like The World Bank and The International Money Fund.

In a closed-door Subcommittee meeting, Senator Naumovski learned that The Central Bank of Russia was about to sign a joint venture agreement with The Peoples Group Bank of China to finance the largest Russian infrastructure project in a half a century. Because he enjoyed the mental gymnastics, and was a bit of a show-off, he was just thinking out loud when he described the Russia/China deal to Christina.

Butch Badger, the Junior Democratic Senator from Kentucky decided to take Mandarin lessons to honor his future in-laws. He asked his fiancée, Edie, to find him the best language coach that money could buy. Edie had dated Senator Naumovski for a short time before she met Senator Badger. She remembered Vlad was taking Mandarin lessons. Since they had remained friends after their affair ended, she felt comfortable asking him for a referral to his language coach. Vlad congratulated her on her engagement to his colleague and was happy to make a referral to Christina.

Senator Butch Badger chaired The Senate Subcommittee on Communications, Technology, and the Internet. His Subcommittee controlled legislation on all forms of cell phones, the Internet, satellite broadcast, broadband, and radio communication.

In a confidential Subcommittee meeting, the Junior Senator learned that Dellio was going to receive a contract to replace all 120,000 of the State's aging computers and that Blueberry had been selected as the State's preferred government cell phone provider. Although she tried to be discreet, Christina heard every word Senator Badger said to his fiancée, Edie, whom he always touched base with before his language lessons officially started.

Senator Sandra Makalowsky, Democrat, from California, was the third most senior Senator and the second most senior Democratic member. She narrowly defeated Republican George Washington Williams in a close primary runoff election in 2007 and was seriously thinking of retiring from the rigors of political life during the next election cycle.

She chaired the Senate Appropriations Committee from 2008 to 2011. She was a wine connoisseur, good friends with the then Governor of California and married to Chad Taylor, President of Bayer Inc. Practical-minded, she wanted to practice her Mandarin-speaking business skills with real life examples, and regularly talked with Christina about her husband's business interests, corporate acquisitions, takeover targets, and research and development projects.

Chapter 51

ESUR

As their friendship deepened, Melodie and Christina had many conversations about how to improve the financial services industry. On more than one occasion, Christina talked about how the vineyard workers on her parents' farm lost much of their meager savings, other than their financial interest in the vineyard, in the 2008 crash.

Christina found it fascinating that you could lose all of your money in a casino and no one cared, yet had to spend hours filling out paperwork to get access to investments where there was a higher likelihood for positive gains. Maybe that was the point—no amount of regulation could protect against a house that held all the cards.

Melodie often spoke about the highly regulated banking system in Canada. Although many Canadian investors had suffered significant and serious setbacks during the 2008 stock market crash, the banks themselves had remained solvent. This was in sharp contrast to Bears Stand, her former employer, and Investment Brothers, Christina's—both companies had played both sides of the house in the Mortgage-Backed Securities Market. Melodie and Christina were convinced that double dipping was not only allowed, it was encouraged.

After listening to Melodie's ideas about the ESUR project, Christina was inspired to create her own spreadsheet and to make imaginary trades of the same stocks as her Senator clients. Three months later, the two women met at Sprouts Restaurant on Georgia Avenue NW, to catch up and to compare notes. They were not surprised to learn that in three short months, each of their imaginary portfolios had returned significant profits!

Melodie had always suspected that U.S. Senators were profiting from insider trading information. The returns on the girls' imaginary portfolios proved it. But they would need to get more people involved to have a large enough body of evidence to prove what was going on and to demonstrate that the Senators were making serious money from their insider trading. To get the evidence they needed for the expose required them to break the law.

"Well, it sounds to me that what you are proposing is that you, or even we, profit from insider trading information, just like our old bosses at Investment Brothers and Bear Sterns. I thought you hated what happened to us. And news flash, the last time I checked, insider trading was illegal. I wonder what Jacques would think if he found out that's what we were planning. I don't know about you, but my parents would murder me if I went to jail. You know I love you dearly, but if that is what you have in mind, count me out," Christina said.

That's when Melodie realized that Christina had put her finger on the one thing that had always bothered her about ESUR—the scheme was mercenary. And of course there was always the possibility that they might get caught, fined, or jailed. For ESUR to align with their personal values, it needed to be more altruistic. Somehow, they had to figure out how to modify their scheme so that it changed from personal gain to something that allowed them to, as Professor C had said so often, do well while doing good. Only then could they justify breaking the law.

Chapter 52

Win/Win

Melodie said, "Let me think out loud here. What if we didn't profit personally, but gave everything away to a charity, like the foundation operated by my friend, co-author and INSEAD alumni, Misha Mikhalov? Alyosha supports the advancement of financial literacy and capability programs in low and middle-income countries around the world. Just last week I received an email from Misha announcing that his Foundation won a U.N. award for their work in Spain, India, and Viet Nam. And I know from our previous conversations that you agree with me that systematic abuses contributed to the recent financial crash. Maybe the markets wouldn't have melted down if people were more financially literate. I like the synergy. What do you think?"

"Now you're talking!" Christina said. "How do you suggest we get a large enough body of evidence, without calling attention to ourselves?"

"What if we had a network of altruistic and trustworthy individuals, who would be willing to make stock trades based on the insider information that we get from our respective Senators? I'm sure my Sustainable Investing Group colleagues from the INSEAD would support what ESUR is trying to accomplish and would be happy to make a couple of stock trades every week or so. And I'm not worried about our trades being flagged for unusual activity because all of us regularly buy and sell stock."

"I agree. Then, we'll be able to prove that our six Senators are making trades and profiting from their insider information. And that will also give us the proof we need to expose the loophole in the law and to hopefully right a longstanding wrong," Melodie said.

"And the Sustainable Investing Club members already have a relationship with the Foundation because we direct a percentage of our book royalties for our co-authored book, Leave Only Shadows, to Alyosha. That's the name of Misha's Foundation. It wouldn't be that much of a stretch to add the profits from our ESUR trades to what we already give. Now that's what I call a win/win," Melodie added.

She continued, "Our imaginary portfolios prove that United States Senators are profiting from insider trading because of a loophole in how the laws are written. When I lived in New York, I met Philadelphia Romualdez, the Pulitzer prize-winning reporter at *30 Minutes*, at my advanced Mandarin language classes. This type of story is right up her alley. Phil is a real go-getter. Although she is a bit pretentious, I've always found her really easy to talk to. If we could prove our case, I'm sure she would be happy to work with us on an exposé, especially because I believe it might lead to another Pulitzer Prize."

"Of course, we will have to avoid getting caught before we have filmed the exposé," Christina added with a smile. "Why don't we set up two teams? Each of us could send coded computer messages to our respective teams. And for security and credibility, I think it's important that neither group knows what the other is doing. In other words, your traders would only trade on the insider information I receive from my Senators and my traders would only trade on the insider information received from yours. That way, anyone that is looking at my trades won't be able to connect my Senators to the information. And vice versa."

"The way I see it, our biggest risk is that we have to send each other the information about what stocks to buy and sell. But if we are smart, no one will know that is happening. Because it is a "blind" study so to speak, I don't think Phil will have any reason to question our data. I think Misha's father—Misha is my school friend with the Foundation—would probably donate the funds to set up the technology that will hide the messages we send to each other. It just might work.

Maybe we can't fix the system-wide corruption, but I think ESUR can help us close a loophole in one," Melodie added.

"I also think that it's important that until Phil is on board and the exposé is in the can, so to speak, that we are not seen in public together. Which means that if you agree with my plan, there will be no more almond smoothie dates together, at least until the information goes live."

"I agree that might be best, but I will really miss our conversations. Isn't there some way we can still communicate while we're gathering the data?" Christina asked.

Melodie and Christina brainstormed different ways to stay in touch while ESUR was operational. They settled on renting a mailbox at the UPS store in the City Center complex. Both Melodie and Christina would each have keys. If ever there was something they felt the other needed to know they would leave a note in the mailbox. If a personal conversation was needed, they would send a text from a burner phone.

After lunch Melodie contacted eight of her Sustainable Investing Group co-authors, Misha Mikhalov, Wayne Lee, Paula Da Silva, her INSEAD roommate, Svetlana Tretiak, Ada Adelmann, JB Washington, Sayid al Farah, and Denzel Sun Mah. Because all were Sustainable Investing Club alumni, had a relationship with Misha's Foundation, and believed in the benefits of ethical investing, they would understand what ESUR was designed to accomplish, and more importantly, would be willing to help. When Melodie reached out to them, only Sy and Ada declined to participate because of work commitments.

Melodie and Christina decided that Wayne, Svetlana, and Denzel would make the trades identified by Christina's Senators and that Paula, JB, and Misha would make the trades identified by Melodie's Senators.

As Melodie had hoped, Misha's father, Sergei, agreed to pay for Misha's time to design the software for Ensure or some other weird name, he pretended to never learn.

Although Misha agreed to create the customized software, truth be told, he was so overwhelmed with the demands of running the various family businesses and coaching the campers that he didn't have the bandwidth to take on more. He reached out to Denzel to brainstorm ideas.

Chapter 53

A Media Connection

Philadelphia Romualdez won the Pulitzer Prize for her investigative reporting of U.S. soldiers' mistreatment of Iraqi prisoners of war—quite a feat for a rookie reporter. It was a fluke that Philadelphia was even in the newsroom when the tip line rang. When she answered on the third ring the caller asked for her colleague, Mary-Lou Tindall.

Philadelphia closed her eyes, crossed her fingers and said, "Mary-Lou is not at her desk—she was technically correct, even if she could see her colleague off in the distance, returning to the newsroom with a mug of steaming coffee clasped tightly in her right hand. Can I help you?"

The caller asked if Philadelphia was a reporter with *30 Minutes*. When Philadelphia said, "Yes, I am," the caller said "I have something for you. What's your email?" Within five minutes, her inbox contained ten photographs of what looked like some American soldiers mistreating and denigrating Iraqi prisoners of war that were being held at an army prison near Baghdad. She smelled a winner. That anonymous call might just be her big break!

Philadelphia pitched the alleged abuse story. Although Jill Stein, the assignment editor, and Mary-Lou's best friend, was skeptical about a rookie reporter's sources or her technical ability to pull off a sophisticated yet gritty exposé, she changed her mind when Philadelphia produced the ten emailed photos.

Jill assigned Philadelphia a camera operator and a researcher. Had Jill known that Philadelphia had poached the story from Mary-Lou she would have insisted that she give her friend everything she had. But Jill didn't know. And Philadelphia didn't tell her.

Philadelphia spent the next three months' investigating the abuse allegations. When all was said and done, a female

General and six of her command staff were charged, and were facing court martial, maybe even jail time. In the end, Philadelphia's Pulitzer Prize was well deserved.

Because her colleagues suspected she had stolen Mary-Lou's story, they did everything they could to make her look bad in front of her boss and assignment editor, Jill. Their treatment reminded her of her years at boarding school where she was bullied because she was not a blonde, blue-eyed, trust fund daughter.

After her Pulitzer, Philadelphia was convinced that her editor was only giving her garbage assignments. Why else would Jill assign a prize-winning journalist to news stories about runaway dogs, grizzly bear attacks, floods, and minor robberies? Instinctively, Philadelphia knew she needed another exposé if she wanted to fulfill her dream of becoming the first Filipina anchor before her 31st birthday, which was quickly approaching.

Before winning the Pulitzer, Philadelphia never felt like she belonged in the newsroom. But none of her colleagues were aware of her feelings because she acted so self-assured. She learned how to feign indifference at Boarding School. The reporters she worked with also didn't know that her career goal was to be the next female Walter Cronkite. They just thought she was a narcissist and did their best to avoid her. That didn't bother her. She was used to being alone and worked better that way.

Philadelphia met language coach and physio therapist, Melodie Beaudoin, at an advanced Mandarin language class when they both still lived in New York. When class started, all of the students were given an opportunity to introduce themselves in Mandarin. Philadelphia made sure everyone in class knew that she was, "A Pulitzer Prize-winning Investigative Reporter." Her award was also prominently displayed in gold embossing on the business card she personally handed to each student after class ended.

Chapter 54

Going Public

When Melodie had enough data to take the ESUR insider trading story public, she felt "Phil" had the experience needed to do justice to the story. "I have her business card here somewhere," Melodie mumbled out loud. She found the right card in her rolodex.

When Melodie called, she thought it best to start with an appeal to the reporter's ego, "Hi Phil, It's Melodie Beaudoin. We met in Mandarin class when I still lived in New York. I live in Washington D.C. now. I think I have your next Pulitzer Prize winning story. Would you be open to getting together over a smoothie at The Peach, my treat, so that we can talk about the story? I'll be in New York to do some Christmas shopping next Saturday. Does that work with your schedule?"

Yuck. Philadelphia hated all that new age, holistic stuff. If she didn't need a good story so badly she would have made up an excuse not to go. But beggars can't be choosers, and she needed Melodie's story as much as Melodie seemed to need her. She replied, "It just so happens that I have some time next Saturday at 11:30 a.m. Does that suit you?"

Melodie booked a return flight to the Big Apple. When she arrived at The Peach, she suggested they order pineapple and blueberry smoothies and a healthy green salad, which weren't quite as dreadful as Philadelphia imagined they would be. Melodie was reluctant to jump right into what she was trying to accomplish with ESUR and eased into the conversation with some background information on who she was and why ESUR was important to her.

"I was born and raised in Quebec, a province in Canada. I believe in the rule of law. One of my brothers is a police detective. I worked at Investment Brothers here in New York before I lost my job in the 2008 crash. I have always been interested in how the US government organizes itself, which is very different from how we do things in Canada."

Melodie continued, "Based on my research, The Senate Ethics Manual says that its Conflict-of-Interest Rule 41(7) does not allow members, officers or employees to derive financial benefit, or to profit, directly or indirectly, from the use of their official position. I don't have your resources, but I have looked at everything I could lay my hands on and have not been able to find any arrests or prosecutions against any Senators for insider trading. And I can prove that at least some of them are doing that."

"In the 110th session of the House of Representatives, on March 28, 2006, Congressman Bryan Bond (D-WA) and Congresswoman Louise Donne (D-NY) recognized there was insider trading going on and proposed an amendment to the Insider Trading Act. Their motion died in Committee. Bond and Donne reintroduced their motion in the 111th session (May 16, 2007) and then again in the 112th (Jan. 26, 2008). Even with amendments, their motion couldn't get any traction and died in Committee."

"My friend, Christina, and I, can prove that at least six sitting U.S. Senators are trading on insider information. We know each of these Senators and have personally overheard all of them talk openly about what went on in their Committees and what stocks they planned to buy, sell or short. Because we wanted to do something to address this illegal practice, we set up an investment team to trade the exact same stocks as the Senators. Our initial seed capital was $1.6M. We had eight traders, which included my partner, Christina, and myself, and six other colleagues. In six months' time we successfully grew our initial seed capital to $2.8M!

When Philadelphia asked why Melodie and her traders didn't just enjoy their profits Melodie replied, "It's never been about the money. None of our ESUR traders, that's what we call our little undercover investment club, personally profited from any of the trades."

"In fact, I've got the paperwork to prove we donated all of our net profits to The Alyosha Foundation for Financial Literacy and Education, a legitimate Foundation, headquartered in Russia, doing financial literacy outreach work, and run by a close friend of mine. None of us traded to make money. We just wanted to shine some light on what we all perceive as a corrupt practice."

"If a private individual bought stock on the basis of insider information, and he or she got caught, they would pay a large fine and probably spend some time in jail. Just look at what happened to Martha Stalwart. It doesn't seem fair that the laws don't apply equally to our government representatives."

"This double standard reminds me of what happened during the financial crisis of 2007/8. None of the executives lost their jobs over a problem *they* created. Only the employees and main street, suffered. Christina and I think the system is stacked against the little guy. It's unfair and we want to do something about it. The insider trading that is going on is just a small part of corruption in the wider system. We think it's time the average person learns what is going on."

It was hard for Philadelphia to hide a burning desire to high five the language coach—Melodie had just delivered what she believed was her next Pulitzer prize-winning story. But Phil had learned to control her emotions a long time ago. She told Melodie that she would pitch the story idea to her editor, Jill. "Maybe I'll ask Mary-Lou if she would like to work the story with me. Or, maybe not," she said to herself with a smile.

Chapter 55

A Disillusioned Patriot

Ted Chen-Williams was a fiercely proud American. He joined the CIA in 1998 after graduating with high honors and a computer science degree from Cal Tech. Everything in Ted's life looked perfect. He had close family relationships, good friends, a sexy girlfriend, and an upwardly mobile computer career with a respected government agency. Yet, in spite of all these positive indicators, by January 2003 he despised every aspect of his life, especially his career.

He did not agree with anything the George W. Bush administration was doing, hated the secrecy, the backstabbing, the egos, and the territory building. Even on a good day he couldn't remember why he had ever considered a career in the CIA. After his girlfriend, Sandy, was killed by a rockslide while they were hiking, a death he felt he could have prevented had he been paying attention rather than taking a selfie, he gave up pretending that his current life was worth living and slipped into a deep depression.

Within days, the fastidious, well dressed, and responsible Ted Chen-Williams started abusing alcohol and drugs. His performance at work took a nosedive. He didn't return telephone calls and missed meetings. He made mistakes on project files. Although his work colleagues were sympathetic in the beginning, after a couple of weeks, they could no longer cover for him and insisted he get professional help. Ted didn't see the point.

His best friend, Temp, was appalled. Although he had been trained to trigger emotional responses and to use them to his advantage, he didn't know how to support his friend. He tried and failed at being diplomatic and his concerns came out as a reprimand, "Pull yourself together man. I met Sandy. She didn't love a wimp."

But Ted was long past caring. He wanted to quit and start over but it was extremely difficult for someone who knew as much about the CIA computer systems as he did, to leave the Farm.

Ted had a good relationship with his boss, June. He asked her to help him figure out a solution. It was clear to June that Ted was depressed and had become a liability. She believed it was unlikely he could be rehabilitated. She decided to go to bat for him and said, "Although it is unusual, in principle, the government is prepared to consider releasing you. Something that might work is that we give you a new identity and kill off the old one, maybe in a car accident or a fire. Leave it with me while I get the appropriate approvals and work out the logistics. But be forewarned. if we do this Ted, there is no going back. You can never reconnect with your family or any of your friends or colleagues. Do you understand?" When Ted nodded yes, June added, I'll get back to you by the end of the week."

That Friday, Ted agreed to every one of the agency's terms. And on March 12th Ted Chen-Williams became the 73rd car fatality victim in DC that year. His only regret was that he could not tell Temp, his mother, or his talented younger sister and best friend, Jade, that he was alive. When Jade heard the news, she was devastated. A week later, his family laid Ted Chen-Williams to rest. His body was too mangled for an open casket funeral.

The CIA resurrected Ted Chen-Williams as Denzel Sun Mah. Plastic surgery lengthened his nose and changed his chin. The surgeons shaved ¼ inch off of his voice box so that his speaking voice sounded different than his original persona. He reshaped his body through boxing and yoga.

Even his own mother didn't recognize him when a "good Samaritan" helped her carry her groceries to her car in late July. The bigger test would be to see if he could fool his little sister Jade. It wasn't long before an opportunity presented itself—his soft-hearted sister was giving a free Labor Day concert in Central Park.

After the concert Denzel went right up to Jade and asked her to sign the cover of the CD he had just purchased. "With pleasure," she said. When she asked his name, and he replied, "Denzel." Jade just smiled and signed. At no point did she realize she had just autographed a CD for her brother. That's when Denzel knew that his physical transformation was complete and that there was no longer anything standing in the way of a fresh start.

Because he had always been interested in business and finance, he decided to upgrade his skills with a Masters of Business (Finance Specialty) Degree from the INSEAD, one of the best business schools in the world.

Chapter 56

A Devastated Sister

Sickly as a child, Jade Chen-Williams was diagnosed with a hole in her heart when she was five years of age. When she was 10, Jade underwent a series of operations designed to repair it. Today, her heart condition was well managed with prescription medication.

Despite the doctor's reassurances, Jade's overprotective parents believed her heart defect meant she couldn't run, jump and play like the other children. Since she spent so much time indoors, her maternal grandmother, a concert pianist, encouraged Jade to develop her musical talents.

Her grandmother recognized that Jade had a natural affinity for the harp and suggested that Jade turn her love of the instrument into a career. It was good advice—during her last world tour, critics favorably compared the young musician to her idol, Lorena McMaster, the most famous female harpist in the world.

Most days, Jade practiced the harp or performed in or traveled to or from concerts. On the advice of her stylist, whenever she performed or made public appearances, Jade only wore John Galliano-inspired Greek goddess togas in white or cream. When people thought of Jade Chen-Williams it conjured up images of an angel whose talent effortlessly created a musical bridge between the inner and outer worlds.

Her rigid practice and performance schedule allowed for few dating opportunities. Because she did not have someone special in her life, Jade was content to have every minute of her time scheduled by her publicist, her manager, her stylist, and her personal secretary. In truth, she was relieved to limit her interactions with the real world and "The many aliens that lived in it."

The only social activity Jade participated in was the occasional black-tie fundraiser or media interview. Most of the men she met while fundraising were over forty. And middle-aged guys didn't have a chance of melting her virginal heart. Her closest (and only) intimate friend was her big brother, Ted.

"One day I'll meet my one true love, get married, and have a houseful of well-behaved, good looking, musically-inclined kids," Jade often joked with her big brother. "Are you and your girlfriend, Sandy, planning to formalize things? I really like her. And you know I would love to have a sister," she asked. She tried to hide her disappointment when Ted answered with, "I'm really not sure if I'm ready for the next logical step."

That conversation took place two months before Jade found out that her beloved brother lost his girlfriend, Sandy, in a tragic hiking accident and a couple of months before he too was killed in a fiery car crash.

After her brother's funeral, Jade slid into a deep, dark, pit of despair. She cleared her calendar, refused all touring requests, and didn't sleep unless it was medically induced. She had no idea how she was going to occupy a world that didn't include Ted, or if she even wanted to.

After one year and several "tough love" lectures from her business manager, Jade scheduled a matinee concert with the New York Symphony Orchestra at Carnegie Hall.

Chapter 57

An Unexpected Pleasure

Misha was a big fan of Jade Chen-Williams, and had followed her musical career from the time she was a teenager. It was fate that he happened to be in New York on business at the same time as Jade's first matinee concert after she lost her brother, Ted. Because her music had given him so much pleasure over the years, Misha felt compelled to do something special for the exotic musician and decided to invite Jade to join him for an early dinner after her concert.

Misha remembered reading that the musician's favorite flower was a ghost orchid. He ordered an impressive display to be delivered to her green room and purchased a front row center seat for her concert. He was confident the $200 he slipped the usher would get him backstage to her dressing room after the concert so that he could extend his dinner invitation in person.

He decided to invite Jade to join him at Maassaa, the five-star sushi restaurant on 75th Street. He was certain that one of the most expensive restaurants in the world, and certainly THE most expensive restaurant in New York City, would remind her that life could still be magical. He planned to send a car to her hotel at 5:30 p.m.

Uncharacteristically open to advances from a stranger, Jade said 'Yes' to Misha's dinner invitation, which was just as much of a surprise to her as it was to him.

Although the twenty available seats at Maassaa were usually booked three months in advance, Chef Maassaa was a family friend, and always made room for Misha or Sergei whenever they were in town.

The offerings were Omakase (no menu). Chef Maassaa selected the five-course meal and the sake, beer and green tea that Misha and Jade would enjoy. In retrospect, Misha realized that he had accidentally made the perfect restaurant choice, because it gave the two young people an opportunity to concentrate on each other, without having to decipher the menu.

At the restaurant, perhaps because they were talking about her brother Ted, who sounded a lot like Misha's friend, Denzel, Jade was uncharacteristically outgoing. As the conversation ebbed and flowed, she noticed that she was laughing more than usual and didn't have to fake interest.

The brilliant Russian computer geek was normally just as awkward in social situations as was Jade. Unlike his brother Dmitri, Misha had never mastered the art of flirting or social small talk. He was much more private and cerebral. Some might even describe him as dull.

Even when he was a student at the INSEAD Misha studied all the time. The only social outlet he allowed himself was the time he spent with the other Sustainable Investing Group members or his immediate family.

But for some unknown reason, at this place and at this time, he was transformed into a brilliant conversationalist. Jade and Misha laughed and joked about everything from cartoons to cartels. Although they had grown up in two totally different worlds, they were pleasantly surprised at how much they had in common, including a strong work ethic and intense loyalty to family.

They were not even shocked to learn that they each loved comic books from the late fifties/early sixties, and both even had an impressive collection of animated cartoons from that era. Coincidentally, they were also both diehard fans of The Rocky and Bullwinkle show. Of course, their favorite characters were none other than the lovable Russian spies, Boris Badenovsky and Natasha Fatale. When they discovered their shared hobby, they laughed even harder.

The two young people were so wrapped up in the moment that neither of them tasted a bite of Chef Maassaa's delicious food. The hours passed by quickly. As the restaurant was preparing to close for the evening, Misha asked for the check.

"We are so grateful that you and your father always find time to visit us when you are in New York. There is no charge. I trust you and the beautiful young lady both enjoyed your dinner. And please give my regards to your esteemed father," Chef Maassaa said.

"Thank you so much, Chef. I'll be sure to tell my father how much we enjoyed your hospitality." Misha replied as he turned to Jade with a smile. Jade took a calling card out of her purse and rummaged around for a pen. She crossed out her agent's telephone number, hand wrote her cell number and handed the card to Misha. "I had an amazing time. I hope to see you again soon," she said. Misha called a taxi for Jade and recalled his driver for himself.

When he got back to his hotel, Misha, the introvert, did four uncharacteristically bold things. He booked the same seat, in the middle of the front row, at Jade's three upcoming concerts at the Teatro dell' Opera di Roma, Tokyo's New National Theatre, and London's Royal Albert Hall.

He reserved the company jet for all three concert dates. He also reserved a suite at the Glitz Carlsberg Hotel in each of the three concert cities and called his florist. He pre-ordered fifty ghost orchids to be delivered to Jade's dressing room before each concert. Then, he made dinner reservations for the two of them at the best restaurant in each of the three cities.

For the first time in his life, Misha was interested in something that wasn't work or education related. He didn't really understand why he felt like Superman every time he thought of Jade. As he sat in the audience in the three different concert venues it occurred to him that he must be falling in love. At least that's what he suspected it was. He had never been in love before, so he didn't really know what falling in love was supposed to feel like. After Jade's last concert at Royal Albert Hall in London, Misha planned to find out, during a romantic four-day weekend aboard the Lady Elena, the Mikhalov family yacht.

Chapter 58

Courtship

The Lady Elena was a 147-foot luxury yacht built by Bloome and Rose and designed by Star Phillipson and Martina Feldman. The master suite was a full-beam stateroom. There were panoramic views over the bow from the comfort of the king-sized bed. The yacht included his and her heads, a Jacuzzi tub and a full Euro shower, a central dressing room, and a study with a sixty-inch plasma TV.

The comfortably opulent interior design included a stunning array of textures, stones, and exotic woods in Elena Mikhalov's favorite colors of beige, eggshell and muted puce. Private stairs led to an observation lounge/cinema and the owner's office. French doors opened onto a private deck with its own hot tub. The fully retractable skylight invited stargazing.

After the London concert Misha and Jade arrived on the Lady Elena just in time for dinner. The onboard chef prepared a romantic supper of spiced sea bass and caramelized fennel, love dumplings, and citrus poached pears. Jade and Misha were satisfied with the feast and with each other. As they looked over the rail at the gently lapping water below, Misha put his arm around Jade and kissed her lightly.

He couldn't believe how "present" he felt when he was with Jade. Misha had never met gentle people—although loving, his hard-as-nails mother and father were intimidating; his twin was too selfish to be kind; and, with the exception of Denzel and Melodie, he didn't really trust his fellow students or his suppliers enough to confide in them. Until he met Jade, the only place he really felt safe was in front of a computer screen.

Misha proposed to Jade under a blanket of stars that first night. Jade made him the luckiest man alive when she said Yes to both his proposal and his suggestion that they retire to their stateroom to seal the deal.

The light from the portal bathed her beautiful skin, which was the color of pulled toffee. He loved how her expressive, almond-shaped eyes danced when she spoke to him or when she laughed at one of his lame jokes. Her voice, her smile, and her touch created a level of excitement in him that he had never imagined possible. They finally fell asleep after two hours of caressing and tasting every square inch of each other's bodies. When they awoke, their limbs were still entwined, and Misha was hard again.

Misha's love for Jade continued to grow. After a year of long distance dating and surreptitious concert going, he refused to stay single for a minute longer. He wanted to get married right away. There was only one problem. And it was a big one.

Because they both wanted a great love, Misha and Jade had vowed to never lie to each other. Misha had confided the truth about his family's many legal and illegal business interests. Her response was crystal clear—she would not marry him as long as he continued to work for his mob boss father.

This was problematic for two reasons. Misha had cut corners for so long he didn't know if he could function in a legitimate business environment again. And if he wasn't making money, why would (or should) Jade agree to marry him? Besides, he wasn't the kind of guy that allowed the woman to pay.

Chapter 59

Denzel's Regrets

While Misha was sitting in the front row, his school friend, Denzel, was sitting in the back row of the darkened concert halls watching and listening to his sister transform space and time. If Denzel had any regrets about his new life it was that he couldn't tell Jade how much he loved her and how proud he was of her.

Denzel knew Misha was crazy about Jade and planned to ask her to marry him because Misha had confided as much to him over beers one night. Although there was no official announcement yet, Denzel was quite certain there was a wedding in the future and that Misha, who didn't appear to be close to his twin or to have many friends outside of The Sustainable Investing Club, would ask him to be a groomsman.

Although Denzel didn't look anything like his former persona, Ted Chen-Williams, because the agency's plastic surgeons were exceptionally skilled, he still worried that his sister might recognize him.

He could only hope that Jade would be so caught up in being a princess bride she would only have eyes for her handsome groom and wouldn't even notice him. He did not have a Plan B if she discovered that her big brother whom she thought was dead, was very much alive.

Chapter 60

Misha's Exit Strategy

Misha needed an exit strategy that gave him enough money to provide Jade with the life she deserved while eliminating his involvement in the family businesses. Unfortunately, the way things stood, his father couldn't operate the family business without him and, because there was so much to learn, the campers were not yet fully up to speed.

Although his brother, Dmitri, was a great spy, he showed no interest in taking over the family business. His mother was consumed by her *OhMy EAU!!* and Lacuna clothing businesses. If anything happened to him or his father, he believed it would no longer be a family business especially if one of his father's lieutenants took over.

His father often talked about the trauma he experienced as a result of his own parents' betrayal. Because he knew this, he cut his father a lot of slack with respect to his demands for total obedience. He knew Sergei would be devastated by his son's disloyalty. He was also concerned that if his father discovered what he was up to he would do everything in his power to derail what Misha believed was his one and only shot at happiness before he had the chance to build his nest egg and marry Jade.

And so reliable, workaholic Misha opened a separate Swiss bank account and started siphoning off 0.01% of the gross revenues of the *OhMy EAU!!* and Lacuna operations. Because he was an honest thief, Misha resolved to stop skimming when he had ten million dollars in his secret account.

He didn't want to hurt his mother and hoped she would never figure out that he was stealing from her. Although her accountants might notice the missing funds, he anticipated they would see the consistently small amounts as rounding errors. And because cash flow fluctuated on a weekly basis, Misha assumed the theft might go unnoticed for years.

Misha rationalized his actions in three ways. First, in the last ten years he had made the family tens of millions of dollars. Except when he was at school, working at the Caisse, or when he stole away to meet Jade, he rarely even took a long weekend away from the business.

Second, the only hope for grandchildren was through Misha, because Dmitri was too narcissistic to love anyone more than himself. Passing on the family DNA was up to him and he wouldn't have the pleasure of doing his duty unless he married Jade—he was surprised at how excited the prospect of marriage and parenthood made him feel.

Third, in the last ten years he had lived on one-third of his $500,000 annual allowance—he donated the other two-thirds to his Foundation. And although he was entitled to it, he had never taken even a nominal salary from any of the other family businesses. Instead he directed the bookkeeper to give the money he was entitled to receive to the hardworking campers. On the other hand, his twin never denied himself anything a life of privilege could buy.

Although it almost killed him, he did not tell his father or mother that he had fallen in love with, and planned to marry the world-renowned harpist. When there was six million dollars in his Swiss bank account, Misha grew tired of the subterfuge. After Sergei and Misha's meeting with the realtors that were working on the purchase of a legitimate ski resort in Austria, Misha asked his father if he could speak to him on a personal matter.

Chapter 61

A Declaration of Love

As father and son settled in the lounge to enjoy their coffee and cigars after dinner, Misha who had very little emotional intelligence, simply blurted out that he had fallen in love with Jade Chen-Williams, a concert harpist, and that he planned on marrying her and fathering enough children to ensure the continuation of the Mikhalov dynasty.

Sergei was surprised that it had taken Misha so long to confess that he was involved with someone. In the last year, workaholic Misha acted more like his social butterfly brother, jetting off here and there and cruising on the Lady Elena, than like a serious businessman.

Fearing Misha was buckling under the pressure of juggling the demands of hundreds of legal and illegal business, Sergei had asked The Iceman to look into what was going on. His loyal consiglieri confirmed there was nothing to worry about—the only thing going on was that Misha was romantically involved with a beautiful musician.

Initially, Sergei hoped his son would tire of the girl but, unfortunately for her, that hadn't happened. He couldn't afford for Misha to be permanently distracted and before too long he would have to take action. Now that Misha had announced his intentions to marry the girl, the timing had become urgent.

Sergei's inward thoughts were at odds with his outward enthusiasm for the happy news. In reality, the business just couldn't afford for Misha to be side-tracked. How could he stop Misha from marrying Jade?

As Misha talked, Sergei let himself speculate—maybe The Iceman, could engineer an accident. Or, Sergei could encourage Misha to investigate an herbal cure for Jade's heart problems. When the herb was identified and purchased, The

Iceman could either poison it or inject the musician with potassium. Jade would suffer a fatal heart attack, just like Elena's Uncle Otto.

Or, maybe there would be a gas leak and the girl would be vaporized in a fiery explosion. It was really a shame. Sergei had seen pictures of her and listened to three of her CD's. She was exceptionally talented and very beautiful and would have given him gorgeous grandchildren.

As Sergei popped the cork on a bottle of Krug Close d'Ambonnay 1995 Champagne that he had been saving for a special occasion, he asked Misha to tell him a little bit about his future daughter-in-law. Quiet, introverted Misha spent the next two hours talking nonstop about how they met, what she looked like, her career, and how she made him feel when they were together.

He talked about how much he admired her upbeat and positive attitude about her heart condition or anything else that got in the way of her achieving her goals. After Misha finally stopped talking Sergei reminded him to call his mother to share the good news. When she was on the line and after her excitement settled down, Sergei and Elena agreed on a couple of alternative dates to meet their future daughter-in-law.

Chapter 62

An Accidental Death

Misha couldn't wait to surprise Jade with the news that he told his father about their relationship, that he had put everything in place that would allow him to quit the family business, and that they could finally set a wedding date. He made a quick stop at the family jewelers, ordered up the family jet for a trip to Tokyo, and just as the sun was coming up, let himself into the condo with the key Jade had given him.

He kissed Jade awake and draped a garland of 100 ghost orchids over her naked form. Nestled within the arrangement was a discreet box that contained "The Forever Heart," a 27.64-carat (5.528 g) diamond engagement ring. Its color was rated as Fancy Vivid Pink by the Gemological Institute of America. He had chosen it because it was as rare and as precious as his bride-to-be.

As she opened her beautiful almond-shaped eyes, Misha slipped the ring on her finger. Spontaneous, happy tears slid down her perfect face. Since Misha had forgotten to bring champagne, they toasted their families, their future, and their love with the lychee juice Jade took out of the wine fridge, located next to the king-sized bed. Early the next morning, the two love birds decided to watch the sun come up from Jade's thousand-foot, rooftop terrace.

They threw on a couple of matching robes, and Misha grabbed the box of Silver and Gold chocolates he had brought as a sweet treat for his bride-to-be. The couple walked, hand in hand through the sliding doors onto the 20-foot terrace.

The city lights still twinkled far below. Although the sun was not yet up, it was already hot. The air was sweet and peaceful because the humans and their vehicles had not yet claimed the city streets for their own. As the sky turned gold then pink, Misha was overwhelmed with gratitude and love.

He pulled his gorgeous fiancée onto his lap and stroked her long black hair. Jade snuggled closer to Misha and whispered, "Were you surprised that I didn't have any sake or champagne in the wine fridge and that we could only toast our love with lychee juice?" When Misha nodded Yes, Jade said, "I have some happy news—we're having a baby!"

"Amazing! I can't believe I'm going to be a father!" Misha said. "You've made me deliriously happy, sweetheart. That settles it! We're getting married next month!" Misha said. He outlined his plans to disentangle himself from the family business. His happiness was complete when Jade agreed to all of his plans. He couldn't wait to meet their child and was confident that Jade would be a loving and attentive mother.

With their arms wrapped around each other, the young lovers were almost asleep when Misha heard what sounded like several angry bees. He was allergic to bee and wasp stings and always carried an EpiPen with him whenever he was out of doors. Since the visit to the terrace was more or less spontaneous, and they were 25 storeys up, he assumed there was nothing to worry about and had left his EpiPen on the bathroom counter.

He wasn't sticking around to find out if any of those kamikaze hornets liked lychee juice, designer chocolate, or pregnant fiancées for breakfast. He threw Jade over his right shoulder and ran like hell for the sliding penthouse door. He didn't slow down until he dumped Jade unceremoniously on the floor and slammed the sliding door shut. Jade laughed as she asked him, "Are you practicing your moves on how to carry me over the threshold? If so my darling, you really need to refine your technique."

Because he was so focused on getting Jade inside, Misha hadn't even noticed that one of the oosumebachi (giant sparrow bees), had sprayed him in his right eye, which had already swollen shut. He screamed at Jade to get his EpiPen.

Jade ran into the bathroom and grabbed the pen. As she turned around, she stumbled on the bathroom mat and almost fell. She righted herself and continued her mad dash towards

Misha who was writhing in pain on the floor. In her haste to get to Misha, she tripped over his suitcase and the protective cap flew off of his EpiPen. She went down hard on the marble floor.

As she fell, Jade accidentally plunged the EpiPen into her right thigh. The adrenaline triggered a heart attack. Within seconds she was unconscious. When he heard Jade crash to the floor, Misha, who was nearly blind from his reaction to the bee sting, crawled over to his unconscious fiancée, and gathered her inert form into his arms.

All of the condo suites had a direct link to the concierge desk that was staffed 24/7. Before he passed out, Misha managed to tell the concierge what happened and to demand an air ambulance. When he came to, Misha was in a private room at The University of Tokyo Hospital. His father and mother were sitting on opposite sides of what appeared to be a hospital bed. Each parent had hold of one of his hands. Misha asked for Jade. He could tell from the look on his mother's face that the news wasn't good.

His mother said, "I'm so sorry son, but Jade didn't make it. She died of a heart attack in the air ambulance on the way to the hospital."

Misha started to sob hysterically as Elena folded her son into her arms. Because he was inwardly happy at the demise of his future daughter-in-law, Sergei found it hard to comfort Misha. Jade was out of the picture, which had always been the goal. And he didn't even have to get The Iceman involved—Sergei loved it when he saved money.

When Misha told his parents that Jade was pregnant when she died, Sergei was momentarily sad. But the business was more important than the needs, wants and desires of any one individual, including one of his twins. He drew Elena and Misha into his arms and settled into the role expected of a loving and supportive father. Lucky for him, Elena and Misha couldn't see his wide grin. He never disclosed that had there not been an unfortunate accident, he would have engineered one.

Misha was devastated and guilt ridden. Had he not asked Jade to get his EpiPen she would not have fallen onto it. He threw himself into work to avoid feeling anything. He never learned his friend, Denzel, was Jade's brother. The two men had become close when Misha started dating the beautiful musician and Misha wanted to share the good news with his friend. Since neither man had many close relationships, they appreciated their evolving friendship. Even after they left INSEAD the two spoke via Skype at least once per week. Their relationship became even closer after Jade died.

Misha assumed that his friend was so understanding, because over beers one night, Denzel had confided that he had lost his girlfriend, Sandy, in a tragic hiking accident. Denzel never disclosed why his grief was real.

Chapter 63

The Hijack of OhMy EAU!!

By the time the twins were celebrating their 32nd birthdays, *OhMy EAU!!*, Elena's bathing suit and lingerie business, had opened over two hundred retail stores in most major cities and had enrolled thousands of enthusiastic Fashion Club Members, worldwide. Elena was also on track for opening one new location every month for the next five years. She had merged the Lacuna and *OhMy EAU!!* businesses under the one brand. Sergei was impressed and somewhat surprised by the extent of his wife's success.

One of the mob boss's strengths was his ability to identify and to act upon opportunities. Sergei was certain there must be some way he could turn Elena's thriving retail business to his own advantage. Besides, he could use the mental distraction, from his ongoing, debilitating, prostate cancer treatments.

Although his doctor said that his prognosis was good and the treatments were going as well as could be expected, Sergei was worried that the therapies were affecting his ability to recall important facts. Recently, he recognized that his memory was not as good as it once was, probably from all of the shots to the head he had taken when he was doing collections for his father, and later, when he was building his own extensive empire.

His doctor attributed his non-existent sex life to his ongoing cancer treatments. Sergei felt sexually frustrated and unfulfilled. He still lusted after his beautiful wife, even though they hadn't made love in the last six months. Sexual frustration made him even more vicious than usual.

One night, as Sergei was settling down in his favorite leather chair and getting ready to take the first sip of his 100-

year-old Louis XIII Cognac, he figured out how he could hijack *OhMy EAU!!* for his own evil purposes.

He would instruct Misha to film the women and men trying on lingerie and bathing suits in the *OhMy EAU!!* dressing rooms. This would give him access to, and control of, the world's largest, and best, live-streamed Peeping Tom show. Of course, he would have to reconfigure the existing dressing room mirrors to accommodate the motion-activated cameras needed for the show. Fashion Club participants would never know that they were participating in a live action strip tease. That was the whole idea. He wanted things natural and spontaneous which meant the "stars" of the show could never learn that they were being filmed.

And just like that, Elena's legitimate retail operation became a front for ubdqt.com (You be damned quiet) the world's largest, voyeuristic website. For $500 USD/month, subscribers would have unlimited access to real-time streaming of adults trying on the sexy bathing suits and lingerie in the perceived "privacy" of the *OhMy EAU!!* dressing rooms.

Dmitri quietly spread the word about ubdqt.com to select contacts.

Sergei knew it was critical to have a small, exclusive, and controllable, subscriber list. With global operating costs of less than $300,000 per year, the net operating profit was enough to discourage driving the numbers up. Besides, the more people that were involved, the higher the risk of discovery.

Sergei knew that with minimal effort, Misha's campers could install a "plug and play" system. The modifications themselves were simple—the campers could remove the existing dressing room mirrors and replace them with new mirrors that had a camera mounted on the rear of the frames. The camera could be fitted with a wire that delivered the signal out and the instructions in. The wire itself would run up to the ceiling and out onto the roof where it could be attached to an innocuous high speed internet connection that could be safely housed in a waterproof junction box. The hard drive attached to the camera encrypted and scrambled the picture. The picture was unscrambled at the main hub where the control system and the ReID software went to work.

Misha had uploaded a library of the faces of every picture posted on social media by every male and female in the world. Although subscribers thought they were watching live dressing room action, Misha's software program scrambled the features and replaced them with another face from its library. In this way, Misha's Re-ID software, effectively "re-faced" and replaced the features with a different face from its library. The software was so sophisticated that it was almost impossible to tell that the "actor's" features were not their own.

Re-ID also "re-rendered" the pattern of the dressing room wallpaper—each *OhMy EAU!!* location used a distinctive wallpaper pattern in its store design. Re-ID substituted the wallpaper of one store, with the wallpaper from another. It also superimposed the images from client's virtual reality headset onto the back wall. That way ubdqt customers could have an identical "POV" experience. This maintained anonymity and ensured that both the volunteer "actors" and their "film studios" could not be recognized.

In new *OhMy EAU!!* properties, ordinary mirrors were installed as part of the construction process. After all code inspections were completed. Sergei sent a team of camp grads to the various locations with instructions to install the new replica mirrors. He told the campers that the substitutions were necessary because the installed mirrors had been recalled for manufacturing errors. He ordered the campers to install the new mirrors after hours so as not to disrupt Elena's retail operations. The real reason was to avoid arousing suspicion. In less than a month, the team of five campers successfully reconfigured the dressing room mirrors in all two hundred *OhMy EAU!!* retail stores.

Sergei was confident about the integrity of the dressing room mirrors. His biggest concern was to ensure footage of any underage "volunteer" actor was deleted. This was relatively easy to do. Fashion Club members provided ID and credit card information when they signed up. Several years earlier, Elena had decided that *OhMy EAU!!* would only accept payment for merchandise by credit card. Since it was unlikely that a financial institution would extend credit to someone who was less than eighteen years of age, he assumed that no minors would be filmed.

ReID had access to the customer's credit card information, as well as to the consents and membership forms on file. To access a dressing room, the customer had to show their membership card. The computer automatically scanned its data base and located the member's file. The cameras continued to roll for members who were over 18 and automatically shut off if the age threshold was not met.

If anyone accidentally stumbled across the Peeping Tom site they would automatically be redirected to the movie trailer for the erotic drama, "Eyes Wide Shut." As an additional level of security, there was a full-time team of twelve camp grads, working on ubdqt.com around the clock and they had strict orders to search and destroy any potential misses by Re-ID. The campers had been trained to be diligent about safeguards."

Over time, Sergei capped the subscriber list at 2,500 people which translated to net earnings of about $15 million per year, a nice, guaranteed boost to an already profitable bottom line, with minimal effort. He recovered the costs to modify the dressing mirrors in less than three months. As ongoing operating costs were minimal; the rest was pure profit.

The campers loved the job. It paid very well and had some obvious perks, including international travel, a generous expense account, and extended time off. When Sergei had five hundred replacement mirrors stored in a secret warehouse, he instructed The Iceman to kill the installation engineer and to dynamite the manufacturing plant.

Chapter 64

The Show Is On

Since Fashion Club Members were not aware that they were being filmed, they were uninhibited, playful and spontaneous which made for some highly titillating filmmaking. A typical hour of viewing might include real-time feed from four different locations, simultaneously. For example, in one dressing room, a woman might be trying on bathing suits—it was abundantly clear to the viewer that at *OhMy EAU!!* the "Leave Underwear On," sign was frequently ignored.

A gay patron might be trying on some revealing lingerie. Or the boyfriend/husband/girlfriend might be in the dressing room with the customer, with a very enticing result. Couples were only allowed to go into the dressing room together if they were both Fashion Club Members. More often than you might otherwise think, there were instances of spontaneous oral sex. More than once, there was even a three-way.

More than one woman played with her parts. A male customer got so excited looking at himself in a particular bathing suit that he stroked himself for twenty minutes. He came all over the dressing room mirror. The prancing and self-admiration were glorious to watch. And Sergei's hidden cameras captured it all.

As an added bonus, ubdqt.com could be configured to reflect its subscribers' specific tastes. Clients could customize their voyeur experience by specifying the body type, age, and ethnicity, they found most appealing. Their subscription included an alert system that would let them know when someone with their preferred body type or nationality, was "on air."

Given the large amount of publicity and legitimate and illegitimate traffic, it was hard to imagine how Sergei and

Misha managed to keep the voyeur side of the business secret from Elena. But it was easier than one might imagine. Elena was more concerned with the buying, merchandising and marketing aspects of the business, and was just not that interested in the operational details which she had delegated to Misha. As Chief Technology Officer, Misha looked after the technological administration of the business which meant that he could do his work undetected.

Neither Elena or the Alyosha board learned of Sergei's and Misha's sabotage—Alyosha became an *OhMy EAU!!* shareholder when Elena transferred 200,000 shares to the Foundation. The Peeping Tom side of business remained separate, and revenues were part of the millions of illegal dollars that flowed into Sergei's many numbered Swiss bank accounts. Throughout it all, ubdqt.com remained a deeply buried dark website

A causal porn seeker would never find the site and no search words turned it up. It was an exclusive club for the richest and most discriminating clientele. An individual could only join the ubdqt.com voyeur community if he or she was referred by another subscriber. It was an inside joke that it was harder to join ubdqt.com than the Marines. No public figure, politician or movie and/or sports star was given access for obvious reasons.

A subscriber could only access the site if they used the right access code. To avoid detection ubdqt.com changed its origin location every twelve hours and the system generated a new access code which it sent to subscribers twice a day. Misha believed all of the security features were robust enough to rebuff hacking. But by far the biggest deterrent for subscribers to have loose lips was the requirement to become a member for life—if anyone tried to renege on his or her financial commitment, The Iceman made a discreet house call, and the matter was quietly resolved. Only death dissolved a subscriber's commitment to ubdqt.com. After five years of operation, The Iceman had only been required to enforce the rules twice.

After Jade died, Misha never cancelled the order to transfer funds from *OhMy EAU!*'s retail account to his own. Although the account had doubled in almost two years, Misha didn't have the stomach to spend any of the funds—that money was supposed to pay for his future life with Jade. Since there was no Jade, there was no future, or at least not one he considered worth living. As his bank account continued to grow, his emotional and mental health began to decline. Although Sergei got what he wanted, the price was Misha's inability to be as effective as he was before Jade died.

Chapter 65

Denzel Sets Up ESHUR

In one of their weekly conversations, Misha told Denzel about Melodie's project. "Unfortunately, I just don't have the bandwidth to design ESUR or to even run the day-to-day activities of The Foundation and the campers are still too green to create such important software. Besides, I already have twelve new technology projects on my plate that I'm struggling to stay on top of. I respect Melodie and believe in what she is trying to do. But given all that is going on, ESUR is nowhere near the top of my priority list."

Denzel replied, "My computer skills are pretty good. Why don't I take a crack at setting up the ESUR system, which should take some of the pressure off of you. By the way, I think we should change the name from ESUR to ESHUR. Ruse spelled backwards is just a little too obvious. The extra "H" makes it less so. I'm only networking and going on the occasional job interview right now. And I love the important work being done by the Foundation. Misha, I know you're strapped. I want to help. I have the time and can easily serve as one of Alyosha's unpaid, part-time volunteers."

"Sounds good," said Misha, "But Denzel, I insist the Foundation pay you for your time."

Denzel laughingly replied, "Whatever you say Misha, but just so that you know, I'm only going to donate my salary back to the Foundation. I have more than enough money to sustain me until I land my next gig."

Denzel set up ESHUR as a very sophisticated encryption and de-encryption system. A custom-designed algorithm did the work of a human that would have interacted at either end of an Enigma encoder. The technology was similar to that used by the Germans in WWII.

Melodie and Christina's stock information was sent to a rolling address. If Melodie was the sender, Christina's computer would receive and then automatically send a re-encrypted message to the three traders in her downline. Whenever the traders went online, the system de-encrypted the stock sign on the screen. The stock sign only appeared on the screen for ten seconds. This allowed the trader to make a quick note. Then, just like the correspondence in Mission Impossible, the communication was destroyed on all involved computers. Although a trail that something was sent might still exist, there would be no record of the message itself.

Chapter 66

System Administrator

The ESHUR trading system worked like a charm. Whenever Melodie got a tip from Christina, Denzel's system alerted the three traders in her down line, and they either purchased, sold or shorted the designated stock. When the stock increased by more than 20% the traders had the discretion to sell. However, when increases reached 30% the software triggered an automatic sell. The traders never covered a short position more than once.

Every three months the eight ESHUR traders transferred their net profits to the Alyosha Foundation. Each of the traders had set up their own home-based, not-for-profit corporation. The eight corporations paid the relatively small expenses of their home-based businesses and ensured all tax filings were up to date. As all the trades were made by their respective foundations, there was no income or capital gains tax with which to deal. The profits were sent to Alyosha, who also received them tax-free which maximized profits. All traders agreed that although they were "stretching" some rules, because they weren't benefitting personally, it was unlikely there would be any legal blowback and even if they were caught the traders would probably receive nothing more serious than a slap on the wrist.

Denzel administered ESHUR from his home office in Mexico City, 3,030 km away from Washington D.C. He relocated there after a sex-filled week with Adelina Aguado. He met the pretty Mexican Airlines flight attendant, at an all-inclusive resort. Although "Lina" was no longer in his life, he had fallen in love with the country's rhythm, food, beaches, architecture, and history and decided to locate there permanently. It was the right decision and he had done some of his best creative writing and IT work since moving there.

One morning Denzel noticed two short power outages on one of the reports he typically ran in his role as ESHURE's system administrator. In summer, small brownouts and momentary power interruptions were just business as usual. The customer service department should be able to confirm if that was the case in this instance. He sent off a quick email, but, because it was the middle of the night in D.C., he didn't expect to receive an answer until the next afternoon.

He then searched Melodie and Christina's computers for the grid reports. As the ESHUR administrator, Denzel knew all of their passwords. It didn't appear that any gateways had been opened and there were no observable breaches. But it was prudent to check, and his CIA training had taught him to err on the side of caution. He fired off a quick email to Melodie and asked her to call him when she was at her desk.

With his skill set it was easy for Denzel to hack into the power company. It appeared that they were running an out-of-date email portal which made it relatively easy to gain access. As it turned out, Jerome White, a junior member of their administrative staff, had in fact, emailed his password to a personal Hotmail account.

Further investigations revealed that someone from the outside had in fact, logged into Jerome's account—many times. Denzel submitted an online incident report to the DC Power's security department and planned to follow up personally the next time he visited Melodie in Washington, D.C.

The "trip wire" he had installed on Melodie's and Christina's computers told him that although there were numerous attempts to break in, none had been successful so far.

As a precaution, he decided to change his process so that if a potential intruder tried to gain access, he or she would only find an empty room. At that point, even a less-experienced hacker would know that he or she had been fooled by a honeypot and would back off.

Although he knew a good hacker could delete any trace of his or her activity after the fact, he made a mental note to run some additional diagnostics when he got a chance. Since there was nothing else that could be done at the moment, he changed into his bike gear and set out on a grueling three-hour ride. Since he didn't feel like working on any Foundation projects or his murder mystery book, he decided to take the rest of the day off.

He touched base with Melodie at 7:00 a.m., Eastern Standard Time, the next morning. She confirmed that her stove clock, and all electric clocks were flashing. She also confirmed that the only clock that wasn't affected was the one with the battery backup. Denzel told Melodie that he would physically investigate her computer when he visited her in Washington in a week.

Denzel was looking forward to catching up with Melodie and attending a hockey game or some live theater. Since he'd moved to Mexico City, he hadn't had anything resembling a social life. That all changed when he met the vivacious, Rosa, a public relations specialist and his seatmate on the flight from Mexico City to D.C.

Other than a short email to tell Melodie that he had arrived safely, Denzel spent the rest of the week touring the Capital with Rosie. He never connected with Melodie or changed her computer configuration before she was murdered.

Chapter 67

The Gig Is Up

Misha cloned the ESHUR trading software and inserted a piece of code that gave Sergei access to all of the traders' encrypted emails, including Melodie's. That is how the mob boss learned of her email to Philadelphia confirming their meeting.

Sergei couldn't afford to have a reporter, especially an American one, sniffing around Misha's Foundation—as Alyosha was an *OhMy EAU!!* shareholder, he just couldn't risk discovery of ubdqt.com. Sergei was content with the stock trading profits he had already made from his personal ESHUR trades. It was a good run while it lasted. It was time to sever the connection. He reached out to The Iceman in the usual way.

Chapter 68

An Ethical Hacker

Born in South Carolina, Jackson Temple Reynolds III, "Temp," to his friends, had an impressive military pedigree. Temp liked the family history represented in his names. Jackson was his mother's maiden name. His mother had always only called him "Temp," a shortened version of Temple, her father's first name.

Like his father, grandfather and great grandfather before him, Temp was a decorated soldier and had served his country with honor and distinction. Thanks to his Special Forces training, his hand-to-hand combat, grappling, knife fighting and firearms skills were at an expert level. He was also highly skilled at surveillance, tailing, and stakeout and could change his appearance at will. His computer skills were off the charts.

The 6' 3" former soldier was also an outstanding physical specimen, which included a full head of wavy black hair, and piercing grey eyes. When he wanted female companionship, he had any number of willing acquaintances he could call. All of them were willing to try and capture the heart or frequent the bed of the mysterious, and charismatic Mr. Reynolds. One of his grateful lovers, described sex with him like making love with a Greek god. But since the Candice fiasco in college, Temp had managed to stay aloof and to avoid any emotionally relevant entanglements.

Since 1998, Temp had served his country as the head of the Financial Crimes and Enforcement Network, an agency within the U.S. Department of the Treasury. Thanks to his efforts, eight felons now plotted revenge from their 6' x 8' jail cells. And Uncle Sam was four hundred million dollars richer.

His boss, Sylvia Goldstein, gave him his nickname, "The Secretariat." Temp liked to think the moniker stuck because his computer skills including his ability to read and create complex, disruptive patterns and computer viruses were on par with the speed and endurance of the Triple Crown winner. Temp's hacking skills were legendary.

Since its inception five years previously, Temp had represented Treasury at the government's internal Cyber Crime Olympics sponsored by the Department of Homeland Security. He had captured the Gold USB (the government Oscar) in all five years he participated. This was an especially noteworthy achievement since the participants were all experienced white hat hackers from different U.S. government agencies. The only government hacker that came close to Temp's level of skill was his best friend, CIA agent, Ted Chen-Williams.

Temp and Ted were both smart, focused and competitive. Both graduated cum laude in the top one per cent of their class—Temp at MIT and Ted at Cal Tech. They thrived on competition and excelled at everything from Texas Hold 'Em, Chess, and Bridge to Sudoku and Mah-jong. They were also both socially adept and highly motivated to serve their country. It was a running joke that Ted could smell a badly made martini from three hundred paces. Temp could tell the difference between a rye, scotch, Bourbon or Irish Whiskey from the same distance.

The two men met at an inter-agency seminar on white-collar cyber-crime. What started out as a casual networking cocktail ended up as a friendly competition over how quickly either of them could break through different firewalls. Points were awarded based on difficulty. At the end of the year, the final score was tallied, and the loser treated the winner to a weekend of golf or skiing, winner's choice.

Temp had won their private competition for the last five years. For his prize, he chose skiing at Breckenridge, Lake Tahoe and Vail, and golf at Pine Valley and Augusta. But this might be Ted's breakout year. Ted had every intention of enjoying the golf course at Cypress Point, when he finally won their friendly competition.

Temp wasn't really worried. He thrived on every opportunity to test his wits and encouraged Ted to, "Bring it on." Bottom line, their friendly competitions made it worthwhile to get up in the morning.

Chapter 69

The Chinese

George Li, and his wife, Edith, immigrated to the United States through Britain in 1981. Everyone that met them was impressed at how well they integrated into the American melting pot. No one knew that the Li's owed ten million USD in gambling debts to Russian mob boss, Sergei Mikhalov, or that they had emigrated to the United States to avoid paying him.

The Li's were no match for a hardened criminal like Sergei. When his American enforcers tracked them down, Sergei was persuaded to let the Li's work off their debt by acquiring classified information, and, where possible, the trade secrets of U.S. companies that might be helpful to the mob boss. It wasn't difficult as they were already passing on this information to the CCP (Chinese Communist Party).

Sergei also wanted the Li's to establish a network of bona fide scientific, academic, and business contacts to ensure an uninterrupted flow of ongoing intelligence. Should they fail to deliver exactly what he asked for, he threatened to kill their only daughter, Edie, in front of them.

George Li was an expert in the use, misuse and development of drone technology for military and commercial purposes and had consulting contracts with a number of U.S. government departments as well as Amazon. He also taught at Temp's alma mater, MIT.

George often worked with Butch Badger, the Junior Senator from Kentucky, who sat on The Senate Subcommittee on Communications, Technology, and the Internet. The Junior Senator often asked him for advice about the use of drones for military purposes. It also meant that George could easily and unobtrusively obtain information that Sergei and the CCP would consider helpful.

George's wife, Edith, was a world-renowned virologist and bioweapons specialist. She had consulting contracts with the Mayo Clinic, the World Health Organization and the Center for Disease Control. Since he sat on a number of biotech and pharma boards, Sergei and the CCP were especially interested in the commercial applications of Edith's work.

When their only daughter, Edie, was sixteen years of age, her parents told her about their arrangement with the Russian mob boss and the CCP. Although shocked at her parents' disclosure, Edie wanted to help and believed that her language and hacking skills would allow her parents to pay back their gambling debt to Sergei much quicker.

She asked her parents to determine if the mob boss was open to her joining the team. The Li's felt Edie was still too young to get involved. Edie threatened to go to Sergei directly should her parents refuse her help. The Li's asked her to at least wait until she finished her Master's degree. Reluctantly, Edie agreed.

After Edie earned a master's in software engineering from MIT her parents felt she was old enough to meet their handlers. The three Li's were going on a family vacation to London, England, after they attended a conference on the future of drone technology in Edinburgh. They would introduce their daughter to their Russian handler, Mr. Ogiyevich, at the conference. The conference also gave Edith an opportunity to transfer a vial of the SARS virus to her Chinese government contact who also planned to attend.

Mr. Ogiyevich was impressed with Edie and believed Sergei would approve of the Li's smart, beautiful, and technologically adept daughter. As an added bonus, Edie was fluent in six languages—English, French, Spanish, German, Russian, and Mandarin which he was certain Sergei would find some way to exploit.

With Sergei's consent, Mr. Ogiyevich gave Edie two dangerous missions. The first was to penetrate and plant a worm on the Treasury Department's Financial Crimes and Enforcement Network computer system. Many members of

Sergei's drug cartel were in jail, awaiting trial on a variety of drug charges, and were facing long sentences. Even with the threat of The Iceman Sergei believed the cartel members would sing unless he could make the evidence against them disappear. Edie's second mission was to access a steady flow of confidential information from a high-ranking U.S. government official or an influential politician.

Edie decided to tackle Ogiyevich's first mission first. She asked Google the name of the Treasury Department head. Within four seconds she had her answer—J. Temple Reynolds III. With a name like that, she assumed he was probably a pretentious jerk. She searched LinkedIn for a current photo. Then she started the hunt. Her initial strategy included visiting the five different coffee shops within walking distance of 15 Pennsylvania Avenue.

Before too long she was networking with all the regulars. In addition to her computer and language skills, Edie was blessed with a photographic memory; and could easily recall names, faces and the circumstances under which they met.

Edie was very attractive, well dressed, and well spoken. She was also a great actress. No one she met or networked with ever suspected that she was anything other than the determined job seeker she professed to be.

Every morning at precisely 6:00 a.m. Edie made the rounds of the five different local coffee shops. She asked everyone she ran into if they had any advice or guidance about how she could land her dream job with The Financial Crimes and Enforcement Network at Treasury.

Most of the time she did not get any useful intelligence, although she did manage to meet two people who said they knew the head of Treasury HR and would be happy to introduce her. Edie gave herself two weeks to meet the elusive Mr. Reynolds. If she failed to do so, she would circle back to these contacts and try the HR route.

Chapter 70

Networking Pays Off

Eventually Edie's networking paid off. On Wednesday August 2, Edie was in the local Starbucks. She said hello to a harried young man in a three-piece, navy-blue suit, wearing a crisp white shirt, and sporting a purple and black striped tie. A pair of purple plaid socks peeked out of the tops of his Salvatore Ferragamo brown leather shoes.

While he was waiting for his coffee order to be filled, the well-dressed young executive was addressed by a musical, female voice, "Hi, I'm Edie, new to the Washington area. I'm looking to land my dream job with The Financial Crimes and Enforcement Network at Treasury. In the spirit of networking, do you have any advice or guidance about how I can meet the director?"

That's when Andy looked up from his phone and got his first glimpse of the pretty, well-dressed, woman who smiled so engagingly at him. She was well worth a second or even a third look, "Hi yourself. I'm Andy. It just so happens I do. Do you know anything about the department or the man that runs it?"

Edie replied, "Only that they are both highly respected."

"Well you may feel differently about your "dream job" and your future boss when you hear what I have to say. Mr. Reynolds is a driven, ruthless SOB. They call him the Secretariat, like the stallion. But unlike the horse, his nickname doesn't come from the size of his heart; it's rumored that he doesn't even have a heart. Mr. Reynold's nickname refers to his speed of mind as well as his work stamina and work ethic. In case you're interested. I've also heard that he lives up to those same traits in the bedroom." Edie clamped her jaw shut to avoid spitting out her coffee at the handsome, young executive.

Andy continued, "Mr. Reynolds is revered and feared by his bosses and colleagues alike. His staff is the best of the best and he hires slow and fires fast. When he took over the original team, he fired three of his subordinates on the first day. He didn't replace them and did their jobs himself for about a year, by putting in 18-hour days."

"90-hour work weeks are normal, and everyone's cell phone is on and at their sides, 24/7—363 days a year."

"Mr. Reynolds sounds like a real go-getter. I admire that. Does he ever get any down time or take a vacation?" Edie asked.

"Not that I've heard, although I do believe he takes himself offline two days a year to spend Christmas and her birthday with his mother. His attitude is that you have to make every day your best day. And I've also heard he doesn't suffer fools gladly. If he hires you, you will also have to be "on" during all hours of the day and night."

"That's some work ethic. Please continue."

"I've also heard that in his spare time the Secretariat played a simulated hacking competition with another driven government guy, who is now deceased. If you do get hired by this man, be very sure that you want the pressure. Fortunately—he plays by the rules. So, as good looking as you are, he won't cross any personal lines. From what I understand, he only socializes OUTSIDE of his department."

"His team is loyal because if you show you can keep up with him, he'll always have your back. Just don't cross him or you'll end up nailed to one. There's more than blood on the tracks, there are dead bodies. Do you still want to meet him?"

Edie nodded "Yes."

"When he is in town, I believe Mr. Reynolds, often has coffee in this little hole in the wall coffee shop. I think it's called Heather's Coffee & Donuts or something like that. I hope you're an early riser because I believe he's there around 5:30 a.m. or some other ungodly hour. I hope that helps. Good luck." With that, Andy raised his grande matcha tea, soy latte with double foam, in an informal salute, and headed out the front door.

The following morning Edie was at Heather's at precisely 5:15 a.m. Weren't her parents always reminding her that the early bird catches the worm? But in this instance, her future boss and his department would be the ones catching the worm from the computer virus Mr. Ogiyevich had conveniently provided.

She recognized Mr. Reynolds from his LinkedIn photo when he came through the coffee shop door at precisely 5:25 a.m. He smiled and nodded at the pretty Oriental woman on his way to the cash. The cashier handed him a black coffee. Temp paid, left what looked like a very generous tip from the happy smile on the cashier's face, and headed out the front door. The whole encounter took less than thirty seconds.

Edie was there the following morning and the one after that. By the third morning, Temp said. "I see you're a regular too. What brings you out at such an early hour? Deadline?"

Edie replied, "I should be so lucky. I'm new to Washington and am looking to land my dream job with the elite Financial Crimes and Enforcement unit at Treasury. I just don't know anyone who can tell me who to approach or what I can do to get my foot in the door."

Temp replied, "Let me think about it," nodded politely and left.

Every day for the next two weeks, Temp saw Edie at Heather's. She didn't indicate, and he didn't acknowledge, that he was the man she so desperately wanted to meet. Although she didn't see herself as a femme fatale, she was good at subterfuge, and was certain an opportunity to meet him properly would present itself.

Since she was obviously serious about joining his team, Temp decided to give the pretty girl a chance at her so-called dream job. One morning, as he was leaving the coffee shop, Temp handed Edie his business card and said, "I'm Temp, head of the Financial Crimes and Enforcement Network over at Treasury, the guy you've been working so hard to meet. I'm assuming you have a copy of your resume with you. I'm prepared to pass it onto HR. Although I'm not hiring at the moment, things can and do change from moment to moment. If something opens up, HR will be in touch."

Temp was overjoyed when HR agreed to interview Edie. Everyone was excited about the fact that she spoke Mandarin. Since his best friend, Ted, died, he had been unable to find anyone with whom he could practice his Mandarin speaking skills. After several in-depth interviews and background checks he instructed HR to make the beautiful analyst a generous offer.

Later that same month Edie joined Temp's team as a junior analyst. She did not tell Temp or HR that she had a photographic memory or expert-level skills in both social engineering and computer hacking. Nor did she disclose that she spoke six languages rather than the two languages—English and Mandarin—listed on her resume.

After she became part of his team, every Friday afternoon Edie and Temp went back to Heather's for coffee, donuts, and Mandarin conversation. They became close, or as close as Temp ever allowed himself to get to anyone on his team.

Edie toyed with the idea of seducing him until she remembered the advice she overheard her mother give her cousin, Richard, when he got his first government job—don't stick your dick in the cash register, because someone might close the drawer.

Besides, Mr. Ogiyevich's instructions were clear—if she was going to seduce anyone it needed to be a high-level U.S. government official or a politician. Although a director of a government department was impressive, if she wanted to save her parents, she had to land a much bigger fish.

Over dinner one night, her father mentioned that the eligible, well-connected, Junior Senator from Kentucky, Butch Badger, was single and an excellent romantic prospect. She'd have to figure out some way to meet the man she was determined would become her first husband.

Chapter 71

A Plan Comes to Fruition

Edie had worked for Temp for about a year before she was introduced to Senator Badger at a Government end-of-year party. The attraction was instantaneous. From the moment they first laid eyes on each other the two good-looking, eligible young people never spent another day apart. No one in the Department, including Temp, was surprised when, three months later, Edie announced she was moving in with the Junior Senator from Kentucky.

Badger was totally besotted with Edie and always looked for large and small ways to surprise and delight her. He decided to celebrate their six-month anniversary with a trip to an exotic sports car dealership. At the dealership, it was obvious that Edie was captivated by a Ferrari red convertible. Edie exclaimed, "I've loved the color red since my grandmother gave me a little red wagon as a birthday gift when I was about two years old. That car is magical. Can we go for a test drive?"

That was all the encouragement the Senator needed. The following Friday, when Edie returned home from another gruelling day at Treasury, it was to a gleaming red Ferrari, festooned in a pearl white satin bow, parked on their curving front driveway. As Badger handed her the keys he said, "Lady in Red is your new theme song."

Shortly thereafter, Badger proposed. He suggested that Edie take a leave of absence from her position at Treasury. Although she purposefully tried to hide the fact that she could manage all wedding preparations as well as a demanding full-time job, it suited her purposes to have her future husband think she was a wide-eyed, overwhelmed bride-to-be. She told him that, in spite of her best efforts, it was challenging to stay on top of the army of caterers, florists, real estate agents and decorators while remaining focused on the fraud, tax evasion, and illegal activities involved in her job. She drafted a leave of absence request which Temp approved.

Early on in her tenure, Edie had installed the worm, and until then, the intruder had remained dormant and undetectable. It would only come to life when it received Edie's specific command to do so. Edie waited for the signal from Mr. O to put the worm into action. With Crispy's drug case coming up, her handler believed the time had come. He also told her that Sergei was prepared to forgive the remainder of her parents' debt if Edie managed to pull it off.

That was all the incentive she needed. After Temp approved her leave she activated the worm. Then she immersed herself in the wedding preparations and never gave Temp, Treasury, or the malware, a second thought.

Chapter 72

A Matter of Professional Pride

On Monday August 19, 2009, black coffee in hand from his favorite coffee shop around the corner, Temp arrived at his office precisely at 5:45 a.m. Although he had been out of the Special Forces for more than five years, he still liked to get a head start to his day.

The office clock said 5:50 a.m. Temp powered up his computer and settled in to reread the case file against drug lord, John "Crispy" Bartram—Mr. Bartram was currently a guest in a maximum-security facility out of state. Crispy had earned his nickname because he used a propane torch to burn the faces off anyone that crossed him. After three painstaking years of building a solid case for Treasury, Crispy was finally going to get some "face time" of his own—with the D.A.

As Temp scrolled through the internal directory, he was shocked to discover that Crispy's complete case file along with 25 other drug and fraud files were missing. He logged out and rebooted. There was still no sign of files. Even the backup files were gone.

Temp gave himself fifteen minutes to identify any other discrepancies. He found at least three. What was going on? Had he or his staff done something that had inadvertently compromised Treasury?

Although he wished he had more time to understand the full extent of the problem, protocol was clear. He called his boss, Lorna Goldstein, at precisely 6:10 a.m. His message said he had an urgent matter to discuss with her and Treasury lawyer, Chantelle Lightstone.

Goldstein called back at 6:30 a.m. to confirm that she had booked Conference Room Bravo for 7:00 a.m. At precisely 6:59 a.m. Temp arrived. When he entered the meeting room Goldstein and Lightstone were both already seated and

Goldstein was drinking coffee from her favorite, "I Love New York" coffee mug, a souvenir she had picked up when she visited the Guggenheim Museum last year.

Without preamble, Temp said, "I've been hacked and believe that Treasury is vulnerable. Three years of work is missing. Important files are lost. This breach is unacceptable to this Gold USB winner. I am not interested in being benched or assigned to another department while the government investigates. I'll save you the trouble. I …"

His boss, Goldstein, couldn't believe what she was hearing. She didn't wait to see if Temp was finished talking when she interrupted him, "For shit's sake Temp, how could anyone fool a world class hacker like you?"

"How indeed?" he replied. Temp stood up, placed his security pass on the boardroom table, nodded to his former colleagues and walked out of Bravo. He briefly returned to his office to collect his coat and the lucky horseshoe, Edie, a junior analyst on his team, had given him the previous Christmas.

As he stood on the sidewalk outside 1500 Pennsylvania Avenue, Temp channeled his fury into resolve. He had a reputation to uphold, and personal failure was not an option. Whatever it took, he would figure out how he had been compromised. And then he would make sure that whoever had forced him to abandon his career, the one thing that made his life worth living, would pay—with his or her own.

Chapter 73

Temp's Preliminary Investigations

It was not in Temp's nature to feel sorry for himself or to wait for someone else to solve his problems. It was clear to him that he had overlooked something or had become complacent in some way.

In the 20-minute window he had before IT changed all the passwords, Temp used his phone to hack into the government computers. His incredible skill and intuition led him to identify that it was an internal hack that had been made to look external.

He then followed the line of site to the original computer. It was Edie's home computer! He didn't see that coming. He thought she was a really sweet kid, a very competent analyst, enjoyed speaking Mandarin with her, and was sincerely happy for her and the Senator. How had he misread her so badly?

Since Edie's hack was completely out of character Temp wanted to find out why she would do such a thing, especially because she seemed happy enough with her life and her job at Treasury. Maybe she was being blackmailed or looking after a sick relative, although he didn't think so—she was engaged to a wealthy Senator after all.

Perhaps the Senator's son, Ron, a spoiled, pimply-faced kid he shared custody of with his first wife, Cookie, was in trouble again. Or maybe Edie was ill and needed an expensive treatment that was not covered by the government insurance plan and needed to sell secrets to raise cash. If Edie was sick, he assumed that she would have confided in him. Didn't she know that he would have crawled over broken glass to help anyone on his team? But a search of her medical records confirmed that she was medically fit for duty.

As his fingers danced across the keys, he continued to think out loud. Maybe the Junior Senator ran out of campaign funds. He had heard through the grapevine that Badger was probably going to lose his seat during the next election cycle. This might make him desperate, even dangerous. But when he hacked into the Senator's campaign account, it looked as if he had more than enough cash to run his losing campaign. "I guess that would have been a little too easy," Temp thought to himself. He continued his investigations.

Although he had figured out that Edie had hacked him, he still wasn't sure why. That would have to wait for the moment. For his own peace of mind, he needed to determine how she hacked him. Then it dawned on him. During their Friday Coffee, Donuts and Mandarin conversations, they often talked shop. He couldn't recall if he told her that he created a new password on his computer every day or if she observed him doing so. Because she had been so careful Temp had never learned that Edie had a photographic memory, insane observation skills, and had in fact, observed his process for password entry.

Regardless of why Edie did it, it was clear that someone wanted him out of the way. But who and why? He couldn't believe Edie had acted on her own and there was nothing in her background check that indicated she was a spy. When he got home, he flipped into her confidential HR files and reread the CIA and FBI reports.

According to the reports, Edie Theresa Li was born in the U.S. to parents of Hong Kong citizenship, who were well regarded in their respective fields. She had attended top schools, had a SAT of 9.7 percent and was in the top 1% of GMAT and GRE scores. She was reasonably athletic and played on a varsity badminton team when she was in college. She graduated 3rd in her class.

He recalled being impressed when he learned she had studied patterning. She had no known political affiliations or obvious credit or addiction problems. She was well liked by colleagues and spent most of her free time with family. She didn't appear to have a huge number of male or female friends. Although Edie dated casually, until she met the Junior

Senator from Kentucky, as far as he could tell, there had been no other serious relationships. This was not unusual. A beautiful, athletic, computer expert was probably intimidating to most men.

In addition to regular trips to Europe and South America where her parents had second and third homes, Edie regularly traveled to Hong Kong to visit April Li, the daughter of one of her father's first cousins. Apparently, April's father, Philip, had lost his mind when terrorists killed his wife, Lotus. Philip had lived in a mental institution ever since.

Edie's parents paid for all of April's educational and living expenses. Although they wanted their cousin's daughter to join them in the U.S., she declined. She wanted to be geographically close to her father, so that she could talk with him whenever he had a lucid moment. Besides, the doctors told her that it was important for his recovery to maintain as much consistency as possible.

Because he was trained to think that way, Temp began to wonder if the whole family duty thing was a cover for something more sinister. Before he became a permanent resident of Castle Peak Mental Asylum, Philip Li had been a top nuclear scientist. Could the parents be spies for China and Edie an indoctrinated daughter? Was the cousin a go-between?

Before he hired Edie, the CIA had looked into Philip and confirmed that he was a relative, in a legitimate mental institution, and that he had a daughter named April who visited him every Tuesday and Saturday. Although the extent of his mental deterioration was unknown, the file indicated that he occasionally had some lucid days. On those days April would get a call from the institution and would make an extra visit.

Temp thought about the implications. If Edie was a plant, she had access to all of the top-secret information on the Treasury computers and she was engaged to a Senator which gave her access to even more. A good play by the Chinese. Being the perfectionist he was, he had to go down the path of determining if his thoughts could be backed up with evidence.

In the meantime, there were practicalities, like getting another job, even if only as a cover for his ongoing investigations. Although he no longer worked at Treasury, he had taken an oath to support and defend the Constitution of the United States against all enemies, foreign and domestic and that was exactly what he intended to do. He wasn't about to be the first Reynolds that failed to deliver on that commitment.

Chapter 74

Unforeseen Consequences

Senator Butch Badger and Edie Li were married two months after Edie left Treasury. All of the Washington elite attended the black-tie affair. Temp was not invited. He didn't care. Until he figured things out, he really had no interest in seeing any of his former Treasury colleagues.

Several months after the wedding, Edie's Ferrari was car jacked while she was stopped at a red light. She was so badly beaten that her face would need years of plastic surgery. And there was so much damage to her body it was unlikely that she would ever walk unaided again.

Before she was put into a medically induced coma, Edie managed to tell police that a homeless Viking that smelled like a fisherman's boot pulled her out of her vehicle and started ramming her beautiful vehicle with his shopping cart. Then, he unceremoniously pulled her out of the car, dumped her broken and bleeding form on the sidewalk and took off in her Ferrari. The car was never found. Although the Senator offered a $100,000 reward to anyone with information that led to an arrest, no one came forward. The local police didn't have any leads or suspects.

The mayor and the media demanded the police find out who had done such a terrible thing. The police interviewed Temp, and everyone else that worked with Edie at the Financial Crimes and Enforcement Network. Everyone with whom they talked said they liked and respected Edie and did not know anyone who would have wished her harm. With no leads and no suspects, Edie's assault and theft case went cold.

By the time Edie was assaulted, Temp had not yet completed his investigation into her betrayal.

Although he would have liked to administer justice with his own hands, he was pleased with the violent beauty of what appeared to be a professional hit. Even if the Washington police were willing to let the matter drop, Temp was not.

Chapter 75

Another Death

A short time after Edie was hospitalized, the Washington police received an anonymous tip that her husband, Junior Senator Butch Badger, was in bed with a minor in Room 765, at the All Seasons Motel on 5th Street SW. When the police barged through the motel door they found Badger, naked and passed out on the king-sized bed, beside an equally naked, unconscious 12 year old boy.

A couple of empty champagne bottles were scattered on the plush broadloom floor, gay porn was in the DVD player, and there was some suspicious white powder on top of the dresser. As a result of the scandal, the Junior Senator from Kentucky was forced to withdraw his bid for re-election and retired from politics to raise horses on his stud farm in Kentucky. He never once visited his bride. He hated hospitals and since she wouldn't know he had made the effort, he couldn't see the point.

Barely a month into his retirement, Badger suffered a freak riding accident. Earlier one fine spring day, the local Sheriff's office had received a report of a bobcat in the vicinity. The Sheriff concluded that the green horse the Senator was riding, panicked, and bucked him off when it scented the big cat. When he fell, Badger severed his spine. Death was instantaneous. His 12-year-old nephew, who was playing video games inside the ranch house at the time, found the body three hours later, and called 911.

Two serious incidents involving members of the Washington elite, reignited media interest in the tragic end to the couple's love story. Under pressure to revisit the matter, the Washington police made a few perfunctory inquiries. They re-interviewed everyone with the same result.

With no new suspects, no new leads, and a huge caseload of current felonies to deal with, they chalked the Senator's death up to an unfortunate accident and Edie's carjacking to nothing more than a despicable, random act. They couldn't have been more wrong.

Chapter 76

Silver Lining

Although Edie's mother, Edith, didn't remember entering the draw for a complimentary cruise to the Amazon rain forest she was delighted to win two, all-expense paid tickets aboard the 5 ½ star Amazon Queen. Edith was not surprised that she failed to remember. Everything had been pretty much of a blur since her daughter's horrific accident.

Edie's parents had both taken extended leaves from their respective positions so that they could be at the hospital every day. The couple was sitting in the hospital coffee shop when they learned of their son-in-law's scandal.

The stress of their daughter's accident and the scandal involving their son-in-law took its toll. George's gout had been acting up lately and Edith's blood pressure had gone through the roof. They were worn down by the sad events and desperately needed to relax and unwind. They couldn't believe their good fortune when they won an all-expenses paid cruise on the acclaimed Amazon Queen. Edith hired a nurse through a respectable, bonded agency, to visit their daughter every day while they were away, packed their bags, and counted down the days until they set sail.

When the Li's arrived onboard, they were pleased to find that the Amazon Queen was everything the brochure promised it would be. After a couple of days at sea, they started to relax. They positively beamed when George won a $5,000 slot jackpot at the onboard casino. The Li's couldn't help thinking that maybe their luck was finally starting to return.

As they were not a very athletic or adventurous couple, they didn't understand why a complimentary ticket to go zip lining through the Amazonian rain forest was pushed under their state room door. Although the shore excursion was well beyond their comfort level, they decided to "feel the fear and do it anyway." It was a fatal decision.

The Li's disappeared on their zip lining excursion. The captain waited in port for 24 hours while authorities searched for them. After a day's delay, the Amazon Queen was cleared by authorities and pulled out. The Li's bodies were never found. Because they had both taken leaves of absence from their respective jobs when Edie was hospitalized, it took several weeks before their colleagues and friends learned they had disappeared. By that time any leads were cold.

Chapter 77

Temp Needs a Job

Temp was too young and not nearly rich enough to retire. He needed a job, both for his own mental health as well as for the sake of his parents whom he had supported ever since his father, a real estate speculator, lost everything in early 2008 when the U.S. housing market crashed. With his skills he was confident that he would be able to secure a new role quickly.

Over the years, many private sector companies tried to recruit him. Temp had seriously considered and turned down several informal offers of employment from St. Clair Associates LLC, a well-respected private security firm run by his university friend, Bob Merilees, a transplanted New Zealander. Bob had purchased St. Clair with a sizeable inheritance from his grandfather.

An early adopter of technology, Bob recognized the growing need for cyber specialists. He added cyber security and corporate espionage to St. Clair's service offering and brought in two colleagues from England to run the European and Eastern European divisions.

Since then, St. Clair had established a reputation for thwarting cyberattacks on public and private institutions. Temp respected Bob's military background and work ethic and thought St. Clair would be an ideal place to land while he figured out his next move.

He located Bob's cell number. "Hi Bob, Temp here. My circumstances have changed and I'm no longer with Treasury. Is your offer of employment still open? If it is, I would like to take you up on it."

Temp knew that Bob had his own government sources and would use them to find out why Temp was suddenly available. "Why don't we meet at 11.00 a.m. at my office on New York

Avenue," Bob said. Temp agreed and hung up. Neither man said "goodbye."

Bob picked up his other cell and made a call to his Washington insider. Within two hours he knew everything there was to know about Temp's sudden change of circumstances and the missing drug files.

Temp arrived at Bob's office 5 minutes early. He accepted the black coffee he was offered by the well-groomed, conservatively dressed receptionist and thought about St. Clair's office set up.

Chapter 78

St. Clair

Unlike the Treasury office, where the Sensitive Compartmented Information Facility or SCIF was hidden behind a secret panel in the Director's office, Bob's SCIF was hidden in plain sight, just outside the main reception area and behind 18" concrete walls. Bob had purposefully located it in plain sight to lull the people waiting in the comfortable reception area to engage in casual conversation. His state-of-the-art surveillance equipment, hidden in the ceiling speakers, recorded everything being said.

His cautious nature had paid off more than once, including the time he caught a potential employee on the telephone, bragging to his girlfriend that he had stolen an ID from a work colleague at his previous workplace. Bob had a zero-tolerance fraud policy. He instructed the receptionist to cancel the interview. The potential employee never found out why.

At precisely 11:00 a.m. Bob asked Temp to join him in the soundproof room. The two men shook hands and greeted each other in a friendly although formal way. "So," Bob said, "You were hacked and had to leave. You've no hand in it as a far as I can tell. Is that true?"

Temp smiled to himself. Bob's statements confirmed that he was just as connected as he suspected. Although Bob and his team, weren't as good as he or even Ted, they were still very good. Temp replied in the affirmative.

"OK," Bob said. "The job is still open, but there are two caveats; the first is, you have to start today. The second is, if I find out you lied to me about anything, and I mean anything, it will tell me I can't trust you and I will terminate your employment immediately." Temp nodded his agreement.

Bob then outlined the generous salary, benefits, and bonus package. Even if he only qualified for half the bonus, Temp and his parents could look forward to a very comfortable lifestyle. So, what they said about working in the private sector was true. Things happen for a reason! Temp replied, "The compensation package is acceptable."

Bob said, "I have a quick assignment for you. You won't be doing much of this type of work in the future, but I'm in a bit of a jam. Our original consultant is on medical leave and will be gone for about a month. We are a lean team and if you don't help out, I will have to do the job myself which I would prefer not to do. If you say yes, the job is yours. Orientation begins now."

"Copy that," Temp said.

Without referring to any notes, Bob outlined the assignment. When he was finished, Bob added, "St. Clair is expanding into Asia and East Asia. I understand you speak Mandarin fluently. If this works out the way I hope it will, I want you as our Asia country chief. And you might be interested in knowing that a country chief earns five times your current salary."

Temp was about to tell Bob that he was fully prepared to prove his loyalty when Bob made it impossible to say 'No.' "St. Clair will also commit the resources to investigate why you were hacked. I have the right government insiders to get the job done which will be harder for a private citizen," Bob added.

Temp was confident Bob would be able to figure out the motivation behind the hack and installation of the worm that had wiped out all of the Financial Crimes and Enforcement Network's current case files. He smiled, held out his hand and said, "Done. Thanks for the opportunity."

Bob smiled and said, "Our office manager, John Berlin, will join us in a minute. He will get you set up so that you are mission ready. I'll leave you two soldiers to sort things out and I'll catch up with you at dinner. Welcome to St. Clair!"

Chapter 79

Onboarding

Bob stood up, shook Temp's hand, and exited the SCIF. John, the office manager, and Bob's assistant, entered. He carried a plain cardboard banker's box with a number stenciled neatly on top and both ends. "OK, Mr. New Guy," John said with a smile. "Let's go through all of these toys," as he handed Temp two phones. One was housed in a protective purple cover; the other in a protective pink cover.

"Don't make any outgoing calls on the phone in the pink case; only call out on the phone in the purple case. You will get two new phones every week. Keep the protective cases and return the phones to the office. Neither phone will ring unless a two-digit numeric key of the week is entered first followed by the year, month and day of your maternal great grandmother's birth date. All of those numbers, in the correct sequence, have to be entered into the phone or the computer system or the devices won't turn on," John said.

"The numbers are encrypted. We change the suffix and prefix every day through another system. I will send a text to the pink phone with the current code. These numbers are specific to you. It might be a ten-digit suffix like your parents' home number or your waist size in inches and so on. If at any point you can't log in, don't call. Text me the date you first met Bob at university. Do you remember that date?" John asked. When Temp nodded in the affirmative, he continued, "And I will get things sorted out from my end," John said. "Copy that," Temp replied.

"Good. I have several things for you to sign including a very comprehensive Non-Disclosure Agreement and you need to fill out this very thick Background Information document. There is also a letter authorizing us to set up a bank account in your name at SNC Financial Services. Your salary and bonus money will be deposited directly into your SNC account."

"I have never heard of SNC Financial Services. Is it a new bank?" Temp asked. "Good question. No, it isn't. You've never heard of it because it a private bank, owned by St. Clair," John replied. "Shall I continue?" Temp nodded his assent.

"Money flows in on the 15th and 30th of each month. Another account will be opened for your expenses. I'll put $20,000 into your expense account later today. A credit card in your name with no dollar limit will be here in an hour. Unlike the U.S. government, St. Clair doesn't waste time on redundant approvals and there is no need for fourteen other "cover your ass" signatures. As far as we are concerned, so long as the expenses can be justified, the sky is the limit. The expenses are reconciled when you file your weekly report. I'll show you how to do that after lunch."

"Unless a case requires a face-to-face meeting with another member of the team, and I've worked here for five years, and can't recall a single instance where that was required, you may never meet any of your colleagues. We don't have lunch and learns, potlucks, or holiday parties at St. Clair. Bob told me that you weren't looking for a touchy-feely kind of place which is good because that's not who we are. We choose people we can trust. While you may work on different teams, and you may talk to and correspond with teammates, you will probably never meet any of them in person. St. Clair shows our respect for your talents, skills and loyalty by enhancing your bank account.

John then asked Temp to place both hands on a handheld device, which scanned his fingerprints. Then he took what looked like a camera from his right suit pocket and took a picture of Temp's eyes. "This device will put all ten of your fingerprints and your eyes into our system. When you get your computer at 2:00 p.m. today, place both hands on the computer base and look into the camera. This will turn it on. Exit the computer as you normally would."

"Your computer is customized to St. Clair specifications. Although a password is required to launch the computer, it only gives you access to the regular partition. Another password is required to launch the hidden one. You obviously understand there are some hazards that go with this job. If you get captured, you may be tortured. So, with two drives you can give the first password to your captors without revealing the hidden drive. I also have two carbon fiber pistols and 500 rounds of ammunition here," said John.

"I hope you don't have any plans for the rest of the day because we have a lot of ground to cover. Bob will catch up with us at dinner." Temp replied, "No plans." John responded with, "Great, I'm starved, let's go grab some lunch. But don't get used to it. As I indicated earlier, I doubt we'll ever eat lunch together again."

John picked up the tab for an incredibly fresh sushi lunch. As John and Temp were leaving the restaurant John suggested they get some fresh air and then work out for thirty minutes. Before Temp could say that he didn't bring his workout clothes, John said, "Don't worry about the lack of workout clothes, we know your size and everything you need is already waiting for you."

Temp thought that he could get used to this first-class treatment. While walking, John turned to Temp and said, "Only Bob and I ever meet with our clients. Since you are going to spend most of your time hacking, you can set your own hours and work remotely."

As they headed back to the St. Clair offices, John talked about how they were driven to be better than the best, and they always had to stay alert, because even the best can get hacked. "Don't I know it," said Temp. John laughed and said, "Bob wouldn't be interested in you if he didn't think you were the best. There are several team members with a similar story to yours. As far as I'm concerned, you can't fix a problem you don't know you have, and a hacker that has been hacked is a better hacker as a result of that rather humbling experience."

When they got to the St. Clair gym, their intense thirty-minute workout was led by a video instructor that included a 7.5 minute warm up and 7.5-minute cool down and stretch. "There are no video workouts that are exactly the same as the one we just did. The gym operates on a key card system. You are welcome to work out any time you wish. Workout times are booked online and other than an orientation like this one, the computer does not allow for more than one person to exercise at the same time. The less you know about your fellow teammates, the better. We reduce vulnerability by having the minimal amount of contact with each other," added John.

The next few hours passed quickly, and Temp was more and more impressed every time he was introduced to a new process. At 5:30 p.m. Bob joined them in the dining room. A delicious buffet dinner was already simmering on a side table. It looked and smelled delicious! There was no wait staff. The wine was already decanted, and Bob poured four ounces for each of the three men. The conversation turned to current events, art, and architecture and ebbed and flowed effortlessly. Temp appreciated the depth and breadth of his hosts' knowledge and realized that he was thoroughly enjoying himself.

Chapter 80

Like a Dog With a Bone

Whenever he had a spare minute Temp thought about the Treasury hack and who might gain by getting him out of the way. All of the missing files were drug related. And the people with the most to lose were the same people that were the subject of those investigations. For example, Crispy's connections to the South American, Chinese, and Russian drug cartels were well known.

International drug cartels were scary smart and had the resources to pay for the hack. Had they taken him down? Did they have something on Edie, her parents, or that cousin in Hong Kong? Were the cousin's sanitarium visits not as innocent as they appeared? Or maybe it was the Iranians? The war on money laundering and on drugs was international in scope.

Every drug crime involved interdepartmental as well as international cooperation. There were many hands and potential holes and a host of ruthless, well-funded adversaries. At this point, Temp could not confidently eliminate any of them.

All of the groups were capable and had something to gain from the hack. From experience, he knew that two or more groups could work together on a joint venture or one-off project basis. As well, all of the heads of the various groups were shrewd businessmen. Although he was sure he had identified the different players and likely combinations, Temp created a spreadsheet to provide a visual of enemies and potential partnerships. But was there another group? Was the theft a ruse? If he wanted to solve the case, he needed to get his very long list of potential culprits down to a manageable size.

No question, it was a rabbit's warren. But a smart human rabbit could take any number of paths and would create at least two different exits. That's what he would have done. "I love rabbit stew," Temp said to himself. "I know how to navigate the warren. With a little more effort, and a little more time, I can give Bob's people the roadmap which will distinguish between the routes going somewhere and the dead ends. I've done it before, and I can do it again."

While Temp didn't have the same resources he had while he was at Treasury, he did however, have something comparable—the St. Clair team. He knew that Bob had a Treasury insider, with access to government resources and who was willing to talk to St. Clair's people. Had Ted been alive, Temp would have trusted him to help. But Ted was dead. He encrypted his research and sent everything to Bob.

Chapter 81

First Assignment

After dinner Bob briefed him on the mission. "I am doing this as a favor. St. Clair does not usually take on these types of assignments. General and Senator Charles Worthington's long-suffering wife, Gladys, wants a divorce. She thinks the General is having an affair with his language coach, a Quebec native by the name of Melodie Marie Beaudoin.

Here is a picture of Mademoiselle Beaudoin. Here is her telephone number, address, Individual Taxpayer ID, and bank account. Please memorize them. Then, Bob provided the General's social insurance, government ID, and passport numbers, his online trading and bank account numbers, and his government and personal computer passwords.

Besides having an affair, our client also thinks her husband is hiding money. We often find our clients' suspicions are true. Last year everyone at St. Clair received a big bonus after we successfully located $30 million in a hidden offshore account. Now, I have to make an important phone call. It should take about fifteen minutes. With your photographic memory I think ten minutes will be more than enough to memorize everything. Temp replied, "Copy that."

Fifteen minutes later, Bob and John re-entered the SCIF. Temp's admiration for the tight way Bob ran has ship increased exponentially. Bob played on his phone while John made sure that Temp understood how to operate the gun and how to log in to the computer and access the hidden drive. At 10:00 p.m. John said, "In about three months we will have a long conference call. I'll send you the agenda about two weeks in advance. Bob is your team lead and your employee number is 383082. Welcome to St. Clair."

Within days of leaving Treasury, Temp had a great job and a team of professionals to help him find out who was responsible for the hack at Treasury. Since he was too wired to sleep, he decided to take his new computer out for a test drive and to start working on his assignment. Internet searches confirmed that Ms. Beaudoin was a language coach and sports physiotherapist. According to her website, she was available to work with clients at any time.

Chapter 82

Surveillance Logs

Day 1: Like most of us, Ms. Beaudoin was a creature of habit—every day, she did most of the same things, in mostly the same order. It was therefore easy to tail her while she went about her usual business—working with clients, grocery shopping, exercising, networking with colleagues, and socializing with friends.

The language coach did not appear to have a steady boyfriend or a pet. By the end of two weeks Temp knew she trained at Knockout Boxing Gym at 7:00 a.m. every Monday, Wednesday, and Friday mornings, and 9:00 a.m. on Sunday. She also had a 6:00 a.m. hot yoga class on Tuesday and Thursday mornings and attended a two-hour advanced Mandarin class every Saturday at noon.

Ms. Beaudoin lived in a rented, executive townhouse at 1118 Dunbarton Street NW, in Washington D.C. in the upscale neighborhood of Washington Heights. Monday morning at 6:45 a.m. after Melodie left for her boxing workout, Temp entered her townhouse for the first time. He gave himself thirty minutes to understand the interior townhouse layout.

Ms. Beaudoin appeared to use the tastefully decorated 20' x 20' foot main floor living room as her home office and language coaching area. Two comfortable couches faced each other in a conversational grouping. A fully equipped coffee station and a small fridge were tucked discreetly into one corner. The modern art on the walls provided interest and energy and contrasted nicely with the more traditional style of her desk.

Her Macbook laptop computer was open on the top of a black lacquer mahogany desk table with leather top designed in the Baroque Rococo Louis XIV style. The desk was strategically placed in the southwest corner of the room. There was a matching, locked filing cabinet underneath it. An oversized 18th century Zinc Oeil de Boeuf mirror hung on the wall behind her desk chair. Light streamed through the floor to ceiling windows located at the front of the space. The overall impression was both restful and pleasing. "Whoever decorated this has great taste in design," Temp thought to himself.

There was a grouping of photos in expensive frames tastefully arranged on the wall beside Melodie's desk. These included several photos of Ms. Beaudoin, as a laughing teenager in a Timber Wolves hockey jersey, and another of her wearing a University of Cornell hockey jersey. There was a graduation photo and another photo of her hugging a handsome, dark-haired man. The family resemblance was unmistakable—probably her brother. Yes, the same man was one of the men lounging beneath a Christmas tree in the family photo titled, "Beaudoin Family Christmas."

There was a separate photo of a good looking, middle-aged man and woman, probably Ms. Beaudoin's parents, because the same couple was in the Christmas photo. Temp took pictures of everything and made a mental note to study them all when he got home. He moved on to the next room.

Ms. Beaudoin had converted the 15' x 20' main floor master bedroom into a fully equipped, state-of-the-art physiotherapy studio. One complete wall was taken up with wall-to-wall mirrors and parallel bars. There was a fully equipped juice and water station on the opposite wall. The clinical equipment included treatment tables, a treadmill, a stationary bike, a hand weight set, medicine balls, physio balls, an ultrasound machine, an e-stim machine, a pulley set and hydrocollator/hot packs and freezer/ice packs. There was an adjoining four-piece bathroom.

A sliding glass door connected the physiotherapy studio to a small, well-kept backyard patio with black slate tiles, a teak and cloth patio sofa with a contemporary stainless-steel frame and black, white and beige designer cushions. An unlit free-standing fire pit was strategically placed in front of the sofa.

A set of locked double interior doors separated Ms. Beaudoin's personal living space from her language coaching office/rehabilitation studio. Her personal space consisted of an open concept, well equipped, kitchen and den. Another tastefully decorated two-piece bathroom was attached to the den.

There were three additional bedrooms located on the third level. Only one seemed to be used. The four-piece bathroom attached to what looked like the second-floor master bedroom, featured a steam shower with six body jets.

Her medicine cabinet held the usual jumble of Tylenol, dental floss, and extra toothbrushes. There were also several prescription bottles including Tamoxifen, Ativan, and Imovane. Because of his work at Treasury, Temp was familiar with all three medications—it looked like Ms. Beaudoin was taking cancer and anxiety meds as well as a sleeping tablet. He casually wondered if Gladys or the General knew about the state of Ms. Beaudoin's health. He took pictures of everything and left. He had been inside the townhouse less than twenty minutes.

Day 2: The second time he entered the townhouse, Temp focused only on Ms. Beaudoin's technology and computer setup. The first thing he noticed was that her computer was far more sophisticated than what one might expect to find in a typical small business.

The complexity might be nothing more sinister than the digital expression of a very private person. He smiled to himself as he opened up the browser to see what web sites the Senator's so-called girlfriend had visited—except there was nothing there. "That's odd," he thought. "Everyone leaves a trail of some sort." He loved a professional challenge and was reminded of how much he missed the friendly competitions he used to have with Ted.

The hard drive contained 150 GB of data, half of which was available. Nothing unusual in that. He next looked at what

Melodie had saved on the hard drive. As Temp worked through the folders and files, his photographic memory kept track of everything. He inserted a USB stick. He would study everything at home.

Day 3: The following Sunday Temp again visited the townhouse at 8:00 a.m. He parked his midnight blue Taurus across the street. He unfolded that day's newspaper onto his lap and put on his fully equipped state-of-the-art HUD goggles. Real-time information on elevation, speed, and time of day were displayed in a small screen located at the bottom-right of his field of vision. He placed ear buds into his ears. If anyone noticed him, they would assume that he was happily occupied with his paper and music while he was waiting for someone.

What he was really doing was surveilling Ms. Beaudoin through the specialty sunglasses. Although the glasses did not look unusual in any way, they contained a pair of infrared zoom lenses. He always used them whenever he was on a stakeout for Treasury. Because the glasses were at home when he resigned, he kept them. He made a mental note to return them when the Beaudoin op was complete.

Every Sunday before she left for boxing, Ms. Beaudoin changed her computer password. Because he was outside observing things, Temp captured the current week's password from the reflection in the mirror behind her desk. Five minutes after Ms. Beaudoin left, Temp was inside her townhouse. He had no problem getting into Ms. Beaudoin's computer and did not trigger the anti-theft and watchdog software that Denzel had installed.

He ran different scenarios in his mind. Perhaps the language coach needed a higher-than-normal level of security because of the confidentiality demanded by the Senators, lobbyists and sports stars with whom she worked. He respected caution and liked people that cared about client confidentiality. Although he spent thirty minutes on his investigations, he still hadn't figured out why Ms. Beaudoin's needed enhanced security, but he would. Unfortunately, the time had come to leave.

Day 4: When he returned home, Temp wrote a key stroke logger or system surveillance program from scratch. His program was designed to monitor and record, in real time, every keystroke Ms. Beaudoin made. Every time the language coach changed her password, typed a word document or an invoice, or sent an email, his program would send the information to his phone. Technology was a big improvement over shoulder surfing which was unreliable.

Temp needed access to all of Ms. Beaudoin's online activities if he had any hope of catching her and the General in the act. His key stroke logger program would provide this information. Moreover, any antivirus software Ms. Beaudoin had installed would only recognize viruses. Regular activity, such as a simple password change, would not trigger the antivirus software and it was unlikely her computer would recognize that her security system had been breached.

Temp returned to the townhouse the following Saturday at 8:00 a.m. He knew from hacking into her calendar, that Ms. Beaudoin would not be attending Mandarin class that day because she had signed up for a special full day "Super Power Yoga" workshop. He believed that this might be his final trip and that he would have uncovered all the dirty little secrets their client, Gladys, was certain were there. He hunkered down for the final push.

Whenever a file was accessed, Denzel's watchdog software would send Melodie a notice. Much like a home alarm system, she needed to enter a code, or the computer would lock up. Temp also knew that if the power went out for more than ten minutes, the entry password to the computer would automatically change to a secondary password, which could only be changed again if three security questions, which Temp didn't have, were answered correctly. He didn't need the security questions. The moment contact was made, Temp's computer would mimic Ms. Beaudoin's computer and her watchdog software would never know that Temp had been snooping around.

As his buddy, Ted had learned when he lost all five of their friendly competitions, it was hard to beat his signature hacking process—instead of copying the files, his computer program took photos of the pages. Ted had teased him that he had figured it out and would win this year's challenge but the S.O.B. got himself killed and he would never know if his buddy would have prevailed. But he couldn't afford to get distracted by a trip down memory lane. There was work to do.

Temp had not expected to find such a highly complex set of gateways. Before attempting to open them, he decided to stop. If this was the level of security Ms. Beaudoin used, what else was she hiding? Was she a double agent or a spy? For some reason her computer set up felt "clandestine."

He was surprised to hear a key turn in the lock, and a male voice, "Cherie, hi, you're early. Sunny and I signed for a package for you, and my sister sent over a tray of those profiteroles that you like so much. Shall I just place everything inside the front door?"

"No. Yoga was cancelled. Just give me a second to get rid of my gear and I'll be right out. I want to get your sister's phone number so that I can find out how to make those wonderful pastries properly. Mine are always lopsided or burnt. Maybe it's my oven which has been acting up lately. Besides, Sunny told me he wants a cookie, and what Sunny wants, Sunny gets."

Melodie tossed her purse and yoga mat inside and headed out the front door. Temp grabbed his own computer and exited into the backyard through the self-locking sliding glass door in the treatment area. Out of the corner of his eye, he saw a golden retriever, he assumed was Sunny, dancing excitedly between Ms. Beaudoin and a dishevelled middle-aged man. He caught a glimpse of the language coach's heart-shaped derriere as she bent down to give the dog his treat. If the General and Ms. Beaudoin were having an affair, the General was a lucky man. A very lucky man indeed.

Later that same evening, Temp was contentedly sipping a whisky. He thought better with a drink in his hand. He gained his appreciation of whisky from his father who had been a connoisseur. Unlike his father, he liked all of the blends, including bourbon, an American Rye, a blended scotch, a single malt scotch, an Irish whisky, a Canadian Whisky, a Canadian Rye and a Tennessee sipping whisky.

He knew that the American Rye he was drinking was very smooth and that it tasted better with a small amount of water. His father believed that neat was less tasty and ice ruined the drink by cooling it and adding too much water when it melted. He disagreed. Temp had one hard and fast rule when it came to whisky—one ounce per day maximum.

Because he only allowed himself a taste, he savored each sip. He worked the liquid over his tongue from front to back and appreciated the burn. Now, what was he going to do about Ms. Beaudoin? Although he was almost 99% certain she was not having an affair with the General, she had far more computer security than was necessary for a small business person. There were still too many unknowns. He knew he had to meet the language coach if he wanted to get the answers. And because he wanted to earn that bonus, he still had to spend some time figuring out if, and where, the General was hiding money.

Chapter 83

Changing Strategies

The following Monday, Temp trailed Melodie to the Knockout Boxing Gym on Joliet Street SW. Earlier, he concluded the best way to learn if she and the General were having an affair was to befriend the French-Canadian beauty.

Temp purchased a guest pass, changed into his exercise gear and joined a group stretch class. When the class finished, he watched Ms. Beaudoin and another female club member duke it out in the boxing ring strategically positioned in the middle of the gym floor. He couldn't explain why he was happy that the language coach was kicking her opponent's butt.

As she climbed out of the ring Ms. Beaudoin couldn't help but notice the sculpted, 6'3" inch stranger. He had deep set, grey eyes, a boxer's V-shaped body and wavy, black hair. Melodie felt that this must be her lucky day because this gorgeous male specimen was smiling and walking towards her. When Mr. Sexy spoke, he said, "Ma'am, I'm wondering if you can help me. I have just purchased a guest pass. I'm thinking of joining Knockout and boxing looks like a good workout. Have you been a member long?" Temp asked respectfully.

Melodie was not surprised that the gorgeous man had the sexiest and most musical South Carolinian drawl she had ever heard. "Two years," Melodie answered as the sweat dripped off of her glistening body and slid onto the scarred wooden floorboards beneath her high-topped clad feet. She took a long, appreciative pull from her bottle of water and smiled at the handsome stranger. "That's a long time. I hope you don't mind, but I've never met a woman that boxed and pardon me, I just have to ask, have you ever been in an actual fight?" Temp asked.

"No, I don't mind. My mother is Ma'am. I'm Mademoiselle—Mademoiselle Melodie Marie Beaudoin. Boxing is a fun workout and helps me manage my stress levels. I am a language coach and a physiotherapist. My job can be stressful and frustrating at times," she said with a musical laugh. "Boxing helps me cope. I mix it up with some yoga and Pilates. I'd be happy to share my routine with you if you think that might be helpful," she said.

"Maybe I will. And my name's Jackson Tiggs. My friends call me Jack. Pleased to meet you," he replied as he put out his right hand to shake hers. "I don't know what to do with these cloth hand and knuckle things. Since you obviously know what you're doing, would you mind showing me how to put them on properly?" Temp asked.

"Happy to," she said. While Melodie was showing Temp how to put on the wraps, he asked another question. "You mentioned you're a language coach. What languages do you teach?" He feigned surprise when Melodie answered, "I am a Mandarin, French and Spanish language teacher. I coach politicians and senior executives on those languages. I also provide physiotherapy to professional athletes and sports celebrities."

"You don't say!" Temp said. "I know this will sound like a pick-up line, but that's not the case at all. I'm not a politician or an executive. But I do need to brush up on my Mandarin language speaking skills, because I will be going to China on business soon and the language coach I was working with is nine months pregnant and is no longer teaching. Are you accepting any new clients, ma'am, I mean Mademoiselle Melodie Marie?"

"Being a politician is not a pre-requisite for learning how to speak a new language. And yes, I'm always happy to work with a new client," Melodie replied with a smile. And that's all it took.

Chapter 84

Walls

Temp hadn't allowed any female to get close to him since his unfortunate encounter with Candice Marsden, the president of his college math club. In his first week on campus, Temp signed up for the computer, chess and math clubs. In addition to his full course load he was also studying Mandarin.

On his second visit to the math club, Candice mentioned that she needed to move a "heavy" table and all of her friends were conveniently unavailable. Being a Southern gentleman, Temp offered to help. Candice looked him up and down and replied, "You seem strong enough. Besides, I've got beer in the fridge." As the beers flowed, inhibitions lessened, and the two healthy students ended up in bed.

Temp fell hard for the future class valedictorian, and they engaged in a very private and passionate relationship for the rest of the school year. Temp was floored when, a week before graduation, Candice informed him that she was getting married to her childhood sweetheart, and after her honeymoon, was relocating to New York, her future husband's hometown, to study law.

Candice's betrayal rocked him to the core. Within a week he had adopted a new dating philosophy—know everything, always be in control, and never get close. He resolved that if a woman wanted to date him, she would have to make the first move. Given his sharp mind and athletic body, there was never a shortage of takers. By the time he met Melodie, his emotions were locked in a vault, and he had thrown away the key.

Chapter 85

Sparks Fly

Melodie and Temp agreed to have coffee together at the Grinds Coffeehouse and Espresso Bar on 20th Street SW at 2:00 p.m. the next day. Three coffees later, they were acting like old friends. Temp spoke French and Mandarin with far better proficiency than his tentative attempts would suggest but he was in character and undercover. It felt completely natural to continue their conversation over dinner at Temp's favorite Asian restaurant, Northern Thai, on MacArthur Blvd. North.

Temp was a trained interrogator and knew what questions he needed to ask to establish rapport. Melodie, a civilian, was like putty in his hands. With little prompting, she talked about job loss, her career, her decision to move from the Big Apple (which she loved) to Washington, D.C. (which she was learning to love—she laughingly told Temp she was even learning how to manage the humidity), to her home-based language coaching/physiotherapy business, to her family in Quebec, her brush with cancer, and everything else in between.

Temp asked, "I know you are a go-getter, but how on earth did you manage to fit a Physiotherapy degree in with your Cornell business degree and hockey?"

Melodie replied, "From the ripe old age of 14, I shadowed the physiotherapists on the on the local junior hockey teams. From the time I was a little girl I was fascinated by the mechanics of the body. I took some correspondence courses offered by Georgetown as there was nothing equivalent in Canada at that time. I worked with a qualified supervisor, and when I lived In New York I got in five hours per week of practical work as a volunteer. By the time I got to Washington I was more experienced than a graduate with two years training. All I needed to do was write the local Board exam and complete a five hour practicum in front of an official examiner. That is how an interest became a hobby, and eventually, a money earning opportunity. My first client was the examiner's partner who introduced me to his colleague on the hockey team. That same person introduced me to his brother, the team captain. They gave me a chance and the rest as they say is history. I guess my hands were really strong after all those years of gripping a hockey stick!"

Melodie couldn't help thinking that, for a man, Temp was both easy to talk to and a great listener. Eventually she got around to asking him what he did to pay the bills. "I do some private detective work for high-net-worth clients who are contemplating divorce and have other concerns about their partners. I'm sorry. I don't mean to be evasive, but confidentiality does not allow me to disclose specifics."

Melodie laughingly said, "I understand. But I must say, I never thought I would have an opportunity to meet the great Hercule Poirot in person." Not knowing her well enough to judge what she meant, Temp wondered if she was teasing him. "Do you mean the fictional Belgian detective created by Agatha Christie?"

Melodie replied, "Bien sûr que oui. Sorry cherie. Yes. Of course I know you are not Belgian, or a fictional character, because if I didn't know those things, I would have much bigger problems than being a breast cancer survivor. Given your profession, I think Hercule is a very appropriate nickname. And just so that you know, Hercule is my favorite Agatha Christie character."

Temp had never been "teased" before, because most relationships ended after a couple of dates. Melodie's comment reminded him of the easy, playful relationship he had enjoyed with Candice before she stabbed him in the back. Before he could stop himself, he sarcastically replied, "Well, if I'm a fictional character then you're one, too. I think I'll call you "Dudley Do-Right."

"Wasn't Dudley Do-Right a cartoon Mountie and a *male*?" Melodie asked with a smile in her voice.

When Temp nodded "Yes" Melodie said, "Well that might explain my lack of success in the love department. Also, if I remember correctly, Dudley Do-Right, was always trying to rescue his boss's daughter. You saw me box. Hopefully you don't think I need rescuing. I have a suggestion. Why don't you call me "Watson" instead? My brother, Jacques, has called me by that nickname since I was 15 and caught our hockey coach taking advantage of underage girls. Besides, "Watson" works better with "Hercule" n'est ce pas?"

When he saw that Melodie was doing her best not to laugh out loud, he started to chuckle. Within seconds, they were both laughing. She was such an open, playful, and honest person. No question, life promised to be a lot more interesting with "Watson" in it.

Chapter 86

A Slow Boil

Melodie looked at the handsome, athletic, charming man seated across the table and suspected that he was so much more than a pretty package. As far as she could tell, everything he did was designed to get the woman to make all of the moves. Melodie had met men like him at work where she was sure two of her male Investment Brothers colleagues had a bet on who would bed her first. They both lost.

Although they saw each other at the gym, and had coffee and dinner at least five more times, Melodie purposefully didn't have sex with the man she knew as Jack. Temp was confused. For the first time, his dating strategy wasn't working. Most women couldn't wait to get him into bed. He wondered if Melodie played for the opposite team, or even worse, wasn't physically attracted to him.

Temp couldn't put his finger on when he started to change. Little by little, his guard slipped. He knew it was happening, but for some unknown reason, he did nothing to stop it. Since Candice, he had never allowed another woman to hold his heart in her hands. He felt vulnerable and confused. He didn't like feeling that he was no longer in control. And he had no idea about what to do about it.

Melodie was also trying to keep her emotions in check. Her almost-boyfriend was the complete package: fit, attentive, sexy, charming, well read, a hard worker, and a great conversationalist. Before she was consciously aware of their evolving emotional connection, Melodie acknowledged that she would do just about anything to get him into her bed, and to make him a permanent part of her life.

She shared her deepest thoughts and feelings about everything and anything—from her breast cancer diagnosis to living long enough to get married and having children (Temp couldn't hide a happy smile when she told him she wanted to have at least three), to fulfilling her crusade to stop abuses of the financial system by elected representatives and greedy CEOs.

Temp continued to be surprised at how much he liked and respected the little French-Canadian girl—despite everything that had happened to her, she was smart, optimistic, and funny. And as he suspected when he first looked into those expressive topaz eyes, she was a tiger in bed! But business was business, and he still couldn't definitively rule out that Melodie and the General weren't romantically involved. He needed to be sure before he would allow her to get any closer.

Chapter 87

Head First/Heart Second

Although they ate dinner and slept together most nights, Melodie still did not know that her boyfriend, Jack, was really former Treasury Financial Crimes head, Temp Reynolds. And Temp didn't tell her. A former Treasury colleague almost blew his cover when he ran into the couple at Northern Thai.

"Hi, Temp. Looking good!" his former colleague said. Luckily, he kept walking and didn't come over to their table. After his colleague had left the restaurant, Melodie asked, "Is that guy a friend of yours? I thought your name was Jack. Didn't he just call you Temp?"

Temp replied, "Elementary, my dear Mademoiselle Watson. I worked with that guy when I took a temporary contract with a government agency. Because everyone in the department knew I wouldn't be around for very long, they couldn't be bothered to learn my name. Before you feel bad for me, I never learned any of their names either. So they just called me "Temp" whenever they addressed me or wanted me to do something. I was OK with that. I really didn't care what they called me, as long as finance had the right name on my paycheck," he said with a smile.

Temp never felt the time was right to come clean about his subterfuge. Although they were together most evenings, he continued to maintain a separate residence close to St. Clair—Melodie bought his excuse that he worked erratic hours and needed the flexibility to come and go as he pleased.

Chapter 88

Temp Mines Melodie's Computer

Although her breast cancer was in remission, her doctors warned Melodie that stress could trigger another attack. "Besides," she joked, "I need my beauty sleep." Temp thought that Melodie was one of the most beautiful women he had ever met so whatever she was doing was clearly working for her.

Melodie still had some residual pain from her cancer surgery. When she was having a bad night, Temp—whom Melodie continued to believe was Jack—was the kindest most loving man she had ever met—got her sleeping tablets and made her a cup of chamomile tea. Once a month the happy couple returned to Northern Thai, the location of their first dinner, to celebrate the current month's anniversary.

She encouraged Temp to treat her townhouse, her refrigerator, and her technology as if it were his own. Although he was getting close to letting Melodie knock down the rest of his protective walls, Temp still did not completely trust the luscious brunette. Which is why he continued to be "Jack," to look for evidence of adultery or espionage, and to mine her computer when she was asleep. Bottom line, he needed to find out why his girlfriend needed such sophisticated security before he could trust her completely.

One night while he was nosing around, Temp discovered what looked like an encrypted file named "ESHUR." Early in their relationship, he had observed that Melodie was a bit like technological roadkill, and often neglected to follow her webmaster's failsafe security protocol for rebooting her computer. This made it vulnerable to anyone with some level of hacking skill which meant it was child's play to break in and snoop around for someone with his level of expertise.

One night, while Melodie was fast asleep, Temp used his key logger software to break the code and to open the encrypted file. It looked as if Melodie and several others were buying, selling and shorting stocks. Was Melodie involved in an investment club of some kind? Why did she need so much security? The whole setup reminded him of a highly secretive and well-functioning multi-level marketing group. Could it be that his sweet little mademoiselle was not so sweet after all?

He assumed Melodie was getting the information from somewhere, most likely her Senator clients, who probably found it easier to discuss things they knew, like their committee work, when they were practicing their language skills. Because his key logger program gave him access to every key stroke, it looked like she was sharing these stock tips with several other people.

He started to follow the trades of the same corporate entities. It was very sophisticated—there wasn't one trade that stood out as unusual. He surmised that Melodie was insider trading but still couldn't prove it. Is insider trading the reason she needs so much security? Does she have enemies? That didn't make sense.

Melodie was the kindest, most decent person he knew. Was she running out of money? He didn't think so. A quick look at her bank records confirmed that she had $55,000 in her savings account. All deposits appeared to be associated with earnings from her business. Another curious fact, although she was clearly making stock trades, it didn't look like she was profiting from any of them as she directed the profits to The Alyosha Foundation. He was a little confused by the Russian connection and made a mental note to find out more about the beneficiary of her largesse. He was also concerned about the illegality of the whole operation and resolved to protect his naïve girlfriend if he could.

The more he investigated, the more impressed Temp was by the elegance and sophistication of the ESHUR software. Despite his skill level, he hadn't yet found the incoming feed or the user.

Whomever had designed it was at least as good as he was, well maybe not that good, but damned good all the same. For some unknown reason, the whole setup reminded him of Ted. But he wrote that off as just a bunch of unconnected bytes and sentimental pap.

Chapter 89

Validating ESHUR

Because he was curious to see how (and if) the system actually worked, Temp started to trade the same stocks as Melodie's ESHUR traders. In addition to Melodie, it looked like there were at least three other people involved and that all four were making the same trades. In six months, it looked like Melodie's traders had almost doubled their initial investment. What he didn't' understand was why each investor donated all of their net proceeds to The Alyosha Foundation. He wasn't sentimental—nothing anyone could say could induce him to give away any of his trading profits. Wasn't it ironic that his current girlfriend could potentially be profiting from the same kind of insider trading that he had once been paid to stop?

Over dinner one night, Melodie casually mentioned that the following week she was going to New York to meet Philadelphia Romualdez, the Pulitzer-prize winning *30 Minutes* reporter. Temp asked, "Why do you want to meet someone from the media?" Melodie replied, "I have a financial story that I think she might be interested in. It involves financial abuse that is wrong on so many levels. It may even be big enough to earn Phil a second Pulitzer Prize."

Temp suspected she was referring to ESHUR. His follow-up questions revealed he was right. He realized the time had come to stop his own ESHUR trades. Bob would probably terminate their relationship if he were to become involved with the media.

Chapter 90

The Games People Play

Since Candice dumped him, Temp had never stayed with a female companion long enough to fully relax and play. When Melodie suggested that they change positions while driving to the restaurant, Temp didn't know what she meant. "I've never had any complaints before. Please tell me specifically what you mean," Temp said.

"Oh Hercule, you are too funny and far too serious. I had something a little more G-rated in mind. And if my delight in the sex department isn't blatantly obvious, I don't know how else to convince you that I love making love with you.

"I was talking about playing a driving game. Let me explain how it works. If you are behind the wheel and we are stopped at a red light, you put the car in park. We both undo our seatbelts and open our respective doors. Then, I run around the back of the car, and take your place in the driver's position. At the same time, you run around the front of the car and take my position in the passenger's seat. At the next red light, we switch positions again. We keep switching positions at every red light until we reach our destination.

"I used to play this driving game any time I was in the car with my brother, Jacques. Because we were having so much fun, it always made the travel time pass quickly and the traffic and the road noise easier to cope with. Do you want to give it a try?"

Temp couldn't believe he was considering participating in such a childish game. But to get to the bottom of Melodie's relationship with the General he needed to keep her relaxed and happy with him and their budding relationship and agreed to play along.

The driving game became part of the couple's routine whenever they were in the car together. No one was more surprised than Temp when he realized how much he actually enjoyed playing it. He smiled when he caught himself wishing for a red light.

One of the things Temp enjoyed about their relationship was it was punctuated by so much laughter and fun. He had always loved board games like Scrabble because playing them gave him an opportunity to test his wits. Because he believed play was serious business, he always kept detailed records of all of his moves and countermoves. Unfortunately, his Scrabble skills had gotten a bit rusty—the last times he played was with Ted when Temp annihilated him by 200 points.

Melodie also loved board games like Scrabble because playing gave her an opportunity to practice the skill of patience. The Beaudouin's had an unwritten rule—everyone agreed to limit their Scrabble "strategic thinking time" to a maximum of 10 minutes rather than the 25 allowed in a professional competition. Because Temp had already told her he was unwilling to have his creativity and options crammed into 10 minutes, a single game of Scrabble could last several hours.

On the rare occasion that she agreed to play, it was only because Temp bribed her with promises of a foot massage and backrub. She recognized there was little she could do to interrupt the great Hercule's game strategy and thinking time or to beat him. She joked that she only agreed to play Scrabble with him when she wanted to catch up on laundry or housework.

Chapter 91

The Downside of Discipline

Over the years, Temp had disciplined himself to only spend his energy on things that were mission critical. At Treasury, he focused on unravelling intricate webs of deceit on behalf of the government while keeping the highly competent and brilliant hackers on the other side at bay. This approach extended to other areas of his life including the food he ate and the clothes he wore. Although Temp could talk for hours about food, wine and whisky from all the main cultures, he'd only learned this information because the knowledge helped him do his job and stay in character more effectively.

Truth be told, Temp would have been happy to eat MRE field rations or to even avoid eating altogether, if there was a pill he could take that would give him the nutrition he needed to function. It was the same for his clothes. Except when he was undercover, Temp never spent any time thinking about what to wear because he always wore the same thing—an exceptionally tailored pinstriped blue suit, crisp white shirt, blue and black striped tie, and sensible black brogue shoes. When he wasn't working or on assignment, he ditched the suit and tie for a sports coat. Even his workout clothes were understated.

One day, Temp tripped over Melodie's yoga mat that had been dumped, along with her running shoes, in the middle of the hallway floor. Lately, this seemed to be a regular occurrence. He was tempted to turn around and to never come back. But this didn't make sense—he was falling in love with the vivacious language coach. Besides, after several months of investigation he did not have any evidence that Melodie was having an affair with the General. He was the one who was not being truthful. He took two deep breaths and willed himself to calm down.

"Melodie. I've tripped over your yoga mat and running shoes. Again," Temp said sarcastically. "Pardon," Melodie yelled from the bedroom. "We really need to talk about this," Temp sternly replied. "OK I'll be with you in a sec," Melodie replied sweetly. Temp went into the kitchen, poured two glasses of Melodie's favourite herbal iced tea, and said, "I'll meet you on the patio. I've got our tea."

When Melodie joined him, she was wearing a comfortable fuzzy pink polka dot bathrobe. A matching pink towel was wound tightly over her wet hair. A few strands had escaped and played peek-a-boo with her mesmerizing topaz eyes. She reached over, placed a heart-felt kiss on his lips, and sat down. As she did so Temp caught a glimpse of both of her rounded breasts. She must have had a very good surgeon because her scars weren't evident in the fading light. He willed himself not to get distracted by his partial erection and softened his tone.

"Watson, because I've always lived alone, and am a minimalist at heart, I've never paid much attention to how important it is to me to have an uncluttered home. When I come over and trip over your yoga gear, I find it hard to focus. I don't understand this, because you keep your language and physio studio impeccable."

"Hercule, I'm so happy you consider my place your home. Please explain what you mean by "hard to focus." Don't you like how I've decorated the townhouse?" Melodie asked with concern. "I just like a place for everything and everything in its proper place. Until this conversation, I hadn't even realized how important having a tidy "home" environment is to me," Temp replied.

"Oh Hercule, my darling, thank you for telling me what's on your mind. Not as an excuse, but to provide a little context, because there were so many of us, life at the Beaudoin household, was always a little chaotic and messy. None of us thought a shoe or two left in the front hall was the end of the world or were bothered by a few loads of unfolded laundry on the living room couch. What was more important to us was making sure that we were all together, safe, happy, and moving forward in life. Although we have different histories, I know these same things are important to you too," she said.

"I hadn't really thought about it until now, but perhaps I'm messy because it reminds me of home and my big, beautiful family. I guess I just miss them. And I know I sometimes leave a trail of shoes, clothing and yoga gear when I come in. I've never thought about how my actions might impact you. Going forward, I promise to pay more attention, or as my friend Christina says, to be more mindful of my actions."

At that point Temp pulled Melodie onto his lap. There was no longer any need to hide what had become a rock-hard erection. Some hours later, as he lay spooning Melodie in post coital contentment, he whispered in her ear, "Thank you, Watson, I don't know how you do it, but you always seem to know exactly what to do or say to make me feel so appreciated and understood. I've never met anyone quite like you."

On another front, his work life was about to get a boost. Through diligence, deductive skills and some creative, out-of-the-box thinking, Temp had located the General's secret TSX America Trading stock account and the $15 million USD it contained. The Secretariat's legendary hacking skills were about to give the General's wife, Gladys, a big payoff and the uncontested divorce she desired. Temp's discovery would also earn the St. Clair team, including Temp, a very big bonus.

One afternoon while he and Melodie were enjoying another iced tea on the patio, and chatting about nothing in particular, Temp realized that, for the first time in his life, he was happy. He knew how to work hard and to do his duty. But medals, a steady paycheck, several gold USBs, and parental gratitude did not come close to the level of contentment he experienced whenever he was with Mademoiselle Melodie Marie. Their easy, loving relationship brought into sharp relief just how empty his life had been before they became involved.

Although the first few times he asked Melodie to marry him had been a ruse to get her to open up to him, he felt differently now. Although he continued to ask her to marry him at each month's anniversary dinner at Northern Thai, he was secretly relieved when she turned him down. Of course, he wanted her to say Yes to his marriage proposal, but to the real him, Jackson Temple Reynolds III, not to some fictional guy named Jack Tiggs. He recognized that he would never have the kind of life he wanted to have with Watson if it was based on a lie.

He was honest enough with himself to admit that his ongoing identity deceit no longer served him. Because he was emotionally tethered to the outcome, he realized it was going to be far harder to unravel the lies than he wished. It hurt him to think that because he was so good at his job he had managed to deceive the only person with whom he wanted to be completely honest. He didn't know if Melodie, who had an extremely well-defined moral compass, would forgive him and he was worried that his disclosure might permanently damage their relationship.

Chapter 92

Bite the Bullet Time

It was bite-the-bullet time. After the main course was served at their current anniversary dinner, on cue, Temp asked Melodie to marry him. True to form, Melodie said "No." But unlike the last three times he had proposed, Temp added, "I will win—I will wear you down. One day you'll surprise us both by saying Yes. I will keep asking until you do."

Melodie sweetly replied: "You know I love you, Hercule. You also know why I keep saying No. Let's go home and celebrate this month's anniversary by having some mind-blowing sex!"

Temp smiled and said, "I'm really sorry kiddo, but I have an unavoidable commitment and the mind-blowing sex will just have to wait. I won't be gone long—I should be back around midnight. I'll wake you up when I get in and we can continue our anniversary celebration then."

After dinner, he called a taxi, dropped Melodie off at her townhouse, and continued on to the St. Clair offices. He needed to swing by the office to get his car and to pick up the engagement ring he had purchased for Watson a number of weeks ago. He would come clean about everything including why he used another name, his own ESHUR trading, his work at Treasury, and his new job with Bob, at their next anniversary dinner—in French St. Maarten!

When Melodie arrived at home the clock in her bedroom flashed 10:04 p.m. It was reasonably early, but for some reason she felt a migraine coming on. As much as she loved Jack, she needed a full eight hours of sleep a night to keep her immune system functioning properly. She swallowed a sleeping pill and went to bed. Her last thought as she drifted off was that she couldn't wait to be woken up by some mind-blowing, early morning sex with the man that set her heart and limbs on fire.

Chapter 93

Coming Clean

Although he had never before considered himself a coward, he had no other word for his failure to come clean the moment he realized his feelings had changed. Which was why he was now thinking that failing to do so was the worst move he had ever made—if he'd been playing chess, he would have lost in the first three plays. Until his recent lapses in judgment, first with Candice, then with Edie, and now, with the ongoing charade with Melodie, the Secretariat had never missed a step.

Since he didn't want to think about what his life would look like without Melodie in it, he distracted himself with running different scenarios. Perhaps he could publicly declare his love with a message on the jumbotron at a Washington Capitals hockey game or from the top of The Capital Wheel at National Harbor while they enjoyed the spectacular views of the Washington area. Or maybe Watson would be more forgiving if they were floating over the Shenandoah Valley on a hot air balloon. On second thought, they were a private couple, and public declarations would probably be awkward for them both.

That was when he came up with the idea of flying to the French quarter in St. Maarten—they both loved French food and spoke the language. He also knew of a great boutique hotel where he could rent the whole floor. This would allow him to control both the mood and the moment. His best idea yet. His thoughts were interrupted when the company cell phone rang. He entered the code. It was Bob.

Chapter 94

Owen

Temp assumed Bob was calling to congratulate him on a job well done. He was surprised when Bob said, "I have something I want to discuss in person, and if it isn't too much trouble, would you mind coming to the office for a quick meeting?"

"I'll be there in twenty," Temp replied.

When he got to the St. Clair offices, Bob was waiting for him. After the two men shook hands, they entered the SCIF. "Will you join me in having a drink of your favorite brand of Scotch?" Pleased at the offer and the chance to enjoy a drink with his benefactor, Temp accepted. He took a sip and felt the familiar burn. He waited for Bob to settle himself and to take a sip of his own drink.

Bob said, "Good work on the Worthington file." "Thanks," Temp said. Although he was enjoying the Scotch, Temp wondered what Bob really wanted to tell him. If he just wanted to congratulate him, he could have done so over the telephone. He waited patiently for the real reason for their meeting.

After another sip, Bob said, "As you have probably guessed there is another reason for me asking to meet other than to congratulate you on your outstanding work. Let me cut right to the chase. St. Clair has the most extensive due diligence process of any security company in the world. Although you are already working as a de facto employee, until we have fully completed all of our background checks, it would be wise to consider our due diligence process as "Ongoing. Are we clear?" Temp said, "Copy that."

"Our research has revealed that you have a son—Owen Talbot-Mercer. Owen is fifteen years of age, an 'A' student with, you'll get a kick out of this, a fondness for online video games, American baseball, and hacking. He is of mixed race, has mocha colored skin, black hair, gray eyes, and is already 5'8" tall. You met his mother, Dr. Simone Talbot-Mercer, a medical student, now a skilled orthopedic surgeon, in New Orleans at Mardi Gras in 1998 while she was on spring break. Does the name ring a bell? We searched Owen's birth records and you are listed as the birth father.

The Talbot-Mercer's live at 715 rue Champagne in Paris, France. Here is their telephone number, and a picture of the boy—I'm sure you are going to ask for a paternity test, but after looking at this photo, I doubt you're going to need one. Other than his skin colour, Owen looks exactly like a younger version of you. I don't know if you knew you had a son and wanted to tell you about this development in person."

When he heard Bob's news, Temp's first reaction was not of surprise about having fathered a child, but that he had not done so earlier. He realized he had been holding his breath throughout Bob's briefing. He exhaled and uncharacteristically gulped down the remaining Scotch.

"Other than the photo and the birth certificate, do you have any other proof that Owen is my son?" Temp asked. "No, I figured you and Dr. Talbot-Mercer could work that part out," Bob replied.

"This is a bit of a shock, thanks for taking the time to tell me about Owen. I had no idea that I had a son," Temp said. Since there was nothing else to talk about the two men stood, shook hands and Temp let himself out.

Temp wondered how Melodie, whom he was growing more fond of every day, would react to learning that he had not only lied to her about his name and background, but he also had a mixed race, teenaged son and prayed the disclosures would not change how she felt about him. He drove back to her townhouse in a daze. Luckily, she was asleep when he got in. He didn't wake her. He recognized that he was not yet ready to have that conversation or to get engaged.

He decided he would only tell Melodie about Owen after DNA confirmed he was the father. And if Owen was his son,

Temp, his doctor mother, and Owen had to decide on what ongoing role Temp would play in his son's life. He must owe thousands of dollars in child support by now. Simone was a doctor, so she probably didn't need the money, but his honor demanded that he fulfill his financial obligations.

Since Bob hadn't yet given him any new assignments, Temp powered up the computer in the 2nd bedroom, went online and booked a first-class Air France flight to Paris leaving at 8:00 a.m. that morning and arriving in Paris at 6:00 p.m. the same day. He kissed the top of Melodie's head and went home to pack. There would be plenty of opportunities for mind-blowing sex. He would send her a text that he had go out of town for a last-minute business trip for a few days and would be in touch when he returned. With Owen in the picture, he was astute enough to realize that coming clean had just become a lot more complicated.

He reviewed what he knew. Simone Talbot was a French exchange medical student at John Hopkins University when they met. She and Temp only enjoyed that one wild weekend together. By the time she found out she was pregnant with Owen, Temp was already in Afghanistan, and she had been back in France for two months. Although she could have tracked him down had she really wanted to do so, Simone didn't think the sexy 'bad boy' she spent forty-eight delicious hours with, was husband material.

With France's highly subsidized daycare system, a loving family, and a bright future as an orthopedic surgeon, Simone could look after all of her son's needs herself. One day he might want to know where the other half of his DNA came from. When that day arrived, she would tell him the name of the bad boy American soldier that fathered him.

According to Bob's file, Owen was born at 8 lbs. 2 oz. at Groupe hospitalier Paris Saint-Joseph on September 1, 1998. Simone didn't appear to regret her decision to go it alone for even a second. Owen was a good baby, and a delightfully precocious toddler. When he was a young schoolboy, he brightened up every day with his antics, his pronouncements, and his discoveries. Now that he was in high school, he loved learning. He was an 'A' student in everything, except in computer science, where he was disappointed if he achieved less than a perfect score.

When she was already established in her medical career, Simone met and married Louis Mercer, a successful software developer. Owen was in grade 1 when she married Louis. Louis liked Owen, and treated him in every way, like a beloved son. If something happened to her, Louis would become his official guardian. More than once, Louis told Simone, "Our son has a truly impressive level of computer skills. He is fearless which makes him so much better than I was at his age. Like a Maestro, he knows exactly what to do to coax an excellent performance out of even the most reluctant code. He is so clever, creative and dare I say, crafty. We have so much to be thankful for," Louis said.

When Simone was approached by Bob's agency, she decided to expedite disclosure of the name of Owen's birth father. She knew her son would be able to handle the information. He was a mature, confident person and had all of his birth father's looks, brains, and charm. Living in cosmopolitan France, it was also likely that Owen was no longer a virgin which meant he would not judge her Mardi Gras weekend.

Owen knew that Louis was not his biological father. His mother had already disclosed that much. Although he had pestered her for this information in the past he had resolved to wait until she felt it was time for him to know the name of his birth father. Until then, he would happily occupy his time surfing the net and working on perfecting his hacking skills.

When his parents used a more serious tone than usual to invite him to join them for a petite dejeuner, he knew something extraordinary was about to happen. His mother looked him straight in the eye and said, "Good morning son. You know we both love you very much and are so proud of the young man you've become. Your dad and I have decided its time you learned the name of your birth father, a little bit of his background, and how we met."

Owen was not even shocked when she told him that he was the product of a steamy Mardi Gras weekend. He hoped he and his birth father would like each other. He couldn't wait to meet him. After eating breakfast, he went upstairs and fired up his computer. His hacking led him to documentation that confirmed Temp Reynolds was an American who used to work for the Treasury Department.

Chapter 95

Temp Meets Owen

Within twenty-four hours of learning he had a son, Temp had checked into the Petit Palais hotel on Rue Rembrandt. He immediately called Simone and told her he was in town for the next two weeks and would like to meet Owen. Simone, who was on rounds when Temp called, returned his call at 6:00 p.m. local time.

Simone told Temp that Owen was excited about meeting him and invited him to join the three of them for a late dinner that same evening. At 9:00 p.m. local time, with flowers in one hand, and a bottle of Veuve Clicquot Brut Yellow Label in the other, Temp was standing outside of 715 rue Champagne. He was certain his life would never be the same when Simone answered the door.

To his surprise, dinner was not awkward. Owen was able to engage in adult conversation and Louis and Simone were gracious hosts. Not only was the family resemblance striking, Temp and Owen acted like family—they joked with each other, finished each other's sentences and talked at lightning speed about computer analytics. After desert was served, Owen wanted to show Temp his computer skills and invited him up to his study.

Owen told Temp that he was the youngest student in the EU to be accepted at MIT. Temp had no right to be proud of Owen, but he was. Simone and Louis had raised a wonderful kid. He was so thankful and grateful to Bob, who had already given him so much already.

Temp wanted to test Owen's level of skill and said, "If you are as good as you say you are, why don't you break into Banque Populaire," Temp said with a grin. "You think that's a challenge? Watch this," Owen replied. The bank was using a software that wasn't in the public domain and hadn't been updated by the publisher. Although Owen was very young, he had a high level of hacking skills and was through the bank's firewall in seven minutes flat.

While Temp was still processing what he had just witnessed, Owen said to Temp, "I think you said you used to work for the U.S. Department of the Treasury? You may think that the U.S. government has the best security in the world, but you'd be wrong. Just give me twenty minutes and I will demonstrate how easy it is to waltz right in the front door or should I say, the back door," he said with a wide grin. And that's exactly what happened.

Temp said, "Owen, that's some pretty impressive hacking. Those skills would come in handy in trying to find out who set me up at Treasury. I've been so busy at my new job that I really haven't had the time to devote to figuring out why my former employee, Edie Li, hacked into my computer and planted a worm that destroyed all of our case files. Maybe you can help, or even better, maybe it's something we can work on together."

Owen replied, "No problem, Temp. I feel more comfortable calling you Temp than Dad. Besides Louis is my Dad, and it would feel weird if I called you dad too. Is that ok? And I'd love to help you find out why your former employee set you up."

Because Owen was a straight A student, Simone and Louis gave him permission to take a couple of weeks off to explore the city and get to know his birth father. Temp and Owen spent the next seven days sightseeing in Paris. They went on a hop-on hop-off sightseeing cruise which included both land and water, visited the Eiffel Tower and the Arc de Triomphe, and wandered through the Louvre and the Musée d'Orsay. They were both surprised at how much they enjoyed seeing the graffiti on the urban art city walking tour.

They ate cheese and baguettes on the banks of the river Seine and enjoyed a picnic in the Champs-Élysées Garden Park. They bought matching black berets at Galeries Lafayette. Owen tried to hide his excitement when Temp paid a street artist to complete a charcoal sketch of them wearing their new berets. He didn't understand how two strangers could look like they belonged together, but somehow they did. That simple sketch would later become one of Owen's most prized possessions.

While they were enjoying being tourists they talked. Owen regaled Temp with anecdotes about school, his friends, and his parents, and Temp talked about his life in the States, his new job as a private detective with Bob's agency, and how he was planning to ask his girlfriend, Melodie, to marry him when he returned home. Based on Temp's description of her, Melodie sounded perfect. And being from Quebec she would speak French! Owen couldn't wait to meet her.

With each passing day, their friendship and trust in each other grew. By week's end father and son were no longer strangers.

Temp and Owen always ended that day's adventure with dinner with Louis and Simone. After dinner they spent at least an hour on the computer together and Temp taught Owen some hacking shortcuts that Owen wasn't aware of before. Owen introduced Temp to the wonders of Dungeons and Dragons. The online game was something they could continue to play together when Temp was back stateside.

Owen couldn't believe how emotional he felt when the time came for Temp to leave France. Temp, who always prided himself on being in control, was similarly affected. More confirmation that his sweet little mademoiselle's loving ways had mellowed him. As Temp gave Owen a heartfelt goodbye hug, he promised to return to Paris with Melodie for a longer visit in the New Year.

As Temp was leaving, Owen said, "I hope mom and dad will give me permission to travel to visit you and Melodie when school ends next summer and before I start MIT. Maybe to your wedding?" With a wink and a rueful smile Temp replied, "I can neither confirm nor deny what life-changing events next summer will bring," and with a wink and another hug he was gone.

Chapter 96

Owen's Friend, Guy

Owen was busy with school and his friends and didn't spend much time thinking about how his life had changed since he met Temp. Within 10 days he had caught up with all of the assignments he had missed when the two of them had explored Paris for two weeks. When Owen could finally breathe again, he called his best friend, Guy St. Cloud, to see if Guy wanted to hang out because his parents were going to the opera, and they would have the house to themselves.

Guy said, "I'm glad you called. I've got something I want to show you. Have your parents left already?" When Owen said yes, Guy replied, "Give me twenty."

When the front doorbell rang seventeen minutes later, Guy gave Owen a quick hug and said, "You're not going to believe what I've found." The two teens ran up the stairs to the study. "We need to turn on my laptop." Guy then downloaded ubdqt.com, a deeply hidden web site. "Whoa, do you see what I see? Is that naked girl real?" Owen asked. "Yup" Guy replied. "How did you get access to the site?" Owen asked.

Guy replied, "I used my "hot spot" access to hack into my dad's laptop to get his credit card information. I wanted to buy some new jeans and had left my credit card at home. I was sure my dad wouldn't have a problem with this because I have used his credit card many times before. After I made my purchase, I was bored and started to read his personal emails. Most were just routine business stuff. But there was one email that wasn't. In it, was a link to this site, ubdqt.com. Because I was curious, I clicked on the link and ended up on what looked like a soft porn site. I couldn't believe my eyes. I never knew my old man was into all that pervy stuff. Ever since then, I have hacked into his email account every day, got the current day's link, and followed it to the site for some cool entertainment."

Owen was a bit uncomfortable with the nudity and spontaneous sex he saw on screen and couldn't believe it was legal. He resolved to talk to Temp about it first chance he got. But he had to admit, the whole set up was kind of sexy. Owen tried to hide his erection, but it seemed to have a mind of its own. When Guy saw Owen squirming in his seat, he just laughed and said, "Don't worry Owen, I'm having the same problem."

When he turned back to the screen, Guy said, "Whoa, what's that? Can those two women have Phoenix tattoos? The only girls I know that are crazy enough to have the Kappa Phi Lambda Phoenix tattooed on their left hip are my crazy, older, twin cousins, Nicola and Yvette. But they live in New Zealand. And their hair and faces doesn't look anything like the girls on the screen. Besides, I thought ubdqt is a French web site. That's really weird. I'll have to ask my cousins if they've tried on any bathing suits lately or if they were supplementing their income with some soft porn. I'm joking. Sort of. I thought I knew my family. With my dad being a voyeur and a perv and my cousins doing soft porn, I feel like my world really sucks. I have to go."

"Calm down Guy, it's probably just a weird coincidence," Owen said. "Probably," Guy agreed. "I still have to go." When his friend left, Owen decided that Temp would understand and called him, but Temp's phone went straight to voice mail. For some reason, Owen felt uncomfortable about leaving a message and made a mental note to try again later.

When Guy got home, he called his cousin Nikki and found out that yes, she and Yvette had gone swimsuit shopping at the trendy new *OhMy EAU!!* boutique that had just opened in their local mall.

"Have you got psychic powers I'm not aware of?" Nikki asked.

"No, I just saw a couple of chicks that reminded me of you and wanted to check to see if you had made an unscheduled trip to Paris."

"Nope, still here in Auckland. The weather is beautiful—80 degrees for days now. Yvette has a wonderful new job as a marketer with Fletcher Building. She also has a sexy new rocker boyfriend. She's been so busy, I was surprised she even had time to go shopping with me. I'm in between gigs and boyfriends. Are you planning to visit us during the holidays?" Nikki asked.

"Depends on mom and dad," Guy answered. "Gotta run. Say hi to Yvette for me. Later."

When he hung up the phone Guy called Owen. "Hi Owen. I just found out that my cousins went bathing suit shopping in some New Zealand boutique called Romeo or something. Maybe it was a sorority thing. I'll have to ask them the next time I see them, which probably won't be till Christmas. I think I freaked out a little. Maybe it's a guilty conscience. I'm thinking I should just tell my dad about what I've done."

But Owen wasn't so sure. Something didn't feel right about the whole situation, but he couldn't put a finger on what was wrong. He and his friend Guy were just kids. He was sure Temp wouldn't judge him and could provide some perspective, but he hadn't connected with him yet. For the first time, Owen didn't feel comfortable sharing information with his dad, Louis.

When Temp and Owen finally connected a couple of days later, he reassured Owen he would look into it and to try and to relax and go on with his life. From what Owen had described it sounded like the people being filmed were novices, not actors. He wondered if they were aware that they were being videoed and that the film was online. He resolved to look into it.

If the screen actors didn't know they were being filmed, it was an invasion of their privacy and illegal. He didn't yet know that the ReID system exchanged the real face with a random face from its inventory.

The site exploited people and exposed them without their permission. That was unacceptable to him. He asked Owen to continue to send him the daily links from Guy. Owen agreed.

Chapter 97

Dreams go up in Smoke

Temp was running late. He had stopped at the office to collect the engagement ring which now rested comfortably in the inside right pocket of his navy-blue sports jacket. Parking was even more of a nightmare than usual and the first vacant spot he found was four blocks away.

It was hard to wipe the happy smile from his face. It was well past time to set things right. As he rounded the corner to Melodie's townhouse complex, he glanced down at the new Patek Phillippe Nautilus Chronograph watch he had purchased yesterday at the Paris airport duty free. The matching women's watch was in his briefcase at the office. He didn't want something as insignificant as a watch to distract his sexy fiancée from the special moment he had planned.

As he rounded the corner he stopped in his tracks. The end unit, the townhouse Melodie rented was engulfed in flames.

The media, medics and police were already there. Sergeant Walter Wilkes, badge 73973, was in charge of the scene. Earlier, the officer had used his cell phone to shoot a video of the bystanders, the street, and the front and back of the high-end townhouse complex.

The Sergeant walked towards a slightly paunchy middle-aged man who was clutching the leash of a golden retriever puppy, who was dancing excitedly between his master's legs.

Notebook in hand, the Sergeant approached the man who introduced himself as Jack Edelstein, the onsite custodian. The officer asked for and received his contact information, his Neighborhood Watch affiliation, and reviewed his conceal carry permit and passport. He then asked Edelstein to describe exactly what had happened and when.

Edelstein was nervous. He had never been part of a police investigation before. He cleared his throat, took a deep breath to steady himself, and said, "At 11:00 p.m., as Sunny and I were returning from our last walk of the evening, we saw a middle-aged man, in a grey uniform, on the sidewalk in front of Melodie's townhouse. He was wearing a Washington Nationals baseball cap. He had a bushy mustache and a bit of a beer belly."

He took another deep breath and continued. "The man carried a portable black tool chest in one hand and a clipboard in the other. A tool belt was hanging off of his waist. Because Melodie had mentioned she was having trouble with her stove earlier in the week, Sunny and I just assumed the man was from one of the big box stores making a late house call." Unfortunately, in his excitement of being part of a real investigation, the custodian neglected to mention the unexplained bang he heard around 11:25 p.m.

Sergeant Wilkes then asked Edelstein if he knew who lived in the burning townhouse. "Of course," Edelstein continued conversationally. "I know everyone that lives here. Mademoiselle Melodie Marie Beaudoin rents the end unit. Lovely French-Canadian woman. She moved here a couple of years ago. She teaches languages, Mandarin, French and Spanish for politicians and she also does some physiotherapy for professional athletes, mostly hockey players, I think. She also wrote a best-selling book on some financial thing. I can't recall the title. I'm sure you can Google it. Is Melodie OK? Sunny and I are really worried about her."

"When I can share any information, I will do so," Sergeant Wilkes replied. He then asked Edelstein if there was any particular reason he was worried about Ms. Beaudoin. A bit taken aback at the question, Edelstein replied, "Her townhouse is burning. Isn't it reasonable to worry about our neighbor's safety?"

Sergeant Wilkes replied. "Of course, besides the fire I mean."

"No there isn't," Edelstein emphatically said.

Sergeant Wilkes then asked if Edelstein if Melodie lived alone. "Yes, although her boyfriend often slept over."

The policeman then asked Edelstein if he had observed any problems between Ms. Beaudoin and her boyfriend. "No, the only thing Sunny and I ever saw them do was hold hands and hug, and the only thing we ever heard them do was laugh. Melodie Beaudoin has a very distinctive, musical laugh. Her parents must have named her for that laugh. It was obvious to anyone with eyes in their head that they were very much in love. One afternoon not that long ago, while we were sharing recipes, we often did that, Melodie mentioned that her boyfriend was trying to talk her into marrying him, and that she was seriously considering his proposal. Since she was a cancer survivor, she was unwilling to say 'Yes' until she was reasonably certain about her health prospects. But based on their loving behavior, Sunny and I believe it was only a matter of time before she agreed. We sure hope she's ok."

Temp found it difficult to move and his feet seemed cemented to the ground. It would be hours before the police and other emergency responders completed their on-site investigations. Since he had no official role, he couldn't see any reason to stay.

Even with all of his native intelligence, cunning and investigative experience, Temp had not foreseen this unexpected turn of events. He thought things were bad when his best friend, Ted, died and then, when one of his work colleagues, Edie, had betrayed him. As bad as those things were, the thought that something had happened to Melodie was even worse.

He allowed himself one minute of self-indulgent emotionalism before his training kicked in. Earlier that same week Melodie had mentioned that she felt like she was being watched. He had dismissed her concerns to being overtired because she had taken on several new language clients and had been working extra-long hours.

Usually, he had excellent instincts. Had he missed something?

Even if it was the last thing he did, he swore he would not rest until he figured it out. He used hi St. Clair work phone to call Melodie's eldest brother, Jacques. The two men didn't speak or meet in person until Melodie's memorial service thirty days after the fire.

Chapter 98

A Professional Hit

Earlier that same evening, The Iceman silently entered Melodie's townhouse. He was familiar with the layout because he had scoped out the townhouse the week before when Melodie was at a yoga retreat out of town. He noticed the jasmine scented candles and wooden match sticks were still in a glass dish on the bathtub rim.

The Iceman observed that Melodie was in a deep sleep. He put on surgical gloves and removed a hypodermic needle, the bottle of Pentobarbital, a plastic funnel, and a bottle of the language coach's favorite wine, a Casa Hermoso Sauvignon Blanc, from his black tool chest. Within seconds he had expertly injected the Pentobarbital into the slumbering woman.

Over the next fifteen minutes, he patiently poured a half of a bottle of wine, through the funnel, down the unconscious woman's throat. He transferred her fingerprints onto the empty wine bottle after he placed her inert hand there.

He then went into her ensuite bathroom, collected the prescription Ativan and Imovane from her medicine cabinet, and the unlit candle from the bathtub rim. He held her jaw open, and force-fed her several extra pills he had crushed, so she wouldn't choke. The language coach never regained consciousness.

The Iceman soaked Melodie's bedclothes in the remaining wine, and loosely wrapped the young woman into what would shortly become her death shroud. While he was returning the pills to the medicine chest, Melodie's inert body rolled off the king-sized bed and crashed onto the wooden floor.

The Iceman collected the rest of his gear, turned on the television set, lit the jasmine-scented candles from the bathroom, and placed them onto her bedclothes.

He remained by Melodie's side until hc saw the blanket catch on fire. He left the empty bottle of wine of the nightstand beside the bed, let himself out of the sliding doors on the main floor, and disappeared into the night. The digital clock on the nightstand read 11:45 p.m.

Chapter 99

Coroner's Report

Thanks to the floor to ceiling ceramic bathroom tile, and Edelstein's quick response, the fire did not completely destroy Melodie's townhouse. In fact, much of the bedroom and bathroom contents were still intact. The CSI's bagged several pill bottles from the medicine cabinet, the melted candle, and an empty wine bottle.

The autopsy revealed that Ms. Beaudoin's stomach contents contained 12 mg. of Ativan (more than five times the recommended dose of 2-3 mg. per day) and 22.5 mg. of Imovane (three times the recommended dose of 7.5 mg. The coroner believed the victim had likely consumed the pills about a half-hour before her death. There was also 0.18 of alcohol in her blood. In addition to having a lethal dose of Ativan and Imovane in her system, the victim had also donned several glasses of Casa Hermoso Jardin Sauvignon Blanc.

The good news, if there was any good news in a situation like this, was that the coroner thought Ms. Beaudoin had been in a coma or was already dead and did not suffer any pain when her body caught fire. He ruled the death an accident. The combination of prescription medication and alcohol likely caused her blood pressure to drop. When this happened, the victim rolled out of her king-sized bed. As she fell, she knocked over the candle, which started the fire. First responders found the charred and still smoking body curled up in a fetal position on the floor.

Melodie's body was released to Jacques Beaudoin, the victim's brother. The coroner declared that Melodie Marie Beaudoin's death was by misadventure. In other words, the victim died because she was doing something that put her in mortal danger. He ruled out natural death, murder and suicide. His office submitted his report and moved onto the next case.

Chapter 100

Temp Loses His Job at St. Clair

Bob called Temp at 8:00 a.m. the next morning. "We need to meet in person. Can you be at the office in an hour? And bring all of your St. Clair gear. There have been some changes I need to discuss with you."

"I can be there in 20," Temp replied.

When Temp arrived, Bob was waiting for him. He invited him into the soundproof room and closed the door. "Take a seat. Remember when I hired you? I made it clear that there would be consequences if you lied to me about anything, no matter how trivial?

"As you know, my team continued to look into your background even when you were on the payroll. They discovered a lie. In the overall scheme of things, it's not a very big lie, and to tell you the truth, I laughed out loud when I heard it. But even a little white lie is still a lie," Bob said.

"What little white lie are you talking about?" Temp asked.

"I know how bright you are Temp. I could never understand how someone who graduated in the top 1% of his Master's program barely passed his undergraduate courses. If it wasn't for your military training and your GRE, I doubt you would have been accepted into a Master's program. We discovered that you paid your cousin to pretend he was you. He attended all of your classes, wrote all of your exams and even graduated under your name, while you traveled and had adventures. That's the funny part. And for the record, I couldn't care less about your academic qualifications. Some of my best employees grew up on the street and don't have any formal schooling.

"What's important to me is trust. This report has shaken my trust. I am suspending you without pay for a month. I will decide if the suspension is permanent within thirty days. John will join us shortly to collect all of the St. Clair property. I'm assuming you brought everything with you. For what it's worth, Gladys was really happy with your report and was ecstatic that you located the General's hidden assets. So was I. Your suspension will not affect your bonus, which you have earned, fair and square. And because I said I would, I will continue to look into why you were set up at Treasury. I just have to figure out if I am willing to trust you again or if I even want you back."

Bob stood up and exited at the same time that John entered the SCIF. John asked Temp to hand over his pass, computer, phones, credit cards, company ID, and his weapons. He then asked Temp if there was anything else he had lied about. Temp said No. John replied, "I hope this will all blow over in a month's time," and extended his right hand. The two men shook hands and Temp left the SCIF. As he looked back at the St. Clair offices, he realized this was the second time in two years that he had demonstrated really poor judgment. Time to refocus—this was more than just a bad run.

Chapter 101

Jacques' Independent Investigation

It had been two weeks since his sister's funeral. Jacques was surprised at how difficult it was to face each day and to put on a happy face for the sake of his parents. He had started asking himself, "What's the use?" more times than he cared to admit. He also became aware of another feeling—guilt. Had Melodie wanted to die? Although it made him sick to even consider suicide as a possibility, he knew she was deathly afraid of the cancer coming back.

Jacques decided to take a three-month leave of absence from his job as a police detective with the SPVM. He did this for several reasons. Part of him had died with Melodie and he needed some personal time to grieve. More importantly, he was itching to figure out what had really happened.

He also needed to assess whether his conversations with Christina, Denzel, Misha and Temp were just the four of them working through their own feelings of guilt and loss or if there was something the Washington coroner and the police had missed. Since he felt worse when he was just sitting around, he got to work doing what he did best—investigating and solving cases.

The first thing he did was review the police and coroner's reports. Then, he turned to the appendix, which included Melodie's death certificate and a printout of the files on her hard drive. There were household files, green smoothie recipes, financial records, contact and client lists, Mandarin, French and Spanish language exercises, family photos, and some YouTube yoga videos.

He smiled to himself because it was so easy to imagine his sister setting up and adding to these files. But there were two files that didn't make sense. The first was a file called The Alyosha Foundation for Financial Literacy and Education, which included financial statements. This was strange for two reasons; Melodie had never mentioned it which was out of character. It was also unusual that she would support a charity that was headquartered in Russia especially because he knew that she believed in supporting local charities.

The second file was saved as, "My Legacy." It included only one page of text, "To my family—I love you all—you live in my heart every day." But he couldn't recall his sister mentioning she had the interest or even the time to write another book. He made a note to ask Christina and Temp about these two files the next time he was in Washington. But in the interim, he would call Denzel and Misha to find out if they knew anything about the legacy file.

His first call was to Denzel. He asked, "Have you ever heard of The Alyosha Foundation of Financial Literacy and Education?" Denzel replied, "Yes, that is Misha's Foundation. Most of the 'Leave Only Shadows' authors donate their book royalties to the Foundation because it does good work. Another reason we support the Foundation is because Misha's father, Sergei, paid for all the printing and distribution costs of our Leave Only Shadows book and the club members wanted to show our appreciation for his in-kind donation. I'm also the Acting Director. I'm volunteering my time until Misha hires a permanent replacement. Would you like me to send you a pdf of our donor package which includes our mission, vision and values, and our current financial statement? The package also describes our current projects and includes a link to our website. Jacques replied in the affirmative. His next call was to Misha who confirmed everything Denzel said.

His third call was to Christina, who was happy to hear from him. She assumed Jacques was calling to talk about Melodie, and launched into a tearful tale of how much she loved her, what a good person she was, and how much she missed her. Christina couldn't believe that it had been almost three years since they went to the 2008 Burning Man. Jacques just listened to her talk—he didn't have the heart to interrupt her.

Chapter 102

Jacques Goes to Washington

When Christina stopped to blow her nose, Jacques told her that he was planning to be in Washington on Friday and hoped to have dinner with her when he was there. When he checked into The River Inn on 25th Street NW, he asked the concierge for the name of the best Indian food in the Capital. The concierge recommended the West End on New Hampshire Ave SW. Jacques invited Christina to join him for an early dinner when the restaurant opened at 5:00 p.m.

Christina didn't understand why she spent so much time getting ready for their dinner meeting. Nor did she admit to herself that she wished she was getting ready for a date with the handsome Canadian detective. When the three of them were at the Burning Man together, she was seeking inspiration, not a date, and saw Jacques as a pal, rather than the vibrant, sexy man that he actually was. Under different circumstances she could see herself happily drowning in those intensely intelligent brown eyes. Then reality kicked in—Jacques was Melodie's brother, and they were not meeting for a date.

She arrived at the restaurant fashionably late at 5:15 p.m. Jacques was exactly where his text said he would be—nursing a beer at the bar. When Christina slid onto the stool beside him, she took his breath away. For a split second, he forgot why they were meeting. Christina asked the bartender for a glass of white from Casa Hermoso Jardin. Although she was disappointed to learn that the restaurant did not carry any wine from her family's vineyard, she good-naturedly said, "That's too bad. Any organic, dry, white Californian, will be fine."

At Burning Man, at Melodie's funeral, and then over coffee and croissants with Denzel, Misha and Temp, Jacques hadn't really paid attention to Christina's beauty. But he sure was noticing how gorgeous she was now. And Christina was just as taken with Jacques as he was with her, especially now that their thighs were almost touching. If she didn't know better, she would swear there was an electric charge passing between them.

Christina was emotionally intelligent which made her just as talented as Jacques at making someone feel as if he or she was the only person in the world. Before too long she and Jacques were sharing childhood stories, he of pranks that he and his best friend Yves Plante had managed to pull off, and she about what it was like growing up on a vineyard. Of course, their lively conversation took place in French.

And Christina was smart. She was as informed about Washington politics as she was about mindfulness—Jacques had never heard of mindfulness before. He was intrigued by her definition, "Mindfulness is paying attention, in a particular way, in the present moment, aided by certain practices to help train attention and develop awareness. A person might study it to become awake and aware, and to develop the ability to stay present and focused."

Sounded a lot like policing. It sounded like he had been practicing mindfulness throughout his career. It didn't matter. He sure was mindful now and he was hanging onto the lovely Christina's every word.

After flirting over several mouth-watering appetizers and a delectable main course (the concierge had been right about his restaurant recommendation), their conversation turned serious. Christina asked Jacques if he had ever heard of ESHURE. When he said No, she spent the next hour explaining what it was all about, and how important the project was to Melodie.

Christina explained, "At least six U.S. Senators that we knew of were trading on insider information. We knew this because they were our clients, three were Melodie's and three were mine. We both listened to them talking about what stocks they planned to buy, sell or short based on the information they learned in their respective Committees. To prove this was happening, we decided to mirror exactly what the Senators did. If they bought, sold or shorted a stock, so did we."

"Some people from her INSEAD Sustainable Investing Club also made the same trades. Each of our six traders, plus Melodie and I, invested $200,000 of our own money. Within six months, our initial $1.6M investment had grown to $2.8M. These returns were well above the benchmark. But before you get the wrong idea, we didn't keep any of the profits. It was never about making money."

"We only kept a very small sum $200,000, split equally between the eight of us, to cover expenses and donated the profits, $1Million dollars, to The Alyosha Foundation for Financial Literacy and Education. Melodie already had a relationship with them. Remember Misha? He was at the memorial and is one of Melodie's "Leave Only Shadows" co-authors. Alyosha was the charity he set up years ago. I also think the Foundation recently won some award for their work. Misha's father published the club's Leave Only Shadows book, paid for the hardware and also took care of the costs of creating the specialized ESHUR trading software. I think Denzel is running the Foundation on a temporary basis now."

She continued, "Because Melodie met Philadelphia Romualdez, the reporter that received a Pulitzer for her story about U.S. soldiers mistreating Iraqi prisoners of war, at one of her advanced Mandarin language classes, she felt comfortable approaching her –about our insider trading story. Philadelphia and Melodie agreed to work together on an exposé that would air in about six months' time. After we set up ESHUR, and well before the *30 Minutes* special was due to air, we were never seen in public together again. And as the team leads with three people in our respective trading teams, we only traded the stocks identified by the other. In other words, Melodie and her team only traded the stocks identified by my Senators and I and my team only traded the stocks identified by hers. That way, none of us could be connected to any particular trade or insider information."

Jacques replied, "That was a really smart decision. You and Melodie really thought about this." Christina continued, "Then, Melodie died in the fire. I've never met Philadelphia, and don't know what she plans to do with the story now." Jacques then asked if Melodie mentioned she wanted to write a book. Christina replied, "Not that I'm aware of. Maybe her boyfriend knows."

He never thought he could love and respect his sister any more than he did at that moment. But he had some concerns—the nature of the trading didn't seem like it was above board and was possibly illegal. Jacques began to wonder if ESHURE had played a part in his sister's death. But it was too early to jump to conclusions.

Jacques asked for the check, paid the bill and the two strolled out into the velvet evening. Before Christina got into the taxi, Jacques asked her what she was doing for brunch on Saturday. Christina said she just had some errands to run and would love to join him for brunch. In less than five minutes Jacques was able to flag down a taxi, a first. He then kissed Christina on both cheeks and wished her a bonne nuit. It was 11:00 p.m.

The next day, Jacques and Christina met at Tim's Bulletin on 8th St NE at noon. He chose Tim's because it was known for its bottomless Mimosa's. If the liquor failed to impress, there was always the restaurant's world-famous eggs benedict, short rib hash and mushroom tart.

The tasty and sumptuous brunch lived up to its five-star reviews. It was hard to rip himself away—if he hadn't agreed to meet the great Hercule, he would have happily extended brunch into dinner with the ravishing Christina. But that would have to wait. He needed some alone-time with his sister's boyfriend. If anyone would know Melodie's state of mind before she died, it would be him.

Chapter 103

More Intelligence

Jacques invited Temp to join him for dinner at The Steak Pit on Constitution Avenue. The hotel concierge had told him that The Steak Pit was one of the top steakhouses in the Capital. Over drinks, Jacques asked Temp if Melodie ever mentioned ESHUR. Temp, who didn't yet trust Jacques replied, "I think it was some kind of financial scheme, but she never shared any specifics."

Temp volunteered, "You know I asked your sister to marry me every month at our anniversary dinner at Northern Thai because that's where we went on our first dinner date. We celebrated all of our monthly anniversaries there. And for the record, she always said 'No.'

"I'm sure you are wondering why I wasn't with her. I was returning from an overseas trip. It was about 1:00 a.m. before I got back. I couldn't get near her townhouse because it was on fire. Not being with her that night is the biggest regret of my entire life."

"Tell me about how she spent a typical day," Jacques asked.

"She saw some clients, did some yoga, went boxing, took in a language class, you know, the usual things," Temp replied.

Jacques asked, "Was she planning on writing another book?"

Temp replied: "If she was, she didn't mention it to me."

Jacques was a bit surprised that Temp's answers were so short. He made a mental note to investigate if his sister's boyfriend had spent any time in the military. He asked if there was anything else Temp wanted to tell him.

Temp replied, "Besides my guilt you mean? I can see it on your face—you think I'm secretive. But I want you to know that I really loved your sister and was planning on marrying her, if she would have me. One of the reasons I was late getting back was I stopped by the office to pick up the engagement ring I had commissioned from Anastasia Hand. I've been carrying the box in my jacket pocket ever since. Now that she's gone, I guess I'll donate it. I've always been unlucky in love."

Temp sighed and added. "There are a couple of things that have always bothered me. A couple of weeks before the fire, Melodie told me that she had the feeling that someone was following her. I dismissed her concerns and told her it was probably her imagination, and suggested she talk to her doctor about her meds. Given what happened, I regret not taking her concerns more seriously. Just another thing for me to feel guilty about."

Temp took a sip of his drink and continued. "As her brother, you know how anal she was about following the doctor's orders when it came to her meds. Because she was taking sleeping tablets, there was no way that she would be so irresponsible as to fall asleep with a night cap and a candle burning. As for drinking, although she allowed herself the occasional glass of beer or wine, I never saw her drink more than one."

Temp continued, "Another thing, I'm sure Edelstein told the police about me. Which is why I was surprised they didn't want to interview me. I just assumed they closed the file when they received the coroner's ruling of accidental death."

Since the conversation appeared to have come to a natural close, the two men said goodnight. Jacques felt like he was about to explode if he didn't get a chance to share how he was feeling about his sister's death. Rather than getting clarity the more he learned the more complicated it all became. He wanted to talk through his assumptions and conclusions with someone that understood. His best friend Yves was on vacation with his family in Hawaii. Besides Temp, the only other person he knew in D.C. was Christina. Rather than drink alone he called her. She agreed to meet him at the lobby bar at his hotel.

Chapter 104

Jacques & Christina

No one could remember who made the first move. It didn't matter. The two athletic and intellectually awake people had been thrown together by a terrible loss. Shared grief broke them open; shared desire kept them that way. Clothes flew this way and that as they fell onto Jacques' king-sized bed.

That night Christina became a new kind of lover, working her body first under then on top of Jacques in a manner that made his excitement even more intense. In the first ten minutes he almost climaxed five times. But Christina tightened and reduced activity and coaxed him to breathe slowly. And for the first hour it even worked.

You would never know that this was the first time they were intimate—they were so comfortable with each other it was as if they had made love a thousand times before. They recognized that until that moment, they had been nothing more than children playing at sex. Grown-up sex was far more physically satisfying and spiritually enriching! Both were amazed at what had just transpired and simultaneously realized that no matter where life took them, they would always be connected. Wrapped in each other's arms, they fell into a deep, contented sleep.

The next morning, they made love before room service brought them their champagne breakfast at 11:30 a.m. and again before they showered. It was hard for Christina to tear herself away, but she had a language client at 2:00 p.m. and needed to return home to prepare.

For the first two hours after Christina left Jacques was in a daze but recognized he needed to focus. He was even more determined to find out who killed his sister or to come to terms with the fact that her death was nothing more than a tragic accident.

One thing that was bothering him was this: why were none of the residents, including Melodie's boyfriend, ever asked to make a formal statement? The only things in the police file were photocopies of Sergeant Walter Wilkes, badge 73973, original photographs and crime scene notes, the coroner's report, and the death certificate. He wanted to know why.

Chapter 105

Edelstein

Since he had already spoken to Temp, Jacques decided to talk to Edelstein, the custodian who had called 911. He explained his relationship to Melodie and the reason for his request. Since Edelstein and Sunny were always open to making new friends, and they truly missed their wonderful neighbor, they agreed to meet Jacques at "Cuppa Beans" on North Street at 4:00 p.m. Edelstein suggested the Cuppa because it was unpretentious; guests were welcome to stay as long as they liked, the staff was friendly, the coffee was great, Edelstein could smoke, and most importantly, they had an outdoor patio, so that Sunny could come along.

Edelstein was animated and articulate and used his lit cigarette to punctuate his points. Jacques didn't have the heart to interrupt Edelstein's stories about what Sunny was like as a puppy. Besides, he had nowhere else he had to be, and the Dirty Chai Latte he was drinking was superb. It was clear from his unshaven face, and food-stained clothing that Edelstein took better care of his dog than he did of himself.

About twenty minutes into a particularly funny anecdote and in an unlikely spot to end the story, Edelstein dropped his lit cigarette into his Latte and said, "I have a searing headache and can't see anything out of my right eye." Just as Edelstein started to topple from his chair onto the floor Jacques noticed the pupils of both of Edelstein's eyes were dilated. Their waiter saw what was happening and called 911 before Jacques caught the unconscious senior in his arms.

Jacques hoped it was nothing more than a bad case of indigestion or an undiagnosed blood sugar drop and that Edelstein would sleep it off. He didn't want to take Sunny to the pound but didn't know what else to do with him. Then he remembered. In one of their chats, Christina had mentioned she always had a dog when she was growing up on the vineyard and missed having a pet, especially now that she had lost her best human friend. Since Jacques had to return to Montreal the next day, he asked Christina to do him a personal favor and to look after Sunny until Edelstein got out of the hospital. She agreed.

Unfortunately, Edelstein was never discharged from the hospital or regained consciousness. He died two weeks after he was admitted. The doctors said that it was likely that his undiagnosed high blood pressure and atherosclerosis had caused a brain aneurism.

Jacques never got a chance to ask Edelstein about what he saw and heard the night of the fire. The only good thing to come out of Edelstein's death was that Christina appeared to have fallen in love with "Sunny, the Wonder Dog" and had de facto adopted him.

Chapter 106

Christina Second Guessing Herself

Christina was also second-guessing herself. Initially, she had thought she might close the books on their ESHUR scheme—it somehow didn't seem right to carry on without Melodie, her co-conspirator and best friend. That was when Jacques, who had not yet finished his investigation into his sister's death, asked Christina to continue trading on the insider information she received from her Senators until he could figure out what, role if any, ESHUR might have played in Melodie's death. Christina agreed to his request. Besides, she hadn't yet made up her mind about whether to pull the plug on the media story about insider trading.

She also started to brainstorm ideas to honor her dear friend's memory. The first thing she did was to make an additional, personal $1,000 donation, in her memory, to Melodie's favorite charity, The Alyosha Foundation for Financial Literacy and Education.

Christina believed that an INSEAD educational scholarship fund was a meaningful way to honor her friend. Since she believed that two heads were better than one, and three heads were better than two, she decided to reach out to Melodie's close friends and former INSEAD colleagues, Denzel Sun Mah and Misha Mikhalov.

Since their initial coffee after Melodie's funeral, Christina, Denzel and Misha had Skyped a few times. When she contacted them to discuss her educational scholarship idea, Denzel said, "I think The Melodie Beaudoin Scholarship Fund is a great idea, I'm sorry I didn't think of it myself, and want to help in any way I can."

"What a great idea, Christina," Misha added. "I also want to help. Why don't I contact the other Sustainability Club Members and see if they are interested in participating? Most of them are very well off and it wouldn't be a financial hardship to ask them to write you a big check. Maybe we can even get them to do some of the grunt work so that you don't have to do everything yourself. Leave it with me and I'll get back to you within a week or so," Misha said.

A little over a week later, Misha reported back with some good news—all Sustainable Investing Club members, would be happy to make a financial contribution and wanted to know what else they could do to help.

Christina was just figuring out what she needed to do and who would be responsible for what. Her preliminary task list included identifying how to fundraise and administer the scholarship fund, defining the selection criteria, choosing the ideal number of recipients in each year, whether recipients would be allowed to reapply for financial support in subsequent years, what information she needed to include on the application form, how she would maintain the scholarship fund, and other related matters.

Since the Sustainable Club members had all agreed to support the project, she would ask Melodie's three traders to join her and Jacques on the selection committee. She also came to a decision on the *30 Minutes* story—she would contact Philadelphia Romualdez herself to determine if the reporter was willing to do the insider trading story with just her. In her excitement about moving forward, she forgot to mention her plans to Jacques.

Chapter 107

Life at the Station

After Melodie died and before they could film what Philadelphia Romualdez was certain would be her next Pulitzer prize-winning exposé, her professional life, which had never been that good to begin with, became unbearable. For the most part, her colleagues ignored her. When they were forced to work with her, their interactions were strictly professional. It reminded her of the mean girls she was forced to deal with when she was in boarding school. Her school mates hated the fact that she wasn't white, spoke French, and walked their illustrious halls not because she was as smart and talented as she was beautiful, but because she had somehow managed to secure the sympathy vote as well as a generous scholarship.

To add insult to injury, her professional adult colleagues, did everything possible to make her life miserable. For example, just last week she spilled coffee on her outfit just before she was about to go on air at the tenth work anniversary party of a charity involved in refugee resettlement. That really sucked, because she normally did not drink either coffee or red wine because they stained her teeth. She was only holding the Styrofoam cup of coffee because she didn't want to drink any liquor before her Muay Thai kickboxing class, which was where she was headed directly after the shoot. She would never forgive the cameraman who had jostled her with his equipment which made the Styrofoam cup of coffee jump out of her hand and onto her the front of her light blue suit jacket and the crotch of the matching trousers.

Had she been more self-aware, Philadelphia might have enjoyed the irony in editor Jill's ongoing battle to find ways to exact revenge. She had never forgiven Philadelphia for her alleged poaching of the prisoner of war story from Mary-Lou.

Because she couldn't go on camera with a brown coffee stain on her suit, Jill gave Mary-Lou the refugee resettlement story.

Rather than being a dog, the tenth anniversary story turned out to be a home run. Mary-Lou got fifteen minutes on camera with Maya, a young Pakistani Nobel prize-winning activist, the unannounced keynote speaker at the tenth anniversary event. Because security was so high, no one, except the event organizers, knew that Maya was the guest of honor. Philadelphia gnashed her perfectly capped teeth in frustration about missing out on yet another opportunity to showcase her beauty and her brains, and to meet the inspirational Nobel prize winner.

Things at the station continued to deteriorate. Philadelphia mourned the loss of her second Pulitzer. She wondered if she had enough information in her notes to pull together something herself and would have liked to talk to one of her colleagues or her boss about her existing research, but she didn't dare. For about one minute, she even considered changing careers. But then she realized there was probably no other profession where she could win another Pulitzer Prize. Just like she had always done in the past, she would figure out some way to persevere.

Chapter 108

Continuing Melodie's Legacy

"Hi Philadelphia, my name is Christina Sinclair-Sanchez. You don't know me, but I was Melodie Beaudoin's friend. I was also her partner on the ESHUR Insider Trading Scheme. If you're still interested in this story, I would like to meet and talk about how we can move the story forward."

The two women agreed to meet at Half Baked on Thomas Jefferson Boulevard Wednesday at 2:00 p.m. The Pulitzer Prize story that was off again, was on again! Philadelphia celebrated by purchasing another pair of Jimmy Cho's. Like her fifth cousin on her mother's side, Imelda, the reporter had a walk-in closet full of status symbol shoes.

Christina had to go to her dentist to get a tooth pulled the Tuesday before she was scheduled to meet with the reporter. The dental office was located one block from the subway, and it didn't make sense to take the car. Rather than a taxi, in honour of Melodie, she decided to be environmentally conscious and to use public transit.

While she was waiting to board the train, an unkempt woman with crazy eyes, pushed her hard enough to make her lose her balance. As she started to fall headfirst onto the tracks, a man in a postal worker uniform put his arm out and blocked her fall. "I've got you. Are you OK?" he said with a look of concern.

"I think so. Thank you so much. I don't know what would have happened if you hadn't been standing beside me," Christina said. "Happy to help," the stranger said. At that point the subway car doors slid open and 25 tightly packed travelers poured out. Christina lost sight of the good Samaritan. She used deep breathing meditative techniques to steady her nerves. By the time she arrived at the dentist she was relaxed and ready for the extraction.

After her dental appointment, she was happy to get home to Sunny who greeted her by racing excitedly through every room on the first floor. She was laughing so hard at the dog's antics that she forgot about the morning's unpleasantness. Since she adopted him that dog had given her so much joy. Sunny and Jacques were the only good things to come out of her friend's death.

Chapter 109

Connecting the Dots

Jacques finished his independent investigation into his sister's death. So much of the information he had uncovered was circumstantial. A feeling that someone was following her and what looked like the irresponsible mixing of alcohol, drugs and candles. He still hadn't figured out what if anything Melodie and Christina's ESHUR scheme and the pending *30 Minutes* story had to do with her death

Jacques set up a conference call with Temp, Misha, and Denzel to review the status of his investigation, to assess if there was anything he had overlooked and to brainstorm next steps. Christina couldn't join them because she had a language coaching session with a new client.

After exchanging brief greetings, Jacques kicked off the discussion with a review of everything he had learned and then opened up the floor. Temp was the first to speak, "Since Melodie was murdered, there I said it, I've talked to every major big box store, and they did not send a repairman. I also reviewed her appointment book and cell phone records, and she did not have any appointments listed for the evening she died. My employer has discovered a loose connection between upcoming Treasury drug cases and the Russian mob. I should have some more info on that shortly."

He continued, "I don't know how or even if this is relevant, but since we last talked at Melodie's funeral, I have learned that I have a 15-year-old son. Believe it or not he is as good a hacker as anyone I've ever seen. Because he is proud of his skills and full of himself, like most teenagers, when I told him my previous job was as an ethical hacker with the U.S. government, he wanted to demonstrate his own hacking skills. I couldn't believe my eyes when he hacked into a local bank in a blink of an eye. I wasn't overly concerned because every teenaged hacker tries his skills on a bank. His name is Owen, and he lives in France with his mother and father."

"Let me preface what I'm about to tell you by saying I'm not a prude and that I believe that interest in sex is very normal for a teenager. Having said that, I am really upset at what I saw. While he was showing off, Owen hacked into a very deep and dark Peeping Tom site called ubdqt.com.

"He explained to me that the reason it was way better than porn was because the people trying on the clothes on camera did not appear to be actors. They just looked like normal people. Although it doesn't appear as if ubdqt.com has anything to do with Melodie's death, I really haven't spent any time pursuing that angle. In the interests of full disclosure, that is what I've been doing since we last spoke."

While Misha was listening to Temp talk about Owen's exploits, his mind started to wander to his personal dilemma. He had begun to lose interest in the Mikhalov family business the moment Jade said 'Yes' to his marriage proposal. Although he had lied his whole life, he refused to lie to Jade. He wanted her to make an informed decision about marrying him.

Before she died of cardiac arrest triggered by an accidental EpiPen adrenalin injection, Misha spent hours reviewing the various legal and illegal family businesses and training his best Computer Camp protégés to take over specific files. During his heartfelt conversations with Jade, Misha got back in touch with his personal values for good that had motivated him to create Alyosha in the first place. He liked that guy. He didn't like the guy he had become. After telling Jade about the various family businesses, including *OhMy EAU!!*, it suddenly occurred to him that he had been living his father's life, not his own. Once Pandora was out of the box it was impossible to push her back in there.

When Temp appeared done Misha chimed in, "I doubt it's even relevant, but I want to mention it any way. Denzel, remember our 'Leave Only Shadows' co-author Cosimo Calderella? I can't remember if I told you that Cosimo threatened Melodie and I. He threatened me because I turned down his job offer to join his family business. For some unknown reason he took my answer as a personal betrayal, rather than as a business decision. I guess I really don't blame him for thinking that way, because a short time later my father's cleaner assassinated Cosimo's father and then we took over all the Calderella's East Asian business interests. After that, I have no idea what happened to either him or his family. Cosimo threatened Melodie because she kicked him out of the Sustainable Investing Club. He left INSEAD shortly thereafter. I don't even remember if he graduated. I never put two and two together until just this second. After he left, Melodie, her roommate Paula, and my brother and mother were involved in a series of bizarre and very scary situations including muggings, property destruction and identity theft. When he saw what was going on and in an overabundance of caution, my father hired some extra bodyguards for my mother and brother and that seemed to do the trick. I don't think Melodie had any other problems after she returned to New York, but I may be wrong. I never asked her, and she never mentioned anything when we talked on the phone. The police never figured out who was responsible for any of the incidents. But my intuition tells me that Cosimo was involved. Do you think he followed Melodie to Washington and continued his vendetta?"

Misha then took a deep breath and added, "I don't want to be associated with my family anymore. I can't live with the never-ending violence and corruption. I planned on leaving the family business to marry Jade. And I'm ashamed to admit it, but I was stealing money from my family so that I could do so. My father is a brutal killer that needs to be stopped. And Jacques, ubdqt.com is one of my father's companies. It is a very lucrative Peeping Tom website run out of my mother's *OhMy EAU!!* retail stores. She has no idea that my father and I hijacked her business. And to further complicate things, my Financial Literacy Foundation is an *OhMy EAU!!* shareholder."

"When Denzel set up the ESHUR trading scheme, which was brilliant by the way, I cloned it. My father and I each made the same trades as Melodie, Christina, and their six traders. In addition to the trading information, my father also received notification of every email that Melodie sent. If she was planning on working with *30 Minutes*, and there was anything in writing, my father would have known about it and would have been concerned about the scrutiny the Foundation would receive as an *OhMy EAU!!* shareholder. I wouldn't put it past him to get his trusty cleaner to take Melodie out, before she had a chance to talk to the reporter and expose the Senators' insider trading. I know my father's cleaner is a real person, he calls him The Iceman, because he insisted that I knew how to activate him, on the off chance that I needed his services."

Jacques was in shock. "Misha your *father* just became my prime suspect in Melodie's death. Based on what you just told us, her death is starting to look a lot like murder, not an accident. Would you be willing to come to Montreal and give a sworn statement?"

Misha replied, "Of course."

Through an abundance of caution, Jacques did not tell Temp, Misha and Denzel that Interpol already had several, ongoing, international investigations into *OhMy EAU!!* and ubdqt.com. Misha and Denzel said goodbye. Jacques asked Temp to stay on the line.

Before Jacques could say anything, Temp said, "Before you say your piece, I have something I need to say. One night Melodie went to bed early. To pass the time I logged onto her computer. By accident I stumbled across some pretty sophisticated stock trading software. Because I wanted to see how the system worked and since I was not as flush as I used to be since I lost my job at Treasury, I decided on a "what the heck" basis to trade the same stocks as did Melodie. The tips were legitimate. In eight months, I managed to turn my $25,000 into a little over $40,000.

"I knew the gravy train was about to end when Melodie told me that she knew a *30 Minutes* reporter from her

Mandarin class and was hoping to interest her in doing an exposé on the Senators' insider trading scheme.

"I am not proud of my actions. For the record, I planned on telling Melodie what I had been doing, but she died before I had a chance. My betrayal cheapened our love. I know I can never make it right. And for what it's worth, I would give anything for a do-over. Is there any way I can do something for you that might balance the scale, even just a little?"

Jacques replied, "Let me think about it," and hung up.

Chapter 110

Shocking Disclosure

A couple of years before he died, and while she was still his protégé, Uncle Otto introduced Elena to his accountant, Alexei Abakov, Founder and President of Abakov Tarakov & Partners. Alexei had looked after all of Lacuna's accounting needs for nearly three decades. Elena knew Uncle Otto trusted Alexei implicitly and when she launched her own bathing suit and lingerie line she retained him to look after all of *OhMy EAU!!*'s accounting needs.

She instructed Alexei to work with her son, and Chief Technology Officer, Misha, to set up the accounting and payroll systems, hire a bookkeeper and accounts payable clerk, and produce the necessary monthly and annual reports.

After *OhMy EAU!!*'s two hundred retail locations had been operating profitably for about five years, the bookkeeper noticed what looked like small amounts of money disappearing from the daily cash flow account. Was this just a rounding error or was one of Elena's employees stealing? After monitoring the situation for about a month, the bookkeeper sent an internal report outlining her concerns, and the dates and amounts of the missing funds, to Alexei, the partner in charge of the *OhMy EAU!!* account.

When he received the bookkeeper's report, Alexei asked the firm's forensic accounting division to investigate. The forensic accounting team confirmed the bookkeeper's suspicions—small amounts of money were being redirected to a numbered Swiss bank account every day. But even with a warrant, Swiss banking law made it a crime to disclose account information to third parties without the account-holder's consent.

Alexei placed an urgent call to Elena and requested a personal meeting as soon as possible. They met at his office on Prochistenka Street the next day. "Welcome Elena. Thank you for agreeing to meet with me on such short notice. You are looking radiant as usual," Alexei said.

"Thank you, Alexei. Although it's always nice to see you, it's not like you to request an urgent meeting. What would you like to talk to me about?" Elena asked.

"There's no way to sugar coat this so I'll just spit it out. It looks like Misha is skimming money from the *OhMy EAU!!* accounts."

"That doesn't make sense. Although he has several Swiss bank accounts, my son doesn't have to steal from me or from anyone. He has never indicated he needed extra money. And if did, he knows that all he has to do is to ask either me or his father. We would never say no to any reasonable request. Come to think of it, we would probably not say no to even an unreasonable request."

"I have no idea why Misha needed the extra money. Our forensic team has identified that every day, 0.01% was transferred out of the cash account and moved to a Swiss Bank account. Although this didn't amount to very much on a daily basis, millions of dollars have already been moved. I know this is upsetting, Elena. I just thought you should know what was going on. Do you want us to report it to the authorities?"

"Thanks Alexei. No, that won't be necessary. Please don't take any further action until you hear from me."

When she left the office, Elena placed a call to Dmitri. "Would you be available to meet me for a cup of coffee at Coffee 1818 on Tverskaya-Yamskaya. There is something urgent I'd like to talk to you about."

But Dmitri had left his cell phone on the pool deck, and it would be hours before he retrieved his messages.

Chapter 111

Surveillance Continues

Since their telephone call, Jacques and Temp, the two men who loved Melodie the most in this world, spoke on the telephone every day. In addition to sharing anecdotes about Melodie, they often talked about their work. Over time, the men became quite close. And the more Jacques learned the more his respect for Temp's analysis and detecting skills grew.

Jacques was the beneficiary of Melodie's $50,000 life insurance policy. In her memory, Jacques decided to direct the funds to Christina's Melodie Beaudoin Scholarship Fund. On a whim, he asked Temp to look into three of the busiest stateside *OhMy EAU!!* locations—New York, Miami and San Francisco. Temp, who was mildly depressed and majorly frustrated, welcomed the distraction.

Temp and Jacques agreed that Temp would observe each of the three locations for a week. Because he knew a law enforcement officer like Jacques would never encourage a private citizen to break the law, Temp "forgot" to tell Jacques that he planned on doing more than simply observing what was going on.

His plans included entering each of the three locations, after hours. He would gain access to the premises by picking the lock—he looked forward to the chance to use his agency skills that were becoming a bit rusty from disuse since he left Treasury and since he had lost his job with Bob.

His first stop was at the Miami location where the retail store was located in a renovated house on Biscayne Boulevard. He arrived in Miami on a Saturday before noon and went to work right away. The only thing he observed were customers and staff going out of a very busy location. He left his post at midnight. The following day, Sunday, Temp was at his observation post at 10:00 a.m. He observed customers and staff going in and out until 10:00 p.m. when the store closed.

At 11:30 p.m. that same night, Temp removed a foldable ladder from his rented truck and climbed onto the roof of the boutique where he noticed a waterproof junction box. He took out a portable screwdriver and removed the exterior casing. There were a bunch of computer cables inside the box. "I wonder what that's about? It's highly unusual to have computer cables on the roof, usually they're under the floorboards," he said to himself.

Temp drilled a small hole in the roof and used the flashlight on his phone to follow the computer cables which terminated behind the change room mirrors, and which were attached to a camera. He needed to enter the premises to confirm his suspicions. At 11:50 p.m., he broke into the retail store. As he suspected, all of the mirrors in the dressing rooms had been modified to accommodate a series of hidden cameras. When he got back to his hotel room, he called Jacques and provided a verbal report.

Then, Temp traveled to the *OhMy EAU!!* San Francisco location on Filmore Street where the scenario repeated itself. At 11:30 p.m. on the second day, he again removed a foldable ladder from his rented truck and climbed onto the roof of the boutique. He noticed the same junction box in the same location on the roof. Once was a design anomaly, twice suggested the modification was purposeful. When he got back to his hotel room, Temp called Jacques and updated him.

Temp's final stop was the *OhMy EAU!!* New York location on Grand Street. That Sunday, at 11:00 p.m. Temp removed the foldable ladder from the back of his rented truck and climbed onto the roof of the boutique. Once again, he noticed a junction box in the exact same location as the junction boxes on the roofs of the Miami and San Francisco stores. He didn't believe in coincidences—this was not random.

When he entered the New York premises he confirmed that the dressing room mirrors had been modified so that they could be used to film the people in various stages of undress.

This seemed to confirm that the *OhMy EAU!!* stores were in fact the source of the soft porn. When he got back to his hotel room, he called Jacques.

Chapter 112

Mystery Shoppers

Jacques and Temp agreed to hire three different bathing suit models to be "mystery shoppers." The only criteria was that each model had to be an *OhMy EAU!!* Club member. Each would be paid $2,000, which included the model's $1,000 fee and $1,000 shopping money. Not a bad return for an hour's work.

The first model was blonde, blue-eyed Laysee. She wore a hot pink sequined baseball cap, white Capri pants and a white tube top, had on pink sandals and several sizes and shapes of pink bangles on her arms when she went into the Miami *OhMy EAU!!* dressing room. She carried purple, black and pink string bikinis over her right arm.

Before Jacques logged onto the ubdqt.com site with Guy's father's password from that day, Temp described what Laysee looked like and what she was wearing. Armed with this information, Jacques logged onto the voyeur site. Yes, there was a woman trying on purple, black and pink string bikinis, but she did not look anything like the woman Temp described. The woman on the screen was an equally gorgeous girl with green eyes, punk green hair and a lip ring. Other than that, everything else, including her street clothes, was exactly the same.

The next day, Temp flew to San Francisco and hired Sam, his second model, as a mystery shopper. Sam received the same payment and instructions as Laysee. Sam's long black hair was tied up into a bun and decorated with an ornate silver and blue butterfly barrette. She wore a pale blue poncho over a silver t-shirt and Tommy Hilfiger jeans. There were 6" silver stilettos on her feet.

Before Jacques logged onto the ubdqt.com site with Guy's father's password, Temp described what Sam looked like and what she was wearing. Armed with this information, Jacques logged onto the site. Just like what happened with the model in Miami, the person trying on lingerie didn't look anything like the woman described by Temp.

The third and final test was with a red-haired, blue-eyed model named Barbara. She was asked to try on a bustier, corset and garter belt at the *OhMy EAU!!* boutique in New York. Barbara was wearing cowboy boots and skin-tight black jeans. There was a New York Jets ball cap on her head, and she sported a matching Jets T-shirt. Barbara selected three bustiers in beige, silver and black, three corsets in black, leopard and paisley, and two garter belts that would work with both the bustiers and the corsets.

Temp described what Barbara looked like and what she was wearing for Jacques. Armed with this information, Jacques logged on to the site with that day's password. Again, everything but the face was exactly as described.

Jacques and Temp agreed that the *OhMy EAU!!* computer was changing the faces of the models. Given his computer background, Temp was impressed with the diabolical sophistication of the software that made this possible. Before he contacted Interpol, Jacques wanted to figure out if any minors were being filmed.

Chapter 113

The Canadian Connection

Jacques was close to a number of constables on the Montreal force including brothers, Claude and Julien Leblanc. He asked the brothers to meet him for a beer and some wings at Charlie's Irish Pub after their shift. When the brothers sat down and ordered, Jacques explained that he was worried the *OhMy EAU!!* retail store on Rene Levesque Boulevard might be taking advantage of younger shoppers. Over the next ten minutes he provided background on the retail store and described the loyalty club perks one of which was access to one of the larger dressing rooms. He asked the brothers to keep an eye on the store and to pay particular attention if they saw anyone that might be under sixteen. He asked them to focus on the shoppers' street clothes. The brothers agreed to help. They were more than happy to spend a little time watching young, attractive females.

The brothers surveilled the store off and on for about two weeks. One sunny afternoon in the third week, they decided to get an order of fish and chips and a couple of cokes from the restaurant across the street from *OhMy EAU!!* They sat on the outdoor patio which had a clear view of the front entrance. Just as the brothers were wrapping up their lunch, they noticed a youngish female who was the spitting image of a young perp Claude had arrested for shoplifting the previous year. The perp, Maxine, was just 16 years of age at the time.

Could that be Maxine who was walking up to the front door wearing a low-cut black, rhinestone t-shirt and skin-tight animal print jeans? If possible, she was even more beautiful than she was the previous year and might even be more beautiful than her older sister, France. The sisters looked so much alike they could have easily been mistaken for twins.

The brothers were both familiar with Maxine's older sister, France, who had just celebrated her 19th birthday with a nipple piercing. Her rap sheet was as long as her chestnut hair and included many top ten hits like possession of cocaine, soliciting, fraud, and identity theft.

Claude had busted France, barely eighteen at the time, for cocaine. As Claude got up, he said to Julien, "I've got this." He could help Jacques and perhaps even save Maxine from following in her elder sister's footsteps. Two birds, one stone. On his way to the *OhMy EAU!!* front door Claude decided his cover story would be that he was interested in purchasing some sexy lingerie for his girlfriend.

While he was browsing, Claude saw Maxine pass a loyalty card to the salesclerk—he later learned the card belonged to France. As requested, he sent Jacques a text describing what Maxine was wearing before she entered the changeroom. After he received Claude's text, Jacques texted Owen and asked if a young woman wearing the same clothes as Maxine appeared on any ubdqt.com feed. About ten minutes later, Owen confirmed that a woman wearing a rhinestone black t-shirt and animal print jeans and carrying blue and red string bikinis as well as a sheer white cover-up tunic over her left arm, had entered a change room.

After she finished trying on the suits, Maxine decided to purchase the red bikini. The clerk ran through France's loyalty card and applied the 20% discount. Maxine paid in cash.

Claude abandoned the subterfuge of wanting to purchase something for his girlfriend and followed the young woman out of the store. When they were on the sidewalk, he called her by name. "Hi Maxine, remember me? I hope you paid for your purchase."

A bit taken aback the young woman replied, "Of course."

"Do you have a receipt? Mind if I take a look into your purse and your *OhMy EAU!!* shopping bag?" Julien joined the two of them on the sidewalk.

"I've learned my lesson," Maxine said as she passed over the shopping bag and purse. "Help yourself."

While Claude peppered Maxine with questions about where she was living, with whom, and what she was doing for money, Julien searched her possessions. France's loyalty card and beginner's driver license were clearly visible when Julien flipped open her wallet. There was a striking resemblance between the two sisters—no wonder the salesclerk thought she was dealing with the older sister, France.

Julien said, "Look you've' got fake ID and while we can't find any stolen merch—we are going to keep the DL—tell your sister you lost the loyalty card—the store will give her a new one and she won't care about the DL if she has graduated up to the next level. You can go—but remember, we've got eyes on you." Claude called Jacques with his report.

The young girl moved off. When she returned home Maxine removed two other G-strings and a cosmetic set from the false bottom in her purse. She had liberated the cosmetic set from a local drug store before shopping at *OhMy EAU!!*

After he hung up with Claude, the French detective called Temp and said, "As you know, Interpol doesn't look kindly on kiddie porn and, like the U.N., has taken the position that child exploitation is a Crime Against Humanity. Maxine is a real underage person, not someone we sent in, so there is no way to claim she was entrapped. Although none of the "actors" we have seen on ubdqt.com appear to be underage, Maxine, an actual underage "victim," takes our sting to a completely different level. And where there is smoke there is probably fire, which suggests to me that there are probably more underage victims."

When Temp called Owen later that night his son confirmed that, as per Temp's request, the teenager had created a video of Maxine's time in the *OhMy EAU!!* change room which he forwarded to Jacques. Temp thanked his son and said, "Well enjoy the replay and try to change hands once in a while!" Although he was physically 3828 miles away from Temp, Owen could feel his father's knowing grin.

Chapter 114

Misha's Betrayal

Viktor Vasiliev, Chief of the Moscow Police Services, and mob boss Sergei Mikhalov had known each other since Viktor was a beat cop and while the future mob boss was still working for his father. For more than two decades, after the incident at Myaso Dichi, Sergei had paid Viktor $25,000 USD a year to call him if there was ever something he needed to know.

Sergei was happy with the return on his investment, especially because one of his twins, Dmitri, was often in trouble. The most recent incident occurred when his son rode Ambrosius Coprius, one of his polo ponies, into the Petrovsky Fountain in front of the Bolshoi Theater, then urinated on the statue of Karl Marx before he fell face down and almost drowned in the water at the base of the fountain. All of this occurred in front of the paparazzi who just happened to be there for an opening of the ballet, "Dance of the Snowflakes."

Because he was also part of the Interpol *OhMy EAU!!* task force, Viktor was privy to the exact timing of the raid and the nature of the charges—conspiracy, pornography, money laundering, identity theft, and extortion. He knew Sergei's wife owned and operated the business. Because of their long-standing, relationship, and as a professional courtesy, Viktor felt obligated to tell Sergei about the planned Interpol raid.

When Viktor called Sergei he said, "I've heard your new stallion has been delivered. I'm going to be in the Corsica area next weekend, and I wondered if you would agree to let me ride him."

For Viktor to override their normal communication channels suggested that he had something important to say. Sergei replied, "Yes, you heard right. He's a beauty. I would love for you to meet him. Why don't you join me at the Estate this weekend?"

Over drinks in the library, Viktor told Sergei that he suspected his son, Misha, was feeding information about Sergei's business interests to someone associated with the Quebec police force and he had it on good authority that a raid of fifty *OhMy EAU!!* locations was planned for November 1st. Although he was in shock, Sergei said, "I understand." The two old war horses finished their drinks and said their goodbyes. Viktor knew it was unlikely they would ever see each other again.

As soon as Viktor left, Sergei placed an ad for a handyman with magical hands on the website InterNationals.com. When The Iceman called, Sergei broke their established protocol and insisted they meet in person. When he arrived at the agreed upon meet Sergei was not surprised when a balding middle-aged accountant, with thick rimless eyeglasses, and dressed in a rumpled second-hand brown suit, sat down at his table.

Sergei didn't waste any time and as the Iceman sat down said, "I have it on good authority that on November 1st police will raid fifty *OhMy EAU!!* locations. When that happens, it will not take long to identify the various shareholders, including the Alyosha Foundation. I am the Chairman of the Alyosha Board. The President of Russia is an honorary patron and will not take kindly to having his name dragged through the mud. I will be arrested. I will not survive in prison. There are just too many people in there that want to kill me. Besides, my prostate cancer has returned, and the doctor has only given me another year. It is not worth living if all I've got to look forward to is a jail cell, a crumbling empire, and an adult diaper."

He continued, "I've had a good run. I've decided to go out in a blaze of glory. Which is why I broke protocol. I have three specific requests—the first is that you shoot my son, Misha, in front of me. The second is that you dynamite his grave three months after his funeral, while my wife Elena, and my other son, Dmitri, are sitting on the marble bench in front of his crypt. The third is that you kill me before the Interpol raid on the first.

"If you agree to do as I ask, in addition to your usual fee, I will pay you a one million USD bonus—in advance. My assassination will be your last assignment. We have done some amazing things together and I have sincerely enjoyed our collaboration."

The balding accountant agreed to the fee and the timeline, shook hands with Sergei and left the bar.

Chapter 115

Sergei's Revenge

Sergei thought Misha was in North America visiting school friends. Little did he know that Misha was in Quebec giving Jacques' team a sworn deposition.

He was aware that the only thing that would induce his son to return on short notice was if he thought something had happened to his mother or brother whom Sergei had sent on an impromptu shopping and gambling expedition to Las Vegas, Nevada. With the time change, mother and son would be offline for at least the next 18 hours. He called Misha.

"Your mother and brother have been involved in a terrible car crash, are both in a coma and the doctors don't know if they will make it. I need you at home right away. Please come. And bring your computer. There are a few things about your mother's company I want to discuss since it's doubtful she'll be capable of returning to work anytime soon or at all." When he hung up Sergei relayed the details of their meeting to The Iceman.

Of course, Misha agreed to return home, which was why he was in his father's study at their Corsica estate. It was 11:00 p.m. on October 30th. As requested, Misha brought his computer. He wasn't worried about losing any of the information or software on it. If his father destroyed his technology, it wouldn't matter –Jacques, Denzel, and Temp already had copies of everything.

Over drinks in the study, Sergei updated Misha on Elena and Dmitri's supposed prognosis. Father and son were putting on their coats to supposedly leave for the hospital when Sergei turned to Misha and said, "I know you've given me up to the police. Do you think you are smarter than I am? I am not so technologically illiterate as you assume I am.

"I knew you were stealing from your mother. I killed your goody two-shoes friend, Melodie Beaudoin, because I couldn't afford to have her tell *30 Minutes* anything about our little side business. And if it wasn't for that fluke accident, I would have killed your skinny, talentless fiancée too. I don't tolerate disloyalty. I would *never* have let you marry her." He swung around and started to walk away.

Before Misha had an opportunity to process what he had just heard, his head exploded in a red cloud, courtesy of a high velocity bullet that had been shot through the open study window. Because of the way Misha fell, the second tap, ricocheted off the side of his head and lodged in Sergei's neck. Both men went down. The Iceman doubted Sergei was dead, which meant he would have to wait for another opportunity to kill his benefactor and fulfill his final contract.

Two weeks after the hit, Misha Mikhalov was laid to rest in the family crypt, in the Novodevichy Cemetery, the most famous cemetery in Moscow. One thousand people, including the President, came to the funeral. Sergei, who was in a medically induced coma, did not attend. If he survived, the once vibrant mob boss would be confined to a wheelchair for the rest of his miserable life. The Iceman had never failed to complete his full assignment. His police sources told him that it was only a matter of months before the mob boss died of stage four prostate cancer. The Iceman decided to let nature take its course and to just focus on eliminating Elena and Dmitri.

Elena and Dmitri didn't know or didn't care about what happened to Sergei. Although they couldn't prove it, both believed that somehow, he was behind Misha's assassination. Mother and son spent many days with their arms wrapped around each other, huddled on the pink marble bench located directly outside the Mikhalov family crypt prominently located in division 2, one of the oldest parts of the Novodevichy Cemetery.

Neither Misha, Nikita Khrushchev or Boris Yeltsin (the latter two Russian leaders were buried in separate sections of the same cemetery) offered any suggestions about what Elena and Dmitri should do next. Even the birds had nothing to say. All of Moscow was shocked when, one cloudy spring afternoon, the beautiful pink marble crypt, along with the bench on which Elena was sitting, was blown to pieces. Dmitri was not with his mother at the time of the explosion. He had moved away from the pink marble bench to take a telephone call. The police did not have any clear motive or any suspects. When the bench and the crypt blew apart, and he was certain that anyone sitting on it was dead, The Iceman melted into the trees. He did not realize that Dmitri was not sitting beside his mother when it blew.

The next day, The Iceman closed the door on his modest life and told his neighbors he was retiring to Greece. He was tired of living unobtrusively and was kicking off a new first-class retirement with a trip to Bora Bora in French Polynesia. He had no specific plans after that.

Chapter 116

A New Dawn

Unfortunately for Sergei, The Iceman's bullet didn't kill him. The Russian president asked the medical staff to do everything within their power to ensure his old friend was comfortable during whatever time he had left.

Several weeks after he was admitted to The Serbsky State Hospital, Russia's leading edge research centre, Sergei had recovered enough to be brought out of his medically induced coma. Within hours, he had bitten his orderly hard enough to draw blood. Doctors increased his medications and made sure he was muzzled whenever he interacted with staff. When Sergei refused to eat, he was intubated.

Sergei told his orderly he could keep the mob boss' Patek Philippe Ref. 1518 stainless steel watch (worth $300,000 on the black market) in exchange for one simple request—to place an ad for a handyman with magical hands on the website InterNationals.com. The orderly agreed to do so, and accepted the watch. After he took possession of the watch, he immediately quit his job and moved to a different town. Had the orderly done what Sergei asked, it wouldn't have worked anyway. The Iceman couldn't care less about any of his former boss' problems.

Every other day, between the hours of 9 a.m. and 11 a.m., Dmitri, the only other family member left alive, visited Sergei in the hospital. Although he suspected his father was behind the deaths of his brother and mother, he could never get Sergei to admit that he was responsible for the hits.

After 45 days Dmitri believed it was time to formally announce his intention to take over leadership of the family business. When his father's seven lieutenants received his request for a meeting, they complied. They wondered if the old war horse had recovered enough to resume control of his multi-billion-dollar operation.

After everyone was seated around the board room table in the Corsica estate, Dmitri wheeled Sergei in. Although they understood Sergei was unlikely to recover from his assassination attempt and would probably succumb to prostate cancer within the next year, the lieutenants were still shocked by the mob boss' appearance. The normally dapper don was unshaven and in hospital pyjamas. There was an IV and a bag of some fluid taped to his left arm. Blood had darkened what looked like a turban wound around his head. While the mob boss was capable of some slurred speech, he had lost his commanding physical presence. It was lucky Sergei was strapped into his wheelchair—had he not been, his body, which was shaking like a leaf, would have fallen onto the floor.

The lieutenants all felt something akin to pity for their former leader and assumed it was only a matter of time before the old war horse died. Everyone assumed they had been called together for Sergei to pass the baton to one of them. They were taken aback when Dmitri, whom they believed was a spoiled playboy said, "As Sergei's only living son, I will be taking over the leadership of the family business. I'm seeking your unanimous support and asking for your loyalty."

The seven knew better than to argue—they all knew the violence the Mikhalov's were capable of. As Sergei lay dreaming and drooling in his wheelchair all seven of his lieutenants swore loyalty to Dmitri. Although they weren't happy with the unexpected turn of events, they all agreed the time was not yet ripe to act.

Dmitri's next act was to secure The Iceman's loyalty. He placed an ad for a handyman with "magical hands" on the website InterNationals.com. and sat back and waited for his father's hitman to contact him. In one of his lucid moments, his father had explained their communications protocol and instructed him to find the hitman and have him finish the job he had been paid so handsomely to do.

As Dmitri waited in vain for The Iceman to make contact, he had his hands full getting up to speed on their web of legal and illegal businesses. He hadn't yet figured out what to do with *OhMy EAU!!* but was confident he would do so.

Chapter 117

Unravelling

Temp sat down with Guy's father and made a strong suggestion that the best thing to do was for him to co-operate.

"What interest do you have in this matter and why should I listen to anything a Yank has to say?" Albert asked.

"I am one of Owen's dads," Temp replied. "I'm also a former director of the U.S. Treasury Department and now work with Canadian and American law enforcement. I know you operate an import/export company, that you used to have a business partner, but he died, and that the company has been operating profitably for about twelve years. I also know that you are married to Helene, a reporter with Le Parisien. You have one son, Guy, who is best friends with my son, Owen."

Temp continued, "I understand you have a subscription to ubdqt.com, a voyeur website. I'm sure you would agree with me that it is illegal to film someone without their consent. This is what is happening in the *OhMy EAU!!* dressing rooms. Even your nieces have been filmed without their knowledge or consent. For the record, I believe you got caught up in something and that before you realized what happened, you were in too deep. I know you have been threatened. My colleagues and I aren't unsympathetic."

"D'accord," Albert said, "I'll help as long as you keep my name out of your investigations and that you guarantee the safety of my family and myself."

"We can do that," said Temp.

"I want it in writing," Albert replied.

"I understand. I need your credit card number and a copy of your latest statement. Then, my colleagues and I will do what we do best—follow the money."

Albert provided a sworn statement. In it he said his business partner, Pierre, introduced him to Dmitri Mikhalov who signed him up for what he described as a little harmless fun. Shortly after Pierre made the introduction, he was killed in a gas explosion, while he was visiting a potential supplier's factory. Luckily, the partners had purchased key man insurance which meant their import/export business had enough cash to continue operations after Pierre's untimely death.

Satisfied that he had all he could get for the time being, Temp provided written assurance that he would do everything in his power to protect Albert's identity. He also asked Guy's father to continue to access the site in his usual pattern so as to not tip off the site owners.

When he returned to his hotel room, Temp called Bob, his former employer. While Bob was a bit surprised that Temp was asking for a favor, he was so disgusted by what he heard that he volunteered the services of his newest specialist—an ethical hacker who could break into any bank—even Suisse if that's where the accounts were.

"Jimmy, that's not his real name, is highly trusted by Interpol, with whom he used to work before I lured him away with a better offer. And I'm still on good terms with Alexandre, his former boss. Why don't I give them both a call and see if we can shake something loose?" Bob said.

Temp was very grateful for the introduction and told Bob to call him if there was ever anything he could do to return the favor. Bob laughed and replied, "I'm sure I'll call in that chip someday—but this is personal—I have four daughters who are frequent flyers in the Washington store."

Because it was the middle of the night in Lyon, France, Bob didn't expect Alexandre to answer his cell phone, but he did. "Hi, Alex, It's Bob Merilees. Your Kiwi drinking buddy. First let me congratulate you on the birth of your son!" Then, Bob outlined the high-level details of Temp's investigation to date. Alex said, "Sounds very interesting. Do you have additional proof? I don't have the proof but my colleague, Temp Reynolds does. Is it ok with you if I give him your telephone number?"

Alex said yes, and the two men said goodbye with the promise to get together sometime soon. After Temp briefed Alex, he encouraged him to verify the information. Alex agreed and within 48 hours had created a task force of trusted team members.

Then, he called Temp to update him on his progress. "As I told Bob I would do, I put the one surviving store owner, Dmitri Mikhalov, under 24-hour surveillance. Our team followed Dmitri to a very large estate in Corsica. Our research confirmed the estate housed a computer camp and a dormitory for the young graduates who stayed on to work for the Mikhalov's after the computer camp. Web research has confirmed that all campers who become employees receive a small salary, access to state-of-the-art computer systems, free room and board, 24/7 access to the estate's various amenities, which I understand includes a cordon bleu chef, an Olympic-sized swimming pool and a stable, a generous expense account and cash bonuses when targets were achieved. The campers also maintain an ownership position and share in the profits of anything created by them while they are on the job. Not a bad gig by anyone's standards."

"We have confirmed there is a backup generator on site to ensure the servers never go down. We can also prove that:

1) The private estate houses a state-of-the-art computer complex, and has its own servers and dormitory facilities that are similar in size and scope to a Silicon valley incubator.

2) The current owner had a brother who is now deceased, who was a very sophisticated software developer when he was alive.

3) With a high degree of certainty, we believe the owners are running a soft porn site out of the estate.

4) The estate uses an inordinate amount of electricity.

Although we've learned a lot, we still haven't figured out how many customers there are and we haven't found the end of the money trail yet."

About a week later Temp called Alex and said, "One of the things the U.S. Treasury department is very good at is getting to the bottom of money laundering. Although the crooks are all different, they have one thing in common—every one of them has a bank account and a banker."

He continued, "My friend Bob's colleague and your former employee, Jimmy, has told me that a credit card trace has revealed that funds are being deposited into a bank account in the Caribbean that was originally set up by some Panamanian lawyers. The funds are moved at least twice a week in various amounts but never more than $9,999 at the same time."

The account owner uses different accounts and banks in every transaction. Eventually, the funds return as sales to legitimate businesses such as a local bank in Corsica and a European River Cruise Line time share. The business is owned by a holding company which has four layers above it all, and that was put together by the same Panamanian law firm. Jimmy has traced ownership to the same Russian family that owns the Corsica estate."

Alex added, "Our team has also identified a person who was living well above a banker's means at the Corsica bank. When this individual was approached for some quiet questioning, he panicked. In exchange for police protection, he sang like Pavarotti. We shared this information with our global partners. Based on all of this intelligence, each partner agency will be obtaining warrants to raid the *OhMy EAU!!* stores in their respective countries."

Chapter 118

Warrants

Inspector Ravelle, a twenty-year Gendamerie nationale veteran, was waiting for magistrat Jean Luc Baptiste to read his file. The Inspector was seeking a warrant to enter the premises of *OhMy EAU!!*, Paris. The raid on the Paris store was part of a coordinated effort to conduct simultaneous raids of fifty different *OhMy EAU!!* establishments in thirty different countries. Interpol was involved.

As the Magistrat reviewed the file, he said: "This boggles the mind. Are you sure it's the stores?"

Ravelle replied. "We believe the dressing rooms in the stores contain hidden cameras behind two-way mirrors. The cameras send the video that is streaming to what we believe is a central location, where it is uploaded to ubdqt.com, a dark web site. Although subscribers can see live stream of the bodies of the patrons trying on clothes in the *OhMy EAU!!!* dressing rooms, it looks like the face of one person is cleverly substituted with the face of another."

"Is it reverse facial recognition?"

"Not really," Ravelle said. "It's more like facial obfuscation or substitution. Although the body is the same, the head and the features are not."

"How did you find this out?" the Magistrat asked.

"An adult with access to the site messed up and, unbeknownst to his father, the son gained access. Since boys will be boys, this young lad shared the site with his buddy. As they watched the live strip action, the two women on the screen had the same bodies, including distinguishable Phoenix tattoos, of his first cousins, but the faces were different. When he got home, he called his cousins and asked if they had been in a particular store on a particular day. They had been. He didn't know what to do and asked his friend if he had any ideas. That friend shared what he had seen with a sophisticated adult who had many law enforcement skills. That individual ran some blind tests and confirmed that the site was, in fact, a functioning Peeping Tom site."

"How did he do that? I'm having trouble believing this."

"One of our U.S. partner agencies brought this to our attention. He hired three different models to be "mystery shoppers" at *OhMy EAU!!* stores in Miami, San Francisco and New York. While they were in the dressing room, each of the three models was live streamed in various stages of undress on ubdqt.com. There was one consistent anomaly. Although the model's bodies were the same, their faces were different.

"Our American partner shared the information with Interpol and the police in each of the cities where *OhMy EAU!!* has a store. To control costs, it was decided to only raid 25% or fifty of the two hundred stores. As required by our international agreements, each partner agency, including the Paris Police, is responsible for completing their own due diligence and obtaining their own warrants."

Ravelle continued. "As part of our own due diligence, I hired Rocky Mountains, a stripper my wife hired for a colleague's bachelor party, and instructed her to shop at the Paris *OhMy EAU!!* location. I instructed Rocky to wear an identifiable necklace and to act in a particular way when she was in the changeroom. Before entering the changeroom, she took a selfie that showed a clear picture of her face, clothing and the three bathing suits she planned on trying on. She draped the three suits over her left arm, one of our pre-arranged signals. About ten seconds after she entered the changeroom Rocky's "live" video stream started. Each time she tried on a bathing suit, she confirmed it was her by playing with her necklace or scratching her right or left thigh. She also filmed everything from her cell phone. We have a copy. To confirm that this was not an isolated event tied to a particular location, I hired Rocky's friend, Bebe Doll, another stripper, to shop at *OhMy EAU!!* St. Tropez with the same result."

"Why didn't your friend just download the video?"

"We couldn't find any trace of the site on our friendly's computer—the site URL "spirals" and there are many blocks. From what we can tell the web site won't allow downloads, but we won't know for certain until we have had a chance to have the hardware and the software examined by our IT experts. We have studied all of the video evidence at least five times and there was no trace of Rocky's or Bebe's actual faces. We did, however, notice a very slight difference, where the movement of the body didn't quite seem to line up with the movement of the head. In other words, the onscreen heads of our mystery shoppers were different than the actual heads of Rocky Mountains and Bebe Doll. But the differences were almost imperceptible and someone watching would have to be very astute to notice any difference at all. Two other things I should mention. Each stripper had a temporary tattoo of a different animal on the opposite shoulder. The live stream picked up both of the temporary tattoos. It is also worth mentioning that based on the cell phone images, the background wallpaper in the change room doesn't appear to match the background wallpaper in the actual Paris and St. Tropez change rooms. In other words, both the customers' faces and the distinctive wallpaper background in the changerooms are being switched. I have never seen anything like this—*OhMy EAU!!*'s technology is really sophisticated."

"Are there any under-age kids in the video?" the Magistrat asked.

"Not the ones we've seen. It should be noted however, that one of our Canadian partners identified an underage actor in the Montreal location and they are handling that on their side of the pond. Our best guess is that the system tries to eliminate the under eighteen crowd as the site owner probably knows there is a high level of extra scrutiny on under-age sites and the risk is just too high. Although well hidden, we believe this group has been operating for at least four years and until now, because no laws appeared to be broken, there have been no enforcement measures."

"Let me play devil's advocate. How is privacy compromised?"

"The privacy of the person in the change room is compromised because he or she is being filmed without their consent. If the person in the changeroom was your wife or daughter, I'm sure you would be concerned. The strippers couldn't hear any technology being activated so we assume that the facial exchange software is always running."

"Does it look like any of the customers or mystery shoppers participated willingly?"

"Our mystery shoppers were told we hired them to assess if the brand's high standards were being observed," Ravelle replied. "We don't believe any of the customers know they are being filmed. There is a CCTV warning at the front door and cameras at the front entrance, lots of stores have that, and it's not considered an invasion of privacy as it is posted and the cameras are visible. We just don't see how that warning could be stretched to include hidden cameras behind two-way mirrors in the changerooms. We also have a copy of the membership application for the rewards program. It says *OhMy EAU!!* can use certain personal data for statistical and promotional purposes. It does not say the information will only be used in aggregation although that might create a "release" of some sort."

Ravelle continued, "It's also worth mentioning that while waiting for a change room to become available, the salesclerk gave Rocky a bit of a commercial. She told Rocky the membership base was huge, 30% of their traffic is from repeat customers, and sales per square foot are almost twice as high as those at most other retail establishments. The clerk also reminded Rocky about the plethora of membership perks including extra discounts when a member shops in an *OhMy EAU!!* store in another city. So, there is lots of worldwide traffic. And with *OhMy EAU!!* stores operating in many different countries, in many different time zones, this is basically a 24/7 operation which makes it a great illegal revenue generator."

"I understand you have retained the services of a defense attorney to create an amicus outlining the privacy issues. What has this person said about privacy?"

"Her report can be found on Pages A-14 to A-92. According to the defense attorney the person is being filmed without their permission in the perceived privacy of their change room. If that person was a relative of yours, I'm sure that you would be pretty concerned that he or she could be identified. All mystery shoppers on shore and off have confirmed that they could not hear any technology being activated when they were in the dressing room, and our best guess is that the software is always running."

"Who owns the retail business? Is it private?"

"It's owned by Elena Mikhalov and her twin sons, Misha and Dmitri. Two of the three, Elena and Misha, are dead. I also believe a family foundation has some shares. There is a rumor that Elena's husband, Sergei, is mobbed up, but so far, it's only a rumor. Sergei is in the hospital recovering from a gunshot wound and prostate cancer. His prognosis isn't good. So, it's only a matter of time before Sergei is no longer our problem. Although the other twin, Dmitri, is a bit of a scallywag, Sergei, Misha, and Elena have never even had a parking ticket.

"I've heard enough. I'm in agreement and will issue a search warrant. When are you planning to do the raid?"

"As you know, Interpol has no police officers or powers of its own and its role is basically as quarterback for the many multi-national operations on its books, including Operation Voyeur. Participation in these joint projects is voluntary. Although foreigners are welcome to ask another country's police to arrest someone or to interview a witness, the host country is not under any obligation to do so. We are trying to coordinate at the same time around the world, so that the *OhMy EAU!!* stores that operate in different time zones don't get tipped off."

"Once the word gets out, this wonderful business will be destroyed. That's really too bad. My wife and our two daughters love to shop there and have been to several fashion shows."

"I'll give you a heads up so that you can ensure your family members aren't anywhere near the stores when the raid goes down."

"I would appreciate that."

Chapter 119

The Raid

Once the search warrants for *OhMy EAU!!!* in the UK, France and the United States were secured the information was passed along to the other twenty-seven participating countries so that the raids of the retail stores could be coordinated worldwide with the raid on the Corsica estate.

At precisely twelve noon in London, England each of the fifty stores and the Corsica estate were simultaneously raided. When Inspector Ravelle who was responsible for obtaining warrants in France and Corsica, and the local police arrived at the estate, the guard at the front gate contacted Dmitri for instructions.

Dmitri asked the guard to put him on speaker phone. He said, "Go away." Then he took a breath and said, "Do you know who you are messing with? Our family is very close friends with President Vladimir Alexandroff. I'm sure his excellency wouldn't look kindly on someone hassling his friends. This is your one and only warning. If you continue this attack on my privacy, I'll use deadly force."

Inspector Ravelle replied, "If you don't open the gates, we will pull them down. And then we will pull you down. We are armed. And Dmitri, this is *your* first and your *only* warning."

Undeterred, Dmitri said, "My team is better armed than your goons. You are trespassing and this is private property."

"You have five minutes to come out voluntarily. After that we will drag you out."

He turned to his lieutenant and said, "Hook up the chains and be ready. Once we disable the gates, make sure the armored truck goes in first. And keep behind it in case Dmitri opens fire."

The moment the truck moved past the gate's entrance they were fired upon. But the team was prepared. Multiple smoke bombs masked their advance, and several groups were able to successfully advance to the main house.

As the police advanced, a team member noticed that there was a helicopter firing up on the helipad located on the roof of the main house. White hat cop hackers had intercepted communications that indicated Dmitri planned to land on his yacht, the *Lady Elena* that was docked in Port De Bonifacio and communicated this information to Inspector Ravelle. He radioed dispatch and asked them to connect him to the navy. Within minutes he was conversing with a coast guard captain and a navy captain who were twenty knots apart. Both were familiar with the Corsica estate. "Let him land on the yacht. We want this guy alive," the Inspector said.

But their intelligence was not good. Rather than heading for the *Lady Elena*, Dmitri's helicopter made a wide pass away from the estate and headed north and then east. Ravelle realized that precious moments were being lost. Fortunately, the quick-thinking navy captain launched his own military chopper. While Dmitri was using a customized chopper, it was no match for the coast guard's state-of-the-art military equipment.

The navy chopper easily gained on Dmitri and forced his chopper to the ground. Dmitri jumped out and made a run for it. Two navy marines fired over his head and to each side.

"Whatever you do, don't kill Dmitri," was heard clearly over their headsets.

Although Dmitri was in good shape, he was no match for the younger marines who were gaining on him. Dmitri was winged in the shin by one of their shots. When the bullet made contact, he crashed to the ground. From a sitting position, he aimed his automatic pistol at his pursuers. He successfully winged the first marine and incapacitated the second.

Emboldened by his success, Dmitri lurched to his feet and fired off another burst. Because he was focused on his pursuers, he never noticed the helicopter pilot trailing the marines. The pilot raised his pistol and winged Dmitri on the other shin.

"Don't move," the pilot screamed and held the gun level with Dmitri's chest while the less injured marine pointed at his head.

Back at the compound, the computer workers were co-operating and the police gathered a treasure trove of other information. But by far, the biggest prize of the night was the server containing the web site and source code for ubdqt.com.

After the raid, the *OhMy EAU!!* retail employees were in shock. The police took down the employees' statements, seized their phones, then let them go with a warning to stay in town. After the successful execution of the mission, Alex called Temp to update him and Bob. "Wow, Corsica police hit the big bad guy jackpot today."

After Alex signed off, Bob said, "A word please, Temp. Glad I could be part of this. By the way, I've checked out your friend, Jacques Beaudoin. If you can help me land him, I'd be willing to consider reinstating you. What do you say? Although I can probably bring Jacques on board without you, I'm assuming because he knows and trusts you, your endorsement of St. Clair would be beneficial."

Chapter 120

The Interrogation

Dmitri was handcuffed and pushed unceremoniously into the back of an unmarked police car and hauled away. Since all of his family members were either dead or incapacitated, the remaining twin was the only one who could be held responsible for all of his family's crimes. At the station, Dmitri asked for permission to use the telephone. Permission was granted. Dmitri called the high-priced criminal lawyer they had on retainer. The lawyer also retained local Corsican counsel—a man with a strong background in dealing with the local police on behalf of some other fairly notorious mob bosses.

The local police had anticipated this move and brought in their own top gun, Giuseppe Stalone, a man with no family to threaten, no life partner, and whose mission was sticking it to the mob. Having lost his father, a judge, his mother, grandparents, older sister, and her three children, when they were all massacred by the mob at a family reunion—Giuseppe lost an eye during the melee—the "advocat" had devoted the rest of his life to eradicating the mob.

Giuseppe identified the perps, made men from the Bianchi crime family and successfully prosecuted the case. The judge who heard the case and sentenced Benito Bianchi to thirty years in prison with no possibility of parole, met his demise through a car bomb.

One of the cops who helped Giuseppe on the original bust was the current chief of police, Marco Sapi—Marco was a young police detective at the time. His girlfriend and several of her colleagues were catering the reunion and were killed when the bullets started flying.

Giuseppe, who was fifteen years old at the time his family was massacred, leaned on Marco who encouraged the bright youth to consider a career in policing. When Giuseppe joined the force, the two men spent much of their free time together. Neither married, but it wasn't because they feared commitment. Both men had suffered at the hands of the mob and weren't' willing to have a loved one be used as leverage or cannon fodder.

Before the interrogation started, Dmitri took his lawyer aside and said to him, "I need to be protected. I need a deal that gets me protection now and also gets me hidden forever. I have a ton to trade but I also know there is at least one very lethal person who has every reason to want me dead as soon as possible. I know that person will come to shut me up and may well be unstoppable."

The local lawyer pulled out his phone and called the lead lawyer.

"Our client is panicking."

The lead lawyer responded, "He's scared for his life, and he should be. I'll be there in less than five hours. See if you can talk Marco Sapi into providing a safe house and around the clock security."

"That should be easy enough," the second lawyer said. "The police are highly concerned that Dmitri has associates who have a lot to lose and who will want to silence him."

Meanwhile, Bob had provided contact information for Giuseppe, which was why Temp was on a three-way call with Alex, Bob's Interpol friend, and Giuseppe, the driven cop.

"Hi, Alex and Giuseppe. Temp here. I know you're busy so I'm going to cut right to the chase. I'd really love to come over and interview this guy."

Alex replied, "That's highly irregular, Temp. Although you have the necessary skill set, the last time I looked, you are no longer employed by the US government and you're still a civilian."

Temp countered. "If it wasn't for my intelligence, Operation Voyeur would never have happened. The arrest and prosecution of a top mob boss, with secrets, money and blood on his hands will give you both street cred for life. I'm pretty sure Dmitri's father, Sergei, had my girlfriend, Melodie

Beaudoin, a language teacher and physiotherapist, assassinated. I need to know which one of his goons was responsible."

Before he could respond, Giuseppe was interrupted by the local lawyer. "Temp, I have to put you on hold for a minute." The lawyer explained to Ravelle, "We need to protect Dmitri because he knows where the literal and figurative bodies are buried. Can I count on your support when I make a formal request to Marco Sapi, the Chief of Police? Dmitri believes that there is someone on the way to kill him and is concerned for his life."

With the support of Alex and Giuseppe, the police chief agreed to the local lawyer's request and granted Temp limited access. The chief replied, "I'll agree to both of your requests. Temp Reynolds is a skilled professional like you and has in fact provided crucial intelligence on Operation Voyeur. Just make sure he is never alone with the perp. I believe he has a personal as well as a professional interest in Dmitri."

When the local lawyer left, the inspector, took Temp off hold and said, "OK. The police have agreed to let you talk to Dmitri. Please get here asap. I'll book you into a local guest house. Bring your bathing suit—time moves more slowly here."

Temp said thanks and booked an Air France trip to Corsica.

After he hung up with Alex and Giuseppe, Marco sprang into action. He ordered his team to rotate safe houses and guard teams. He also asked his superiors for more money—keeping Dmitri safe was going to be very expensive as well as dangerous. 12 hours later, when Temp arrived at the police station, Dmitri's interrogation was already underway. Dmitri had played a lot of cards in his life, and he gave up each piece of information slowly and strategically. Like all good negotiators, he had a deal bottom line and wanted to make sure he had some cards left if he ever needed to use them.

On the surface Dmitri looked like a directionless playboy squandering family money and partying till dawn with more drugs and booze than common sense—but appearances can be deceiving. Many drinks were poured without booze and the drugs were often palmed or hidden in his pockets. As the real heir to the throne, he was always on the job. Dmitri had been groomed and nurtured in ways that Misha had not been. Although he assumed his father's mantle willingly, he knew one person in this world wanted him dead more than anyone else, and that man was his father's hit man. Dmitri assumed his father's cleaner was responsible for the deaths of his mother and brother, which meant it was only a matter of time before The Iceman came looking for him. Dmitri knew far too much to leave alive.

Chapter 121

The Iceman Cometh

Two people converged on Dmitri's location—one was there to extract information from him, and one was there to kill him. Each had close to the same level of technical skill. However, the one with the most to lose had an advantage—his continued peaceful retirement and perhaps even his life.

The Iceman had been in contact with Sergei's police informant, Viktor Vasilyevich, who came through with the safe house location. But the "kill and escape" window of opportunity was limited and there was minimum time to complete the meticulous preparation for which he was famous. He knew he was rushing and that made him nervous.

The Mikhalov hits were supposed to be his swan song. Unfortunately, he only injured rather than killed his former boss, Sergei, and Dmitri was not with his mother when he blew apart the pink marble bench she was sitting on outside the Mikhalov family crypt.

Although he was pissed that his perfect record was tarnished by his failure to complete his last assignment, he continued with his plans to retire and had been enjoying a quiet life full of health and wealth in Bora Bora. When he first started his retirement journey, he didn't have any close friends or lovers. The Iceman didn't care. He concentrated on fitness, discovered he enjoyed music and food and kept his mind sharp by reading newspapers in five different languages every day. He also started taking cooking classes and was learning how to prepare Polynesian food in a traditional pit oven.

One evening after cooking class, he noticed Luna, a fellow classmate, smiling at him. Despite his cautious nature, he found himself returning her smile. The Iceman wondered if a love interest was the missing piece in his otherwise serene retirement life.

The Iceman was a successful killer because he knew how to compartmentalize his deeds. He did not have regrets and never woke up in agony over any of his past kills. Guilt was for the weak. And he was anything but weak. For the next three months The Iceman and Luna practiced their cooking and love-making skills. Time passed quickly.

Everything was perfect until The Iceman saw an article in Le Parisienne that indicated Dmitri Mikhalov, the heir to *OhMy EAU!!* was in police custody. Then and there, he decided that it was a matter of self-preservation, that he cleaned up the mess he had inadvertently created when he failed to kill the mob boss and both of his twin sons. When he was done, if she would have him, he planned to marry and build a wonderful new life with Luna.

He told Luna he had some family business he needed to take care of and would return in a couple of days. The Iceman flew to Paris and rented a car under one identity. He hid the car in some brush 500 meters from the main thoroughfare. He changed into another disguise and caught a bus downtown. Then, he took a ferry over to the island of Corsica.

He hid behind a dumpster located three hundred meters away from the Corsica police station. From logic and experience he knew that the station would be heavily guarded. He also assumed that the cops were planning on moving Dmitri to a safe house. That's what he would have done. The Iceman decided that his best chance to make the kill was during the transfer.

The police station had two sides, as well as heavily guarded front and rear entrances. The station roof was connected to the roof of an adjoining building. The west entrance opened onto an alley. There were 3 unmarked police vehicles parked nose to tail in the alley. From his spot behind the dumpster, he observed each hooded and cuffed prisoner being frog marched into the back seat of a different police cars. All of the men appeared to be about the same height and build as Dmitri.

At the mouth of the alley, the three cars took off in different directions, one turned right, one turned left and the other continued straight. With no eyes on the inside, The Iceman didn't know which of the three cars held Dmitri which meant he had to kill 3 hooded passengers and 3 armed drivers in about twenty-five seconds. The noise would attract armed reinforcements. There must be some way to reduce the number of targets or to change the location of the battlefield.

That night The Iceman went to the local library. Using one of the public computers he studied maps of the downtown area. He identified three potential escape routes for himself. He also went onto the local police web site to see if he could identify any of the officers that he had seen in the alley. That's when he found the piece of information that would give him an edge.

Constable Fabio Ferro had joined the Corsica police force after his professional driving career was cut short by a horrific crash. Although he still drove for fun, his injuries didn't allow him to race professionally. A wall full of testimonials and awards for heroism and quick-thinking validated the veracity of his career choice. His most recent commendation was for saving a choking baby.

The article also noted that the Constable's dad, a former Formula One champion, had taught him how to drive. His excellent driving skills had been used to good effect on many other occasions, including the time he chased down a very nasty armed robber traveling at high speeds in difficult driving conditions. Given his extraordinary level of skill, The Iceman believed that Fabio would be the cop tasked with driving Dmitri to the safe house.

When he was doing his research in the library The Iceman was not tempted to look at the help wanted ads—he was in Corsica to clean up loose ends and had no interest in resuming his previous career. He never saw the ad posted by Dmitri's lawyer for a handyman with magical hands.

First thing the next morning, The Iceman rented another car and parked it a couple of streets over from the police station. He took out his burner phone and called up a local tour company and arranged for a private island tour. He needed a flexible start time and was prepared to pay extra to get it.

He was burning through a lot of aliases and disguises and hopefully was not going to need more than what he had brought with him. Disguises were expensive and while he had lots of money, his cash had to last for a lifetime.

Chapter 122

Working the Angles

Dmitri had been ferried from the safe house to the police station for another day of questioning. In the morning, the out-of-town lawyer arrived. The local lawyer and the out-of-town lawyer conferred with Dmitri and with each other. Then, Temp arrived.

The next day and after Dmitri's third night at a different safe house, Temp was given the first interview slot. With a senior detective sitting beside him and Dmitri's out-of-town lawyer sitting at the table with Dmitri, Temp started the questioning. At first, Dmitri wasn't sure why Temp was there. After several preliminary questions, it became clear the American was trying to figure out who had killed a woman named Melodie Beaudoin and if the Mikhalov's had ordered the hit.

Dmitri knew his father had instructed The Iceman to kill Melodie because he didn't want any media scrutiny of *OhMy EAU!!* It was a big card to give up. "Ok" Dmitri said. "I'll give you the name and the description of my father's hit man and two other jobs I know he completed for us. I never learned his real name. My father always referred to him as The Iceman.

"If my father's hitman is not here already, he will be here soon. I believe my twin brother, Misha, betrayed my father. He wouldn't be able to get over my twin's disloyalty and I wouldn't put it past him to tell his hitman to take everyone out. The hits on my mother and brother were successful. The only reason I'm still here is because I had stepped away from the bench outside my brother's tomb, where I had been sitting with my mother, to answer a call from my bookie. I feel it in my bones that The Iceman is on his way to finish the job. I have lots of information I can share but won't be able to provide any of it if I'm dead.

"I have two examples that prove my intelligence is legitimate. First example, Scotland Yard has been working on the murder of a judge for three years now. The only people who know what killed the judge are me, The Iceman, the police officers working the case, and the coroner. The authorities deliberately withheld the cause of death from the media. The autopsy identified two causes of death, with one being the most likely. I can confirm they are right. Second example, remember the CEO of Emeralds International that business Sergei tried to buy but was rebuffed. The Iceman killed the CEO with a potassium overdose and then bribed the coroner to say that he died of a heart attack. Authorities don't think he was murdered but I can confirm that he was.

Dmitri continued, "It is probably wise to let you know what you are up against. The Iceman never uses the same kill method twice. He always works alone. His planning and level of detail are first class—he could plan a rocket ship to the moon and identify three different escape routes if he got stuck. No one really knows who he is—he's been at least 50 people that I'm aware of so it's impossible to profile him. He has a thousand faces and can look like a woman in one moment and a man the next. He has never been caught and to the best of my knowledge, his fingerprints and DNA are not in the system."

"I believe he's coming to shut me up. He's my worst nightmare and I'm his because I'm a witness for the authorities who want to cut his retirement short. That is why I'm prepared to trade my life and my freedom for his. In exchange for my information, I want long-term protection, a new identity, and access to my personal funds at the Suisse Bank."

But neither the out-of-town lawyer or Temp had the authority to make a deal with Dmitri. The only people who could make a deal were behind the two-way mirror. Temp and the out-of-town lawyer left the interrogation room and walked over to a secondary break out room where they were joined by Giuseppe, Marco and the head prosecutor.

Temp recognized there was much more on the line than figuring out who killed Melodie and that he had to tread carefully. The head prosecutor turned to Giuseppe and Marco and said, "Perhaps we shouldn't go through channels—if Dmitri is right The Iceman must have someone on the inside and we don't want that person to know that we know. At least not yet."

Temp said, "I have a trusted connection."

Giuseppe laughed, "Of course you do. And we would be most grateful to find out who that is. But Temp, and I say this with the utmost respect and gratitude for your help thus far, you are a civilian and it's personal for you. If this is as big as you have suggested, it's time for you to step away and to trust us to take it from here."

Temp knew they were right. Time to turn his attention to something he was trained to do—get into the mind of the Mikhalov's hitman and figure out how The Iceman was likely to take out Dmitri. Then he could share this information with the authorities. He turned to Giuseppe, Marco and the head prosecutor and said, "I'll meet you back here at the end of the day and we can debrief once Dmitri is back at a safe house."

It had been an intense morning for everyone, and Temp was feeling a little jet lagged. He decided to get a coffee and clear his head. Two hundred yards away from the police station was a café that had been a consumer's choice pick for their coffee and croissants. He ordered a double espresso and sat down. It was time to focus. In one way he respected the ingenuity and the intellect of his opponent.

Four pieces of information deserved further study. Based on the not-so-shocking revelation from Dmitri, he now understood that The Iceman was a disguise and escape specialist, who used a different MO every time he was activated for a hit, and who was not in the system. It would be challenging to catch a wily opponent who was basically a ghost.

He refocused his mind on the planning pieces—his opponent had very little time to plan the op including escape routes. The cleanest, and fastest way to kill someone from a distance is to use a rifle for the hit.

Temp made a long list of questions in his head and called Jacques who was both happy to help 'noodle' the issues and pleased to hear there was a potential turn in the case. "Call me back in 20," said Jacques. "I want to be looking at the town on Google earth when we talk. Temp walked the mile back to his guest house. When he was settled, he called Jacques.

"Ok," Jacques said, "Let's start from the top as they say." They both laughed. With military precision, Temp summarized the interview with Dmitri and his assessment of The Iceman's potential strategy. When Temp was finished speaking, Jacques landed in exactly the same spot as Temp—Sergei's hitman was probably going to shoot Dmitri. "The Iceman would be rushed and would not have the time to do any meticulous planning. We both agree that escape routes will determine mission success," Jacques added.

Temp said, "At some point within a two-hour window the locals will move Dmitri to a safe house. Giuseppe and Marco are being extremely cautious. They will dress Dmitri and the two decoys in the exact same clothes, hood them, and then load three different vehicles. As before, each car will go in a different direction."

Then, Jacques and Temp studied Google earth on their computers and independently determined the most likely position for the kill shot. Again, they both landed on the same spot—an elevated door stoop hidden behind the dumpster on the same side of the west door of the police station. That location offered a clear shot from 150 meters—an easy shot for an expert marksman.

"If there are three of them how will the assassin know which one to shoot?" Jacques asked. "If he shoots the first one out of the door, I'm assuming Giuseppe and Marco will ensure the others stay inside the police station."

"Yes," Temp replied. "If the shooter waits until the two decoys and Dmitri are all outside the building, I'm assuming at least one passenger, hopefully not Dmitri, will be shot. The others will take cover while Giuseppe and Marco and the other police officers return fire. I'm assuming their officers are adequate but not expert marksmen.

Chapter 123

Flaw in the Ointment

Jacques said, "Flaw in the ointment." Temp laughed. "Don't you mean fly in the ointment?"

"No," Jacques said. "When I used to run my theories by Melodie she would say flaw in the ointment as a joke! Since this is as much about her as it is in taking down a voyeur site, let's call our operation, "Flaw in the Ointment."

After an hour of noodling the problem, all of the scenarios they dreamed up offered good escape routes. Given that all of the nearby shops, stores and restaurants had front and back entrances that opened directly onto the alley, escape was almost guaranteed.

Temp thanked Jacques for his time and said that he was going to mull over their conversation. They agreed to touch base before Temp went back to the police station where he planned to share his theories with the rest of the law enforcement team.

Before he landed on his preferred scenario, Temp decided to walk the alley and assess the vantage point from behind the dumpster. Could someone have the same idea? Temp saw someone behind the dumpster and that person was leaning on his elbows and had a coat pulled over his head in exactly the same spot he and Jacques had identified. He felt and saw the person take a deep breath. As a trained shooter himself, he knew it was going down. He ran towards the shooter.

Chapter 124

The Confrontation

Temp was unarmed. He knew if he yelled, the shooter would probably be able to get at least one shot off, which meant Temp had to knock the shooter off balance before he managed to kill Dmitri. He stopped long enough to pick up a loose stone. While continuing to run forward, he threw it hard. The stone hit the shooter's ear and the gun discharged. Temp kept running forward. Although he was armed with little more than his balls and his brains, Temp was determined to take the shooter down. He took a breath, hit the ground and rolled towards the shooter's feet. He connected. The shooter went down.

As he stood up Temp realized the shooter was also on his feet and fighting back. Temp took a quick hit to his jaw and countered with a well-placed shot to his opponent's eye which landed, but only managed to make the shooter flinch. Before Temp could get in another shot, he was hit across the head twice more. The speed at which the blows were delivered was extraordinary. He blinked once, hit the deck, and passed out.

After he knocked down Temp, The Iceman scooped up the rifle shell, tore down the collapsible rifle and put the pieces up his sleeves and down his pant legs. Before he left, and once he had resolved to abandon the op, he deposited the pieces in 7 different trash containers well away from the Airbnb. He threw the unused bullets and the empty shell casings into the ocean.

He also destroyed the hard drive of his laptop by driving over it in the car and burned the passports and related identity and credit cards. The police were able to trace the credit card used to pay for the Airbnb to an account in a Suisse bank. The Airbnb account was brand new, and the email account used to open it had been deactivated.

Sometime later Temp woke up. He lay with his eyes open for a minute assessing his circumstances. With a start, he realized he was in a hospital bed. From a distance, he heard a calming voice say, "Hello, my name is nurse Michael and I'm glad to see you are awake. How do you feel?"

Temp found his own voice and croaked out an answer. "Sore, my head hurts."

"Not surprising. Your head took more than one blow," nurse Michael gently said. "If you like, I can give you something for the pain."

"Not yet. I need to know what happened first."

The nurse called a number he'd written on a piece of paper. He handed the phone to Temp who pressed "send." A male voice answered. "Temp is that you?" It was Inspector Ravelle.

"Yes," Temp replied.

"We are glad to have you back with us," said Ravelle. "It seems …"

Before he could finish his sentence, Temp interrupted him. "Is Dmitri still alive?" he asked.

"Yes!" said the inspector emphatically. The good news is the shot went high and the shooter missed. The bad news is we didn't catch the shooter. Dmitri is convinced that it was his father's hitman. Did you get a look at him, Temp?"

"Not really, his face was partially covered—did the security cameras catch anything?

"No, the alley at that end has no camera. We think he ran past you, turned left and went into a back door of a restaurant fifty metres or so down the alley. The sous chef said a man wearing a hat and a scarf knocked her over as he ran past. It all happened so quickly she really didn't get a good look.

"A line cook who was coming out of the employee change room believes he saw the back of the head of someone with long red hair running through the kitchen and heading towards the front door. The person was almost at the front door when he turned, and the line cook also caught a glimpse of a scraggly red beard. But the only person with a beard we saw after the incident was a priest going into the church.

"A local bus driver dropped a tourist out near the birding area, but he didn't have red hair or a red beard. We searched the area but didn't find anything. The shooter is definitely a master of disguise. He or she managed to change his appearance at least three times in about five minutes.

"We stumbled across a fresh hole, with a shirt and scarf in it, but that's it. We arrived probably ten minutes after the shooter and set up a roadblock on each of the four roads leading away from that area and the alley, but our roadblocks only managed to inconvenience the locals. We also searched every vehicle within a two-block radius. We have concluded that the shooter beat the roadblock. We've activated our official and unofficial sources in the surrounding towns but haven't yet received any actionable intelligence."

"Maybe the shooter doubled back," Temp said.

"Good point. As a preventative measure, we will move Dmitri to another safe house in another town this evening."

Chapter 125

An Active Situation

The Iceman's left eye hurt and was a bit blurry—he assumed the person that hit him must have had some military training or spent some time in a boxing or MMA ring. He blinked and acknowledged his opponent's skill—it had been a long time since anyone had gotten close enough to deliver such an impactful punch!

The Iceman recognized that his lack of preparedness was a big vulnerability. He always made it a point to know as much about his target as he could. Since he was often required to outsmart the police, he had studied them extensively and knew how they were likely to respond. But something else was bothering him. And then it clicked. He knew that face from a photo in a filigreed silver frame he observed on Melodie Beaudoin's bedside table. He assumed the man in the photo was either a relative or a romantic partner. Either way, his presence at the scene looked and felt "personal."

The officers predictably returned Dmitri to the police station. That delay bought The Iceman the time he needed to circle back, "borrow" a car and wait for the police to move Dmitri to a new safe house. When the police made their move, he just followed the lead car to the new location. Two hours later The Iceman checked into an Airbnb conveniently located five doors down the street from the safe house. It was a remote check-in, so he did not meet or interact with anyone. He powered up his laptop and started to plan three different escape routes.

Chapter 126

New Plans

Temp woke up after a well-needed nap. He let his mind wander and an hour later he came up with a new plan. At his request, Nurse Michael, who was working a double shift, loaned Temp his personal cell phone. Temp called Inspector Ravelle. Pretty soon Giuseppe, Marco and the Inspector were all clustered around his bedside. Ravelle's idea was to have the lead car driven by one of his cops who used to be a part-time professional race car driver, from the set of the movie "Wild Card", act as a diversion.

"Let me think out loud here. The shooter may not have figured out how we know that he's here to kill Dmitri. He may not even care. Why don't we leave Dmitri as bait at the safe house? Put your best cops with bullet proof vests and some fire power into the three cars. Let's have a mouse with teeth. I suspect our shooter isn't used to being set up or watched—Dmitri has told us that besides being very dangerous, The Iceman is always in control. In fact, we believe he is so skilled, he could easily get off three shots which means the lives of the stunt driver, our officers and their respective decoys are in jeopardy. The only upside is the shooter will reveal his location."

"OK," said Inspector Ravelle. I'll see if I can get three brave volunteers and we'll see if we can't smoke this Iceman out."

Temp suggested the team run a series of zig zags with the drivers crisscrossing each other at very high speeds. "Our ultimate objective is to protect Dmitri—if we capture or kill The Iceman—that's a bonus," Temp said.

"If we run the zig zags right and the shooter falls for our ruse, he'll give up. Even if he doesn't and goes to the safe house, Dmitri will be in a bullet proof safe room. The Iceman knows it would be suicide to try and storm that particular castle," added Temp.

"We will only need a few extra men—chances are this guy is working alone—Dmitri says that's the way he likes to work," Ravelle said. "We also understand from Dmitri that while he worked for Sergei, The Iceman infiltrated many a prepared "fortress." Dmitri believes it would be a mistake to underestimate either his resolve or his skill," he added.

With that, Giuseppe, Marco and Inspector Ravelle left with the promise that they would let Temp know how it all went down.

Inspector Ravelle added, "We are going to see if we can work out where The Iceman is staying—there are no hotels close by. Don't worry Temp, we'll get the job done. Just try and rest and leave it to us."

Temp reluctantly agreed. The "Secretariat" was bushed and needed to sleep.

The Iceman was also in planning mode. Over the past three days he had managed to get in twelve hours of rejuvenating sleep, exactly what he needed. His preparations and his mind were now crystal clear and he was ready to focus on the problem at hand.

The night before he had stolen a car and at 8 a.m. the next morning, drove it to the long-term parking at Ajaccio Campo dell'Oro Airport. The Iceman took the free shuttle to the VIP hangar where a local pilot was waiting for his private aerial tour of the coast. He planned to get off of the island by boat. A Google search identified three marinas where a private vessel could be hired and he wanted to identify the best option. After the tour he took the shuttle back to the long-term parking and stole another car. He then returned to his Airbnb and waited for signs of movement in the safe house.

He observed three unmarked police cars arrive at the safe house. Three drivers got out and stood by their cars and three hooded people were led to the cars. They were all wearing the same clothes and were more or less the same height and build as Dmitri. Then, he noticed their shoes. No one was wearing the same shoes as Dmitri—Julius, Nike's Black Wide Sole Combat Boots, that cost his father about USD $1925 as a birthday gift. He recognized the brand because he owned a pair.

The Iceman mumbled to himself. "They either think I'm around or they're being cautious. As he wandered over to the bathroom located at the side of the house, he noticed that the three unmarked police cars were zig zagging through the neighborhood. But that didn't fool him. The shoes told him that Dmitri was still inside the safe house.

Chapter 127

Working the Odds

The Iceman pondered the situation. Was there an extra analytical brain in that police station? It certainly seemed so. Could that be the person that hit him? It was clear the police knew he would try and take Dmitri out.

Getting to Dmitri in the open was The Iceman's preferred and the cleanest option for the kill. But the cops kept their target safe in the easily defended police station or at a safe house. Whether he made the hit in the open or somehow got to Dmitri in the station, he knew his odds of success were extremely low. He also knew he would have to make a move soon. The longer he delayed acting increased the chances of capture. It was clear there were only two moves: leave or quickly go after the target.

It turned out Dmitri had given the police too much credit—they hadn't even thought about the boots. What they did know was that, sooner or later, The Iceman would have to make a move. Dmitri was in a Kevlar vest and there were seven, heavily armed, battle-tested officers protecting his cell. Moreover, the cell itself was located at the rear of the station behind two front steel doors and the cell door could only be opened by a card reader and an iris scan. The doors also prevented direct enemy fire from a distance.

The Iceman was betting that the police knew just enough about him to conclude that he was probably responsible for a number of unsolved homicides and his capture would mean an automatic promotion for the lucky officer. He assumed Dmitri was singing, but whether like a canary or an Aquatic Warbler was anyone's guess. It didn't really matter. Anything that Dmitri gave them was too much information for a man who wanted to stay a ghost.

The Iceman played it all back and forth in his mind. Logic told him to leave and find another time. This opportunity had been ideal in one way—a quick hit on a what was (until today) a relatively unprepared team. For the first time in his professional career, he was not certain about what to do. He didn't have any specialized equipment, and there was limited time to prepare. If he could make it through the sally port unscathed, he knew he would be met with armed resistance from a thick blue line. Lousy odds.

Although he didn't have many moves, he identified two potential openings. One was that every hour at least one person came out front for a smoke and the second was the cleaning team arrived at noon. It had been four hours since the convoy of cars had left. If he could hang on one day longer, he might be able to exploit the cleaning staff or the smokers and use one or all of them as human shields. He assumed the cleaning staff were there every day, but he wasn't certain. One thing he did know was that smokers took cigarette breaks multiple times every day which is why he decided that the smokers held the key to his success.

"I don't know everything about my enemy," he thought, "and that's a lesson my mentor drilled into me. Even if you assume they are better than you, you don't know how much better which means that you don't know how to counter their strengths because you don't know what they are. You also haven't found their weaknesses and made a structured and meticulous plan to exploit them."

The Iceman hadn't thrived this long without sticking tightly to a plan. Since Ivan was killed, he never had to improvise, and he'd never been followed. In the last three days he had improvised and had been followed. He concluded the police will let their guard down later—but not now.

Chapter 128

The Iceman Melteth Away

Reluctantly, The Iceman decided to abandon the op. He walked to the car he had hidden and drove towards the airport. He left the car in a secluded part of the airport parking lot, changed into another disguise, and caught the airport shuttle to the hangar where a bored "flic" was checking ID's.

The Iceman had taken the registration out of the car and had copied and printed it with his portable printer so that it matched the name on the French passport he was carrying. The flic looked at the registration and said, "No driver's license?" The Iceman replied, "No, my son took my wallet this morning by mistake and I'm having to use my back-up credit card which thankfully I had tucked into my passport, or I wouldn't have a Euro to my name."

He offered the Credit Agricole card to the flic who laughed and said, "Bet the cash will be gone when you get your wallet back!" He handed the ID back, and smiled at Monsieur Pierre Marchand from Paris. "Have a good flight," and then he turned and gestured to the next passenger in line.

As he walked forward, the next passenger in line asked the flic, "Why the extra security?" The flic replied, "There's a bad guy on the loose. We're looking for an ID without a Corsican address." He gestured to a group of five people in a corner—those people are non-residents, so we'll give them another look."

The Iceman nonchalantly walked over to the private airline counter and asked if the pilot he had arranged for a 4 p.m. take-off was available. The counter agent nodded and replied, "Your pilot has just finished filing a flight plan to the Coast. Please wait here for him to return."

Fifteen minutes later the Iceman's private rented plane was airborne. As the Beechcraft climbed into the clouds he started to relax. He figured he would have twenty-four hours of lead time to get away. When the plane landed in France—he made his way to the train station and once there headed back out to the coast by bus and then boarded a ferry to England where he donned his last disguise and used his last identity.

He would make another opportunity happen in the future. Although it was probably going to be harder to find Dmitri, he reckoned that the police would move him to Paris because Dmitri was a big fish which means he needed a big pond. He was going to have to find some trusted eyes in Paris—something he had only done once before and he had dealt with that loose end in the same manner he dealt with all of his assignments—quietly, effectively, and permanently.

He only had one trusted ally—so reliable and so good that he knew that certain special undercover teams and private police used him as well. He connected with one of his forgers, told him what he needed and set the wheels in motion. The usual terms were agreed upon with a significant bonus paid for eyes at entry points to France.

The Iceman knew it was a risk to bring in the spotters. If Dmitri was killed his "trusted eyes" would know they had played a part in some operation but wouldn't be able to connect said operation to him. Even the forger didn't know his real identity and The Iceman intended to keep it that way.

In London, The Iceman headed to a mailbox near the Chelsea Football Club Station, collected the new identity the forger sent there and found his way to a quiet hotel to think about the next steps—he liked north London and the Blues were his favorite football team. He opened up the new lap top he had purchased at the airport gift shop and contacted Luna to let her know that he was fine and missed her, but had met up with a few work colleagues and wanted to catch up. "Don't worry, I'll be back before you even have a chance to miss me."

He had never been in love before or had anyone love him back. He liked those feelings and he wanted them—it was the best he had ever felt in his life.

He refused to let Dmitri take that away from him and he knew that his future happiness hung on his ability to successfully stay under the radar.

Chapter 129

Putting the Pieces Together

As predicted, the Corsican police were beginning to put the pieces together. They located a stolen car near the airport. The car registration was missing. The shuttle bus driver confirmed he had picked up someone near the car port pickup spot. The driver also confirmed that the unidentified male in the surveillance picture the police showed him looked like the dark-haired, mustached, 5'11" middle-aged man he dropped off at the terminal.

An airport police officer remembered a man proffering a car registration with matching passport and credit card. But he didn't have a mustache. He estimated his age to be around forty. In addition to having a little beer belly, the man also wore thick eyeglasses.

The Corsican police eventually figured out The Iceman had taken a private flight to France followed by a taxi to the train station. Although the security cameras caught the same beer-bellied man arriving at the train station there was no sign of him leaving. Where he had gone or what transportation he used to get away remained a mystery.

The owner of the Airbnb opposite the police station confirmed a nondescript man in a rumpled business suit had prepaid for three nights' accommodation but had only stayed one. Registration was remote so the property owner never met his guest. The view of the front and side doors of the police station were clearly visible from the second-floor front bedroom and an experienced person could easily remain unseen. Although the owner thought he might be the same man the police were pursuing, she couldn't swear to it in a court of law.

The Corsica police expanded their search. They interviewed every homeowner, Airbnb, hotel and guest house within three kilometers of the police station. They learned nothing of value. Then, they got a tip. One of their more reliable informants reported seeing a tall, overweight woman leaving the train station and taking a bus to the ferry going to England. Police thought they were looking for a man and dismissed the tip as not credible. The trail went cold.

Although the Corsican police assumed The Iceman was heading to London, without a name or description it would be hard, if not impossible, to identify or locate him. Who was this master of surveillance and disguises? The police had grudging respect for him.

The police continued their search for a partial print and any hair left on any disguise or in any car. They needed the perp's DNA. The Iceman was sure he had covered his tracks. Although he was sure his DNA wasn't in any government data base, he couldn't afford to take any chances.

He bleach-bombed each getaway car and changed into a new disguise every time he moved from one location to another. He wiped everything down in the bedroom and bathroom at the Airbnb. He even shook out the sheets from his two-hour nap into the bathtub and then ran the shower to wash away any hair.

Two more days passed, and the police moved Dmitri to a safe house without incident. "He'll be back," said Dmitri. "It won't be long. He's never failed in the past. He's probably still here working on a plan."

The police took down the roadblocks and cancelled the airport and ferry checks. While he was still in France and before he returned to Washington, Temp decided to spend a couple of days with his son, Owen. But first, he had to get out of the hospital. He assumed he had missed his one and only opportunity to avenge Melodie's death.

Chapter 130

Reflections

Temp was tough and fit. While he had never had a concussion before, when he woke up the next day, he felt more like himself.

His doctor said, "While I recommend you stay and rest for a couple of days, you seem to have recovered really well. Go for a walk for an hour and if you notice anything such as headaches you should not only stay, you should want to stay! If you don't experience any additional concussion symptoms you are free to go. If anything changes, please come back right away."

Temp took a shower, changed into his street clothes and went for his walk. When he returned an hour later, he tracked down the doctor and thanked him for his help. The Doctor wished him well and the receptionist called Temp a taxi. Temp returned to the Corsica police station.

The local Police Chief and the prosecutor were sad to see him go and wished Temp well on the next chapter in his life. Temp said, "You and your team deserve the accolades and I'm sure the Dmitri bust will reap dividends for years to come."

"We couldn't' have done it without you," chorused the locals. Temp turned, gave a thumbs up, and walked outside to a waiting taxi. Truth be told, he couldn't wait to see Owen again.

Father and son enjoyed a long weekend together and then it was time for Temp to head home. On the Air France plane, Temp relaxed and allowed his subconscious to review his brief encounter with the man he assumed was Sergei's hitman. He believed The Iceman was probably responsible for Melodie's death and that at some point in the future he would identify and track him down. His ego required him to do so.

He begrudgingly acknowledged that his adversary was probably the toughest and most wily opponent he had ever faced and he was going to need help. As he settled into the flight he believed the Melodie Fan Club, including Christina, Jacques, Bob and Owen, would be a good place to start. Of these, his evolving relationship with Owen was the most fulfilling. He still hadn't figured out what to do about the missing piece of his heart.

Chapter 131

An Unexpected Scoop

Philadelphia Romualdez, a FNS *30 Minutes* reporter, just happened to be on holiday in Paris, France when Operation Voyeur—the *OhMy EAU!!* and ubdqt.com—story broke. Fellow reporter, Mary-Lou, wondered how her nemesis always seemed to be in the right place at the right time. Since she was already on site, editor, Jill, had no choice but to ask Philadelphia to cover the breaking news story.

"I am here in Paris, France with Jürgen Starke, Secretary General of Interpol. Earlier this morning, local police in seven countries, backed by Interpol, arrested more than twenty-five people allegedly connected to *OhMy EAU!!* cyber "voyeur" pornography sites. Through Operation Voyeur, Interpol helped law enforcement by identifying and sharing intelligence leads with each of the seven affected member countries. Mr. Starke, please tell us why this raid was so important?"

Mr. Starke stepped up to the microphone, cleared his throat and read a prepared statement. "Thank you, Philadelphia. As the world faces an ever-increasing range of terror threats, international cooperation between law enforcement agencies in our member countries has never been so important. None of our work on Operation Voyeur, would have been possible without the support and input from police departments in Canada, the United States, Italy, France, Brazil, Russia, and South Africa. I look forward to working even more closely with all of our global law enforcement partners in the future and honestly believe that our collaboration benefits citizens worldwide."

"Chief Denis Fornier of The Service de police de la Ville de Montréal, Canada, is also here with us today. Chief Fornier, do you have anything to add?" Philadelphia said as she handed the microphone to the Chief.

"Yes, I do. Our collective efforts and cooperation in Operation Voyeur have made a positive impact in combating cybercrime. We will continue to work with our international law enforcement partners to aggressively pursue these criminals around the world. It is good to see each partner in this investigation working towards the same goal: to catch and prosecute the suspects who are responsible for exploiting unsuspecting citizens especially our vulnerable children."

Chief Fornier handed the microphone back to the reporter, who said, "Thank you Chief Fornier and Mr. Starke. This is Philadelphia Romualdez, *30 Minutes*, with this special report. Good night."

Chapter 132

Epilogue

At Jacques' request, Denzel who had been given Misha's laptop, shipped it to Temp, who had a short term lease on a flat in France for himself, and his son, Owen. Father and son successfully deconstructed Sergei's computer system and passed information on over two hundred illegal enterprises to Jacques and Alex.

Jacques' investigation further confirmed that Sergei had, in fact, commissioned Melodie's execution. Just as Misha had speculated, his father couldn't afford to have anyone from the media poking around and calling attention to any of his businesses, especially *OhMy EAU!!*

Their research also revealed Sergei had been blackmailing Edie's parents, who would do just about anything to get that particular monkey off of their backs. When Edie completed her mission to plant the malware on Temp's computer, Sergei instructed The Iceman to eliminate all witnesses, including Edie, her Senator husband, and both of her parents. Temp finally had his answer about why Edie, a junior analyst, planted the worm.

Denzel recommended Jacques interview Misha's mother and father. But by the time this request was made, Elena and Misha were already dead, and Sergei might as well have been.

Although Temp never returned to the government, he was happy Jacques' investigation cleared his name. Two years later, his record for the most Gold USB wins still stood.

After a one-month suspension, Bob offered to reinstate Temp. He was still thinking it over while he spent time in France with Owen. Eventually, he decided that if Jacques agreed to work with Bob, he would rejoin St. Clair. He was confident Jacques was interested in anything that provided another reason to spend time with his girlfriend, the lovely Christina.

The Alyosha board offered Denzel the job as the full time Executive Director of the Foundation. He accepted the offer and was in the process of actualizing Misha's dream of making financial literacy an educational prerequisite for every degree, everywhere in the world; setting academic standards; and establishing the Foundation as the Financial Literacy Registrar.

Denzel delivered Misha's financial literacy speech to the U.N., in which he stressed that in a global village, financial literacy was just as important as reading, writing, and coding. He received a standing ovation. More importantly, the speech resulted in the formation of a Special U.N. Financial Literacy Subcommittee. He was optimistic that global change might actually happen during his lifetime.

After it was published, Denzel's murder mystery book, "Killing Wall Street," spent more than seven weeks on the New York Times Best Sellers List. He and his girlfriend, Rosie, were thinking about taking their relationship to the next level. In the meantime, they were getting to know each other and having a lot of fun.

The Sustainable Investing Club members, including Denzel, continued to publish annual updates to "Leave Only Shadows" and to direct the lion's share of royalties to The Alyosha Foundation.

Six months later, *30 Minutes* aired a special on insider trading and Philadelphia was nominated for her third Pulitzer Prize—she received her second Pulitzer for the Operation Voyeur story. A new bill to close the Senator's Insider Trading loophole was once again before Congress, but politics being politics, Christina and Jacques doubted the greedy establishment would ever be willing to kill the goose that laid the golden egg.

Jacques and Christina often wondered whether Melodie's plan to reveal the Senators' insider trading scheme was worth her life. Then again, if things hadn't unfolded exactly as they did, Jacques and Christina might not have started a romantic relationship, Christina would not have adopted Sunny, the Wonder Dog, and they would not be making plans for the three of them to enjoy the Trois-Rivières Hiking Trail next month.

Jacques and Christina were thrilled that "The Melodie Marie Beaudoin Scholarship Fund" had enough money to give out 10 educational scholarships and the bursary committee was currently in the process of reviewing applications for the upcoming academic year. The couple had also recently decided to join Bob and Temp at St. Clair.

Until they figured out exactly where they would set up house, Jacques and Christina took turns commuting to each other's location. When she was in Trois-Rivières, Christina and Sunny spent as much time as possible with the clanging, banging and laughing Beaudouin's. She didn't miss her best friend quite so much when she was in the presence of Melodie's boisterous brothers.

Life was so much more exciting and fulfilling since she and Jacques had found each other, and they were both cautiously optimistic about the future.

Authors' Notes

Additional References:

https://www.investor.gov/introduction-investing/investing-basics/glossary/insider-trading

April 4, 2012: https://en.wikipedia.org/wiki/STOCK_Act

July 21, 2014: https://www.integrity-research.com/washington-insider-trading-probe-could-become-biggest-ever/)

July 22, 2017: https://investmentu.com/why-congressional-insider-trading-legal-profitable/

August 16, 2018: https://www.congressionalinstitute.org/2018/08/16/can-members-of-congress-engage-in-insider-trading/

May 24, 2019: https://www.nytimes.com/2019/05/24/business/dealbook/insider-trading-act.html

https://www.amazon.com/Throw-Them-All-Out-Politicians/dp/0547573146

https://www.businessinsider.com/congress-insider-trading-earmarks-real-estate-nancy-pelosi-rich-tax-payer-money-2011-11

https://truepundit.com/crime-pays-bandit-nancy-pelosi-pockets-6-million-in-amazon-stock-profits-insider-trading-scheme-involved-purchase-during-congressional-coronavirus-meetings-before-u-s-retailers-were-forced-to-clos/

https:///www.npr.org/2021/09/21/1039313011/tiktokers-are-trading-stocks-by-watching-what-members-of-congress-do

Acknowledgements

As *A Convenient Ruse* evolved, we consulted with, bugged, begged and bribed a fair number of people who took time out of their own busy lives to help us with our project. We are most grateful for their input.

In particular, we would like to thank our narrative/story editors Barb Amsden, Shirley Crockett, John Eberhart, Muriel Fishman, Mikel Fromstein, Susan Gould & Shelley Springall.

We would also like to thank Piroska Bata for her medical advice & guidance, Kevin Best, for his marketing prowess, Cameron Freeman for rescuing Suzen's technology (on multiple occasions), Lewis Stoate & Anthony Sukdeo for their IT insight, Sara Carrick and Donna Carrick of Carrick Publishing for their confidence and support, and the Metropolitan Toronto Public Library, Main Branch, where we spent many hours working in pod 3 on the 2nd floor.

A Convenient Ruse would not be as good as it is were it not for your combined input and support. We are most grateful that you took the time out of your busy lives to make a difference in ours.

Also by Suzen Fromstein

Suits and Ladders: Ten Proven Ways to Keep Your Job Safe (with a few jokes thrown in)

Want To Inform, Influence And Entertain Like A Pro? Simply Recognize The Seven Deadly Sins Of Public Speaking And Then Avoid Them. Includes a Bonus Section, co-authored with Mike Nemiroff, on How to Add Humor to Everything

The Grin Reaper—a Humorous Look at Death & Dying (with a few jokes thrown in), co-authored with Mike Nemiroff.

Suzen Fromstein

Suzen is a freelance business writer and content creator, speech writer, and book author. Her three published books (two business and one comedy) are available on all e-platforms with a print-on-demand option from Amazon.

A Convenient Ruse is her first murder-mystery novel.

Suzen Fromstein
416/471-3845
suzen@suzenfromstein.com

TJ Stoate

Tim has 40 years of experience in corporate finance advisory work, banking, and investment syndications. Portfolios under his management have exceeded $100 million in committed funds and have included residential real estate, construction transactions, commercial loans and equity investments. Tim has arranged senior debt, mezzanine financing, subordinated debt, and equity investments for early stage and growth businesses. Currently, he is the VP of Impact Investing for The Atmospheric Fund and specializes in environmental enterprise and project finance.

A Convenient Ruse is his first murder-mystery novel.

TJ Stoate
416/274-5421
tjstoate8@gmail.com

Made in the USA
Columbia, SC
14 June 2022

61716808R00214